NIGHTHAWKS
AT THE MISSION
MOVE OFF-WORLD. MAKE A KILLING.

INCLUDING SEVERAL BONUS SHORT STORIES SET IN THE NIGHTHAWKS WORLD
WRITTEN BY JASON ANSPACH, TODD BARSELOW, AND FENTON COOPER

FORBES WEST

NIGHTHAWKS AT THE MISSION

Copyright © Forbes West 2014

Cover Illustration Copyright © 2014 Forbes West

Names, characters and incidents depicted in this book are products of the author's imagination, or are used fictitiously. Any resemblance to actual events, locales, organizations, or persons, living, dead, or undead is entirely coincidental and beyond the intent of the author or the publisher.

All rights reserved. No part of this book may be reproduced or transmitted in any form or by any means whatsoever, including photocopying, recording or by any information storage and retrieval system, without written permission from the publisher and/or author.

This edition published by special arrangement with Auspicious Apparatus Press, 2016.

http://www.apparatuspress.com/

ISBN-13: 978-0-9966628-4-0
ISBN-10: 0996662847

DEDICATION

To the producer, Junko Forbes,
always two steps ahead of me.

TABLE OF CONTENTS

Thanksgiving 1
Network Interview 19
Queen Mary 31
Solomon's Bay 59
To Mission Friendship 71
The Ritual 83
Mission Friendship 91
The Flash Storm(When the Levee Breaks) 95
First Day 103
Christmas 131
The Temple of Kern 139
The Burial of the Dead 155
The Road Back to Mission Friendship 183
The New Normal 201
Showdown at Mission Friendship
(The New Normal, Part Two) 221
Sarah's Dream of an Off-World Ranch at Midnight 259
Last Night at Mission Friendship 271
The Magician's Highway 283
Death by Water 307
What the Thunder Said 321
Epilogue 333
About the Author 339

LAST MEAL
By Jason Anspach 341

OH DIYOS IN THE OBERON
By Todd Barselow 353

THE LAST LAUGH AT THE END OF THE WORLD
by Fenton Cooper 367

Dunbar-Weiss English Dictionary
Published January, 1999, Cape Town, South Africa

Ori·chal·cum
Function: *noun*

Etymology: Latin (from the Greek *όρος, oros,* [mountain] and *χαλκός, chalkos,* [copper or bronze])

Definition: a strong metallic element obtained only from THE OBERON (OFF-WORLD). In spite of the etymology of its name, ORICHALCUM is always blue, with shades and imperfections that can only be discerned by certain machines and individuals with TETRACHROMACY before actual use. When the element is connected to a small electrical charge and placed next to a person's body, he or she may exhibit extraordinary power(s) or influence from an unknown, possibly supernatural, source (e.g. summoning of fierce creatures, production of lightning, ability to heal the sick or dying, shapeshifting, control over fire, control over localized weather conditions) with the proper mental focus. Each shade of the element denotes a different extraordinary power or ability. Its usefulness for modern society was discovered by FRANK MORGAN (see NETWORK, history of) in 1995.

— See element table.

CHAPTER ONE:
THANKSGIVING

Sipping on your third beer of the evening, staring out at the off-world night sky just outside your bar's little patio space, you think about how far away from home you are, how you've become increasingly crazy, how you've fallen in love with a person that you barely know who is officially in love with someone else, and how you've ended up millions of miles away from your adopted hometown.

You dimly realize through the alcohol and Adderall-induced haze that it all kicked off one not so fine Thanksgiving at a beach house in California.

It is last Thanksgiving. You're at Tyler's and Jaime's beach house (well, their parents' beach house) and the semester for City College is done; you've just managed to grab an associate's degree. Tyler's and Jaime's parents are good people. They like having any friends of the family stay over at the beach house for Thanksgiving, and so you are there instead of being at home.

Tyler and Jaime are twins; they look alike, they sound alike, but are nothing alike whatsoever in their personalities and their moods. You like Tyler—the funny one, the out of control one—and you've been dating him since high school ended, but he's an ass and perhaps you should find someone better. You see him currently being an ass out past the pool area downstairs. He's wrestling Steve, his old friend from high school, and his other buddies are cheering them on. Tyler and Steve are older than you, still in a four-year college doing their degrees in "Business Communications".

Tyler is picking Steve up and then slamming him back onto the grass area by the pool with a barbarian scream. Steve is laughing maniacally. Tyler looks to you and says, "My woman! My woman, Sarah, do you like what you see? Are you not entertained?"

You shake your head, in a mix of fake and real disgust. The two of them go back to wrestling.

You are the only girl there besides that stick creature Courtney, who has a room-temperature IQ and who constantly insists that the waves are caused by flying fish and not the wind, "like, you know, everyone, like, thinks." Courtney mentions this to you as you are watching the waves break instead of the on-going wrestling match.

You smile and nod, then leave her, pretending to have to go to the bathroom after rolling your eyes so hard they make a sound. "Tell my boyfriend, after he's done beating on poor Steve there, to come and grab me."

You pass other partygoers who are sitting on couches and chairs sipping wine and other drinks and jabbering about whatever white, Orange County adults in their thirties to fifties jabber about. They are complaining about the Mexican illegal help they've hired and the President of the United States all in the same breath, hitting the highest and the lowest of society in one blast of white upper-middle-class bitterness. This rich house you are in is decorated in a comfortable little fall motif, and little turkey decorations dot the living room's landscape.

You decide to wander upstairs to the third floor, your bare feet bouncing up the carpeted steps, where Jaime, Tyler's mellower and stranger clone, sits at a computer in the hallway office. Tyler jokes it is strange European pornography that he watches on the computer. In actuality, Jaime just likes to research whatever he can about off-world.

You found this out when you slept over one night when Tyler's and Jaime's parents weren't there. Jaime doesn't go to Long Beach City College like you or the University of Southern California like Tyler—fact is, he could have gone to Harvard if he'd wanted to, but it seems he is always biding his time, waiting for something. His parents always let him be on that subject for some reason.

Jaime is deep in thought. You come up beside him and clap your hands hard next to his ear, making him jump nearly fifteen feet into the air. Jaime wears button-down shirts and designer jeans, unlike Tyler, who is currently dressed like a trailer park drug dealer in a ragged black T-shirt and old, faded jeans.

Jaime holds his ear and whines in his most conspicuously not-Tyler way, "Ow! Christmas goose! What did you do that for! I'm looking up stuff that's really important."

Your eyes become slits. "You looking up people doing the wild thing, huh? Naked pictures of European people being naked together, Jaime? Hmm?"

Jaime ignores you for a moment and licks his lips. "Some stuff like that. No, Sarah, I'm looking, I'm looking—was looking—for off-world photographs."

You cross your arms. "Those are illegal, Mr. Jaime."

Jaime shrugs. "Doing illegal stuff can be amusing."

"So you really are Tyler's twin brother." You look over at what Jaime is busy picking out. Authorized drawings of those Antediluvian cities and orichalcum batons and sketches of Ni-Perchta agents, or Ephors, come up on his Google search for images.

Jaime turns to you as if reminded about something and has a very serious look in his eye. You wonder what exactly has gotten into him. He says, "Come on back to my room."

"That's a little forward, Mister," you say with a smirk. You walk down the hall to Jaime's room, which is covered in off-world stuff including maps and sketches, plus an Off-World Network recruitment poster for the first temp settlers back in Settler's Campaign, 1995. His bed is unmade, his clothes and underwear strewn about as if he put a bomb into his laundry hamper and let it explode inside the room. Jaime closes the door behind you, making you wonder a bit about his intensions.

The advertisement seems to be brand new and fresh, and reads in very noticeable block letters:

ADVENTURE AND A NEW LIFE AWAIT YOU.

START YOUR MOVE TO THE OBERON TODAY! CALL 1-800-OFFWORLD TO SEE IF YOU QUALIFY FOR SETTLING! (AGES 18-45 ONLY)

The stylized symbol of the Off-World Network, the blue and white circles overlapping each other, takes up the rest of the poster's space.

In a different, smaller typeface under the symbol are the words:

BROUGHT TO YOU BY THE NETWORK: NEW WORLD, NEW FRIENDS.

The Network is a chartered corporation of the Federal Government of the United States.

Jaime sits at his desk with his dark, open laptop and swallows compulsively.

There's a sort of sinking feeling in your stomach. Something bad is coming but you don't want to hear about it; you don't want this bad idea brought out into the not-so-fresh air of Jaime's bedroom. Idly, you finger the crucifix around your neck.

"Tyler's made love to Courtney on the side. *Is* making love to Courtney on the side. Present tense," Jaime says simply, staring at you.

Your world drops out from under you. It feels like your head is full of sugary soda, with fizzes and pops that block out your thought processes. You drop the cross, letting it swing from your neck.

"Making love? As in?" you say, weakly.

"Recreational sex," Jaime says, biting his lip. "Here. Well, not here, in the bedroom, you know, but here, in the house. I can hear 'em around two a.m. when they think I'm asleep, but I'm not asleep. Courtney's loud. Did you know she thinks that flying fish cause the waves here in Seal Beach? That's really amazing."

You sit on Jaime's unkempt and unmade bed. You let out a big sigh, as if your whole body is full of air and you've just expelled it all at once. "I, actually, I'm actually a...well, I haven't done that yet. I kind of thought, marri-" You let the word drop in mid-air.

"Me, too. Oh, and I think Tyler made, made love with your friend Christine. She's your best friend," he says, not picking up on the social cue you have just provided him. He looks around, as if unsure what to do next. You don't cry, not yet.

"Well, this is a very happy Thanksgiving." A part of you is hot, embarrassed, and angry all at once. You know of Tyler's reputation and his troubles but he always seemed, deep down, beneath all the play-acting and the crap, to be a good person. That is obviously a lie. You've put up with Tyler for so long because you thought, well, he is about four years older than you, perhaps he will, one day, maybe, just maybe, grow little by little.

Jaime looks suddenly worried. "Don't tell Tyler, please, but I had to tell you."

You shrug. "Yeah, sure thing." You look around his room at all the sketches and artwork about The Oberon; part of your mind has shut down from the information overload. There's an artistic poster of a wintry, tundra-like scene showing blasted-out black castles, woolly Afer cattle, and pine trees scattered around craggy gray peaks under a perpetually overcast sky.

"Looks like the Wicked Witch of the West's castle," you say, staring at the poster. In bold, black letters it says *Castle of Kadath* and has the symbol of the Network stamped on it. The sight of the poster sends little chills up your spine.

Jaime follows your gaze. "It's a place I'd like to go to. Actually, I can go there, technically, but I have a problem. A big problem. It's an issue I have that's preventing me from getting into The Oberon. You know my family has money?"

You smile. "No, really? With this beach house in Orange County? I thought, gee, I never..."

"Well, it's true," he says woodenly, again not picking up on the now less-than-subtle cue. "My father has money, and I've got a little bit that's all mine. I saved some of my Best Buy pay."

"Uh huh," you say, half-listening, the impact of what he's just told you now hitting you hard and deep right in your guts. A tear leaks out.

"My cousin Steve just got LR'd from The Oberon because he went, well, insane, and so he doesn't have anyone to leave his little house to," Jaime continues, even though a flash flood of tears is now flowing down your cheeks.

"I'm s-sorry," you stutter. You wipe your eyes with the end of one of Jaime's blankets, and then smell it by accident. Stunned by the amazingly weird odor, you put the sheet back onto the bed in disgust.

"You don't have to cry over him, Sarah. He just got LR'd—leave requested—since he's completely insane. He's had issues." You look up incredulously as he keeps speaking. "Apparently, no one liked him. But he likes me a lot since I always asked him questions about The Oberon and his life there. So he left me his property. There's a Triumph motorcycle, ori-modified for infinite range. And I always—"

You're now staring at the carpet, still crying as he rambles on. You look down on your well-manicured feet, with your brightly painted purple toenails shining through. Tyler bought that little treat for you.

"Well, I got my money, and I want to move to The Oberon to sketch and draw all that's there—something that's still legal to do. But the new immigration rules from the Network say all new immigrants have to be married couples between eighteen and twenty-five years old if they don't have any sort of college degree. So I can immigrate to The Oberon and live out my dream right now, but I have to be married since I don't have a degree. And I got to marry someone fast because the solstice portal will be open on the twenty-second of December. I'm just...Marriage is such a big deal; you want to find the right one, you know, and I have to make a decision right now...I don't want to wait two to four years through college."

You rub your temples, sniffling. "Sucks for you," you say. Memories of Tyler keep flooding into your head, making you feel worthless and embarrassed and stupid all at once, like how a child would feel if they were struck after wetting their pants. You know it isn't your fault but a part of you—that unforgiving part—says that you probably did something to attract it, to deserve it.

You look at the Witch Castle of Kadath poster again through bleary, tear-filled eyes. The scene really does look like that black rock castle the Wicked Witch of the West lived in.

You wonder if that poster depicts a real place.

"So would you leave for The Oberon right now, if you could Ty- Jaime?" You sniffle again, curse to yourself, and wipe your nose with Jaime's bed sheets. He catches you doing that again and frowns.

"Uh, well, yes. Yes, of course. It's my dream. I mean, it's a new world there, a real new world. No more Starbucks or McDonald's or terrorism or global warming—it'd be like a real life fantasy adventure every day. I want to be a dayhawk, too, you know, on the side, if I get the chance—that's their nickname for legal salvagers."

"And we, I mean you, you could make lots of money?" that mercenary part of you enquires. "People make a lot of money off ori and all the salvageables, don't they?"

Jaime nods up and down rapidly. "Oh, indeed! It's like the California Gold Rush all over again. It'd be fun for anyone. I can't wait to get out there and just...just wander and explore and sketch."

Part of you is so disgusted with your surroundings and so angry and so disturbed all at once that you blurt out: "You wanna get married, Jaime? Go to The Oberon? Have a little adventure away from it all?"

Jaime looks stunned. "Well...well...I'm going to ask this Chinese girl I sorta date, Pachinko. If she says yes by tomorrow, I'm in and we're gone. I know her; she's a math tutor over at Cerritos College, but, well, yes in answer to your question, yes I would. I would definitely. And I'm sort of with her."

You nod, deflated. "I have—had—a sister who lived in The Oberon."

"Raquel?" Jaime says.

You shake your head. "Rachael. Married a man, Ian Zur. She was one of the first doctorates from Solomon's House University. Xenoarchaeology. She always said it was a good place to be..."

Jaime raises an eyebrow. "Quite the sister—but she's dead, I mean, passed on, isn't that right? I didn't-"

Tyler bursts into the room at that moment, sweaty and with his arm around Steve. All of his other douchebag buddies are with him, too, standing around like the absolute goons they are. "Who's up for drugs?" he stage whispers. "Who wants drugs? Drugs? Drugs for you Jaime? Sarah? Steve here just got his Medical Marijuana card, and so everyone's doing drugs on the roof tonight, right?" Tyler sees that you are in tears and looks concerned. "Hey. What's going on, sugary sweet? Sweetie McSweetums, Cutie McCutes?"

"You've been with Courtney. You've been with Courtney, that's what's going on. And Christine."

The look on Tyler's face, eyes flicking to Jaime, tells you everything in a moment.

You stand up, wiping your eyes, and slam Tyler hard right in the balls, making him double over in pain. Your right arm is pretty strong from all those softball practices. "Cheat on me with Courtney, you bastard!"

Courtney, who is standing near the back of the group, takes off as you plow through the rest of Tyler's friends. You chase her down the hallway, and she squeaks in fright. You stop running and wipe your nose with the back of your hand, laughing as she almost jumps down an entire flight of stairs.

Jaime pops his head out of his bedroom for a moment, looking concerned.

"Well, maybe I'll see you off-world? Let's make that happen, right, Jaime?" you say, as Tyler's confused friends look on in amazement. Jaime gives you a thumbs-up.

"It's a deal!" You return his thumbs-up and leave the house. As you exit, you see Tyler's new black 2012 Maserati; California license plate *TylerIs1*. You pick up a loose brick from the small garden outside the front door, feel the weight of it with your right hand, and then throw it through the windshield in one epic smash, sending a thousand little pieces of glass all over the place and setting off the alarm.

You walk down the street under the afternoon sun, feeling chilled but also strangely liberated at the same time. You shake out your arms, punch the air directly in front of you a few times, and keep walking.

You walk to your car, which is a beat up 1995 Honda Civic POS painted that ugly post-apocalyptic primer. You get three feet down the partially sandy beach road only to find out that the engine light you have been unfortunately ignoring is right about something; your car's just died.

You leave the thing in the middle of the street, making the quick calculation that if you are in The Oberon by next year—which is fast approaching—no one's going to be bothering you about abandoning the car. So you leave it here, in the middle of a suburban street, and hop on a piss-smelling bus.

You remember that you are poor and without a father who can gift you a Maserati.

Later, as you chew on a fingernail on the bus ride to work after riding it from Tyler's house, you see a large billboard across the street. The advertisement is already fading from weeks of sun and rain but you can just make out the block letters:

ADVENTURE AND A NEW LIFE AWAIT YOU.
START YOUR MOVE TO THE OBERON TODAY! CALL 1-800-OFFWORLD TO SEE IF YOU QUALIFY FOR SETTLING! COLLEGE GRADUATES WANTED!
OFFWORLDNETWORK.COM

The stylized blue and white symbol of the Off-World Network takes up the rest of the billboard's space.

You take out your cellphone and start to dial. After ten minutes on hold, a helpful operator finally comes on the line, and you talk all the way to work. The operator tells you what you need to do in order to apply.

Half asleep behind the counter at Subway, as lifeless as a doll, you wait for the customer to make up her mind about whether she wants pepper jack or provolone on her sandwich. Your green shirt and hat are covered in grease stains and probably bits of mustard that have been misplaced. When the customer finally decides on pepper jack, you start to put on provolone by accident, ask if she wants bell pepper and onions with that, and can't be bothered to listen to her response. Out of habit, you look up. You've asked her a question, after all. She's a tall woman, forty years old, beefy but not fat. Thick glasses cover her face. She is someone who can definitely put you down pretty quickly.

"I asked you a question. I asked you a question, Miss. Why are you putting provolone on my sandwich? Did I say provolone or did I say pepper jack?"

You blink a couple of times. "Oh, sorry, I'll take it off..."

"I want you to start over. I want you to start over right the hell now."

You look up, confused. "You want...wait, what? A new sandwich?"

"Damn right, I want a new sandwich. You got that provabone crap all over my sandwich."

"Provolone. Not provabone," you reply. You start to smolder, getting angrier and angrier. One eye starts to twitch a little. You reflexively grab onto the cross around your neck.

The customer behind her is snickering and muttering something to his friend. A few "Yo, dawgs" are thrown about in muttered whispers.

"I can just take it—"

"Is there a manager here? I want to talk to a manager right damn now," the customer says, raising her shrill voice. She is slapping the counter with her palm. "You have not been concentrating on my meal at all. This is just poor customer service, Miss, and I believe that some compensation is in order."

You stand quietly for a second, biting your lip. "Look, I'm sorry, but I can just take the provolone off." You start to remove the little triangle slices from the wheat bread. "See? There."

The customer snaps her fingers in the air. "I don't see a thing except for poor customer service."

One of the other customers is filming the exchange with an iPhone and snickering. Your manager, an Indian man in his late forties by the name of Rajendra, comes out and apologizes to her. The woman asks for compensation, stating that she is there every day (which is not true, this is the first time you've seen her). The manager offers to give her a free set of three cookies. You watch this in absolute disgust, and mutter about this being bullshit.

"What did you say to me, Miss? You want to say that to my face?" One of the other customers is cracking up about the whole exchange while still filming with his phone.

The manager asks you to finish making up her sandwich. You smile a little and just leave, walking straight out the front door after tossing your apron into the garbage.

When you arrive at the small two bedroom, one bath Marina Pacifica apartment that you share with your mother, you trudge up the stairs after a half hour bus ride that would normally have taken you just five minutes if you'd had your now broken down car. It is bare, sparse, cold to look at. It's not dirty, per se —it's even got a little bit of a view—but it has a soft prison cell décor: old, bland furniture and a bland carpet within soft beige walls. You sit down on the couch, turn on MTV, cry a little, and stare at meaningless television. Before long, footsteps outside your apartment tell you that your mother is now coming home. She opens the door almost as if she is bursting into the apartment to make an arrest.

"Sarah! So your car's broken down again? And how are you gonna fix it without me paying for it?" your mother cries, her voice shrill. As she gets closer, you can see the lines on her face and her perpetually watery eyes. However, the years can't take away her good looks that she's definitely passed down through her genes to you.

You don't say anything at first. Your mother relents for a brief second, sitting down at the dining room table. You don't say anything but turn the TV's volume down.

"Oh, just go goddamn mute, I don't give a rat's ass." She blows out her breath and takes a moment to look through the contents of her purse for something. "I'll call Triple A tomorrow, but..." She slaps her hands together. "Next time I'm going to really kick your ass, sweetheart. You don't take care of anything. Anything."

"I took care of it and I can pay," you say and your mother just waves her hands around, humming at the top of her lungs so she can't hear you. She does this all the time, and it makes you want to scream. It's so childish and surreal you now just feel a sort of crazed pity and hatred for your own mother. "Could you listen?" you ask, dejectedly. "I broke up with Tyler."

Your mother replies with a dismissive, "Thank you for telling me that. It's really fascinating, the love life of a teenager."

"I'm twenty." Your mother stares at you for a moment, looking like she wants to ball up her fists and take a swing at you. "I'm moving to The Oberon," you add, offhandedly.

Your mother looks like all the life has left her body for a moment but she raises up her defenses again and her angry self quickly returns. She walks over and flips the muted channel to something else.

"What on earth for? You really hate being around normal people?" she says, her voice sharp as she sits in the loveseat watching an old pirate movie —*Captain Blood,* you think, with Errol Flynn. Swashbuckling pirates are fighting each other, slashing with cutlasses and shooting cannonballs at each other's ships.

"Jaime sort of turned me on to it. I called the local Network office, and I qualify since I have an associate's degree. I have to go in for an interview, but they have a lot of settling slots available." You cough into your hand.

"Fantastic." Your mother rolls her eyes, saying the word like it is loaded with poison. She steps out of the room.

Unconsciously, you take a look at the framed picture of your smiling sister that's hung on the wall behind the TV for the past few years. It's actually a framed copy of TIME Magazine with the headline *Professors of a Different World* next to it. She was a tall, attractive brunette with hazel eyes, and the picture was of her on a balcony somewhere.

You stare at the picture for a while. The television is now showing flickering images of the game show *Jeopardy* before switching to a line of jabbering commercials for random products, cars, and orichalcum for everyday use. Your mother returns to the room.

"Your sister was a professor—a professor of Xenoarchaeology—and she's missing. She knew everything—and I mean everything—about The Oberon and she died out there. You are just a naïve little bitch of a twenty-year-old girl who doesn't know her asshole from a hole in the ground. I'm sorry to talk so crude, but you know it. You know it."

You stare at her for a long time. "I'm twenty years old. I don't need to listen to you," you say coldly. "Since Rachael disappeared and Dad died, I'm just your punching bag."

"You are not going to The Oberon. Period."

"I'm going." You stare right into her eyes.

Your mother lights up for a moment, smiling. "Sure! Sure, just go, go on out, go to The Oberon. Enjoy that life. Be like your sister—someone who thought they knew how to handle anything and everything until they wound up missing one day. You go and do that." Your mother has this hideous smirk on her face that makes you hate her even more, which you didn't know was possible.

She squints at you. "I say it's wrong. There's nothing for a little girl there. It's nothing for a girl to be dealing with, I just know it. There's only—what's the word I'm looking for? Promises of money and death. But you go ahead, my little girl. Go ahead." She sits right next to you, her eyes looking straight into yours. "Sarah, you need to remember something. Something very specific."

"What?"

Your mother slams your arm hard with a closed fist, making you yelp with surprise and fear. "There'll come a time, little girl of mine, when you won't have me or anyone else to tell you what's right and what's wrong. Remember that! There's only that small, still voice inside that can tell you that. You can either listen to it or ignore it. You can't just have some outside person tell you that. And what does that still voice say to you now? Does it say to play around in The Oberon, make your mother sick with fear? Or does it say to stay here?"

You shake a little and start to cry. Your mother tells you that she's taking a nap because she's tired after work, but catching the look on your face, her voice softens a little. "You will never do it, because you're weak. Right, sweetheart? You are a weak person. You're not like your sister at all. She was strong, and you are weak. You're weak compared to her." She holds your chin in her hand and looks you in the eye. "You will never do anything like going to The Oberon because you are weak. Unlike your sister, unlike your father—it's no fault of your own." She caresses your cheek for a moment and then lets you go. "We can go to Hof's Hut. They have a Thanksgiving deal, two for one. We'll split it, real cheap and good. You like that, right, sweetheart?"

You nod.

You pretend to go to sleep early that day, occasionally looking at your phone. Text after text from Tyler come in, at first apologizing about cheating, then wanting to talk, then calling you a bitch, and then calling you something that rhymes with punt and starts with a C.

It's midnight and you sneak into your mother's room. She's asleep with earphones still in, listening to some odd relaxation music. You grab a prescription bottle of Vicodin off her bathroom counter and sneak out again. In your lonely little room, where a muted TV plays old episodes of *MASH*, you pop a couple pills and wash them down with a gulp of water from the sink. You sit down in front of your computer, boot it up, and delete photograph after photograph of you and Tyler during happier days. You then eliminate him completely from your Facebook account and change your status to "single".

After a little bit, the Vicodin hits your system and you get a bit angrier. You find a box of letters from Tyler, and before you know it, you rip each and every one in half with a dull, drug-induced slowness, muttering curses to yourself as you shred every bullshit little note, every scripted lie. In one of the letters, Tyler talks about marriage a little, in hesitant and specifically vague terms. You rip it up.

When you are all done, you look at the prescription bottle of Vicodin, thinking of what you could do with that right now, what you could do to yourself with that. You take another pill and put the bottle back into your mother's room. Stoned on prescription pills, you jump back on the computer and start cruising the Internet, coming upon the Off-World Network's settler recruitment site.

Good Morning LA ABC 7 KABC
Aired November 21st, 2012

David Ervine: Anchor
Seen ten months ago, it has been confirmed that it should appear over The Oberon skies around June of next year. And now, Karen, I think we are getting what has become the most popular part of the show. Let's take a look at California Weather Control over at Grissom Island in Long Beach.

CUT TO

Karen Whitemore: Presenter
Thank you, David. Sorry, Southland, even though you were looking at a nice weekend full of sunshine, here's Aaron Sizemore from the Off-World Network...

Aaron Sizemore: NWS Orichalcum User (Weather Control)
Good morning.

Karen Whitemore: Presenter
Aaron is an experienced orichalcum user with a level five rating. He is here with his baton, embedded with the rarest type of orichalcum to be found in The Oberon. Now, Aaron, the Department of Agriculture is looking for a small storm for the area because we are a little bit behind in rain volume, is that correct?

Aaron Sizemore: NWS Orichalcum User (Weather Control)
That's correct, Karen. The Department of Agriculture is concerned about what little rain we have had so far, so it's our job to make up some ground so we can avoid a drought. I know everyone watching is probably going to hate me for doing this, but I'll have to begin.

Karen Whitemore: Presenter
Literally raining on their parade?

Aaron Sizemore: NWS Orichalcum User (Weather Control)

[Long pause] Sure. Now I'm going to ask you to back away about one hundred feet—you and your crew there—and I will begin the process in—checking my watch here—in exactly two minutes.

Karen Whitemore: Presenter

Now, David, as I am sure you are watching right now, we are moving away from Aaron who is now in this wide open space on Grissom Island. This island is open and uninhabited. It gives the ori user the best view of the sky and keeps him away from all the possible interference that can happen if this were to be done in a city environment. As you can see behind me, Aaron is exhibiting the ori glow—which, since he is highly skilled and trained to conduct weather control, is turning the air around him to a deep green. Weather control has been, of course, the most successful ori practice to come from off-world and is responsible for those perfect summers that have been such a boost to tourist areas like Long Beach or San Diego.

However, as much as I think everyone would love to be consistently rain and cloud free, we do have to ensure that agriculture in the area is taken care of, and so we do need maintenance storms like the one Aaron will be creating. The Weather Service tells us that every time an ori user takes control of the weather it costs the taxpayers forty-four million dollars. This includes the user's training and time and also that this particular ori is worth forty-three million for every gram, which is always useless after the weather has been controlled.

As you can see behind me, Aaron is levitating several feet above the ground; his arms are outstretched and his eyes have now taken a strong appearance of almost pure white light... If you can still hear me right now, David, beams of green, almost like lightning, are spreading from Aaron's chest, eyes, and hands and are now bouncing across the entire sky. He is descending downward, and the green bolts are disappearing. He is back on the ground and back to his usual self. I'll give him a moment to rest, and then we can go over there and ask him. Oh, he's come over here, David, and he's-

Aaron Sizemore: NWS Orichalcum User (Weather Control)
It's a rush, it really is, I tell you that much. I don't think anyone will understand—but it's something else. Phew...It's a feeling that you are actually one with the Earth, but it's a bit much. It's very exciting...

(Loud thunder clap drowns out audio.)

CHAPTER TWO:
NETWORK INTERVIEW

You end up on a street corner in downtown Long Beach the very next day, outside the Off-World Trade Center building, staring up at the height of it. The sign confirms that you are in the right place. You look in desperation at your watch, and Mickey Mouse is letting you know the unfortunate—five minutes late to the interview, 11:35 am. You get a face full of warm, wet wind and diesel fumes as you move down the sidewalk. Rain is coming down hard, soaking the dress clothes and coat you have worn for the interview. The heels you wear hurt your feet.

You walk into the first floor of the Trade Center and past the glass doors that separate a very small throng of protestors proclaiming "Stop the settling!" and "No blood for ori!" A statue of a Ni-Perchta warrior in full armor with an ori-staff and a model of the Ni-Perchta city of Solomon's Bay laid out on what looks like a giant stone palm are centered in the lobby.

You pass them with barely a glance, rushing inside, and see a glass elevator that carries you to the fourteenth floor of the building.

Waiting outside Christopher Lee's office takes two hours; you have to stand in line with other prospective settlers and candidates for direct employment with the Off-World Network. It's a very motley group, mostly women ranging from your age to their fifties.

You made the mistake of getting a free cup of coffee earlier and now you have to pee. You'll have to hold it until the interview is finished since the recruiter is asking you inside, holding a manila folder in his hand. "No, there is no relation between myself and the other Christopher Lee," he says, after he shakes hands with you. Mr. Lee states this in a delightfully British accent as you step inside his large, almost football field wide office that looks over the Long Beach Harbor. He is a slightly bucktooth man, middle-aged, no wedding ring on his finger. He sits behind his desk, his gut slightly extending over the smooth mahogany desktop. A new Macintosh is perched on top of his desk. He wears, to your non-surprise, the blue jumpsuit uniform of the Network. It's that goofy NASA flight suit wannabe outfit that apparently all the Network employees off-world dress in. On his left breast are the two overlapping circles of the Network, and on his right shoulder is a British flag patch.

There is a female employee in his office, click-clacking away on what looks like a courtroom stenographer's machine. She's Japanese; you can tell by her round features and the rising sun flag on her right shoulder. She never speaks to you once or interjects in any way.

"I...I'm sorry?" you say, not understanding what Mr. Lee is talking about, not understanding what being related to "Christopher Lee" means. You nervously pat your damp head, shifting in your seat, with your plastic-covered resume held uncertainly in your hand. The Japanese stenographer click-clacks away on the machine every time someone speaks.

"Christopher Lee? Dracula? The Man with the Golden Gun? The Wicker Man? Saruman? Count Dooku?"

You swallow nervously. "The Shit...I mean Sith Lord?" you ask, vaguely remembering something.

Christopher Lee shakes his head. "No. If popular culture was something to be graded on, Miss, you really would've been docked a few points there. Never heard of Lord of the Rings? Really? The Hobbit?"

You start to freak a little bit, thinking to yourself that you should have. "I don't know anything about Dracula or uh, a Syrup-man. I'm sorry!"

Christopher Lee shakes his head and says without emotion, "I'm teasing you. That's what we call an "ice-breaker" in the corporate world. Something to liven up the mood." He looks at you again, and brings a pen out and starts marking something on your file.

Your heart beats faster and faster, and your hands shake a little. "Huh."

Christopher Lee clicks a few things on his keyboard, and checks out the application you submitted online before you went to bed last night.

He keeps speaking, looking over your file. "Now, where it asks for your job objective statement, you've put down, and this is a very interesting quote for me. "Livin' in fear ain't livin' to me. I'm armed with a gun defending the free. They blew it in 'Nam, shot up my friends. I'm back in the street, the fight never ends. I was born with a gun in my hand. I'll die for my country but I'll die like a man"."

A moment of dead silence. The recruiter stares at you, looking straight into your eyes.

Your jaw drops. "Oh shi...I mean, shoot, that's, heh, heh. I was copying and pasting lyrics to a Manowar song for my friend online as this, well, well, it's a funny story. It's not a funny story, really, well, I guess it's funny...I actually wanted to use my SSR position so I can gain that free slot into Solomon's House University, and then maybe into Xenoarchaeology. Like my sister."

"That's a shame, really. We don't have many twenty-year-old, female, Vietnam veteran/ vigilantes prowling the streets," Christopher Lee says without batting a single eyelash. A slight curl on his lips suggests that he wishes he could laugh but can't.

You slowly raise your hand and start to speak. Mr. Lee informs you that this isn't a classroom and that you can put your hand down.

"While that objective statement was—original—to say the least, you left out your hobbies. We like to know everything about our settler candidates, within reason and within the law, so please, enlighten me."

You have to think, and then you make the mistake of being too honest. You look to the mahogany ceiling. "I like to do LARP," you squeak out.

Massive silence. You can even hear the slight hum of the computer booting up an application.

"You think doing a drug would be an acceptable hobby?" Mr. Lee says.

"It's...it's not a drug, it's..."

"Ah, a sick, sexual deviant thing? You're just a young woman barely out of your teens, I mean, what is this country coming to?" the recruiter continues, his face turning red. Mr. Lee bites down on his lip openly, as if he wants to say something but can't.

"No! No, please, it's about role playing," you almost yell.

"Role playing?" Mr. Lee looks more disturbed, his eyes half-lidded.

"Wait, it's like, like D-Dungeons and Dragons, except we go outside and act it out live. Well, actually, what I like the most is Dagorhir—you use foam swords, foam javelins, and you have to be in character. You make your own uniform; it's like theater but with sports mixed in, but you have to stay in character. I was Queen of the Realm for one day. Tyler and everyone used to make fun of me, but..."

After a moment, Mr. Lee clears his throat. "Continuing on, then." He writes something down with his red pen this time. Your stomach feels upset.

"There are three hundred and seventy-six different people looking to get official settler status in The Oberon, and that's just today. We ask that those who wish to settle with us directly and work for us be of the highest caliber and highest character. The Oberon is a place unlike anything of this Earth, indeed it is not of this Earth, hence the common name "off-world". The Oberon is a very different place, a golden land of opportunity and advancement. We accept only the best there, and those who are the most open-minded, to be a part of our Network system."

"You're serious that The Oberon is that great? Because I only wanted to go to a dangerous and unstable place myself..." You chuckle nervously, trying to retrieve the situation. You blurt out something else that you hope makes some sort of sense in the long term, taking a leap into the dark to see if you can land on the other side. A moment passes and you feel this horrible need to rush out and use the toilet. Your gambit works.

Christopher Lee laughs after a moment, seeing you are joking. "That's good. That is good." He turns serious. "But no more joking, Miss Sarah. Laughing time is over, as the Simpsons would say. You have an associate's degree from Long Beach City College but you are single, which barely qualifies you to even have this meeting for possible settling. Now, based on your age, prior work experience, which is, ah, Papa John's Pizza for three months due to what you term "wrongful termination", currently at Subway, and your associate's degree, the only position I can guarantee you as a probationary settler is to be a Settler Service Representative, or SSR, at one of our Missions, one of our tower settlements. Your job there would to be help maintain the tower's settlers and see to their needs, and to attract other human settlers to live inside the settlement so we can expand. Immigration is still open to everyone who can charter a boat out to Point Nemo, so there are many settlers still outside the Network system. Your job would be to help attract the undocumented into The Oberon for their own safety and protection. We are looking to fill our homes at Mission Friendship, Mission Hazelden, Mission Passages, and Mission Wonderland."

"Oh, I see, you mean, like, like renting them houses inside the settlement? I heard about this on Discovery. The Network is basically like a human housing authority."

"We do more than that," Christopher Lee says. "We do a lot more than that. We are not some simple property management company. The Network..."

He launches into a five-minute monologue on what the Network does exactly, but since you are so nervous and have to pee, you barely pay attention to what he is saying.

"...chartered by the mandate of the Witch-Lord and the United States Government to fund and run all human police, all human settlements, and all large mines and salvage operations. We work closely with the natives. There is no colonization here. We are under the Witch-Lord's law."

"Of what?" you ask, fidgeting a little. You really need to pee.

"Miss Orange, what did I just say?" He taps the capped end of his pen against his teeth for a moment.

"Well, that the Network has to do what it has to do and there's a lot of ins and outs and complications to the situation, but that you need all the help you can get," you reply, praying that you've hit it on the head, or near enough.

"Indeed," Christopher Lee says, slowly nodding. "Indeed. Well put." You don't know if he is joking or not. "Let us run over a few situations and see how you would handle them..."

After a few scenarios are given to you about how to rent a place, how to deal with a fire emergency, or how to deal with an attack by Ni-Perchta; you think your answers, in comparison to what has gone on before, are correct and sound. Then again, you're not sure.

Christopher Lee sits back in his leather chair. "Well, we are making settler assignments and choices by 4:00 pm today. We will give you a call back by five. If you do not receive a call, it is because we have found a better-suited candidate on the list."

You look around to see if you should stand up. You do, slowly. Mr. Lee shakes your hand deliberately. "Be seeing you," he says, smiling.

You are sitting alone at the In-N-Out next to Pacific Coast Highway in Seal Beach, watching new drops of rain splatter against the window—another day of the orichalcum-produced maintenance storm. You are downing a Double Double—hold the lettuce—and sipping on a Coke with too much ice, staring at your Mickey Mouse watch. You've just paid out your last eight dollars for this meal.

A cheesy container and a box of dwindling fries sit in front of you. If Christopher Lee was telling the truth, it will be around 5:00 pm that you'll find out if you're going to The Oberon.

It is now 1:30. The lunch hour rush has passed so you are virtually alone, except for the anonymous attendants working the drive-through window. Time will drag out. Every hour will not be quick enough. You stare out the window, thinking of Tyler, your mother, and your future here on Earth disappearing.

The window faces Pacific Coast Highway turning into Main Street, and you watch the cars splash and stop their way through the downfall. Cheap-looking old Buicks, brand new Fords, and little curvy Toyotas swing by; a limousine drives by as well. A bus discharges its already soggy patrons onto the street. They rush across the long crosswalk towards a once-white, now gray, office building next door, ignoring the old, homeless man soaked to the bone holding a *Will Work For Anything* sign.

There is a very long line of people waiting to get into that gray government-style building across the street; they're mostly young, some older, with umbrellas out or hooded sweatshirts covering their heads as they shuffle forward, one sneakered or flat shoe at a time. The blocky office monument on the small green lawn outside the government building reads: *California Unemployment Services.*

You think for a long while about your sister. She is—was—a smart woman who thought a lot about the world and what it meant to be alive in it. She was philosophical without pretension. She won scholarship after scholarship in school, was always athletic, driven, always focused, and different—in a word: scary. She graduated UCLA, then Yale; already mentioned in a small article in the New York Times about the up and coming women of the Ivy League by the time she was just eighteen. And then she got married to that Ian Zur and had been in The Oberon for the last ten years, doing God knows what. She never called and never wrote past your thirteenth birthday. It was as if she had moved to the dark side of the moon, which you guess The Oberon really is.

If they say no to you joining, if you don't get the Network job, where could you go? Back to your mother and her bullshit? You aren't going to college next year—you and your mother are broke—and you've finished City College. Tyler had talked loosely of marriage, maybe, in the summer, and somehow you'd read more into that than you should have, making no real, decent, future plans. Besides, college is bullshit for a bachelor's degree in this economy—four years and $40,000 later to find out you're qualified to work at Starbucks.

You watch as a young, fresh-faced couple step out of the rain and into the restaurant—a blonde-haired, blue-eyed boy with a blonde-haired, blue-eyed girl, about your age. They are smiling and laughing, shaking off the rain, enjoying each other's company. They make their order, choose a table, and the boy brings the girl her soda fountain drink. They look at each other, touch each other's arms, laugh at what you are sure is nothing.

You pick up your food and toss it out, not hungry anymore, and leave the restaurant to step out into a gust of rain, umbrella in hand.

You put it up and try to avoid looking at all those poor faces queuing in the unemployment line, each face full of dull despair mingled with dying hope. You wait for the bus going in the opposite direction and then head back towards home.

With a jerk of your key, you open your apartment door and walk into your bedroom. It is empty and dark; the blinds are drawn, and there is only the slightest drumming of rain against the window. A bed unmade, a low-volume TV left on an Evangelist station, and a chair with your cat, Slinks, perched on top of it.

Slinks blinks twice, looks at you, and falls back to sleep, a curled-up classic tabby. You look at your watch as you close the door. It's 2:05 pm, according to Mickey Mouse.

"Hello," you say. Slinks looks up, blinks again, meows something, and goes back to sleep. "Good to see you."

You lock the door behind you and crawl into bed, your wet coat still on, though you do manage to kick your heels off. You pull the covers up to your head and try to sleep.

You look at the red digital alarm clock: 2:07 pm.

You start to cry a little, a sort of mild sob. Think of Tyler and his cheating. It has made you finally look at where your life is going—your precious life, your one life, and you are here, in miserable Southern California, going nowhere, getting nowhere, feeling nothing, doing nothing, with an unfeeling, unloving mother. What should you do?

You don't sleep but you aren't fully conscious either. The cat decides to get up, stretch, and then perch himself near the top of your head. He purrs the day away.

"Thanks for that," you say sarcastically, as you feel his furry body brush your head.

2:15 pm.

You start to think too much. Your dead father wouldn't mind you joining him in Heaven, would he? You think not. Why are you thinking this?

Slinks abandons his position.

2:38 pm.

You turn over and stare at your cellphone. They will call at 5:00 pm, you remind yourself. If they don't call, you'll go to Heaven; a place of eternal whiteness and warmth, where the trees always give cool shade, the water is fresh, and there is no work to go to, only sweet music to listen to. The days never end and all the people you have ever known sit together in perfect understanding and harmony...

2:52pm.

If you don't get this "job," what will you be?

An eternal nothing; a young woman with no future worth mentioning, nor past worth studying. Why are you making this job into something bigger than it is? It's a CSR job—customer service—a rental agent job. But there is a feeling just at the back of your skull, a feeling that by getting to The Oberon, somewhere so different than anywhere on Earth, that maybe just getting your foot in the door will lead to something very, very great. This is not a rational thought but a feeling that is tugging at you.

You drift off to sleep and wake to find that some time has passed.

4:57 pm.

Three minutes until their phone call. Time moves oh so very slowly forward. You grow more scared and rationality leaks away from you. You think strange thoughts. When it is night and perhaps storming outside, you will take off all your clothes, let the cool rain wash over your skin. You will walk out into the waves; you will start to swim ever forward. When it gets too cold, you will fall asleep in that mother ocean...and you will let the sea take you. You will only see the moon before you slip under...

4:59 pm.

They should be calling. One minute from now, you will know how the entire rest of your life will play out.

5:04 pm.

You sit upright in bed, your fists clenching and unclenching over and over again. You mutter under your breath. "Call...call...call, you bastards, call...Call..."

5:05pm.

A ring. You grab the phone. "This is Sarah Orange."

"Hello, Sarah, this is Christopher Lee. You are hired..." His voice seems a million miles away. You fake your way through the rest of the conversation, saying everything appropriately, then thanking him. Shaking, you hang up the phone and lay it back down, pulling the covers up tighter.

Later there is a knock at the door. It's Jaime, looking frantic and in need of something. "Pachinko, Pachinko is out."

"Pachinko is out?" you ask, confused at first and then remembering exactly who Pachinko is. "Oh, Pachinko. Are you sure you're pronouncing her name right?

Jaime ignores your enquiry. "Pachinko is out, Sarah. She attacked someone at the Math Lab with a pair of scissors. I need to get married to get out there." He lowers himself onto one knee.

"Sarah Orange, will you marry me?" For a moment you almost forget it is Jaime—you look at that face, that kind face with bright blue eyes, and slide into a different reality where it's actually Tyler asking you for marriage. That charming Tyler is asking you and you say...

Then you snap out of it, biting your tongue for a moment. It's just Jaime, his slightly-off twin brother.

NIGHTHAWKS AT THE MISSION

CHAPTER THREE:
QUEEN MARY

You sit by your apartment's broken Jacuzzi, bundled up in a sweatshirt, looking up to the stars you can barely see through the orange haze of city lights. You are thinking things over, haunted by your mother's words from days earlier. You have been slowly and secretively preparing for your off-world escape.

Tyler has called you twenty-four times. No one else is around; you sit on a cold deckchair by the lit-up pool, alone, thinking over your life. The constant city sounds, sirens, cars driving by, televisions, and your neighbors talking do not distract you in the slightest from your meditation.

Coming over the small wooden bridge shaded by the oak trees that lead into your apartment's courtyard area is a thin, older man, maybe in his early sixties, in a three-piece old style suit as gray as his face and hair. He is whistling into the wind. You can't help but notice that there is a charred electrical smell—like a socket has burnt out or when your TV pops a fuse—when he appears.

He stops midway on the bridge over the small creek. "Feeling alone, Miss Sarah Orange?" he asks.

You swallow, feeling very alone now; there is no one there at this particular moment except for the people in their apartments around the courtyard. "No," you call out.

"May I step over and speak with you?" He waits before making his move.

"Um...okay."

"Good." He smiles and walks over to you. Before you can say anything, he speaks again; cultured ooze pours out of his thin lips. "Oh, the things I know about you, Miss Orange."

You stand up, ready to do a little bit of fight or flight. "Pleased to meet you, Mr...."

"My name, well, for now, let's say it's Scratch. I often go by that name in New England." He titters like a girl. "Old joke."

"Oh," you say, looking for an easy escape route. That sixth sense that something is very wrong is needling the back of your head. Thunder cracks, very close by.

"I wouldn't leave, Miss Orange."

"Wh...what do you want?" The wind picks up making it hard to be heard. You wonder where the storm has come from; it was seemingly peaceful just moments ago.

The old man's eyes light up and he smiles, revealing a set of yellowing, uneven teeth. He puts a finger up to his lips, shushing you. From his pocket he takes out a small, gray, dented, and very old-looking box with a button that has a large crack running through its middle. Scratch presses it, and you suddenly find that all sounds from the outside world have stopped—no city sounds, no sound of the wind, not even the chatter of your neighbors or the sounds of their televisions. He puts the device back into his pocket. The whole world has been muted except for you and him.

"That's better. Why, Miss, I'm here to congratulate you! Your sister has left to you this particular item in her will."

"My sister is not dead," you say.

"She's not only dead, she's really most sincerely dead." Scratch laughs and then catches the look on your face, a look of pure horror. "Apologies." He motions for you to sit down, and he sits down opposite you on another deckchair.

"Oh, Miss, I do apologize, but this item was left in her will for your family in particular. Unfortunately, it did take a long time—she had to be considered legally dead and the item had to clear Network customs and well, you know how bureaucracy is. Someone took its listing, put it to the bottom of the pile and then forgot that the pile existed in the first place." He laughs with that titter again, frightening you. "She went missing leading an illegal expedition to somewhere on the other side of The Oberon, maybe even past the Burzee, no? Quite the explorer, she was."

He gives you a small leather book of parchment that has a cloth strip binding it together. It is about the size of a thick wallet.

"It's the Voice of the Four Winds, or the Book of the Witch-Lords of Mir. It's an original made out of Afer skin. It has pages of prayers, spells, a complete map of The Oberon itself, the Rosetta Stone page—where it translates fourteen Earth languages into the Antediluvian standard hieroglyphics. It's a rare book to have outside The Oberon."

You open it carefully. On the first page is a collection of circles and lines drawn in black ink. Little thunder bolts sign the corners of each page.

Scratch, looking at what you are seeing, reads what it means. "And over the world, nor stop, nor stay, the winds of the Storm King go out on their way..."

The simple nature of these words and the unknown that lies behind them is terrifying. You suddenly don't want to take it. You bite your lip. "If I refuse to take it?"

Scratch tilts his head in amusement. "Refuse?"

After a moment you can see that his eyes have turned a deep green after being a light hazel. "Of course you can."

"H...how much?" you ask quietly.

"How much is it worth? How much is it worth? Oh, it's worth a good amount of pennies. But never sell it. You must never sell it. Keep it on you at all times."

You feel as if something has slapped you hard across the face. "I will never sell it. I will always keep it."

Scratch begins to walk away, humming to himself, and then turns back to you. "Be seeing you."

You notice for the first time that Scratch has companions with him—three tall men in black coats and black fedora hats with almost bone-white skin. As you watch them leave, you start to shake a little, not sure if what just happened actually happened or was only in your mind.

The private gym that a long time ago Tyler gave you access to is empty at this hour, as it mostly always is, and time stretches out; you can't sleep and don't want to think anymore. So you work out by yourself. You throw your sweatshirt off, stretch, and, just because you can, do a random handstand, letting the blood flood your head and push out all those thoughts that come up like little poisonous buoys floating in the surf of your mind. When your handstand ends in a summersault, you catch a glimpse of your slightly sweating self in the mirrored wall, and spot the hanging boxing bag.

Falling into the fighting stance you were taught a long time ago, you lightly kick at the bag, once, twice, three times. You throw in some medium punches, wanting to keep it to an easy exercise but as those thoughts start to finally intrude, you go at it, biting the inside of your lip hard. You punch the bag as hard and as fast as you can for a minute straight. Both your hands and feet sting like hell. You finish with a little combo, hurting your right hand a little. There is blood in your mouth.

You stare at the bag, sweating profusely now, thinking of Tyler and wishing that the bag was your ex-boyfriend's face. You cry a little again, but shrug it off with another combo to the bag. Next you run for five miles on the treadmill; the only sounds you hear are the running of the tread's motors and your feet slapping against the belt.

You steal your mother's Volvo that morning. You've packed two suitcases: one with your personal stuff, like pictures of your sister and father as well as yearbooks and other things; the other suitcase is full of clothes. You managed to pack up everything in the middle of the night, silent as a ninja.

Digging your phone out of your purse, you dial Tyler's number and wait impatiently for him to pick up.

"Hi, it's Tyler."

"Tyler, it's me. I..."

"You know what to do. Beep." It's his voicemail. He's probably asleep. It's three in the morning, after all. He'd better be asleep.

"Tyler, we need to talk. Can you meet me somewhere? Call me. Please." You hang up and toss the cell onto the passenger seat.

You drive through the deserted streets of Long Beach and Seal Beach, seeing your old hometowns for the last time, killing time until the sun rises and Tyler wakes up.

You call him again but aren't surprised when it goes straight to voice mail. Again. Frustrated, you sigh and toss your cell back on the seat. No point leaving yet another message.

The next few hours pass slowly. As the sun begins to peer around the horizon, you try one last time and finally get through. "Tyler, we need to talk," you tell him.

"Yeah, okay," he says sleepily. "Come on over."

You roll down your window and toss the phone into the bushes as you speed towards the beach house. You won't be needing it where you're going.

It's 7:00 am when you arrive at the beach house, which is empty and cold compared to how it was at Thanksgiving. In the living room, you stare at the waves as you wait for him to come down from his bedroom. When he does you look at him like he is a completely new person. His hair is disheveled and his eyes are red with heavy bags under them.

"Sarah," Tyler starts, swallowing compulsively. "Sarah, I am sorry about that, about what happened."

You sit on the leather couch, listening to him spout on about his need to apologize and that it was "just sex, just sex." You stare at him for a good moment, saying nothing; Tyler finally chokes up a little.

You tilt your head. "Yes?" you ask.

Tyler shrugs. "Look, we don't...we haven't had sex, you know, and that's, that's something...you need to have that in a relationship."

"I was waiting until marriage, Ty," you say coldly. "We were going to be married, weren't we? We never said it totally, but there was that—I don't know what you want to call it—implication, there."

Tyler starts to cry a little. "But I'm a guy, Sarah. I need it. I want it. Sorry if that sounds selfish, but shit, I do. Your friend Christine, and Courtney, they understood. They weren't, uh, you know, weird about sex."

You stand up. "I need to use the bathroom." He nods and sits down on the couch you've just left.

You go upstairs, pass by the bathroom, ignoring it, and make it into Tyler's bedroom. On the dresser next to his king-size bed is a nightstand, and on it is a wallet with *Bad M*F*cker* embroidered on it. You open the wallet and take out all the money—a good collection of hundreds and twenties, equaling $1,240—and put it into your jacket. You also see his Rolex watch, and snatch that—he once told you it was a gift for turning eighteen and was worth $8,000 new, so you could probably get a third of that at a pawn shop. You walk down the hall to the guest bedroom.

Lying in bed, stomach down with bare back showing, is Courtney.

You reach into your jacket and slowly take out the heavy gun you've brought with you, cock it and even point it at the sleeping traitor. Stare down the gun sight and aim it right at the back of her pretty little head, savoring the moment just a little.

You pull the trigger and the gun makes a dry click sound. Courtney snuffles something in her sleep. You smile.

Downstairs again, Tyler sits on the couch. "Goodbye, Tyler," you say evenly. You take one last look around his house. "Oh, here's your little present back."

You hand Tyler the gun. He sniffles a little.

"You can keep it," he tells you. "You were the only crazy Wild West girl around here. Every week you'd be out there." He has a weak, sad smile on his face.

"I wanted to give it to you and Courtney so bad," you reply coldly. "But I can't keep it. Goodbye."

Tyler feels the gun, pops the cylinder, and drops the bullets into his hand. "You brought it over, uh, loaded?"

"Oh, I guess I did," you say and walk away without looking back.

You meet her at something called The Spot, some local little breakfast-lunch café open only until two p.m. That she showed up at all must have meant your one voicemail had gotten through to her—something, maybe a tone in your voice, a choice of words, had imparted the important message. She didn't decide to ignore it, as was the case sometimes.

Your mother, always early, sits by herself at a small outside table facing the Pacific Coast Highway, her round sunglasses making her look like an aging Hollywood actress trying to be discrete. She sips her coffee, acknowledging you with a stiff nod.

You sit down, sick to your stomach, thinking about Tyler. And Courtney. And what you were—you try not to think about what you were capable of earlier.

She doesn't bother with formalities of any kind.

"You are going off-world, then?" your mother says, her voice low. You can barely hear her over the light traffic whizzing by the front of the café.

"Looks like it," you mention, before being interrupted by the waitress who asks you if you want something to drink. You ask for an apple juice.

"Apple juice," your mother says quietly, sipping at her coffee. "Very adult of you."

Before you can say anything, your mother blows out her breath and takes another sip of coffee before putting together her words.

"Quick, isn't? Never knew they were that desperate for settlers. That's too quick," she insinuates.

"Maybe." Your apple juice comes and the waitress retreats as you ask for another moment to look at the menu. Before you sip on it, you take the straw out and place it down on a napkin. This might make you look a little older.

"Don't go." She puts down her coffee with a clang and some of it spills out over the top of the white mug. "Please. Don't do it." She stares not at you but at the traffic whizzing by. "Why are you doing this? For God's sake, I'm begging you not to. I really am. We're…we're all that's left of our family. Dad. Your sister. You know…" She chokes up a little. "I can't bully you into staying, I guess. I'm sorry I did that." She whimpers.

You spot the waitress out of the corner of your eye catching the scene of your mother sobbing behind her sunglasses. When she sees that you see her watching, she quickly starts counting napkins near the cash register.

You relish this a little, your mother's defenses—her anger and her hysterics—have crumbled beneath your determination to go to The Oberon.

Even so, your lip quivers a little before you respond. "Oh, that's good. From bullying to guilt-tripping. Why should I stay? I mean, what do I have here? What do I really have? Why should I even want to stay?" you say, about to tear up a little yourself. Anger trickles into your blood, a cold anger caused by years of hurt and shit being thrown your way. Anger once buried down deep that's now been dredged up and returned to the surface like a foul oil.

"I've got nothing here. I've had my whole life to realize that I've never had a mother. Just a bitter woman needling me and pressing on me my whole life. Not really a mother. You can blame it on what happened over the years. Your bitterness. Your nastiness. But deep down you and I know the truth. If you really gave a shit about me, you'd get over that. You'd find it within yourself to do that. But you know what you are? Just a bad person that bad things have happened to. You understand? What happened was just extra for you, just extra bitterness and hurt and anger on top of a miserable and angry life. "

Tears pass out from under your mother's sunglasses. She doesn't say a word but she quietly cries, crying more than she did at the funerals. You wait a good minute before continuing.

"Let me tell you about a little girl. She was a little awkward and a little different from the others, had a stutter she had to e-erase. But she grew up and people stopped teasing her. But she wanted to be better than everyone else, so she hooked up with a boy who probably wasn't good for her but he was rich. And by being rich herself by marrying this boy, one day she could get away from all the memories, the bad memories of the past. But that just blew up in her face. So now she needs to go out there and get money any which way she can to finally bury the past. So she goes off-world. Does that explain enough for you? Why would I stay?"

You stand up to leave, abandoning your mother to her own fate. You wipe a tear from your own face before you climb back into the Volvo after nearly knocking over the waitress on your way out. You see your mother one last time in your rear view mirror as you go down P.C.H.

Your cab pulls up to the Queen Mary. You had dumped your mother's car off in a parking lot next to the Courthouse. The Queen Mary strikes you as a stately throwback of a cruise liner. The Network brochure you got at their local office mentions that the old ship, which looks to you like a kissing cousin to the Titanic you've seen in movies and books, was originally launched back in the 1930s, retired in the 1960s, and then re- furbished and re-launched a few years back since all the other, newer ocean liners with all their electronics would have mechanical meltdowns every time they went into The Oberon. The ship is a majestic piece of black, white, and red machinery, and its three smokestacks are already pumping out a sizeable amount of pollution into the gray and very overcast afternoon air. A thousand seagulls fly around the parking lot next to the launch.

You hold the brochure tightly in one fist, your tickets tucked safely inside, and you hold your small crucifix in the other.

The yellow cab pulls up behind idling buses and cabs and other random cars that swing in and out to drop off a passenger or three. Jaime says awkwardly that he has forgotten his cash, and you dig some out from your purse.

"No problem, honey," you say sarcastically. You pay off the cab driver, who pulls out with a screech.

"Did the courthouse thing feel, you know, strange? We're actually married, Sarah, that's something. That's really something." Jaime looks at you sheepishly, one of his eyes slightly blackened. He holds up his left hand; new golden wedding ring in place.

You hold up yours and clink your ring against his.

"We are married," you marvel. "Your uncle the judge was very nice to come in on his day off. How's your eye, Jaime? Tyler didn't hurt you too bad, did he?"

"Meh. What did you think of the...wedding? Weird, right?"

You nod. "It was kind of the opposite of every girl's dream. Look, Jaime, no offense, but this is, uh, an open marriage, you understand that, right? No offense? We'll work together as partners, like we said. We'll figure that out when we get out there."

Jaime has to think over what you've just said. "Oh, no, no, none taken. You're not really my type anyway," he says. "We have to do that again, though, you know that? Three hundred and sixty five days later, we have to do it in a Witch-Lord Temple in order to stay."

You feel sort of slapped in the face by his earlier comment and are about to reply when you see something amazing. You both watch as a couple of longshoremen, in their black and yellow safety vests with red hard hats, lift a couple of large metal crates the size of cars into the front hold of the Queen. The thing is, though, they are not lifting these crates with cranes, but telekinetically with the aid of their batons. A telltale green glow comes from these telescoping batons. They have orichalcum stones embedded into their grips. The two longshoremen point at the crates with their batons; the crates float upwards towards two more longshoremen standing on the Queen. They "grab" the crates in mid-air with that telekinetic power that comes from their telescoped batons. The large crates, that must weigh thousands of pounds, bob for a moment in the air as the second team of longshoremen grabs them.

"That's orichalcum power. The longshoremen now use telekinesis ori, which is cheaper and more cost effective than cranes," Jaime says. You are both pretty young but the orichalcum thing is still a little off-putting to the both of you—you didn't originally grow up with it like kids nowadays, so there's always that little moment of reality disconnect when you see something on the news or someone using it in real life. A couple of other people quietly watch the scene as red-capped valets and bellboys scurry about with pieces of luggage and other random items.

"Stuff like that is going to be all over the place in The Oberon," Jaime says and walks to one of the metal platforms that leads into the Queen. He almost disappears into the darkened interior of the ship, but stops by the line going inside. A couple of baseball-capped security guards wait nearby, as does an aged cabin stewardess charged with checking passports.

NIGHTHAWKS AT THE MISSION

As you wait on the edge of the giant gangplank that leads into the Queen, a bad feeling grows in your stomach. A cool breeze caresses your skin. You think how irresponsible this is, how impulsive—but then you realize, what's to stop you? There's nothing really there for you in the O.C., no real future expectations. The sad fact of the matter is that you were just planning to go to college and help Tyler grow up a little, and that fell apart. Jaime, in his own almost criminally-nerdy way, is leading you towards something better than what waits for you here. You know it inside; you feel it. But at the same time, there is a slow and awful dream-like sensation, this feeling of upcoming danger you can't exactly shake. Your palms sweat a little and your heart starts to pound. This is an adventure, you admit to yourself. This is something more extraordinary than anything you've ever done—and all because you got burned by a relationship with a man who looks exactly the same as the one you are now in a sham marriage with.

Suddenly the salty smell of the sea and the whiff of diesel that permeates everything in the air becomes stronger, carving themselves into your memory. And, with that last thought, just as your fake husband waves for you to come on in, you step onto the metal platform. It clangs heavily under your sneakered feet. There is no one to see you off.

After settling into your cheap little cabin, you stand on the starboard side of the ship. The cabin has cigarette burns on the carpet and smells like vomit in one particular corner. When you saw the room, you and Jaime gave each other a look about the one bed. Jaime laughed nervously, then shut his mouth after looking at you.

Jaime leaves to grab some coffee, and you stand next to the railing, feeling a chill as a fresh breeze blows in. A red-capped valet, an older black man with a kind face, comes by and taps you gently on the shoulder. You turn down the volume on the iPod and stop the Manowar that's ringing through it.

"Miss, make sure you stuff that away with the purser by the time we get to the Nemo Gate. Otherwise, it's gonna cook, okay?"

You look uncertainly at your iPod with its Hello Kitty cover. "Cook?"

The valet nods. "Honey, with all that EMP out there, it'll pop the moment we go through." Your confusion must be apparent because he shakes his head and continues. "You know, EMP? It's like a signal that comes off the A-bombs when they blow 'em up? Well, The Oberon is just full of it bouncing around and it blows out all the electronics. I mean, why d'ya think we're on the Titanic's younger sister? This thing should be a museum, not an ocean liner, but all the new liners are almost like NASA built 'em, too much electronics—they would break down two seconds after they crossed."

"Is this thing safe, then?"

The valet looks around as if seeing the ship for the first time. "Well, if it's not, I'll save you a seat on one of the lifeboats." He winks and starts to leave, but then turns around to say another word to you. "Oh, and make sure you don't get caught with a camera—it's a UN rule. No pictures allowed!"

Jaime skips around the corner, his steps almost bouncing down the old deck, carrying two cups of coffee. He gives you one.

"No electronics? No iPods, no laptops?"

Jaime sips his coffee a little too quickly and dribbles some down his sweatshirt. "Uh, yeah. I forgot about that whole thing..."

You squint at him. "I didn't know that, Jaime. Jeez."

He grows quickly defensive, not making eye contact. "You didn't read up on anything about The Oberon? I mean that's like, like the first thing they say, Sarah. Really..."

"How do people get around?" you ask. "Horses? No cars? Sending mail by carrier pigeon, maybe? Is there electricity? Hopefully there are toilets..."

"Sometimes," Jaime says, giving you a sidelong glance. "There's books inside. A really good one is *The Oberon* by Frank Morgan."

You stare out into the ocean, glancing at the skyline of Long Beach, California. "We really doing this?" Before he can answer, a foghorn blares out three times.

"I guess we are, Sarah," he says, brushing his black hair back as it's blown around in the wind. "I'm so excited I could almost spit!"

You, being in a dark mood, mock him to his face. "Oh goodie!" you say, then walk down the deck with your coffee. Jaime looks hurt when you glance back at him. You feel bad for a moment, but just for a moment. You take a sip of coffee and spit it out over the railing just as he comes up and switches coffees with you. "I usually put in about six sugar packets and fill half of the cup with cream. Sorry about that."

You nod, say thanks, and sip away.

The knowledge that you are going to a completely different place is unreal and heavy. The feeling of thin ice under your feet is there as well. Perhaps the cracks are already forming.

As the Queen Mary chugs out into the open ocean, the briny smell of seawater steadily streams into your nostrils. Seagulls cry. There is the continuous blasting horns of tug boats. The Long Beach skyline, full of condo towers and high-rises, cranes and floating docks, gradually diminishes. The coastline slowly disappears into the distance and you feel a sort of relief, a sort of stillness in your chest, as you realize that you have done it.

A pre-recorded, cultured female voice comes over the loudspeakers. "The Off-World Network and the Witch-Lord of The Oberon welcome you aboard the Queen Mary and wish you well on your journey to The Oberon off-world settlements. And now your host, Morgan Freeman, who will join you at certain stages of the journey."

People begin to clap and cheer, thrilled at their upcoming excursion. There's a slight pause and then Freeman's deep voice speaks; an uplifting soundtrack plays in the background. "Today, you begin your voyage to a place once found only in the imaginations of the writers of fiction—a place like no other, a place only opened to outsiders after centuries of isolation.

"Fifteen days from now, you will have crossed the great blue expanse of the Pacific Ocean to the oceanic pole of inaccessibility, the furthest point in the ocean away from all landmasses, or as the sailors once called it, Point Nemo, in reference to Jules Verne's Captain Nemo.

"And there, on the day of the southern hemisphere's summer solstice, December twenty-second, you will see the phenomenon that Frank Morgan, the discoverer of The Oberon, famously called "God Moving Over the Face of the Waters"—the opening of the great Nemo Gate, the largest one in the universe.

"As we start our first steps towards going off-world, let us take a moment to appraise the potential fruitfulness of that far-off place."

The Queen Mary steams towards a massive structure that sits in the middle of the ocean, a technological monstrosity that is the new ori-reactor, a sixty story, quarter of a mile wide steel pyramidal structure that tapers off into a narrow flattop. Blue and orange lights dot the structure, and the reactor center has the telltale whitish hue around it, noting the active use of power-producing orichalcum. Waves crash and crest onto its base. Small ships with construction cranes and other equipment are docked next to it.

"This project, if successful, will be a Network reactor, Solomon's House One, built with the plans of the Antediluvian civilization that has been extinct for six thousand years. When fully constructed and brought finally online, this first reactor will potentially be able to generate enough electrical power to light every household, factory, shop, and school from Los Angeles to San Francisco. Pure white orichalcum, the mineral used for energy consumption, will be this and other reactors' lifeblood, delivered to all of us by the sacrifices and discoveries of young prospectors and free settlers who live life on a new frontier."

Freeman's recording continues. Nearly everyone on board is as young as you or only slightly older.

You take a deep breath, enjoying these moments of absolute freedom but also feeling like you've just been cut adrift. You feel very much alone at that moment, though Jaime is beside you. He's too interested in the reactor to be of much company. Finally, he pats you on the shoulder twice and gives you a little hug, and you find yourself responding.

You wake up on your side of the bed in the little cabin. Jaime sleeps with his feet towards your head, and your feet point towards his. His feet smell, and you're a little disgusted every time you wake. You've been doing this little routine for a couple of weeks now, as the liner makes its way across the South Pacific. You're sick of it and sick of yourself for having set up this whole thing to begin with. *What the hell just happened?* is now your running mantra.

You flip on the bathroom light, brush your hair, and stare at the mirror for a few moments. You roll your eyes at your mirror image, then pull on jeans and a jacket and step into the deck's hallway. The lights flicker for a moment. It's almost like walking through the lobby part of that Twilight Zone Tower of Terror ride you went on with Tyler a few months ago. Tyler was so scared he ditched you in line because he heard about the drop and was too much of an effing you- know-what to go on. The hallway is vintage 1930s horror—dust covers all the beautifully ornate crown molding and the almost-Victorian style lighting.

Up ahead, the door leading to the outside deck has been left propped open, and you step through the heavy doorframe. From the deck, you look out onto a millpond ocean. There is a full moon highlighting the lack of new waves.

Partially illuminated by the moonlight and the glow of lights streaming through the portholes is a young man, older than you, with slightly ruffled blond hair and a pair of white Ray-Ban sunglasses tucked into the neck of his black T-shirt underneath a black cloth jacket. He stands there, waiting alone, as if he knew you were coming.

You say hello to him curtly and he says, "Good evening" right back at you.

Dry white lightning rolls out over the horizon without a single thunderclap. Little balls of lightning, blue and orange flash and dip into the far distant ocean, rise again, and disappear into the greater darkness. "Good Lord," you say, startled. There is a spread of three green balls of lightning that each fly towards different points of the compass and disappear.

"What is that?" you say.

"Ball lightning phenomena coming out near Point Nemo. It's starting to open. I knew we could see it now. It'll be like this for a few hours, then nothing. And then something incredible, like God opening a hole in the universe. Didn't you hear the orientation stuff? About what happens when we actually go into the Gate?" he asks with innocent wonder, not mocking you.

You blink several times. "I wasn't paying attention." A strong wind blows from somewhere far off, pushing you both towards the outside deck walls. He doesn't say anything further.

"Sarah. Sarah Orange," you say. "I'm sorry, what's your name?"

"Guy Farson," he says. You shake his hand with one fluid motion, and he continues to watch the display outside the ship. "First time to The Oberon?"

"Yes," you say. "It should be fun."

Guy smiles and looks like he wants to say something but holds his tongue. "That's one way of putting it." He rubs the thin layer of stubble on his cheeks, as if thinking about something. "I have no idea why I'm volunteering this information. I sort of "dayhawk" for a living. What do you do?"

You wonder what the hell a dayhawk is, but then remember. "Oh?" you say, chuckling. "Me and my, my, uh, Jamie, are goin' to be dayhawkin', too. I guess. Well...At a place called the Super Sargasso region." You keep talking despite Guy's obvious lack of interest. "He'll be, uh, grabbing salvageables, is that the right word? It'll be a hoot." You realize how retarded that sounds but Guy doesn't say anything.

"Maybe I'll be seeing you out there. I go out that way sometimes." He takes out a silver flask and has a sip from it.

"Is that alcohol?"

"No. Not at all." He looks at you sideways.

You nod quickly, feeling a chill, laughing a little. "Goodnight."

Guy leaves, watching the electricity play out over the far waters as he continues to walk down the deck.

December 22nd, 2012
Summer Solstice (Southern Hemisphere)
Point Nemo

You sit on the bed, feeling Jaime's forehead. "You're not burning up with fever, at least. That's a good sign."

"I feel like I got to throw up again." He gets out of bed, rushes to the bathroom, and closes the door behind him. You hear a vile noise come out of him, and it makes you wince. When he stumbles back to bed, he looks pale green and compulsively wipes his mouth. "You go on ahead to the party. I'll be here until this calms down. I won't miss it, I swear I won't miss it..."

You sigh and stand up. "Look, Jaime, if you need anything, please, uh, well you can't call me, but call the porter, okay? Don't suffer with being sea sick."

Jaime groans and closes his eyes. "Please get me up when the portal opens, okay? Please?"

After a moment you leave the cabin, closing the door quietly behind you.

The party is in full swing, the chants of well-wishers and the clanging of glasses echoing throughout Winston's Lounge. *Happy Summer Solstice* reads the large white and blue banner that hangs across the mirrored wall directly behind the bar. The lounge faces the darkness of the ocean ahead of you. Cigarette smoke fogs every corner. Couples dance on the large tiled floor in the middle of the space while a Huey Lewis and the News cover band sing something about a new drug. TVs are being taken down and put into storage by men in grim, gray overalls, armed with ladders. They're trying to get the equipment out amongst a sea of partygoers and the curious.

You sip on a Shirley Temple and watch people mingle, dance, laugh, drink, and celebrate as time ticks down towards the portal opening at exactly 3:00 am, as it does every solstice. It is 12:18 am right now, according to Mickey Mouse. You slept most of the day in anticipation of the late night. Lost in thought, you ponder where you're going. Anxiety fills every pore of your body. You sit there with a sick stomach and an aching and racing heart.

Guy Farson is in a sort of business-casual suit, complete with loose tie. A lit cigar hangs out of one side of his mouth, and he has a bottle of Johnnie Walker Blue Label scotch in one hand. He wears sunglasses. "Oh god, I love Huey Lewis and the Blues," he says, trying to be heard over the music as he sways to the beat.

"N-news," you say, nervous. The young man you've only just met the night before seems drunk.

"What?" he practically yells, sitting himself down at your table with a thump. Your Shirley Temple almost tips over onto the white tablecloth before you grab it.

"It's uh, uh News. Huey Lewis and the News."

"Jews?" he says. "I always thought that was an odd name for a band, innit? Huey Lewis and the Jews." You look around desperately for an easy out.

The band finishes up their song and tells everyone that they'll be back in ten minutes to play up to the opening of the Nemo Gate. The noise level dies down a bit. Farson takes your glass, drinks all that is left of the Shirley Temple, and pours the Walker over the leftover ice. He flips an unused white coffee mug and splashes some into it for himself.

"I don't drink alcohol. I'm underage," you say with firmness in your voice. You stare at him for a good moment.

"And I'm really twenty-eight. I don't drink except on weekends. I don't lie to friends, borrow money from family, and I go to church only on Christmas and Easter. Anything else you want to share? You ever do drugs with a stranger?"

You shake your head and stand up. He holds up a hand and takes a drink of his scotch. "Look, Sarah." He licks his full lips as if thinking for a moment, trying to get over some sort of hurdle to speak what is on his mind. "Let me tell you something, Miss Orange. I'll leave in just a minute, but I think that you must be a very interesting girl." He looks around and then moves closer to you. "Let me explain."

You cross your arms, hopefully looking tough. "You're by yourself here—no friends that I can see. You just signed up, no problem, with no one else. So you must have quite a sense of adventure—going alone, as a young lady. Not a lot of people can do that. I mean, money is tight back in the USA but still. I was watching you as you came in. Everyone here is with somebody, 'cept you and me. And I know why I am alone."

"Maybe you're right. I always wanted to have an adventure. But you are also wrong—I'm here with my husband."

Guy tilts his head. "Who isn't here now, is he? On the biggest night of the voyage?"

You shrug. "He's sick."

Guy nods his head up and down, grinning, clapping his hands together. "Sick or not sick, I'd be with a pretty girl like you. You know, I'm sick of cake-ass niggas like him."

You laugh a little and look away from him.

Guy continues. "I love meeting people who want to break the mold. I was the same way, too. Or still am, I suppose. Well then, do you mind if I spend this solstice talking to you? I am by myself."

You look down for a long moment and then straight into Guy's eyes—well, sunglasses. "What exactly do you do in The Oberon?"

He pauses and downs the contents of the coffee mug. He licks his lips. "I'm the point man for a co-op called Tokyo Sex Whale. I didn't make up the name, I swear. I know it sounds just...well, anyway. I'm the first one into the old buildings in the cities. I get first look at old Antediluvian-made stuff that would just blow your effing mind. Incredible stuff is just lying around, waiting for the absolute taking. I'm the guy in the radiation suit with the pistol and the orichalcum baton jumping down dark holes, doing things that are questionable in retrospect." He looks out the window for a moment, as if lost in thought. You look at your watch. 12:30 am.

"In a few hours, you're going to have left the US for the first time and will be doin' something very different than anything you have ever experienced before," Farson says, almost as if talking to himself.

You have to choose between leaving and just letting the man talk.

Guy leans back. "Have a drink with me, dear. To the Winkie Country!"

"What?" you say, holding your glass up. "Winkie Country?"

"Never heard of that? From the Wizard of Oz. That's the nickname for The Oberon. Winkie Country. The part of Oz where the Wicked Witch lives. People call the Ni-Perchta natives Winkies because some asshole thought it was funny a long time ago."

You and Guy clink glass and mug together and then slug down the scotch. It burns your throat and makes your eyes water. You cough long and hard.

"Good stuff, no?" he says, with a mischievous smile. "Like Gene Hackman says, don't get too used to good scotch. It's more expensive than drugs."

You and Guy talk the evening away. He tells you about what he's done, where he's been, where to go in the Winkie Country. You try to light your first cigar but Farson's cheap lighter keeps blowing out. You give up and let the cigar just hang there, then take another sip of scotch. Guy Farson keeps on; it's like a one man, one audience member show.

"Somebody said that the whole thing, being in Winkie Country, is like this old David Gilmour song. It goes: 'When you've come in you're in for good, there's no promises made, the part you've played, the chance you took, there are no boundaries set...'"

You nod, making as much sense out of it as you can. You can barely hear him at this point, between the people and the steady pop beat of some fast Huey Lewis song from the band. After a moment the band transitions into something slower and sweeter; the physical gyrations of the crowd break down into slow dances.

"Let's do this thing that all the screwing kids are doing. Let's dance to whatever this song is," Farson says, slamming the table with the flat of his hand and almost knocking over the bottle of whiskey.

"Sure." You get up, putting the unlit cigar into your pocket, and stretch. It is now 2:45 am. Farson looks pleased with himself. "Happy to be stuck with me."

He stares at you. "Excuse me?"

"Name of the song," you croak.

He takes you by the hand and dances with you, leading you awkwardly. "My sister taught me to dance a long time ago, and told me not to go for the ass grab until thirty seconds into the song."

You raise an eyebrow.

"She was a weirdo." He caresses your ass for a second before you take his hand off. "Still got what I wanted."

You giggle a little.

The lights dim and brighten, signaling something is about to begin. Farson puts his blazer back on, then takes you roughly by the hand. "Let's go get a good bird's eye view, shall we?"

As he elbows or otherwise slams others out of the way, you follow dutifully behind him through the heavy doors that lead to the deck outside. The warm Pacific wind blows steadily, increasing in power. You feel slightly drunk after your one and a half drinks. Children in pajamas, slightly-to-fully-intoxicated adults, and the crew are all hands on deck, waiting for the big show to begin. You can see the other lights of the small fleet, waiting, each ship full of settlers to The Oberon. Guy takes out another cigar and lights it, lighting yours as well. Your cigar blows out after a second.

A crack of thunder rolls along in the distance. Guy points to the crow's nest, that single white tower that juts up from the deck. He goes over to the mast, nonchalant, and climbs up the ladder, ignoring the obvious *Do Not Climb* sign tied to a rung. After a moment's hesitation, with the wind blowing your hair this way and that, you spit out the cigar and begin to climb, looking at all the white stars that mark the thick black sky. You get all the way to the top, thirty feet up from the deck, without being detected. Everyone is looking out over the ocean instead. Even the crew, who are mostly away from their posts at this time.

There is a heavy wind from the west that almost blows you and Guy completely off the ladder. Deafening metallic horns, a mix between a foghorn and the cry of a whale, echo out over the entire ocean. The wind and the horns then stop. Lights in the sky begin to flash.

The once black sky fills with a bioluminescent cloud of blue and gray light. It takes over the southern horizon. The light comes from the right and quickly passes to the left. Streams of gray clouds, partially obscuring the original light, are generated from some far-off source. Others coming from the opposite direction meet these streams. A red and orange cloud—long, thick, distorted—cruises over the ocean with little pinpricks of white flashing in its core. It is the size of an island, maybe thirty or forty football fields across, and high up into the heavens. Where it came from you cannot tell. It has just simply appeared. Guy takes off his glasses and whistles out loud. A rumbling begins and the cloud stops in front of the ship. Dry lightning flashes all around. As the cloud dissipates, a thick column of water rises up to the sky, so large and awe-inspiring that it reminds you of something out of those old newsreels that showed the hydrogen bomb detonations in the atolls.

After the water descends, there is utter stillness, no lightning, no clouds, no horns. No sound.

Miles upon miles wide, blacker than the night it is framed against, stretching from one end of the horizon to another, is the primary Nemo Gate. It is a superstructure so large it seems it has enveloped one end of the Earth, with a distinguishable peaking towards the middle. At its center it is blacker than black, emitting no visible light.

The Nemo Gate is the height of the Empire State Building in New York. Its perimeter is covered in fantastical and frighteningly large sculptures of creatures, either strange dragons or cephalopod in shape with long and terrible tentacles. Smoke trails from each sculpture's mouth. Designs of armored humans and Ni-Perchta wielding serrated swords also decorate its sides. The sea does not lap against the Gate's sides; it has stopped dead in its tracks against the massiveness of the thing.

Finally, as if the whole entire Gate is a giant television slowly switching on, the utter blackness that has been at the center changes. Lights flash in its dark center.

As if you are looking through one incredible window, you can see another world in the middle of the Gate. The portal is open. You can see that the ocean leads into some *other* incredible ocean, and that on the other side there is not a night sky, like in our world, but a brightening morning sky with seven ghostly moons shining through the heavens. Strange manta ray-like creatures fly in the distance, their tails trailing across the sky.

"Good Lord," you whisper, your hand over your mouth.

Farson smiles. He has these beautiful gray-blue eyes. "We'll go through and dock at Solomon's Bay, and in seven weeks, the Gate will disappear like it was never here. It won't open again until next June." Your eyes meet, and you look at each other for a moment too long. You kiss him lightly on the lips.

"Hee hee," he says. "Your husband doesn't know..." He motions for you to climb down from the crow's nest. You do, and endure a scolding from an officer or someone official-looking. Guy disappears into the crowd.

You find Jaime there, in his pajamas and jacket. He looks slightly upset. "You didn't wake me up," he says in a sad whisper. His forehead is glistening with fever sweat.

No one dares to be the first one to move away as everyone drinks in the incredible sight of the Nemo Gate and the view into another planet.

"Oh, snap, sorry. Sorry about that. Jeez, did you see it?"

"I did. Barely in time," he says. "Who was the guy?"

You shrug. "Guy. Guy Farson."

"Meh," Jaime mutters and then explodes into an excited burst of energy. "Wasn't that freakin' awesome? Oh my God, we did it! We're gonna cross! We are going to cross big time!"

He looks much healthier and happier now, much more himself. He takes in the view with a sigh as he looks over the shoulder of another girl your age. He talks to her, smiling and laughing. You excuse yourself and walk back to the now empty and cleared lounge, suddenly feeling a little ill. You make it to the women's bathroom and stare at the mirror for a long moment, seeing a slightly disheveled, tired-looking young woman with brunette hair. After splashing some cold water onto your face and exiting the bathroom, you run into Guy walking down the hallway. He sees the look on your face.

"I'll see you on the other side," he tells you with a kind smile. His eyes look over your shoulder. You follow his gaze and see a massive black wall advancing forward, seemingly eating every part of the Queen Mary. It is passing through the Nemo Gate, you realize with a start, and Guy puts a hand on your shoulder. "It'll be over in just a moment. It doesn't hurt."

The black wall advances to the point that it is just a few feet away from you. You inadvertently step backwards onto Guy's left foot, and he hisses a little in pain. Then the wall hits you, along with a particularly strange feeling of being pinched on every square inch of your body. You see only blackness for one moment, and then you feel like you are watching stars explode and a white ring grow and grow.

A moment later you are again standing next to Guy, who pats you on the shoulder again and turns to leave. Reality hits you very hard—you are now in The Oberon, millions of miles away from anything you've ever known.

Guy turns back to you, waits a moment, tilts his head and asks, "Will I see you back at the lounge?"

You slowly nod, and then shake your head. "No, no, Jaime. My Jaime is going to be..."

Jaime comes into the corridor, happy as can be. "Eighteen more hours to Solomon's Bay! Eighteen more hours! I'm going to go take a nap! So tired and so sick!" He turns to leave.

You tell his back, "I'll come take a nap soon."

"Okey dokey!" He claps his hands together twice and yawns exaggeratedly, then continues to walk down the corridor; you wait until he is well out of earshot. "I'll see you back in the lounge," you tell Guy.

He asks you if you want something to drink as you meet him back in the lounge but you shake your head. The room is now full of bright morning sun, filling every inch of the lounge, still in full party mode, as dawn streams in. You breathe in the air of the new world, feeling a sense of accomplishment—a minor sense of accomplishment, but one all the same.

Lost in thought, you don't notice that Guy has just brought you a glass of champagne. Couples dance to the new wave of music coming from the band that's playing during this early off-world hour.

"All of our dreams can come true, if we have the courage to pursue them." Guy raises his drink to you and you clink your glass of champagne against his.

"Cheers." You sip the bubbly. "Thanks for the drink I didn't want. Whose quote is that?"

"Motherfucking Walt Disney. But it rings true, eh?" He gulps his wine and leaves his emptied glass on the counter. "See you in Winkie Country." He leans forward and kisses you for a long time.

"Good luck out there."

"You taste like alcohol, schoolgirl," he says with a wink.

NIGHTHAWKS AT THE MISSION

CHAPTER FOUR:
SOLOMON'S BAY

You make it back to the bow where the Queen Mary, now under a darkening and dusky but still very much daytime sky, is steaming forward to your first stop, that medieval city you once saw as a model back on Earth.

You find Jaime again, looking so happy and excited, until he looks at your face and seems to remember something very important. His look scares you so badly that you immediately and unconsciously touch the little crucifix hanging from your neck. "What? What is it?"

Jaime swallows a few times. "I forgot. Well, Sarah, I forgot about the whole, uh, well…"

"The computers and the iPods, right? You forgot to give them to the purser. Oh Jesus, I even talked to the purser, Jaime. People still use their computers carefully out there, now my Hungry Birds scores, my Manowar songs…"

"Angry Birds," Jaime interjects.

You are too annoyed to keep speaking for a moment though your mouth keeps up a sort of speaking motion. "Whatever."

"Hey, you forgot to wake me for the coolest part of the trip! So there!"

His stupid mistake has put you into a really nasty mood, squashing away any fear and trepidation and replacing those feelings with anger and annoyance. You keep your face in a tight frown for the next few moments until the first firework goes off in the sky, welcoming you into The Oberon.

Large bonfires have been lighted on that far-off shore. They flicker under this massive statue you see in the distance—a statue so large it almost seems to block the setting sun–of a creature with two faces: one angry, one calm. It holds what looks like an entire medieval city. In the center of its large palm, on a real or artificial hilltop, is a very large building made out of a dark wood that looks to you like a Buddhist temple set on top of a giant wooden barge with oars sticking out of its sides. Giant flags or sails are at the four corners of this temple, facing towards the almost-set sun.

In the other hand, forever floating above its palm, are seven massive stone spheres,. You read somewhere that these spheres representing the seven permanent moons. A crown of demonic-looking skulls adorns the statue's brow. The stone has been cut to look like flames are surrounding the statue.

Jaime points out the city. "Solomon's Bay, Solokon-Bi in Perchta. First stop."

You see these custom fireworks, spruced up with orichalcum, being set off in celebration of the first ship coming through the portal. Some of the fireworks look like little robots dancing across the sky, while others, detonated just seconds before, keep burning in the sky for minutes afterwards. Pyrotechnics made to look like scary bats and dragons fly back and forth over the sea. You watch in awe.

At the very end, right after a gigantic finale when it seems like every firework in the world is shot off at once, the blue and white overlapping circles of the Off-World Network symbol appear in the sky.

The Queen Mary is now docked next to the palm of the statue's hand, which holds the city of Solomon's Bay. The Queen is in actuality floating in the air next to the city in the statue's palm, bobbing on top of sheer nothing. Other ships from the portal fleet are nearby, as well as some strange others that are also floating in the air next to the palm. Small wooden ships with red Chinese-style sails that jut out from their sides hang from strong ropes wrapped around large blimp-like balloons. Some are heavily modified and even have a couple of cars hanging from their sides on hooks; the cars are either being used for ballast or being transported, you really aren't sure. One of these airships floats out over the ocean, disappearing into the distance.

You and your husband disembark amidst a sea of other humans stepping off the gangplanks and platforms and onto the stone docks of the city. area right outside the docks is listed in your brochure as the Free Market. It is a large space full of open shops under three- or four-story stone towers where you assume the city's Ni-Perchta live. Most of the towers have flat tops. There are a few that are ten stories tall with slanted, wooden roofs of premium craftsmanship. Only a few buildings have glass in their windows—the rest just have shutters and silk curtains that flap in the sea breeze. You follow Jaime, who is carrying all the bags.

"Sarah, could you carry some of this?" he whines.

"Consider it penance for the computer screw up back there. I just lost all my Mano- I mean Bieber songs. All my Justin Bieber songs."

"Bieber sucks donkey..." Jaime mumbles, and you shoot him a look.

"When did you start talking like that?" you ask.

He shoots you a look back but says nothing.

You see your first Ni-Perchta up close. This one is helping a couple of humans into the back of his horse-drawn wagon, which is not so much a wagon as an old El Camino station wagon on moldy rubber tires.

Bunches of Ni-Perchta aliens are standing around, doing business in the same way they have for hundreds of years—their fantastical and medieval lifestyle mostly seems unchanged; their clothing and demeanor are things from a fourteenth century golden age. Humans and Ni-Perchta wander about. Only a couple of buildings have electricity. The smell is incredibly strong—a mix of random spices, Ni-Perchta candles, and the steamy smell of tasty things cooking.

Some of the shops are makeshift cafes. You see one where a couple of people and Ni- Perchta are cracking open the boiled shells of bright red trilobite-like things. A sign showing a painted picture of one of the creatures reads *Boiled Trilos* in English. The restaurant-goers are stripping off the shells and chowing down on the meat. It looks like they're composed of one giant lobster tail underneath the shell.

Seeing a Ni-Perchta close up after years of hearing rumors and reading explanations of their features is frightening to you—beings as intelligent as any human being, but they are not human. Their skin color is gray-white, making them look almost as if they are the inverse of a photonegative. Their eyes glow a little red in the darkness, but you read that in regular daylight they are a dull gray. Their ears are slightly pointed. Other than that, they are very human-looking, though everyone seems to be on the tall side. From all the scientific reports you've read in *Cosmopolitan* magazine, you know that it is possible to have kids with them, though the Ephors, the police of the Witch-Lord, will kill or abduct any product of such relations.

You nudge Jaime along, quietly berating him for staring at the Ni-Perchta driver. "Look around for a cab," you tell him. "We're going to Nikh-Cunm Station for the steam mono." He nods in understanding, but then trips over something sticking out of the cobblestone street and falls over, right onto your bags.

You curse under your breath, picking him up as a few humans and Ni-Perchta look over at you. "Quit making a scene, Jaime," you say.

"You quit making a scene!" he replies loudly, attracting even more attention.

At this moment, you see the Ephors for the first time; there is a group of five heading over. They come from nowhere, the Ni-Perchta warrior-police of the Witch-Lord of The Oberon, and are dressed in gold and green armor that is as ornate as it is tough, made of individual plates that almost look like hand-crafted leaves or feathers. Each wears a half-mask made out of black cloth to cover their mouths, and the one in front wears a half-crown with one wing. Each is armed with a long, serrated blade and an ancient-looking black ori-staff with a few small orichalcum stones embedded in the hilt.

Jaime looks so happy to see them as they come up to you; they're about six feet away. You touch your little crucifix necklace.

"Oh wow, Ephors! I've read about them," he says before the lead Ephor lowers his half-mask and stares at him. Then Jaime says, "I've read about you. Hi, I'm Jaime Van Zandt and this is Sarah, er, Sarah Orange. I don't think we changed the...well, sorry, let me start again." Jaime spoke in accented and stilted Perchta. You can recognize only his name and your name in his mini speech.

The lead Ephor holds up his right hand and speaks in clear, if accented, English. "I am Dwelka Storma, and I am the Ephor inspector of off-world barbarians and their customs."

"I was talking," Jaime says, annoyed, and you look at him as if he has just grown another head, then put out a hand nervously, which the Ephor pointedly ignores.

"You bring Jesus Christ and his teachings here?"

You and Jaime look at each other, confused, and then Jaime panics. "Um, no. No, Morgan Freeman on the loudspeaker told us, uh, not to bring any Bibles or Korans or the secret books, and we haven't. You...your people..." Your eyes grow wide and Jaime makes a motion like he has this all under control. "Your people do not like converting, people being converted."

Dwelka Storma smiles a little. "So there isn't a group of packages marked oranges that contain thumb-sized Bibles made in San Antonio, America, on that ship you just came in on?"

You shake your head repeatedly. "I only go to church at Christmas. I'm not a Bible smuggler, if that's what you think."

Storma comes forward and grabs your crucifix necklace in one armored hand, twirling the little cross piece. "Of course that's what I think." He lets go and calls out in Perchta, a sort of lyrical language. It sounds to you like Japanese being spoken by someone with a Russian accent. The four Ephors back up as Storma steps to the side.

You notice that humans and Ni-Perchta in that crowded place are watching this scene play out, and your heart starts beating hard. You think something awful is about to happen. One of the Ephors expands his ancient steel staff, which extends out nearly three feet and glows a grim green. Lightning shoots out from it, striking you and Jaime with one concentrated bolt that knocks you out for a moment. You fall on your back, your body quivering from the shock, your teeth rattling. You taste blood. Jaime takes most of the blast and is completely out. Someone in the crowd screams.

Tall, dark shapes that you see through your clouded vision march towards you quickly in a tight formation. You can barely move; half of your body is numb. You try to scream but only a slight squeak of air gets past your lips.

One of the Ni-Perchta Ephors flips you over onto your stomach, hog-tying you as you pass out.

You wake up on a straw bed in a small stone cell that's maybe the size of Tyler's bathroom back on Earth. It takes you a while to come out of it, and your head hurts as bad as when you fell off your bike and knocked it on the ground two years ago. You ask Jaime to turn off the goddamn radio, but then you notice that he's messing with the lock on your jail cell door with a small screwdriver and, you think, the hairpin that used to be in your hair.

There's someone screaming in an alien language in a way that scares you. You shake with adrenaline and start to breathe heavy.

"Where are we?" you say in a raspy, dry voice. Jaime drops his screwdriver and looks around. He then shuffle-crawls away from the cell door. Dark shadows cross his face as he moves away from the meager torchlight that illuminates the dungeon. You sit up and take some straw out of your hair. "Where are we?"

"Temple of the Witch-Lord. We are under arrest for Bible smuggling." He kneels next to you. "Crazy." You look at him incredulously. He pats your shoulder. "I asked for the Network rep, but they seemed to ignore me. Can you believe this?"

Jaime mutters something about this being exciting. The screaming stops.

"Plenty exciting," you respond, palms sweating and your heart increasing its pace. "What's the penalty for Bible smuggling?" you ask. "Oh God, we stay here for a few years?"

Jaime shakes his head. "Oh no. No, it's either being released in Gug territory to be eaten, or decapitation. They don't do trials here. I'll just have a hand chopped off because I'm the accomplice; you're the actual suspect. And you'll be..." He doesn't finish his sentence.

You swallow.

"I have a plan. I break the lock on this door, and then we sneak down the hall. The Ni-Perchta are not really on top of proper law enforcement procedures. I still have that," he gestures to the screwdriver, "and then we get to the American Residents' House in the Forearm Quarter."

"Are you nuts? This isn't a video game. They could kill us for escaping. Oh my God."

Jaime nods rapidly. "I'm...I know, but God, I'm scared, Sarah, and we..."

You hug each other. There's a large and bloody gouge on Jaime's back. "Something bit me in here. You believe that?" he tells you. "When I was asleep."

You nod, hugging him tight and then letting go. You feel in your back pocket that book you were given by Scratch, ages ago it seems, and take it out for a moment, then put it back. You think about how it would be back home—the cops would take everything out of your pockets any time you were arrested. Jaime is right—law enforcement procedures are really lacking here.

"Wait, you don't need to pick this lock," you say. "Let me look." It's a simple combination job from Earth, something you remember from high school. Kneeling down, you notice it has forty digits. At least it's not something strange, like a Ni-Perchta lock. It's just a rudimentary, run-of-the-mill Master lock that can be cracked.

"Are you serious? They lock their jail cells with these? I had that lock in high school on my locker," you whisper.

"Los Alamitos High had these locks, too—The Oberon is amazingly third world," Jaime says. "So advanced yet so behind." He continues. "Forty digits means, of course, sixty-four thousand combinations. Which leaves us S.O.L."

"Look, Jaime, I want you to follow what I have to say, okay?" You can hear your voice trembling. "I'll keep an eye on the corridor. We can hack this cheap thing. Here's what you need to do." You don't want to touch the lock yourself as your hands shake too badly. Jaime puts his hands on the lock, looking at you with amazement.

"First thing, dial the lock back to zero. Okay. Pull down on the shackle thing." As you continue to give him directions, you can hear boots click-clack down the stone floor of the dungeon, coming closer at first and then just fading away. Next he discovers the number and you write it down in the dust of the dungeon floor.

Sweat starts to beads up on your forehead as you remember this trick. You listen, still crouched next to Jaime, your knees hurting.

"Okay, pull down the shackle." He does so and then starts slowly spinning the combination dial clockwise. "Find where it gets stuck twelve more times..." you whisper.

"Okay," Jaime says, still looking at you like you've just lost your mind. He seems to be going through the motions now. Jaime reads the numbers back to you. You and Jaime jot down the rest of the numbers by writing in the dust of the dungeon floor.

"Okay. Ignore all the ones that are between numbers. So you should have only five left because seven of those numbers are in-betweeners. 6, 16, 26, 28, and 36. Okay. Which number is the odd one out, Jaime?"

"28, Sarah."

"Okay. Jaime, this is the third number in the combination. What's 28 divided by 4? 7. Any remainder, Jaime?"

You look at Jaime, who is incredulous that you are asking these questions instead of just telling him the goddamn answer. "No."

You stand up, stretching your legs. "Next step is that you take that remainder number, which was 0, and keep adding 4 until you have gone around the entire dial."

You think for a moment and carefully put those numbers down in the thick dust of the dungeon cell to help you remember.

"Jaime, one of those numbers is now your first number. Last step here—to find the second number—what do you have again, what's that remainder number?"

"0, Mom," Jaime snaps at you.

"Add 2 and that's your answer, so add 4 to that until you are all the way around the dial. So what's those numbers? Uh, 2, 6, 10, 14, 18, 22, 26, 30, 34, 38, that's it. And now you have your second combination number. Write it down in the dust if you need to." Panic sets into you a little bit, eating away at any remaining confidence as you think of the Ni-Perchta returning.

"Try 'em out. Remember, your third number is 28."

He starts to spins the combination dial and runs through the gamut for a couple of minutes straight before you hear some footsteps get closer. "Hurry, Jaime," you whisper, your heart thudding in your chest. He spins the dial twice but has no luck. He tries the next combo and this time the lock pops open with a snick. You luck out big time.

"Isn't the Internet the best?" you say, as you slowly open the cell door.

Jaime kisses you on the cheek, stunning you. "Okay, then," he says, wiping his mouth as he heads out the door. The two of you tiptoe down the corridor, walking deeper into the dungeon; it has a funky smell, like an over-chlorinated pool mixed with mildew. You see other humans and Ni-Perchta in their small stone cells, some looking beaten and neglected and one with terrible burns. There are no guards down here; the Ephors seem not to worry at all about their prisoners.

At the ends of each corridor are long halls, softly illuminated with blue light that echoes with the sound of water. You almost scream and pee your pants when you look down one corridor and see what looks like a spider the size of a Volkswagen suddenly move by, its red eyes jutting out from meaty stalks that follow you with dull interest. Jaime steadies you with his hand on your arm.

In one of the cells is a Ni-Perchta hanging on the back wall in chains, passed out or dead.

"Okay...where do we...how do we?" you ask. You remember your book but for whatever reason it doesn't seem to be working or active in any way.

There is a strange doorway, unlike anything you have seen before, made out of red and orange light that's sunk into the stone of the dungeon. It glows incredibly bright, but Jaime isn't taking any notice of it or even looking in its general direction. The door is shaped in the same manner as the Nemo Gate—large and peaked at the top with elaborate sculptures of dragons, people in armor, and, oddly frightening to you, squids.

You point to the door. "Jaime, are you seeing this? What is that?"

He looks at what you are pointing at and then at you as if you have become mentally challenged. "Rock, Sarah."

You ignore him and walk up to the doorway, which seems to become brighter as you approach, and step through the door. Jaime yelps behind you. Once through the door, you find yourself outside the dungeon and out in front of the Witch-Lord's Temple, standing on the edge of a black band of cobblestones ringing the courtyard of the temple structure. Jaime appears a moment later.

Red light flashes from three of the cobblestones. Each display a Ni-Perchta hieroglyphic which slowly fades away into little red blurs that you can barely make out. Despite it being daytime, torches are being lit in the courtyard by robed servants dressed in purple and black.

Dwelka Storma and another Ephor stand nearby, discussing something in Perchta. No one else is about. Storma spots you. The other Ephor, a younger apprentice you guess by his youthful look, quickly covers his shock. Storma looks as if this happens all the time.

"Do not move. This will be short and to the point. I will personally execute the two of you within a minute unless you give me your contact in the Christian underground. When we took in the barbarian hordes under the order of the Witch-Lord, we did not ask for a religious takeover of the entire Four Lands. You will give me your contact or be killed," Storma says, looking very cold and dangerous in his Ephor armor and by the look in his eyes. You feel truly helpless, and Jaime lets out his breath. You take an involuntary step backwards. You've almost passed the black band of cobblestones now; you've been slowly creeping back since Storma began his speech.

He blinks quickly for a brief second but keeps up the stony facade. The other Ephor cannot stand it any longer and tries to pick you up telekinetically by snapping out his ori-staff and using it on you. Jaime quickly makes a move and falls backwards, knocking you to the ground and barely past the black band of cobblestones.

Storma screams out a curse in Perchta and then recomposes himself. "This Ephor and I offer our apologies. We have no excuse for our actions. We have improperly imprisoned you." He takes out his serrated blade that's almost as long as you are tall and gives it to you. "We offer our lives in apology."

The other Ephor gives his blade to Jaime, who takes it in both hands and looks it over.

"Thank you, but no," you say simply, happy to be alive. You drop the sword onto the temple's courtyard with a clang, and Jaime places his sword on the ground as well. "May we leave?" you ask, wiping your sweaty brow.

Storma looks incensed, crazed even. "Of course. You will be escorted to the mono station."

Jaime grabs your elbow and you walk quickly out of the courtyard. Other Ephors start to walk towards you.

Storma picks up his blade and chops off the head of his companion in one fell swoop, sending up a geyser of blood out of the other Ephor's bloody stump of a neck. You scream, and Jaime yelps and jumps back.

Storma walks away, leaving you speechless.

CHAPTER FIVE:
TO MISSION FRIENDSHIP

You wait in the steam monorail station. It has a wooden platform like something out of the Old West and is located on the utmost end of the statue's palm. You and Jaime only have one bag with you. Some Ephors, who haven't spoken a word or made a gesture except to pat your arm or drag you to the side so you can hop the mono to where your job is, have led you here. They mutter a few words of Perchta to Jaime, who chatters something back.

"Next monorail is at noon." He points to a very large and oddly-made clock standing in the middle of the platform. Hundreds of people, and a few Ni-Perchta helpers, are scattered around the clock with luggage and supplies, like little pickaxes and home-made dynamite. Each numeral on the clock has a picture from The Oberon—a single prospector for a one, two pictures of the steam mono to represent a two, and so on. The hands of the clock are almost on the twelve, which is a picture of twelve Baleen dragons in mid-flight.

The steam mono pulls up, a strange barrel-shaped train covered in Plexiglas except for the almost-bottom of the train, which looks like stainless steel riding along a series of iron wheels. A miniature choo-choo engine pulls along the entire contraption, and a car marked with a red 5 is yours to take all the way to the end of the line, Mission Friendship/Funeral Breaks.

Jaime bows to the Ephors and helps you board. "What a neat monorail," he says. "Better than Disney."

The mono's big cushioned seats recline. Seated in front of you is a hairy and slightly chubby Englishman with a red beard. He speaks a thousand words a minute to his tiny girlfriend. They both wear protective clothing and are sporting crossbows, knives, and grenades on their belts. They laugh and pinch each other, sharing what you hope is a cigarette.

"Well, that was interesting back there," a very pale Jaime quietly says.

"Yep," is the only thing you can say. The train car reeks of a million cigarettes, and the red leather seat has abrasive cracks that dig into your back. You finger one under your bottom and stare at the peeling pieces, afraid to look out the window for some odd reason, believing that if you do, you will attract more attention to yourself and lead the Ephors back to you.

"Why did they let us go? Christ, what was it?"

Jaime speaks in a very serious, very scholarly tone. "We made it past the black band that rings around the Witch-Lord Temple. To the Ephors, who never allow escapes, it means that the three gods of the Witch Lands guided you to freedom. Your escape proves that the gods favor you and is a presumption of innocence. All your crimes are forgiven. Mine, too, I guess." He smiles and pats your knee. "Holy cow, that was interesting. Did you see those cobblestones light up? I think that's a combination to get in and out. Thank God we got out of there."

You stare forward, still shell-shocked. "There is no God," you mutter. Your crucifix is gone.

Jaime breathes a sigh of relief, but only for a moment. "Good move, finding that hidden door and screwing with that lock. When we got past the black band, they had to let us go. The Ephors allow no one to escape, but if you do, it's the will of the gods and all is forgiven. That's incredible. That's really incredible."

"I'm really, really happy to move off-world with you, Jaime." You nod and tear up a little.

"By the way, how did you know how to work the lock?" he asks, before you shoot him a look that tells him very clearly to stop talking.

"I'll tell you later."

"You're full of surprises, Sarah Orange."

"We have only your bag with some of my stuff. They burned all the rest." You think of your whole history burning up in minutes, leaving you with nothing to tie you back home. You are a ship without an anchor in an unchartered sea.

"I know. Sucks." He touches his bag. "Well...Your computer is here." You swallow your anger against him for ignoring your pain.

The train lurches forward and chugs its way north into another Nemo Gate at the edge of the statue's palm. After an explosion of white light and a thunderclap, the train passes through the Nemo Gate and Solomon's Bay drifts away behind you.

After two hours, the great, green expanses of The Oberon and the white- and iron-colored mountains come into view. Pine trees and odd rock formations jut out of the land like knives stabbing at the sky. A green reflector sign, like something you'd see hanging on top of an American freeway, states from its position above the train tracks that you are entering the Super Sargasso Sea region and its prohibition of Ni-Perchta alcohol use. *No Night Salvaging Permitted* is also splashed across the sign in bold white letters, as well as *No Unregistered Firearms.*

Jaime has fallen asleep and his head rests against your shoulder. You stare out the window, still a little shaky from the whole possible-decapitation-then-escape thing.

The train's chugging motor runs and runs and you feel increasingly sleepy. Outside, bugs splatter against the glass walls of the mono car. A long black highway covered in yellow Xs runs over the next hill and beyond. Each yellow X flashes under the overcast sky, and there is a single yellow car, a small one, traveling in the same direction as your train. Thick, dark clouds stream across the sky, casting long shadows onto the grasslands as the train passes through.

The "old man rock 'n' roll" being piped into the car keeps you occupied for a while . Dull, flat news is reported every two hours. The opening bars of the ELO song *Here is the News* plays as its opening theme.

A random person reads the news in an over-professional and over-cultured voice. Fireworks and festivities are still permitted until a week after Bonfire Night and the Network warns yet again that alcohol is illegal in The Oberon unless you have a personal liquor consumption license. Failure to pay the license fee is punishable by fine or a stay in a Witch-Lord Temple and eventual LR-ing. By the sixth reading of the same report you have memorized every word.

The train travels for hours in the high grass along a large river. Chunks of rock and little mesas dot the plains, breaking up the land into large bits. The river is wide, blue, and almost surreal. Its current is impossibly quick, as if it is being forced out of a water cannon; there has to be something artificial for it to be churning so quickly. Every inch of its flow is like the worst rapids you can remember from back home. Little canyons are cut into the land, this way and that, breaking the ground up here and there.

You start to nod off, little by little. The radio plays an old song, *Big Log*.

You fall asleep to Robert Plant's melody.

The cool air of the underground along with a smell of moisture and mold flows into the car, waking you up. Jaime is already awake. Almost everyone else has gone, although the Englishman and the girl he is with are still on board. The train car is ablaze with illumination from hidden lights in the glass frame of the steam mono. The train is going through some sort of giant subway tunnel filled with looming statues that look over everything. You are pretty confused as to where you are. Jaime looks very happy.

"Just went into an old subway tunnel for Sargasso-uh, Sargasso-3. Thousands of years old. Pretty nuts, huh?"

As you pass through another tunnel, your train switches tracks. A giant hole in one side of the tunnel leads into a greater darkness. You look out the window and are scared by what you see. Tens, if not hundreds, of deep green eyes watch from the deep shadows. They're maybe a few hundred yards away. The train has picked up steam and is now going faster. The green eyes move—and then nothing. Blackness again. You hear a howl and a moan as the train pulls forward.

"Mummies. The Antediluvian people weren't all wiped out. Some got into shelters and, unable to feed on any fresh blood, all those human-turned-vampires went feral and turned into sort of mummified zombies. They just go on and on unless someone puts them down. Forever mad. They're desperate for human blood." Jaime is way too happy about the subject.

"Your sister died of Bevan's disease, isn't that right? That's basically what these guys have," he says quite innocently.

"No, she went missing but had the symptoms of that disease before she did. And thank you for reminding me."

A surge of green eyes rush forward, coming closer and closer to the train and its Plexiglas casing. In the light reflecting off the train you see one of them up close for a second. The thing's features, once human, are grotesquely pale; deep, dark shadows ring this female mummy's eyes. The eyes themselves are bloodshot and as yellow as custard, filled up with complete and hateful rage. Tears of blood dribble down the ragged remains of whatever clothing the mummy had been wearing. You are too scared to even scream—you sit there and quiver. You reach for your crucifix, which is long gone, and feel nothing but thin air.

"Another two hours to Mission Friendship." Jaime yawns. "Two hours! I can't believe it." The train pulls out of the tunnel and back into the light of day, passing through another round of grasslands. Only the occasional tree, like one of those out of an African safari picture or documentary, breaks up the endless plains ahead of you on either side of the river. Each tree has a wide, umbrella-like canopy which is the hiding place for things that could be mistaken for birds.

The Englishman turns around. "Did you see that?"

You nod as Jaime pipes in. "I saw it, too! This is the greatest trip I have ever been on! You know this is the most exciting thing—we got a story for you guys..."

The Englishman nods vigorously. "Actual zombies, Lord above, I have been waiting for this my whole life! I said to myself back in Liverpool, I said, 'Well, now, John Boston, here's...' Are you crying?"

You are. This little trip is turning into an unmitigated nightmare. You're finding things out that perhaps you should have researched before you left, but didn't because you were, well, under the weather emotionally.

"I'm John Boston." You shake his hand.

"Keira Love." You shake hands with the woman.

"Anyone else want to do a Valis wheel? Hmmm? Got it off a dealer in Stonetown," Boston says, taking out a silver pipe that has what looks like a miniature electrical fan set into its end. The strong odor of ozone and sound of atonal music fill the train car as Boston sucks at the end of the tube. Blue smoke comes out of the fan as it whirls around. He takes out a match, lights it with his thumbnail, and puts it inside the silver tube. "This'll help calm you down. You want it?" John offers the tube.

As Jaime looks on, you decide to take a hit. Anything that helps you relax and forget what just happened is worth it. This would not be a real change in pace from the pot you've smoked a couple of times before. You take a hit and immediately feel light-headed and happy, and also sort of scared that reality has suddenly become a little more real all at once. After another drag you cough. Your coughing barely obscures the atonal music coming from the pipe. "Oh shit! That was—hoo boy." You give the pipe back to John.

"This is fun! This is what couples do!" John offers the pipe to Jaime, who shakes his head.

"No, I couldn't. I've read three online accounts about doing a Valis wheel. One post said that you feel very relaxed, and the other two said you won't stop screaming for the next forty-eight hours." You look at Jaime in horror.

Keira Love takes a hit and then starts screaming loudly for a long, uncomfortable moment before giving the pipe back to John. "Always good." The sound of her voice is a little strange, as if she is trying to mimic an English accent.

It is dark now, and the blazing light inside the car has become soft illumination that allows you to see the seven moons of The Oberon for the first time. The white forms peek down from high above in the star-filled sky. There is a slight rumble of thunder, perhaps the beginning of a storm coming out of the Sargasso Breaks, perhaps something else, Jaime says. Dry lightning plays out against the western skies, revealing a flock of luminescent manta ray-like creatures, their tendrils drifting behind them in the wind.

You are very close to the Mission Friendship/Funeral Breaks. Regular pine trees are now making their appearances, and the mountains seem to be closer than ever, crowding out the rest of the land. The train begins to ascend a little bit, going up the single track.

"Up." Boston laughs to himself. "Spelled backwards it's fuck you."

The train slows down as you hear the Ni-Perchta begin to sing something a cappella, in almost funeral dirge tones, somewhere off. You can hear this music thump through the monorail.

John and Keira are passing the Valis device back and forth. You feel more than a little light-headed at this point, and the world is beginning to run a little on the slow side.

That ozone smell and atonal music from the Valis wheel are getting to you. It is fully dark now, the only light coming from the seven moons and what you see in the distance.

There is a stone palace in the middle of a green grass field. It's large and looks like it should be somewhere like Tibet or Bhutan, a Dzong-style fortress with high, windowless walls, a Chinese-style rooftop, and two massive doors made out of what looks like wood and iron. The Dalai Lama probably had a place like this once upon a time.

Connected to it is an apartment tower; a good-sized one, maybe twenty stories tall, give or take. Lights are on in some windows, and a couple of swirling searchlights reach into the heavens above, painting the sky over and over with small circles of light. It is made out of concrete and stands out significantly from the rest of the land. Balconies jut out from the sides; the top floor has one wrap-around balcony that isn't separated like the others.

"I think that's it." You take out the small brochure that was stuffed into your pocket. *Mission Friendship—A Place of Warmth and Protection* states the brochure's front page, next to a painting of the Dzong and apartment tower structure.

There is another, thinner tower connected to it by three concrete walkways which looks as if it is set up as observation point—glass windows surround the topmost part. Farther away is a large, walled village; it looks like something out of *The Lord of the Rings*. Wood-timbered homes stick their heads out over the walls. A large wooden bridge crosses the rushing river separating you from Mission Friendship. A lumber mill also spans the entire river and is right next to the bridge.

The train slows.

"And here we go," Jaime says in a guttural voice before coughing a few times to clear his throat.

"The Joker said that before he blew up a building in *The Dark Knight*," you retort, seeing double. "Nerd."

"That's the joke."

"I think this is the best capital D drugs I've had since I was thirteen at that Prodigy concert at Glastonbury." John Boston coughs. "You ever seen that old movie, *The Jerk?* Remember that cat juggling shit?"

Jaime looks confused and you have no idea what John Boston is talking about. "Was that about cats being juggled, or a cat juggling shit?" you ask with a slur.

John Boston shrugs "These cans are defective!" he calls out. "Steve Martin—it's a funny film."

No one laughs. "Was Steve Martin the guy in The Blues Brothers?" you ask.

No one says anything for a long moment. Keira laughs, stoned. "I should really slap you hard."

You laugh, and so do Boston and Jaime. Keira slaps you hard, stunning you.

Boston laughs, and even Jaime laughs a little, nervously. You are startled. Then you hit back once, twice, and three times, making Keira tear up. Her face is really red and starting to swell. Boston stands up and snaps out the ori-baton he had hidden on him with such force and points it at you, lifting you up and out of your seat. Invisible strings seem to pull you out of your seat.

"Hey, now, girl. All quiet on the Western Front," Boston says, a scowl on his face. He looks like he is about to do something else just as a Ni-Perchta monorail attendant in a shimmering rainbow-colored tunic walks into the car. Boston drops you right back onto your rump.

You have arrived at your new home, after almost getting into a full-on fistfight with strangers who were once friendly. "Last stop," the overhead speakers say. "Funeral Breaks village. Mission Friendship. Star in the Mountain."

You get off the train and step onto the very empty stone platform. Boston and Love walk over, looking sheepish. Love also looks a little angry. Boston speaks up. "Look, my friends, I think things became a bit heated. A bit strange. Drug use makes these situations happen." He snickers, and Love laughs.

You and Jaime look at each other. Boston and Love put out their hands to shake with you and Jaime, and you do so gingerly. "We'll be working on-site in Sargasso-3, out near the old boat quays. Our radio frequency is Quay-two-five-six."

Boston hands you his powder-white business card embossed with the words *Boston-Love Dayhawk Co-Op*. "We check up on the world around 4:00 to 6:00 pm each evening. Give us a call if you're in the area. Stop on by."

Jaime nods. "We may just do that. The old boat quays in Sargasso-3, that's about a mile or two from the Nemo Gate that leads to the old reactor, right?"

Boston nods slowly. "Yes, if you can get near the place—the wreckage and the machines down there...You don't own that site, do you?" Jaime smiles a little. "Oh, I wish. But no, just read up about it. Sounds neat."

Boston blows out a raspberry. "That's a bad deal friend—that's a death zone. Ask anyone. I mean that whole defense system is up and running. It's very strange. It's more than a reactor should be. That place is locked down, shut down, do not enter. Unless you've got a defense key."

Jaime shakes his head. "Uh, no, just curious about it."

Boston shrugs. Love speaks up, in a sort of stilted speech, changing the subject quickly. "I'm sorry about the... what happened back there. Have a better one. Radio us."

You and Jaime thank them, though a cold feeling is running up and down your spine. A place that is considered a death zone does not seem like a place Jaime should be working in. You laugh and laugh, making everyone uncomfortable, and then start to tear up again.

Boston says something about maybe being wrong, but you take it as him trying to downplay what he just said.

Jaime gives them your new home address at Mission Friendship and tells the couple to come by whenever they have the chance. Boston and Love are picked up by what looks like an old Pontiac muscle car being driven by a Ni-Perchta male in dark war paint. They drive off down a dirt and cobblestone road that leads into the mountains at the far end.

You see Mission Friendship and hear the rushing water of the river very close by. Ni-Perchta are singing somewhere in the distance; their songs echo in the valley. It's very cool out and a breeze blows down from the mountains. Everything smells fresh and of pine. Jaime tells you it's about a fifteen to twenty minute walk to Mission Friendship from the station's platform.

You look to your left, up a snow-capped mountain on the other side of the river, and see something you've just heard about on the monorail train. Star in the Mountain.

Jaime nervously blathers on. He'd probably mentioned it before, but you hadn't really bothered to ask him what it meant, figuring it was self-explanatory—which of course, it is.

Over two hundred stories tall, Star in the Mountain is a glass and steel star, a single giant building in the shape of an actual multi-pointed star. Its mid-section is like a glass bowl and its points, which are dissimilar in size and length, stretch upwards and outwards. It is set into the side of a mountain, like God's own Christmas ornament. One point of the star has broken off, taking a piece of the mountain with it. The rest seems to be in good condition. There's an odd reddish light around it, somewhat faded, and you wonder if it's the moonlight being reflected.

"That star can hold up to one hundred thousand people, if not more. Star in the Mountain is the one of the few left that's still intact," Jaime says in a whisper.

"So are we supposed to..." He nods at Mission Friendship. "Do we walk it? What's the instructions?"

You only stare up at the stars in the sky as you wait, not thinking and not listening. The constellations are so different, so jumbled up compared to what you can see on Earth. Seven moons drift overhead, amazing you. Somewhere Earth is there, you suppose, up in the middle of all that.

NIGHTHAWKS AT THE MISSION

CHAPTER SIX:
THE RITUAL

Far away there is what looks like an old-school police cruiser painted yellow, blue and white, its headlights flickering on and off. It seems to be signaling to you and Jaime, who are still on the badly-lit station platform with the idling train. It has a rough double tap rumble to it, like something's wrong with the muffler. It's at least thirty years old and definitely not American made. More Europeanish in style. The words *Mission Security* written in English and Perchta decorate the sides of the vehicle.

The cruiser pulls up. Two young guys, both in black leather uniforms, pop out. Each one has an ori-baton, a pistol, and a sawed-off double-barreled shotgun attached to his belt. They call out to the Ni-Perchta train workers in Perchta before coming up to you two. The Ni-Perchta are busy off-loading some cases from one of the monorail's cars.

"Who are they?" I say. "Cops?"

Jaime blows out a raspberry. "The Ephors are the only cops to be really scared of, Sarah. No, these are just Counters, uh, Mission Security, who work as, well, security for the Network Missions. They actually operate under the Bill of Rights."

The two men shake hands with the Ni-Perchta in the Ni-Perchta way: one hand closed up in a fist touching the chest, the other out and shaking in one smooth pumping motion.

"They look like college students. Just like us," you say, watching them.

Jaime suddenly becomes nervous. "Be careful what you say to them," he whispers. "You don't know how they'll turn it. We love each other very much and are happily married."

He kisses you on the cheek, which is now the second time you have kissed since you've been officially married.

The Counter with glasses and long hair speaks to you. "I am Tadeo Marcelino, and this is Robert Fuller." He puts out his hand to you and then to Jaime.

Jaime says, "We're married, me and her, and this is great. This is fun, this is what couples do." The inspectors shoot you and Jaime a weird look.

A single eerie horn blasts out over the dark, empty land, like a call from a dead Viking's tomb. Other horns begin to blow, from all directions. You hear what you assume to be other Ni-Perchta out in the darkness, far off, calling out to each other.

"This is the night of the comet's return," Robert says. "It signals something to them—a chance for change, incredible change. You see the moons up there—those are the Seven Sisters of Night. And with the comet here, it's the return of the Eighth Sister—the one that'll fight with the other sisters before passing on. The Eighth Sister is important—she determines the future of all. The Ni-Perchta know the exact hour when this comet will return every century. Incredible, isn't it?"

"Oh, yes. I knew that," you say.

The Counters gesture to their cruiser. "Let's take you over. There's a local nomadic tribe. They like to know those who work and live at Mission Friendship. They are not like the city Ni-Perchta who hate our guts but smile to our faces."

"They're called covens, Sarah," Jaime pipes in.

Robert Fuller nods. "Yes, that's correct."

Jaime looks very happy to hear that.

Tadeo continues. "A lot of your future neighbors are there, too. The Coven of Upper Sargasso has welcomed you all. All are welcome."

"All are welcome, all welcome. Go into the light. There is peace and serenity in the light..." you say in a high and creepy falsetto voice, making Jaime and the inspectors look at you. "Never saw Poltergeist? Huh. I'm sorry I'm still a little high..."

"Highly exhausted," Jaime interrupts. He takes our luggage and puts it into the back of the cruiser.

You come up to an open grass area with a single tree in the middle. Two Ni-Perchta males are spraying something on this tree using an old garden hose connected to a small tank. A few other Ni-Perchta set it on fire; its entire form is now blazing and crackling under the dark sky. The smoke and the smell of the burning wood reminds you of Halloweens past when you used to have bonfires at Bolsa Chica beach.

The Ni-Perchta sit around on what look like giant carpets, watching the tree engorged in flame. You and Jaime and the Counters jump out of the cruiser. The Counters and, oddly, even Jaime, call out to the Ni-Perchta in Perchta.

It certainly looks like they are happy to see you, and they offer you a place on their rough carpets. Meat and a sort of red milk are offered but you and the two Counters gently refuse. Jaime refuses as well after a moment. One Ni- Perchta brings out a small wooden baton, and with that strange little power of telekinesis that only orichalcum can give, pulls a group of branches off the burning tree and sets them into a circle of rocks to make their own separated bonfire for cooking skewers of meat that hang limply from rusty bayonets.

From over the horizon you see lit torches and hear the stamping of feet and the creaking of wagon wheels over the grasslands. More Ni-Perchta gather towards the burning tree, coming from all angles.

Jaime rubs his hands together, excited. "Must be somethin' special!"

The Ni-Perchta approach in pairs and groups, some with fully decorated wagons adorned in garish colors like the old Gypsies back on Earth. Others arrive in small, rotted out pickup trucks and cars twenty or thirty years old being towed by hairy cows that have six devil-black horns on the sides of their heads. These are the Afer animals. A few dump trucks, covered in beads and wind chimes, pull up as well, loud and jangling.

One regal-looking Ni-Perchta drives up in a rusted Ford Mustang with no doors and chains on its tires, being pulled by nothing but Detroit horsepower coming out of a bad engine. This older Ni-Perchta wears a sort of black headdress; three straight, black Afer horns poke out of each side.

The Ni-Perchta call out to each other, laughing or singing their funeral dirge songs.

The women are beautiful, their platinum hair waist-length around angular faces, their eyes glowing red in the dark. They wear almost see-through blouses and tunics that are every color of the rainbow.

Some of the males and their children set up large drums. With heavy smooth sticks the Ni-Perchta start to pound the drums in unison, creating a steady, thundering beat. Whistles and flutes begin playing; there's a distinctly Asian sound to them. Poles are raised that have wind chimes on top of them. The drums continue to beat in rhythm, slow, steady. The two humans with you, the Network boys, stand to the side, observing. Some humans come out of the dark. They have come by wagon or crappy 70s-era cars, and are about your same age or a little bit older.

The drums beat a little more quickly, then a little more quickly. The Ni-Perchta dance in a large circle, spinning slowly around in their own individual circles. They chant now, something you would hear at the entrance to Hell, you suppose. They stop.

"Oh Lord," Jaime says, pointing to the sky. A comet, white and glowing, streaks across the sky, as large as one of the moons. It blots out some of the stars as it passes.

One of the Ni-Perchta speaks a few sentences. You assume that he is the chief judging by his headdress and the way the other Ni-Perchta pay attention to him.

The drums beat again, slowly this time. The chief sends over a little Ni-Perchta girl, a cute one, perhaps in her very early teens, who has something wrapped in a cloth.

She gives you a collapsed expandable baton, one like all the others that humans carry around. It's brand new, shiny. It has empty slots to put in orichalcum stones; only one slot has a blue-white orichalcum stone fitted into it. In tiny letters you can read *Telekinesis* above it.

"A goddamn weapon. Sweet," you say. "I refuse."

Jaime looks at you funny. "Refuse? You are a Force-Fire. Like me. It's sort of interesting. They want to make sure you are okay. They are so happy you'll be working at Mission Friendship."

You nod and then look around like you've just woken up from a deep sleep. "What's a Force-Fire?"

"A resurrection of a local hero. Sort of like the concept the Tibetan Buddhists have about tulkus. You are a great soul, they say, but you just don't know it yet. Apparently, me too. We escaped from those dungeons—they all know this." Jaime looks confused, but excited at the same time.

"Wow. Great," you respond, disinterested.

"Of course you can refuse it. But that's, that's..."

"Do I have to thank them? Thank you guys. Thanks." The large crowd of aliens stare at you with red reflecting eyes. One Ni-Perchta sharpens a sword in the background. You think you see Guy Farson somewhere in the background, too, but you aren't really sure. A shadow of that good-looking man disappears into the darkness. You feel a little scared now as you are surrounded on all sides by the Ni-Perchta.

"Can't believe we did that." You reflect on what happened not even a full day before. The Counters look at you curiously, exchanging glances.

"Thank you," you say to the Ni-Perchta girl who is still standing next to you. The Network Counters and Jaime nearly trip over each other trying to get the translation out.

"Why did they just give it to me?" you ask.

Robert speaks to you in a whisper. "The chief says that it will help protect you as your past life comes into your present life."

"You should give a speech," Tadeo says.

"A speech for what? I don't know why. This is some silly stuff, guys. I just got through some shitty twenty-four hours and you're springing this...this craziness on me." You cough and then nod to the entire crowd of Ni-Perchta. You decide quickly that perhaps you should say something. A long moment passes. You speak loudly and clearly. "I'm sorry, but I don't want to be an emperor. That's not my business. I don't want to rule anyone or conquer anyone. I should like to help everyone—if possible—Jew, Gentile, black man, white. We all want to help one another. Human beings are like that. We want to live by each other's happiness—not by each other's misery. We don't want to hate and despise one another. In this world there is room for everyone. And The Oberon is rich and can provide for everyone. The way of life here can be free and beautiful."

The crowd looks confused, and the Ni-Perchta say nothing as one of the Counters translates for you.

"It's from *The Great Dictator*. I had to memorize it for drama class. You're welcome," you whisper to Jaime. He looks confused.

"Humphrey Bogart was in it?"

"Never mind."

The crowd cheers for an unknown reason after the Counter finishes, and you realize you are definitely still high from the Valis wheel. The speech sticks in your mind. You haven't thought about that movie in a long time, nor have you thought about that Charlie Chaplin speech. The speech means a lot to you actually, though you don't share that information with anyone.

The other humans come out of the crowd and walk over to you. The first you meet are the Cartwrights, a young couple from England who apparently run a lumber mill or some such enterprise befitting a name like Cartwright. The man, Wellington, "Call me Wellington," he says, after you call him "Devo" for no reason, is Mission Friendship's head doctor. His wife, Temperance, cuts up and sells the trees around the Funeral Breaks to local Ni-Perchta tribes. You ask if the Ni-Perchta are too stupid to figure out how to use a saw blade and she laughs nervously and tells you no and that what you just said is a bit racist.

You also meet the Page sisters: two girls, one skinny with horn-rimmed glasses named Treena and the other chubby with bouncy blonde hair called Winniefreddie. They run the bar inside Mission Friendship, the Benbow Inn.

"Fantastic!" you say. "Now can one of you bounce on back to the Benbow and get me a drink?"

"So sorry," Jaime apologies. "Time to go, Sarah."

In the back of the cruiser on the way to Mission Friendship, as Jaime is still beaming at his surroundings, you take a look at the baton the Ni-Perchta gave you. Though their concept of who you are is quite ridiculous, you find them giving you the baton to be a very nice gesture.

CHAPTER SEVEN:
MISSION FRIENDSHIP

The Ni-Perchta go back to their caravan homes and their trucks and cars to relax and perhaps sleep the night away. Though the smaller bonfire has petered out, the tree still burns, fully engulfed yet strangely not falling apart.

You see it behind you as you drive towards Mission Friendship, passing over the wooden bridge across the river. Someone has left strange white graffiti on parts of the bridge's wall.

A wanted sign is pasted onto one of the pillars of the bridge. It says:

WANTED—CHARLES MATHIAS, LEADER OF MATHI-AS-PETTY GANG.

A hand-drawn and faded picture of a man with curly red hair has been copied onto the poster.

Convicted Murderer. 25 Million Dii-Yaa Reward, Alive or Dead, from Ephors of Kadath and Bureau of Off-World Affairs.

A dragon-like symbol is stamped at the bottom of the poster.

You mean to ask Jaime about it but Mission Friendship is ahead of you. As you get closer, the Mission looks like it is half out of the movie *Kundun* or *Seven Years in Tibet* and half like it belongs in Vegas or Dubai. The glitzy ugliness of the apartment tower arbitrarily grafted onto the old stone dzong is jarring to you.

NIGHTHAWKS AT THE MISSION

You are mildly excited about what you're about to get into, curious more than anything else. A monument sign states that, yes, this is indeed Mission Friendship. The Counters park the cruiser outside the massive wooden doors of the old part of the Mission; the doors are ajar. Behind them is a set of glass doors, leading to the interior.

The Counters unlock the glass doors of the building and then turn on the lights. In the lobby, a pair of desks—each with stacks of brochures and a computer on top, along with a printer—face you head on. There are a couple of glass-walled offices off to one side. . The electronics all have a funny-looking, metallic cage over them. One of the Counters grabs a clipboard and a yellow packet full of keys from one of the desks and leads you to the elevators.

The lobby is as big as a soccer field and has within its stone walls three all-American shops—a McDonald's, a Subway, which makes your skin crawl a little, and a Starbucks. Though the lobby looks like it had once been the inner courtyard or hall for the great palace, now it's just a glorified food court. Off to the far right corner, away from fast food row, a smaller shop with closed doors , has a wooden sign stenciled with the words *Benbow Inn.* The smell of French fries is both comforting and overwhelming. A large marketplace, closed off and behind steel bars, seems to be your local grocery store. It takes up most of the lobby.

Hanging on one wall is an incredible painting—it's of a wizard, you think, perhaps a representation of the Witch-Lord himself. The figure is covered in shadow, holding a gnarled staff. A white light shines on this figure but it only highlights his outline and never his features. A small plaque with an inscription written in English, Japanese, and Perchta confirms your belief: *The Hidden Witch-Lord of The Oberon.*

Radio Oberon is playing an old fifties doo-wop song through concealed speakers.

The men from Mission Security take you to a row of elevators. You find yourself lowered, not brought up a floor. Stepping from the elevator you peer around some dingy basement-like area. The light here is pale and barely illuminates anything. The MS men take you to your front door, which opens to reveal a fairly large two-bedroom place. Bland furniture and appliances fill up the space, and there is no television, just a large, old-style radio, apparently an antique rescue from the forties.

There are no windows, which depresses you further. The walls are blank. A welcome basket sits on one white counter next to the sink, and you find the refrigerator fully stocked with bland goodies.

The Counters check through the place quickly. Robert makes notes on how the place looks. This is your moving in inspection, you realize dimly. Jaime is doing all the talking.

He finally calls you over to sign off on the last few bits of paperwork, and when you do so, he hugs you for a second. "New home for you...us. Kind of cool, huh?"

It's all a bit too much for you and your stomach heaves for a quick and painful moment. Jaime mentions to the Counters that you've been feeling a little sick lately, which explains "the silliness you do."

Near the back of the apartment, you spot a single white door that is ajar, revealing a bleak-looking toilet, and make your way to the back in order to use it. Perhaps it's every emotion you've had since arriving hitting you at once, or perhaps it's your foolishness in doing drugs catching up to you, but now you feel sick to your stomach. You make it into the restroom, close the door behind you and stare into the mirror for a long moment, seeing a slightly disheveled, tired looking young woman with brunette hair. You turn on the cold tap, running your hands through it and then splashing it onto your face for a good minute, feeling the water run over your hands, your face. The basin is filled with cool water now and you become fixated on it, staring at it, skimming your hand over its surface.

Blackness. No sound. No feeling.

There are strange tones, something not of this world; sounds that only the dead can hear, you fear.

You stand up in a stupor, shaking your head, and stumble out of the bathroom, swinging the door wide open. You feel drugged.

And then you see Dwelka Storma, same armor, same mask covering the bottom half of his face, the half-crown. The Ephor warrior stands there, sword drawn. You hear the strange tones again and feel as if you are falling. The vision of Dwelka Storma fades and disappears, to be replaced by your sister—a woman you haven't seen for a very long time. You see Star in the Mountain for a brief second.

The vision disappears. The two Counters are helping to your feet, and Jaime gets a cup of water for you.

"We can go to sleep in a little bit. You okay, Sweetie McSweetums?"

You shake your head, thinking that you just imagined what he had said. Tyler would say that. Not him.

CHAPTER EIGHT:
THE FLASH STORM (WHEN THE LEVEE BREAKS)

You wish the Counters an awkward goodbye as they leave your new home. You and Jaime watch from the front door as they walk down the hallway to the elevators.

Jaime nudges you. "Want to get something to eat? There's an observation area on the roof. And grills." He checks the refrigerator. "They've left us Network Beer. Alcohol, Sarah. Take a look. Oh and they left personal liquor license forms to fill out in the refrigerator..." Jaime shakes his head. "I don't know why they left them in the fridge."

Your mood picks up a bit at that news, and you take a closer look. "You're the man now, dog," you reply.

Jaime hands you a white fluffy towel with the crest of Solomon's House University imprinted on it, and you take a shower in the second bedroom's bathroom. You stand in the shower for a long time, maybe thirty minutes, running that hot water all over, scrubbing away the memories of the train trip and the day in the dungeon, cleaning underneath your fingernails, and washing and rewashing your hair with little hotel-style shampoo bottles.

As you dry yourself off, you look in the mirror. You don't know if this is possible but you look like you've lost more than a few pounds, like a skeleton with two red coals for eyes.

Wearing an oversized Solomon's House University sweater and sweatpants that smell of mothballs and were part of your move-in gifts, you walk out of the bedroom and look for Jaime. You see a note on Network stationery—he is at the observation lounge at the top of Mission Friendship.

After a long elevator ride to the top, you emerge on the rooftop to encounter not a single resident. There's an incredible view—the mountains, the stars, Star in the Mountain, the walled village, and the train station far off. Clouds drift across the night sky with all those different stars looking back down on you and the seven ethereal moons orbiting above. There are little, round, neon-green birds sitting on the railing. Behind you is a fire pit that burns steadily in a giant brass centerpiece, the fire crackling and puffing as the logs split from the heat. The air is tinged with fragrant smoke. A strange robot, skeletal and ancient-looking, beeps away, watching the fire and stoking it constantly.

Jaime has found an old, portable transistor radio, and is grooving to yet another rock and roll classic. His eyes are closed as he sways along with the music.

You watch him awkwardly wiggle his knees back and forth for a good few minutes before you touch him on the shoulder. He jumps a few feet straight up into the air.

After turning down the radio, he leads you to where a couple of wicker chairs are set up with a tray table next to each. "Found all this stuff up here." Each tray table is complete with a sourdough sandwich, empty glass, and small bag of Doritos. It feels like no one else is here at the Mission.

"Quite the view here, hmmm?" You nod in response, looking at the dinner intently. "Glass of milk, uh, Earth cattle, perhaps? Water? Pre-mixed virgin pina colada?" Jaime opens a large plastic red and white cooler that he's brought from downstairs. It has the Network symbol on it. It's full of ice and beer bottles strangely covered with the hammer and sickle symbol and the words COMECON BEER, plus a few other beverages. The Network is not stingy when it comes to welcoming you to its Mission.

"Milk," you say. "Still feeling a little loose from the whole train thing..."

He pulls out a bottle and pours you a glass. You down half of it in a single gulp.

He sits down in his own chair after grabbing a dripping bottle of the Hammer and Sickle. He takes a bottle opener from his pocket and pops off the bottle cap, which he then throws over the railing. You're too high up to hear the clink of it falling against the road. "This is fun; this is what couples do," he says, looking very content. "Boy, I hope no one was down there..."

You eat with relief. Jaime takes out an old Casio digital wristwatch, a cheap silver thing that would have looked dandy on any frugal gentlemen from the 1980s, and tosses it to you. You look confused.

"Not really my style..." You toss it back, and he immediately tosses it right back to you with a grin. "Keep it on, Sarah, and watch the clock. When the digital screen goes out, that's because of the EMP blast. When you see a blank face on the watch, that's when it happens."

"When what happens?" you ask, looking over the watch.

"When it happens, you'll know it."

You nod, still looking at the watch, feeling weird. There seems to be a charge in the air, a sort of static heaviness over everything.

The sandwich is great. It has meat inside that tastes like lobster and is buttery, somewhat hot, with a spicy mayo sauce all over it. The sourdough, interestingly, is fresh. "What's in this sandwich? It's so freakin' good," you say.

Jaime shrugs. "Wish I knew. Something alien, I guess. Maybe like those trilobite meat things we saw back at Solomon's? I got it from this little deli shop on fifteen."

That stops you from eating any more of it. You pop open the Doritos bag and are about to plop a chip into your mouth when Jaime abruptly stands up and walks away. When he comes back, he has that large, boxy transistor radio he had earlier. Moving the tray table to the side with a scraping sound, he puts the boxy radio on his lap with a groan, turns it on, and starts to fiddle with the dials. There is this funky popping sound, then a repeated buzzing noise. A warbling of static comes in and out of the transmission. You eat in silence for the next few minutes, listening to the noise, munching on chips as Jaime fiddles with the radio.

Finally, an old Led Zeppelin song with a steady, thumping beat blasts out of the radio. "Got it," Jaime says. "Now we got music again."

"Old man rock 'n roll? Still? Good god, it's like being on your dad's boat back that one day last summer. You remember that? Shit, he put Jimi Hendrix's greatest effing hits on loop for two hours. It was soooo annoying. I actually became happy after a while that Jimi choked on his own puke, and that's a mean thought. 'Hey Joe, where you going with that gun in your hand'. 'Hey Joe, where you going with that gun in your hand'. Oh man."

Jaime laughs hard. You eye him, realizing something but not letting the thought hit the conscious surface of your brain at first.

"Yep, I thought that, too. Not the Jimi choking to death part, that's really, really mean Sarah, but, you know..."

As you laugh, the watch face goes suddenly blank. "It just went dead, Jaime," you say.

"Storm's a coming," he says, rubbing his hands together.

The Led Zeppelin song is interrupted as the radio cuts out into an eerie emergency band drone. The announcer, a woman with a crisp English-sounding accent, comes on.

"We interrupt this radio broadcast to update you on the special flash storm warning for the Super Sargasso Sea region. Any and all persons within five kilometers of the center of Sargasso-3 Antediluvian city must take immediate shelter. We repeat, this is a flash storm warning..."

And then the storm starts. The black sky, once pockmarked with white stars and several moons, is covered in a fast movement of clouds. The wind becomes stronger and there is a rich, droning sound. The roof shakes so much that it rattles the glass of milk off your tray table and knocks it to the floor, shattering it. Neither you nor Jaime actually hear the glass break over the discordant warning sirens going off and the roar of the wind. The sky lights up, red, then blue, then red again, and then it turns into an almost fiery orange.

You walk to the edge of the observation deck and watch the fantastic display. A ring of white circles spreads out from some distant location, swirling in and out of the clouds, making at first a chain of circles and then shooting from the sky to the ground.

You lose your footing for a moment due to the wind and stumble to the side. Green lightning sporadically shoots out in all directions. The entire world seems to light up in white flashes as bright as millions of flashbulbs popping at the same time.

The sky turns a deep bluish-green and becomes incredibly thick with clouds. A sound like a thousand angry screams comes forth from the sky.

"You're not who you say you are, are you?" you cry out to Jaime. He doesn't hear you.

The wind becomes its strongest now, rattling the multi-paned windows in Mission Friendship with flashes of white that become more and more frequent. It seems that the whole world is being bashed into whiteness.

Jaime gives you a funny look, his mouth moving soundlessly. "I am Jaime Van Zandt," he finally says.

The storm stops. There is now utter stillness. The clouds disperse. Stars once hidden begin to shine again. A dog barks in the distance and a crow caws back.

You wonder about Jaime but let it go.

"I'll get myself outfitted in the Funeral Breaks in the morning, and then I'll be off to go check out my little modded bike," he tells you. "You remember me talking about that, right? I'll be off doing what I want to do—sketch and salvage. God, can you believe we are standing on another planet?" Jaime shivers in excitement. "In the morning, I'll be off to grab the bike and go. And the road leads ever on and on." He looks so happy. "You'll be okay here, right? I mean, it looks like the Network don't even know about our little, ah, excitement back in Solomon's Bay. The Counters never mentioned it once." He crosses his arms. "Lord, we just started an adventure."

"Must you leave so soon, Jaime?" You notice once again how exactly he looks like Tyler.

"This is what I've wanted to do my whole life, Sarah." He smiles. "Be myself, in a strange land. Thank you, Sarah. You helped make this happen." He kisses you on the cheek. "I'm living my dream."

You stand on the deck, listening to the music coming from the radio and looking at the sky.

"Okay," you say. "Okay. You go out there, and do your dream—and I'll start mine here." You manage a smile.

Later, you lie awake in your basement apartment with the lights off, trying to sleep but unable to. There is a note on your welcome basket about meeting for work tomorrow at 9:00 am. Jaime can't stand it any longer. You watch quietly as he gets dressed in the middle of the night, throwing on a leather jacket and a backpack. He walks to the kitchen and comes back with a water bottle from the refrigerator. You get out of bed, studying what he is doing.

"You're leaving now? It's three in the morning."

Jaime shrugs. "Night-time is the right time. Can't sleep, gotta walk."

"But it could be dangerous out there," you squeak. "Really, come on. Go to bed and leave at daylight."

Jaime shrugs again. "Why? There are all-night inns in the Funeral Breaks. It's a twenty- minute walk to that walled village. I'm up, I'm ready, and I'm going to go. I want to see that Triumph waiting for me in the Free Zone. Besides," Jaime takes a sawed-off shotgun with a pistol grip out of his backpack and stuffs it into his belt. "Counters had an extra shotgun just lying in the trunk, loaded." He breaks the gun open, takes out two red shotgun shells, and reloads it. "Loaded, right. If they come and ask, play dumb. But they won't. My personal intellectual assessment of people like that, based on what I have read, is that they will be too embarrassed about having lost the gun to either report it or try to track it down. I'll be fine. It's time for the adventure to begin."

Jaime opens the apartment door slowly, peeking out. "Look, Sarah," he whispers. "I think you came off-world with not the clearest and most rational reasons. I really do. So can I give you some advice?"

"Give me advice? Call me irrational? Says the guy who makes a really big assumption and steals a gun?"

Jaime smirks. "Look, what I'm saying is this. We are here on another planet. Don't end up doing the same thing you did back on Earth. This is such a cool situation."

"Jaime?"

He looks you over and shrugs his shoulders. "You should come with me. Just leave. What are they going to do? This isn't Earth. All the old rules of life just went out the window." When you shake your head, he steps out the door, leaving you to spend the next five hours awake and alone in your new basement apartment home. Your phone, which you didn't even know you had, rings and wakes you up just as you start to doze a little. It's one of those old style rotary telephones, older than you, and the noise scares you to full consciousness. A woman on the other end yawns into the phone as you pick it up. "Dee Ricco, Mission Manager, how can I help you?"

You state she called you, not the other way around. "I'm Sarah Orange, the new Settler Service Rep."

"Oh, my God. I'm so tired from last night. My apologies. Oh jeez, I just wanted to call you to check in. Did you and your husband have a good night's rest?"

"Yes, we did."

"And you got our goodie basket and our note about today? Did you get all of that?"

"Yes, thank you."

"Oh joy! Great! We will see you at nine sharp!"

You get slowly out of bed, bleary-eyed, and shower and dress. Your stomach rumbles, and your legs and arms ache from all the tension of the last few days.

Bored and over-tired, you start to sing that Led Zeppelin song you heard last night. "Cryin' won't help, prayin' will do you no good... Mama, you got to move..."

CHAPTER NINE:
FIRST DAY

In the lobby, you can smell the hot coffee brewing automatically in one of those glass-walled offices off to the side. A strong-looking woman, mid-thirties, blonde, is brewing it and it smells wonderful, the fragrance filling the large lobby. She wears the Network flight suit tightly, her breasts about to pop out, with a white scarf around her neck to show some individuality. The front glass doors are still locked—it isn't officially start time. Ni-Perchta and human workers are starting up at McDonald's, switching on fryers and grilling whatever needs to be grilled.

The woman welcomes you into her office with a wave. She introduces herself as Dee Ricco, Mission Manager. Still attractive in some ways, although the wrinkles and over-tanning have caught up to her. She isn't as thin as she perhaps once was; she mentions to you twice that she needs to get back into "fighting shape". You are wearing your own blue wannabe NASA flight suit with the American flag on your right shoulder. She gives you a once over, seemingly sizing up the competition.

"It's really good to meet you. I understand, just loosely, you had some issues with immigration?" She sips her coffee, half-lidded eyes watching you closely.

You sip on your own mug, nodding. "A little misunderstanding. Just a small delay. Thank you for understanding."

"Of course!" Dee tosses her long blonde hair casually to the side. "This isn't America or even Europe. We have to operate on their time, not our own." Dee glances out the window of her office. "Well, I'll have you shadow me today, helping you with touring Mission Friendship, how to sell one of our places, how to do work orders for our maintenance team. Our maintenance is good—we have Ernesto, who has been here since the Morgan discovery, believe it or not, and Te-La-Calles, the Ni-Perchta foreman. All of our...Buenos Dias, Ernesto!"

A slightly paunchy Mexican in his mid-forties passes by. He walks over, eyes on the ground, and opens the glass door of the office. "Buenos Dias, Dee! Hello, hello." He puts out one of his big hands and shakes with you. "The new SSR, eh? You had a good train trip all the way?"

You nod. "Fantastic. It's beautiful out here. Very nice. I even got to see the comet ritual." Ernesto's eyes meet Dee's, as if they're sharing a little joke.

"Oh, yes, yes, you know that's a rare one," Dee says.

Ernesto leaves. He waves to someone you don't see as he goes, and in a moment you meet him for the first time. Shorter than you, slicked back hair, he comes into the office with a gleaming, white-toothed smile. He has a briefcase in hand and over his black flight suit he's got a holster, just like a police detective back home. A pistol sits there comfortably.

"Our new SSR. Great to have you on board. Jake Alexandros. I'm the Bureau of Off-World Affairs agent here at Mission Friendship. I'm, sort of, your friendly representative and advisor from the US Government. I help work with the Network people and locals." He chuckles and so does Dee, again at some inside joke.

"Good to meet you. I heard you and your husband were delayed a little, but got in safe and sound. Good, good. Well, I know that our Dee here is set to help you out through the day but I'll be here, too. Oh, jeez, what time is it?" Jake swings his gaze to his watch. "Nine oh five. Oh well, let's get these doors open and start touring today, shall we? We want our tower up and running for the day!"

You see a tall Aryan superman walk over and open the glass doors of the lobby. He wears the same motorcycle cop-like uniform as the rest of the Counters. Armed with a submachine gun and carrying an ori-baton heavily studded with different types of orichalcum on his utility belt, he introduces himself in a heavy Afrikaner accent. "Oscar Botha, Chief of Mission Security, Madame. I am the ori-man around here, just in case the Winkies get out of line."

Jake nods and pats him on the arm. "Botha keeps us safe at night. There's been so many—misunderstandings—between us and the indigenous population."

Botha gives you a once over and nods. "Quite right, sir. Quite right. The Winkies need to know we are not afraid to live here in the colony." He winks at you. "How's your husband doing?" he asks intently.

"Oscar, Oscar, remember about the word 'colony.' We don't use that word here. 'Settlement' is more appropriate," Jake reminds him. You and Botha ignore him.

"Left me for another woman. Rat bastard," you say, perfectly true acting behind every word.

Botha takes out some gum from his pocket, offers you a piece. You politely refuse. He stuffs his mouth and starts smacking away at it. "Your husband is an interesting fella, yeah? Just takes off on you the first day you are here."

You frown. "He's, he's, unfortunately, he used to beat me as well."

Dee looks shocked and sad and puts out a hand, rubbing the top of your own. "Well, sweetie, no more of that. If he's gone, Botha won't let him in."

Botha laughs. "Nope. I'll put a bullet in him first, and then I'll let him in. Wife-beating scum."

You start to nod rapidly and sniff the air, as if about to cry. "Yes, yes. Terrible." You muster an amazing emotional act. Afterwards, you do not understand your outburst against Jaime and why you made up such lies and decided to slur his name. Something unconsciously bubbled to the surface and your anger and your sadness at his departure has made you say something less than sane.

Dee gives you the grand tour of the place and people trickle out of Mission Friendship. Half of them are the middle class of Network life—Ni-Perchta overseers—in their neat flight suits, but the rest are independent owners and operators in their mining gear or their Kevlar armor. Some greet you with kindness and courtesy, others ignore you. An old school bus painted blue and white pulls up in front and takes people to their respective places of work in the area—the Darling Mine, Mine 357, the Scales Mine, and Orichalcum Refinery.

There is a gym on the fifteenth floor of the apartment tower, a full one with weights and exercise bikes, and there's a heated pool on the sixteenth floor. An old man is swimming naked, and Dee smoothly asks him to put on his swim trunks.

"Why?" he asks. "Is this not proper? I mean, Dee, this is not the United States. What law are you enforcing?" He says this with his wrinkled and very naked carcass barely covered by a towel.

Dee smiles thinly. "But, Mr. Bern, let us remember that we have by-laws here on Network property as well as the US Constitution."

Bern jumps into the pool, showing off his wrinkled and concave ass. As he pops up to the surface, he states, "Well, call the Counters, see if I care. Roll the dice and let's see what happens, champ."

Dee turns and smiles at you, gives a fake laugh, and leads you back to the elevators. "The old man loves to play around. If people don't get the joke..."

You're confused.

"You're from Long Beach, right?" Dee asks. "Me, too."

Another elevator pulls up before she finishes her thoughts, revealing the three Counters, Botha, Robert, and Tadeo.

You catch Botha yelling, "This is the deal. Get some goddamn clothes on, you old bastard!" at the top of his lungs just as the elevator doors close.

You are shown empty apartments ready for rent, priced at twenty-eight thousand Dii-Yaa a month, or two thousand dollars a month in real money. You wonder why they are so expensive, considering that most of the apartments have the same amount of living space as a Volkswagen Beetle. As you look over the new appliances, specially made without electronic components in order to avoid the EMP bursts, you ask why the rent is the way it is.

Dee replies smoothly, "People want to live with people, not with the Ni-Perchta. Except for the crazies. So they are more than happy to pay to live inside a real settlement, whatever the damage to their paycheck. Besides, they pay nothing in US taxes, so they still come out ahead. And the Network is a corporation, albeit one with a unique mission. We need to generate income in everything we do." She smiles at you, a wide and white smile, predatory and unkind.

You don't say anything as she rambles on. "Our mission is to make The Oberon a modernized world through progressive renovation and development. The Ni-Perchta here live as we did back in the fourteenth century. Illiteracy is found in almost seventy percent of the native population, child marriage is common, and slavery is legal. The Witch-Lord knows this, and he works with us to make this a proper and decent place to live."

You nod. "Of course."

Dee leads you back to the elevator. "Wanna see something neat?"

You nod, already terminally bored by the entire experience. The elevator reaches the highest level of the apartment tower and opens to a small hallway that leads to two black doors. Dee walks ahead and pops open the doors with a key from her key ring, revealing something else entirely.

The penthouse suite is tastefully furnished, larger than most houses back on Earth, and takes up the entire floor. It's a modern art masterpiece made into a home and over six thousand square feet, according to Dee. She walks you through it, showing off the wall-to-wall closets, the Jacuzzi bath, the incredible almost-three hundred sixty degree view of the world around you. All the furnishings are here. It's an empty but fully-stocked palace waiting for a person to move right in.

"Nice place," you state, meaning it. It's done up in a sort of Arab motif, with striped pillars and gold furnishings adorning the place. The floors are tiled and covered in some spots by Persian rugs.

"Only for the best," Dee says. "Seventeen thousand dollars a month. Quite the place and only for the best."

For someone who has lived only in cramped, crappy apartments or slept over at someone else's house, the size and luxury of the place hit you in the gut and right in the back of the shoulder blades all at the same time.

"Anyone renting it?" you ask.

Dee shakes her head. "If you can get someone to rent it, I've got a great bonus for you." You raise an eyebrow. "Oh?"

"Sixty-five dollar Network voucher," she says, indicating that this indeed is something to work for. "You get the most expensive place rented, you can get a nice little meal downstairs for a couple of days," she says with a wink. "I know."

You nod, looking over the place in open envy. Dee seems to be reading your thoughts. "Not like you or me could grab a place like this," she says with finality. "But maybe in the next life."

You end up back at your desk with the computer, waiting for Dee. There is a young Asian girl at the other desk, looking very, very tired and hung over with heavy bags under her eyes and her long black hair slightly askew. Jake comes over to her. "Ohayou Saki, when did you clock in today?"

Saki yawns and speaks with a light Japanese accent. "Probably, like, five minutes ago. Hello." Saki stands up, smooths her blue uniform out, and shakes hands with you.

"And what time is it, Saki?" Jake says. Saki nervously chuckles.

"Um, five after ten. I'm sorry, Jake, it's just, well I was feeling like I was getting the flu again."

Jake nods. "Dee and I have to go to three oh one—they're moving back to Earth before the portal closes. Show Miss Sarah here how to take down work orders."

"No problem!" Saki says and you and she watch Jake leave the room. Saki mutters something in Japanese and goes back to the computer. Within a moment, she's back to playing *Super Mario Bros. 3* on the computer.

"Oh hey, sorry, you want to..." she starts.

You sit down at your desk and look over the notes you've been taking about your new job. "Oh, I figure we got about six more hours in the day. I want to type up my notes beforehand." You smile. "How is your day going?"

"Shitty," she says. "Woke up from being so drunk last night in the Funeral Breaks at this, uh, speak-easy run by an American. On Moondog." She looks slowly over at you, realizing she's said something terribly wrong. "Kidding, kidding! I never leave the Mission past curfew without permission."

You nod, and she turns slowly back to her computer. "You want to see a work order now? I have to put one in for the guys; there's a broken faucet in four twelve."

"Sure," you say. A thought jolts you a little bit. You are doing exactly the same thing that everyone else is doing on Earth. The same exact type of corporate job that everyone else is doing. You look down at the tiled floor for a moment, thinking.

Saki says, "Hey, don't forget, day after tomorrow is Christmas. You got the invite to be at the observation lounge?"

You nod. "Oh yes. Thank you. In that goodie bag, thanks. I got the message."

The day ends as it started—with you barely interacting with anyone. The miners start drifting in about the time you are going to wrap up for the day. 6:00 p.m., Oberon Standard Time. You are surprised as Dee pays you immediately for your work in Dii-Yaa money. One thousand four hundred and thirty-five Dii-Yaa to be exact.

"Witch-Lord law," she says. "Have to be paid daily. Oh, you know, there was one thing." She leads you over to her office. "Sorry, I know you're probably clocked out, but here's a rundown on people looking to get a 'dayhawk' license for Sargasso-3." She pulls out a small folder with long thirty-page forms. "These are the salvage license forms—Form twenty-seven bee dash six. Now they have to be approved by myself, then cleared by Jake as the Bureau agent." Dee grins. "How much do you think a license costs?"

You shrug, not terribly interested. Dee smiles. "Twenty thousand cash, up front." You fake surprise. "Straight to the Network. You sell a license; you get a hundred dollars out of that. Sound good, Sarah?"

"Sure. But isn't that expensive? I mean that's…"

Dee keeps smiling. "Sarah, we have a contract from the Witch-Lord and the Bureau that states we have the right to charge whatever is appropriate. This is market appropriate."

"Yes, but wouldn't that put people…I mean, would make people do things illegally instead?"

Dee shrugs. "Not really our problem, Miss Sarah. Besides, it's for their own good. If you have a good amount of money you can avoid most of the danger out there because you have the means to have your expeditions properly funded."

"Any way around that?" you ask, innocently.

Dee grins. "I wouldn't know anything about bribes, if that's what you mean..." She shakes her head. "Nope. You want to see our little salvage and ori showroom in the back? I mean, if you need to run off back home..."

You shake your head, not really interested but not quite ready to say no to your new boss.

She nods to the door, jabbering away as she leads you back beyond the elevators and the lobby. Past the mural depicting the Witch-Lord is a metallic sign bolted over a couple of large steel doors reading:

Official Ori and Salvage Buy Center for Sargasso-3 and *JUST SAY NO TO ILLEGAL ORI AND SALVAGE SALES. SMUGGLING IS A CRIME.*

The wholesale prices for the orichalcum is in the thousands of Dii-Yaa, but a quick conversion in your head finds them to be pretty reasonable compared to what was being sold back on Earth, especially the telekinesis ori. A large bulletin board to the side explains in English, Spanish, and Japanese that they have:

Non-Human Non-Ni-Perchta Control Ori! 20K D-Y-Taurus. Telekinesis Ori! 15K D-Y- Leo.

Fire Control Ori! (High Danger!) Mkt. Price. Sagittarius. Electrical Ori! Mkt. Price. Libra.

You walk through the steel doors and discover a Nemo Gate—a small one, only big enough for one person at a time. You enter and in a moment you are in some underground place you know not where. Dee materializes and leads you into the shop run by a few Ni-Perchta under a human overseer. Stepping inside, you feel as if this is the most insane antique shop you have ever seen in your life. There are items on shelves that stretch up the entirety of the stone walls. Radio Oberon is playing over hidden speakers. The room is lit by gaslight, making it dark and dungeon-like. Why no electricity is being used is never explained to you.

There are no customers inside, just the glass counters full of random stuff and old-fashioned cash registers. There are old statues of the man-beast things from the Antediluvian cities and lots of old guns, including something called an ori-projector. It looks like a haphazard mix between an M-16 and a flashlight, hooked up to a backpack. There is also random junk, historical pieces, traditional Ni-Perchta armor, and clothing that looks medieval.

You look into the glass counters, seeing things you have never heard of before—a jar of Remembers, also known as school pills; five pills for three thousand Dii-Yaa, or one Krugerrand (no US dollars accepted).

These pills are, according to the cards in the glass cases, guaranteed to give you increased intelligence for a temporary period of time, and you will be able remember any event for the next hour with one hundred percent perfect clarity and recall.

There are strength pills as well: "guaranteed to increase physical strength by 200% for three hours."

Golden belts that emit a "body shield to deflect physical blows or gunfire" are also behind glass and so are large, hollow boxes: "an infinite storage device when hooked up to electricity."

And, of course, pure orichalcum pieces line one wall, ready for re-sale.

"Everything you ever find or mine out there has to come through us. The Network's economy is bigger than Belgium's," Dee says, looking around the shop. "You know where we are?"

You shake your head.

"Neither do I. Once the Gate is shut off for the evening and the doors weld themselves shut for the night, no one can get in or out. If anyone tries to rob the place, the doors close and the room gets gassed. Even the tiniest bit of shoplifting. A little Antediluvian machine does everything. Thank God, too. If someone had access to all this stuff that the legals sell to the Network in this sector to re-sell back on Earth..." She makes a mock shivering motion.

Alone, back at your apartment in the basement, you turn on the radio and grab a beer from the refrigerator. You sit on the couch, listening to the only radio station coming in—Radio Oberon out of Solomon's Bay. You drink and fall asleep on the couch after filling out the license form.

Later, you wake up in a stupor and realize that Radio Oberon is now playing some old type of radio play, something from the 1940s or '50s. You like it—there's a weird freshness to such an old-fashioned show, with its melodrama and the faint scratching of vinyl.

"Tired of the everyday routine? Ever dream of a life of romantic adventure? Want to get away from it all?" the narrator says on a recording made before your own mother was born.

"We offer you... escape!" a second narrator shouts like a used car salesman on amphetamines.

Vincent Price rambles on about a lighthouse that's apparently surrounded by jellyfish and sharks and smells like death. Then the narrator has an adventure or something against rats and blind tribesmen while smoking a pipe to hide the stink of death.

The show ends in half an hour and you are not tired, not tired at all; you want to explore a little. It's 10:25 pm, according to the wall clock. The rules of the Mission state that you cannot leave Mission Friendship without a pass or escort from Mission Security at this hour. But the Benbow Inn, the bar inside Mission Friendship, is open until 3:00 am.

Standing outside the Benbow Inn, you try to see if anyone is around or working at this place. The doors are closed. You suddenly feel weird, dejected, alone, hopeless, all of those feelings put together into one hideous emotional cocktail. Finally, Treena and Winniefreddie, the Page sisters, open up the place, and you walk inside.

The Benbow Inn is apparently nothing but four walls and an incredibly small version of the Nemo Gate that girds the Pacific twice a year. Treena and Winniefreddie have disappeared, apparently having gone through the Gate itself back to, well, wherever they have just gone to. A neatly printed sign hangs from a cardboard cut-out of John Wayne. *Step on in, Pilgrim! One second away from cold beer and fun!*

You hold onto the side of the Gate, bracing yourself, but then give up and feel this sort of pull as you go through the middle of the Gate. There is a thunder crack and you can see, for just a brief moment, everything at once—your past, the present predicament, scenes of the future, all in a flash, in a jumbled mash that you can barely remember after being pulled through the Gate. Then you see a thousand stars exploding and have the sense of watching a white ring of light form and grow.

You are on the other side of the Nemo Gate, which is next to a pair of heavy wooden doors inside the actual inn. Looking through the massive plate glass windows at the front of the inn, you watch as a light rain pours steadily down onto a turtle and duck pond, scattering the little animals. Green grass-covered hills covered by the night are just a moment's walk from the porch of the Benbow.

You also spot Mission Friendship's modernistic tower miles away. A large sign bolted to the front doors of the Benbow states: *No Access Beyond This Point For Any Network Settlers Past 10:00 pm.*

The Inn is deserted, despite it being 10:30 pm. The wooden booths and the tables with red checkered picnic tablecloths are empty.

The front bar is decorated at one end with the giant skull of a Baleen dragon—"quite harmless if a bit large in real life," Treena explains later—and hundreds of framed photos from around the world fill every nook and cranny. The ceiling is decorated as if it were the night sky, with the seven moons. Dark but homey, the place has that rich smell of years of spilled beer. It also smells of eggs—there is a large clear glass jar of deviled eggs sitting in the middle of the bar, reminding you of a place in Long Beach your dad once took you to. A plaque that states *ILLEGAL TO HAVE ALCOHOL WITHOUT A PERSONAL LIQUOR LICENSE—WITCH-LORD LAW* hangs above the bar.

An apron-wearing Ni-Perchta male with one side of his face heavily scarred watches you from down a hall that leads to a true, old school Viking dining hall area. An open fire pit covered in hot coals is in there, with large bits of meat being grilled under a partially- opened roof. You realize that the bar section must jut out a little bit from Mission Friendship itself.

You yell out to Treena and Winniefreddie, who are stalking about the place. "Hey! Hello!"

They seem to want to ignore you, but walk over slowly and meet you by the bar. "Hey there, yourself, girl. What's up?" Winniefreddie says, looking bubbly. "Good to see you. Sarah, right?"

You nod. "Need something to eat and drink. You guys are open, right?" you say, friendly. "How much for a beer and uh, you guys got something heavy? Burgers? Steak? Somethin'?"

"Of course. For a price," Treena, the skinny one with horn-rimmed glasses, says, walking around the counter. She creeps you out at first with her weird voice that sounds like Bullwinkle being castrated by hot oil. "Five hundred Dii-Yaa." She bats her eyes four times in quick succession, fluttering them at you behind her glasses. Her voice returns to normal. "Please. Sorry, I get excited talking about money."

You look at the star-painted ceiling. "That's, that's, um, well it's fourteen Dii-Yaa to the dollar, so that's, um..." You look at Treena. "It's thirty-five bucks. You really get so much business here?"

Treena and Winniefreddie look at each other. Winniefreddie speaks up. "Well, yes, yes we do. Yes we do. Yes."

The Ni-Perchta walks over, waving his hands. "You pay? Is Exeurncalles! Is Exeurncalles!"

"Yeah, yeah, I understand, but I have to pay."

"Is Exeurncalles!" the Ni-Perchta says, looking at Winniefreddie and Treena.

You peel off the red Monopoly money bills Dee paid you and give them to Treena, who looks all too happy to grab them.

"Yeah, yeah, shut up, ya stupid alien," you say as you hand over the cash. The Ni-Perchta still yells in the background. Treena nods appreciatively and stuffs the Dii-Yaa into her cash register.

You shake your head. "Freakin' alien, huh?"

Treena and Winniefreddie look annoyed at what you just said. You watch as the Ni-Perchta man leaves and goes back to his cooking.

"You girls into drinking? No one else here, and I don't want to be the lonely drunk," you say dejectedly, feeling sickened by the last couple of days.

Treena and Winniefreddie look at each other, shrug. "I always love shooting the shit with a new resident," Winniefreddie says.

"Is Exeurncalles! Okay!" the Ni-Perchta male yells out.

You give him the finger, and he ignores you. "What does 'Exeurncalles' mean?"

Treena and Winniefreddie smile to each other. "Means you should, uh, show respect to the festival days. Ni-Perchta have rules against drinking. Forget Tek though, he's just a little pious, that's all. Forgive him."

"Beers on us. You are our only customer," Treena says, walking behind the counter. "I'm supposed to inform you that you need to have a personal liquor license registered with the Mission Manager. Do you have a liquor license?"

"I...uh, yes, not on me," you say, meeting Treena and Winniefreddie's eyes.

"The hell with the Ephors," Treena says. "Fourteenth century fools trying to boss us around. If it wasn't for the ori we'd probably never come here except for a curious vacation."

"He cheats on you with two different people, and then has the balls to blame you for not doing the 'hey-hey'?" Winniefreddie mock shivers. She is sitting on one of the bar stools, her chubby figure angling to get a comfortable perch. The storm outside has picked up. "Is he a psycho?" she continues, as you stand behind the bar drinking out of a copper cup you just refilled with the tap.

Treena plays solitaire on another cracked red leather stool. She looks annoyed, since you've been belaboring the shit out of this story, and pipes in with her opinion. "Yeah, he sucks and needs to die in a car fire. Now, can we move the hell on?"

The giant dragon head that hangs over the restroom doors watches you and the others with glass eyes that reflect flickers of light from the fireplace you just lit up after you complained to the Page sisters. You find that you like them a lot and enjoy talking to them.

A regular rainstorm is going on outside. It is at a steady, hard tempo. With only a few lights on and with the centered fireplace-stove giving off light from burning logs, the place is both grim and homey at once. A fully decorated Christmas tree is in one corner. You wonder how they got away with the tree. Perhaps since Christmas is such a secularized nothing holiday back home that even the non-religious love, you figure that Christmas trees get a free pass.

You notice for the first time that dollar bills are stapled across the ceiling; people have signed them from wherever they came. A couple of the bills are noticeably red notes instead of green dollar bills—Dii-Yaa money. One says *Guy Farson*, you think. You realize you've been staring at it for a while. If it wasn't for the Nemo Gate next to the back door of the Benbow, you would think you were in some ancient pub back on Earth.

"That was my feeling, yes, Treena, but then what you were saying... And yeah, he's, wow," you say, turning on the beer tap and putting your mouth on the end. "God, I like to drink now."

You're joking but there is a bit of reality behind your statement. Alcohol, you notice, makes things feel just distant enough that you can think for a simple moment. It calms your nerves and your stomach enough to make life tolerable, and masks the shittiness you feel. With increasing doses, alcohol makes life fun again. You have noticed this since the Queen Mary. Guy offered you a drink then and you remember how your mind stops racing, slows down and you know you can think more clearly after a drink.

Winniefreddie wiggles some more and then takes out a cigarette. She mumbles something under her breath and looks through her pockets for a lighter, doesn't find one, and puts the cigarette away.

You stop. "Did you just say he's probably a vampire? I don't think this...wait, there are vampires here, in The Oberon. You think? No, no that's... I mean, the ancients or what you call 'em..." You think of the dead city you went through.

Winniefreddie looks away and mumbles something about you about to be educated, so you move on. Treena takes out a small .38 pistol and a blue expandable baton that's collapsed. It has a single blue orichalcum stone in the handle. She lays it out on the counter. "You should go back there and blow his brains out. This is my gun and my baton, totally untraceable to you. You understand me? Totally untraceable."

Winniefreddie quietly asks, "Can we have a beer to calm our nerves?"

You nod and bring out a copper cup for each as well as two bottles of home-made beer with tags stating *Tokyo Sex Whale*. You are running the bar now, for no particular reason. Treena takes the beer bottle without looking and twists off the cap. You look at the bottle again, with its blue whale wearing a sailor's cap. The name is awfully familiar. The whale is destroying what could be downtown Tokyo, while women in bikinis run away. *Tokyo Sex Whale* is written in colorful, neon lettering.

Winniefreddie tries to open her bottle with her teeth until she sees Treena make a twisting motion with her hands. "Look at me, Winniefreddie, look at me."

"Where you guys, I mean, let me say that again. Where you guysss es from?" you slur.

"Seal Beach, originally," Winniefreddie says. "Graduated Los Alamitos High School in 2006."

You lick your lips. "You gotta be shitting me! You shit me not! God, that's me, too, me freakin', too! I graduated in 2011! Jeez, that's awesome! We're all from Seal Beach!" You are very happy to hear that and high five the two girls, hard. "This is fate. I attracted this. I attracted this big time. You ever read *The Secret?*"

They shake their heads.

"What are you guys doing out here?" you ask.

"Selling alcohol, pretty much. We make our own beer. Tokyo Sex Whale. Want to get out there to the Sargasso-3 Free Zone. California Gold Rush time, you know? Sargasso-3 is supposed to be barely hit, and so a lot of flush dayhawks are paying ten bucks a beer. You can't import alcohol into The Oberon, but we can make it," Treena says, her face down.

You look at the bottle again. "Tokyo Sex Whale. That's—you know Guy Farson, don't you? Dayhawker, right?"

Treena and Winniefreddie become very still. "Nope, never, uh, heard of him. Why do you say that?" Treena asks.

You look at the bottle again, thinking, but don't say anything.

"We really wanted to get into dayhawking ourselves, but we don't have anyone to teach us, you know? And the license fee... If you want to do it legally and in the daytime, it's a lot of money or special favors to the Bureau agent here," Winniefreddie says. Treena looks at her as if she has said too much and she quiets down.

"I want to do that. We're all California girls. We can handle ourselves out there in the big bad empty, can't we?" you say.

Winniefreddie nods. "Hell yeah. Hell yeah," she says repeatedly. You put out your sloshing cup full of cold beer. "Here's to underage drinking and bad decision making! We got to go into dayhawking, right? I mean you guys don't want to just own this place, right? You guys got here just a little while ago too, right?"

Treena and Winniefreddie look at each other. "Right, right, and we own this place, right."

The Ni-Perchta male walks behind you three, shaking his head and yelling, "Is Exeurncalles!"

"Shoo! Shooooo!" Winniefreddie and Treena say. He goes into a back room marked *Private*. You see a little cot set up for him to sleep on.

"Do you guys want to see something nuts? The book? That the Network Rep brought me back in Long Beach? From my sister. I looked it up online. It's a very rare thing to have, and it's supposed to be very helpful with dayhawking," you say.

Treena shrugs. Winniefreddie nods with excitement.

You put down the copper cup and run back to your apartment—which means going through the Nemo Gate again with a crack. You bring out the book, slap it down on the counter and open it up.

Winniefreddie looks like she's just won the lottery. "Oh snap, it's the *Necronomicon*! Have the walls started to bleed and are the stars right? Where's the section where we can raise the dead from their dreamless sleep?"

You ignore Winniefreddie's ramblings on H.P. Lovecraft, excited about telling your story. "*Voice of the Four Winds* or something, he said. Not the *Necronomicon*. I don't know what that is. You can read stories, look over maps. I've read a lot in here."

Treena finally rouses herself, pushes back her glasses, and looks over the book. "Are you thinking about selling it?" she asks. "It has to be worth something."

"Yeah," you say, meaning it but feeling that it will never happen. Looking at the book again gives you a chill. It's quiet for a long moment with the logs crackling in the background and the storm playing outside the front doors.

"These books are pretty rare, Sarah, so I've heard," Treena says. "These books, these are really strong religious artifacts, too. Like our Bibles or Korans. Sort of a translator/GPS/gospel for the natives, the Ni-Perchta. How'd your sister get it?" She flips through the pages. "And it's blank, Sarah."

"And it's worth a shitload of money, I think... wait, what?"

Treena nods without looking up from the pages. "Oh yeah. You smell that, every time you flip a page? Smells like electrical burn. Just, sort of, drifts up from the page. What is this?"

Winniefreddie spits out half of her beer, spraying the book and you. "Oh man, we can use this! I know what this is. This is a tetrachromatic version of their book—that's why we can't see it, but I guess you can. Man, we make money so we can hang out with you and you'll be like, 'Winniefreddie, you want to go places and do things and not work 'n' shit?' And we can drink Hankakins instead of Budweisers, and the men we hang with will all look like Abercrombie and Bitch models except without the douche factor. Right?" She high fives you hard and you are barely ready. You shake your hand because it hurts. "But wait, you said you can read certain things. How does that work?"

You wipe your front with a towel after spilling some beer on yourself. "Sounds awesome to me, too. The word is Heineken. Not Hankakins." You look at the book. You can see every hieroglyphic and a map showing the entire Oberon with the four regions—Burzee, Quadling, Super Sargasso Sea, and Nikh-Cunm/Former COMECON Territories.

"Do I look like I'm Russian like Hitler? I don't speak the language," Winniefreddie says, chugging her beer and placing it on the counter. "Chalk up another one to the Maniac. I can't read a thing, though. You must be tetrachromatic."

Winniefreddie and Treena look at each for a long moment. "Yeah, you must be," Treena agrees. "You know what that is, right?"

"Seeing extras coloorrs and shit," you slur.

"Seeing extra colors beyond the normal spectrum, right."

"Cool." You start to gargle with beer and dribble some onto yourself. "My future is in beer dentistry... Hey, hey, got a question. Why are we so locked up tight in the Mission? They afraid of the Ni-Perchta that much? I mean, Jesus, what's the big deal? They are strange but they ain't, you know, Cthulhu flying up into your face and shit, you know?"

Winniefreddie and Treena smile at each other. "There's a lot of...creatures... around. I mean, more like in Sargasso-3, but still, you can see things out there, late at night," Treena says.

You nod as if you really understand this. "Where is everybody?"

The Page sisters shrug. "It's Christmas Eve. Everyone is with family, Sarah," Winniefreddie says.

Treena comes up with an idea. "We should go to the Breaks, girls! Hang out at the bars on Moondog Street!"

You high five her hard, making her cringe. Winniefreddie nods her head. "Oh yeah."

You and the girls actually walk the green and hilly fields at night, taking a good fifteen to twenty minutes to get over to the walled village of the Funeral Breaks. Walking on a cobblestone path, the three of you are doing a stumble-and-talk to the town's edge. The high wooden and stone walls greet you with ambivalence and the gate leading inside has a green reflector plate, like a highway sign back home, stating that the walled village of the Funeral Breaks is a designated census spot. A mix of cars and motorcycles and even a few short buses are all over, parked in front of the village, each modified with extra lights, metal plates, and other things to armor them.

A single yellow Karmann Ghia stands out amongst all the other cars—clean looking, snub-nosed, a 1970s hipster-mobile. A Ni-Perchta kid, maybe thirteen, sits on the hood of a '55 Chevy that's dying of rust, smoking a Valis pipe. He waves to you and points to his pipe. You ignore him. A slight drizzle falls from an overcast sky, creating a mist.

Just steps away from passing through the gate, a Ni-Perchta in simple, medieval-style armor steps out and asks what your business is. Next to him is another Ni-Perchta in a blue military uniform, human style. Winniefreddie responds, "Going to Moondog Street, sir knight."

The Ni-Perchta frowns and lets you pass. You look him up and down, still a little weirded out by seeing a true alien up close and personal.

The village itself is a good size, with winding and narrow streets snaking off in all directions. You walk on mud and cobblestones, avoiding the stares of the few Ni-Perchta still on the street. Their homes and shops are shuttered closed and all street lamps are doused. You walk in almost pitch darkness with only a few Coleman lamps left in windows and on street benches to guide your way. Ads for bars and restaurants dot the street, pasted onto Ni-Perchta homes.

Coming around the corner after avoiding a couple of fat, drunk humans munching on carrots, you and the girls make a beeline down the street where the music, the shouting, and the yells are coming from—Moondog Street. Electricity is on in this section of town. The whole street is lit in neon. Women with green and red body paint covering their breasts appear. A couple of homeless human street musicians thump their musical shit through the air. Multiple bars, and what you assume to be strip clubs, dot the street. Ni-Perchta women alongside human women call out to you for lap dances and make obscene gestures. Cigarette smoke and the smell of food blow by with every gust of wind. You even hear firecrackers—or what you naively think to be firecrackers—popping off. Christmas lights are piled on buildings that look like they were built in some medieval Lord of the Rings world.

"I'm so far away from home," you say, bumping into a girl with no top who's using body paint as a bra. In the distance there's the guitar riff of *Money for Nothing.* You spot signs stating *Human Only* and *Both Races Allowed* in many of the shops.

Winniefreddie and Treena look at each other. "Green Man?" Treena says. They stare at each other for a good moment and then nod.

"The hell is this place? Did we just wake up in that part of *Back of the Future Part Two* where Biff controls everything?" you say over the yelling and people shouting things to each other.

Treena shrugs. "Shit, basically. Thunderdome meets the village of Bree."

You see Livesey's Green Man. It's a very large stone tavern standing in a field of high grass that perhaps was a common area or park at one time. Old wooden picnic tables dot the bare ground in front of the tavern. An odd yellow, red, blue, and white flag flies from Livesey's Green Man—you've seen that flag once or twice since coming off-world and you try to make a mental note to discuss it sometime. A wooden statue of a person, well done and very intricate, stands outside the tavern, seven feet tall, painted a dark green. A string of Christmas lights, reds and greens, is strung around the statue. People are all over; the place is busy this hour.

Each man and woman, all pretty young, has one of those orichalcum batons, with maybe a couple or more stones set into it, and each has a crossbow on them as well.

Everyone has a red or yellow plastic tag on his or her chest or arm. They all look tired. Men and women talk in pairs and in groups. Some have metal chainmail armor on, others thick, leather, padded motorcycle jackets and even old riot gear helmets.

You walk up the front stairs and swing open the heavy wooden doors. The Green Man is one part roadhouse, one part casino, and one part place to get stabbed. Stepping inside as a twenty-year-old girl, you feel very alone and very overwhelmed in this dim, partially lit place.

Passing a cardboard sign that says *Check All Weapons! NO EXCEPTIONS!*, you come across an odd scene. There are roulette tables—those big wheels that spin so you can bet whether or not the tag will land on a 1, 5, 10, or 20. Men in bowler hats are dealers in probably rigged card games, and salvagers with stacks of money are laying down bets on craps tables left and right or duking it out over poker. A thick smell of cooking meat, cigar smoke, and sweat permeates the entire open space. A salsa and chip bar is off to one side, looking appetizing if unhygienic.

"Oh snap," you say, seeing something that turns you on like nothing else. The two girls watch you as you drift over to the casino.

"Blackjack!" one of the old women dealers cries out and claps her hands. The other players look pissed, folding up their cards and giving them back to her. They are playing with bundles of red money and casino chips. You take a look at the table between chip bites. One shoe. The dealer is only using one card shoe to deal, so the cards are barely getting mixed up.

You're pretty good at math. When you were small, you used to play a little casino night with your dad and could always count the cards—you were doing that when you were eleven, twelve years old. You move over to the blackjack table. Treena and Winniefreddie shrug and walk over to the bar to pick up a libation or three. They ask if you want something to drink and you reply, "What do you think?"

NIGHTHAWKS AT THE MISSION

You sit down just as another player is leaving. The old woman dealer in a bowler hat gives you the dirtiest look in the world, her wrinkled and over-made-up face seeming to crack with petty hate. "You of age, Missy?" she says.

You stare at her and say nothing. The old woman shrugs. "It's another planet anyway. Who the beep cares, amiright?"

She starts to deal out the cards. From that one shoe, you think, amazed at how this place is being run. You know from television that casinos back home, in Vegas, usually use six shoes to prevent what you are going to do. With six shoes there would be so many card combinations that no one could ever figure it out. In this half-assed Oberon, they didn't think of it at all.

You get your first card: a queen. You start to play; beginning very carefully, scoping out the territory, seeing how they flop down. Next to you sits a guy who looks like an older, more beaten up version of Brad Pitt and a very attractive older woman with heavy mascara who is drinking beer from a copper cup. With two other players, the dealer and you, you'll have no problem figuring the flow of play.

A human waiter comes by and asks if you want a beer. "Of course," you say. "I'm old enough." The dealer gives you a fake smile with nice golden teeth. You start to drink the beer, feeling pretty good now. Treena gives you an extra beer. She blows a raspberry after seeing you already have one. You are about to destroy this casino, you just know it. One shoe! *Holy Christ, what an opening,* you think. You cross yourself in front of everyone before the second deal, muttering a prayer to God, thanking Him and His son and the Holy Spirit, too.

It is about the fourth deal when you start winning big, figuring what is in the shoe and at play. You get dealt a queen and a deuce—this combination is usually shit, but you know that there's a nine coming up, and there it is. From then on in, you blow up Livesey's Green Man.

You play and play and drink and drink, beer after beer, in copper cups and plastic cups, depending on what the Ni-Perchta waiters can throw to you. You see your mountain of chips in clear, double vision, and scoop the mountain into a plastic bucket that somebody handed you earlier. A crowd has gathered, quite amazed at your dexterity and also waiting to see if at any moment you will be hauled off for cheating.

You fall off your stool, still holding the bucket upright, not spilling a drop of beer. You laugh hard, managing to stand up with the cup of fresh beer and the bucket of casino winnings. Seeing that everyone is looking at you, you take a bow. The older woman with mascara is laughing very hard and gives you a thumbs-up. Older Brad Pitt is there, laughing, and you decide to go up and kiss him on the mouth for no particular reason.

"Alright! 'Kay, thanks, bye!" you yell to the casino, the other salvagers cheering you on as you grope your way across the place to the bar counter where the Page sisters are talking with the bartender.

A bouncer comes over, a thick, big-bellied bastard with a bald head. "I'm the bouncer here, and I am asking if you need assistance to your vehicle," he says before you respond.

"Why don't you bounce on over and get me a drink, then?" You wink at him and stumble backwards. He just looks annoyed and leaves.

You manage to face the bartender. "Ch-change 'em out." He shakes both his heads, looks at the four Page sisters, and then takes your chips. He opens a door marked *Private* behind him.

You stand there rocking out to music that may or may not be there.

After five minutes he returns and gives you your winnings. You count the stacks. Five hundred thousand, five hundred Dii-Yaa or, in real money, thirty-five thousand, seven hundred and fifty dollars. Not too bad.

You give a few thousand bucks to the Page sisters, who shake your hand, then stuff the rest into every available pocket.

"We gotta be hanging out with her more, man. We gotta. We just gotta, we gotta, we gotta..." Winniefreddie says.

You and the Page sisters keep drinking until all the words coming out of your mouths become slurred and slow versions of themselves. You three laugh the night away and dance in some club connected to the Green Man with people who look like the Manson family. Human bands play typical club songs.

The three of you stumble out of Livesey's Green Man laughing like the inebriated hyenas you are. Dawn has arrived in the Walled Village. There is still some music playing somewhere.

Exiting Moondog Street, you are back in the true Ni-Perchta part of town, trying to roam back to the Benbow.

Flush with a bit of cash, drunk and happy, you three come onto a disturbing little scene when you exit the walls of the village. Next to a parking lot is a group of humans surrounding a group of Ni-Perchta who are on a makeshift wooden platform. Ni-Perchta guards in armor and in soldiers' uniforms stand by. Even in the little you can see, there is a handmade sign stating: *Dawn Auction of Assigned Persons.* An excited Ni-Perchta rambling in Perchta is pointing at the Ni-Perchta in chains. The auctioneer touches their arms, their legs, pats their behinds as he speaks as fast as any auctioneer back home. Some of those in chains are children. A small, weasel-like human is shouting out the translation at the same time.

"What is dis?" you slur, pointing. You still have a plastic cup filled with beer in your hand.

"Assignment auction shit. The Ni-Perchta, if you get caught—caughted, I should say—doing a non-violent, non-religious crime, they sentence you to be bought as someone's slave for five to fifteen years, unless they release you early. For minor, little transgressions. Failure to respect the Witch-Lord, petty theft under five hundred Dii-Yaa, stuff like that," Treena says, and then burps. "I'm gonna puke."

Winniefreddie pats her on the back. She hiccups and gives her a thumbs-up.

"What? Slavery? You kiddin' me?" you ask. A little Ni-Perchta girl is crying her eyes out as some pedophile-looking human raises up his hand to purchase her service. There's a sick feeling in your stomach. "Whoa, whoa." You step forward and take out all your cash. "How much? How much?" Everyone watches as you rush through. The crowd parts to let you in.

You walk back to the Benbow with the Ni-Perchta girl, who holds hands with a couple of other Ni-Perchta kids; you've bought them as well.

Treena and Winniefreddie stare at you in wonder. "You just spent all that cash on these little Oliver Twist bastards," Winniefreddie says. "Jesus, you got some heart. Brains, no. Heart, oh, yeah."

Treena shakes her head. "No, no, it's a good thing, Winnie."

"I got no idea where you can go," you tell the children, "but you can go." They look at you in wonder, their eyes wide.

The Ni-Perchta girl speaks haltingly in broken English. "My...my dad...he up that way."

You turn and see that a Ni-Perchta male has been following you the whole way from the village. He's tall, regal looking, and afraid.

"Hey! Screw the Witch-Lord! I escaped from his dungeon, and you can all escape, too! Fuck the police!"

Winniefreddie looks at you sideways. "You're that girl?"

You sober up a little, staring as the children run off. "Winniefreddie's right. That was stupid. Drinkin' makes you do silly things. There goes, how much money? I still technically own their contracts, right?" You look down at a piece of parchment that was given to you, and then throw it away. You notice it just sits on top of the soil. You kick up some dirt and halfway bury it, then slap Winniefreddie on the arm and start to dance a bit. "All day, all night, all day, all night. What the fuck..." You and the other girls dance and giggle in the morning air.

"Going to get more money, right girls? Right, girls? I went to Spain and saw people partying..."

Winniefreddie and Treena look at you and say almost at the same time, "You're good people. We'll be in touch."

CHAPTER TEN:
CHRISTMAS

You barely manage to wake up, dress, and go to work the next morning. No one is there but Oscar Botha, who's sitting at your desk with his feet up. He's already unlocked the front doors. "Happy Christmas, Miss Sarah," he says. "No family like me, eh? Spending the holiday alone?"

"Jeez, I feel silly. It's Christmas. No work today."

"For you," Oscar Botha says, chewing and snapping his gum and staring at you angrily. He smiles, showing it to be a joke. "I honestly don't care about working on holidays. I have—had—a family in Mission Hazelden but they went home. I don't mind working on Christmas." He seems to get lost in thought. "Ever spend time in Suid-Afrika?"

"Can't say that I have."

He grins. "No reason a white girl like you should unless you need to. Otherwise, the blacks there, they'd jump all over you like a pack of wild hounds. Give you something permanent to remember them by. The blacks there—they don't have education, family, things like us—you and me. Not even like the Ni-Perchta. Be careful out there if you go."

Your skin crawls a little. "Merry Christmas," you say, cutting him off.

Botha watches you turn to leave and laughs a little to himself. He goes back to playing solitaire on your computer. "Oh, and Orange?" You turn. "You do know you have tomorrow off as well? And the rest of the week? This isn't the States, Sarah. We get nine days off for Christmas—Christmas Eve until January second."

You go back to your downstairs apartment home, avoiding everyone again and sealing yourself into your lair. The radio drones on and on. You down a couple more beers from the refrigerator and notice that there are now Tokyo Sex Whale ones in there; you don't remember buying them.

You take out your laptop and try to boot it up, but you just see a scrambled screen that's completely screwed up. You sigh and decide to sit on the kitchen floor. "No more Facebook. What a shame." You take the laptop and smash it against the tile floor of the kitchen; you pick it up again and smash it as hard as you can against that cold surface, angry, pissed, and enraged. You are on your own here, literally millions of miles away from home. With no one.

"No more Facebook." You start crying a little bit. "Oh money, money, money, come my way and take me away..." you mock pray.

You wake up from a three-hour nap and head back upstairs to the Benbow. As you pass through the lobby, you finally see people. Young people with families are getting together, hugging each other, driving off in old cars to God knows where. Oscar Botha is receiving Christmas gifts from residents who seem to either like him or are afraid of him. They nod a hello to you. The Benbow is closed, although the little door clock says that they should be back by now.

Treena is the first one to arrive, giving you a weird look as you're hovering around the door. You go through the Gate right after her. You help her by cleaning up, and then spend the rest of the day playing Clue, Simpsons Edition, once Winniefreddie comes back.

The Ni-Perchta cook, Tek, hovers in and out of the bar/restaurant area like a specter of ill will, with glowering looks and half-lidded eyes for anyone who dares to look him in the face.

Winniefreddie wins Clue for the second time in a row, and she lets you know it by tossing the board up in the air; the pieces are thrown everywhere. "No more need to play, eh ladies? When I keep winning!" she says, leaving the room dramatically and then returning with a flourish.

The rain has stopped and, while you're still a bit hung over, you decide to ask them the question you've had on your mind all day.

"Okay, guys, here's what I got planned for us. We are going to get—what was it Tyler, I mean Jaime, was mentioning? A license to go dayhawking, right? Let's get that going, set up our little business together, like we said last night. We can save up some cash or I can win..."

"Co-op," Treena says.

"Co-op? Business? What's the difference?" you ask.

Winniefreddie rolls her eyes. "A co-op is a co-operative—that's the only sort of business that's allowed here. No business in the sense of profits to be generated for just one person. Everyone has to get a share."

"Okay, okay, co-op. We sign up all together and we go and do this."

Winniefreddie and Treena look at each other and shake their heads. "Not so fast, Sarah. I mean, you seem like a great person but we just met. The Four Lands are a bit...what's the word I'm looking for? Or phrase, Winniefreddie?"

Winniefreddie coughs into her hand. "Screwed up. We have to think about this. I mean, you got a good advantage with that crazy vision where you can see certain things, but we have to weigh everything. We've had a good little co-op ourselves for a while selling off-world beer and running this place. And we have to ask our currently silent partner."

"It's goddamn Guy Farson, right? I remember him saying Tokyo Sex Whale on the ship, so stop screwing with me. You guys nighthawk, right? Isn't that right?"

Winniefreddie and Treena look around to see if anyone heard you talking so loud, but no one is there but Tek. Winniefreddie speaks. "No, it's not Guy Farson. Okay? Not Guy Farson." They nod though, indicating yes on both counts.

"It is Guy Farson," Treena whispers. "But keep it down. We'll talk more in a bit."

You spend some time sitting by the window of the Benbow, sipping on instant coffee as the day turns from dark and stormy to sunny and clear. "Screw off-world," you say to no one in particular. You think over the events of the last few days, sickened by the death at the Witch-Lord's Temple and the loneliness of this place. Working at an office millions of miles from home? Screw that. Drink and be lonely? Screw that. You think only of leaving this place now and forgetting this experience.

You go back through the Nemo Gate and see Oscar Botha sitting at the front desk, playing on the computer. Guy Farson is in the front part of the lobby, a backpack in hand and an unlit cigar hanging out of his mouth.

Oscar looks up for a moment and then looks back down at the computer. "You know I have half a mind to just punt you back out there with the rest of the garbage, Guy Farson. You have no legal right to be here."

Guy walks over and puts his hand on the counter. "Then do it, Apartheid. Otherwise stop giving me lip every time I make a stop-over to a legal settlement." He smiles at you and nods towards the elevators. You follow him over and ride the elevator down to your apartment. That Charlie Brown Christmas song plays on your old radio as you and Guy say nothing to each other.

"Good to see you," you finally blurt out.

He nods at your surroundings. "Neat digs here. Very fashionable. Very, very fashionable."

You nod.

"You thinking about leaving The Oberon?" He stares right at you.

You swallow. "What gave you that impression?"

Guy smirks a little and lights his cigar. "I would. If I saw someone get their head chopped off in front of me and wasn't ready for it. I mean, I've seen some screwed up things: people mind-scorched out in the cities, Ni-Perchta lynching, a Ni-Perchta guy with no legs fighting a Ni-Perchta guy with no arms for money. But I'm sort of used to that." He blows out some smoke. "You might lose your security deposit with all this cigar smoke. Apologies."

"How did you..."

Guy smiles and asks you where he can dump his ash. You grab a bowl out of one of the kitchen cabinets and set it down on the glass table in front of him with a clang.

"Have a contact or three in the statue city. You escaped also with a Jaime Van Zandt —your disappeared hubby—from a Witch-Lord Temple. That's a neat trick. One that hasn't been done in, oh, forever. Indiana Jones must've date-raped your mother twenty years ago.

"You've also got the Voice of the Four Winds—that's a good book to have. A really good book. The Ephors spotted it on you back in Solomon's Bay. It can be a big help out there in the wastes with those map pages. A really big help. And from what I gathered from Treena and Winniefreddie, you might be a tetrachromat, which is quite the mouthful but very helpful. So with those two bits of information, I realized you're good for our team."

Guy puffs out more smoke, filling the room with that aromatic tobacco smell. It is strong but not stinky—probably expensive.

You think about asking him more about tetrachromacy and the book but you don't care anymore. You really don't. You just want to get away from all this insanity.

Guy mentions an oil painting at the Benbow Inn. You nod that you saw it while you were there. It's a beautifully done painting of a city that looks at once more ancient than anything on Earth while at the same time much,

much more high tech. A post-apocalyptic, ultra futuristic city, all by itself. "That's a painting of Sargasso-3, one of the last really untouched Antediluvian cities. Treena painted it, did you know that?"

You shake your head.

"I have talked to a contact—he's a dee jay for a pirate station you might've heard of—the Old Man at Midnight. He also scouts out locations and paths to get through the old cities. He buys and sells things. A good man. Now, he did not find this himself but..."

You listen as Guy talks on. You even hear the monorail whistle twice somewhere not too far off, echoing through the mountains. So you think.

He finishes by saying, "That is where your book and you all come in for your time. There is a chance to earn thousands of dollars' worth of good salvage out there. That city is full of valuable things. You even told the girls you want to dayhawk. Which is not going to happen. I ain't paying a corporation twenty thousand bucks for something they really don't own. I did one year and it was literally the gayest experience I had since me and my friend Henry slept in the same bed back in ninth grade. But nighthawking, now we're talking.

"Look, I'm not going to waste your time, give you a little pep talk. That's not my style. I'm not going to waste your time with anything metaphysical or make-believe hopeful. You can go home, you can go back on the mono, back onto the Queen or maybe the Duke of Lancaster, and you can forget this whole thing—but you will go back with a definite loss and not with a potential profit. But you work with me, you may make enough money in one night to start building a new life. You can wipe away whatever happened here and back there with money. Money isn't everything, but it is a real tool to get somewhere. That is reality, not fantasy."

A couple of tears trail down your face and you speak up. "That's why I wanted to come out here." You think of your sister for a moment, the sister you knew, the sister in your dreams as well.

Guy doesn't say anything for a minute. His face is totally expressionless. His words, put on or not, have an effect on you. The thought of returning back home to your mother and admitting that you are weak and helpless and nothing like your sister makes you want to vomit.

"So, so how do we do this?" you ask.

"Well, let's do a little milk run..." Guy leans back and smiles.

You put on a blue Network windbreaker over your NASA flight suit and wait on the couch until it's nice and dark outside. You snooze for a little bit, both fascinated and scared about this opportunity that you're jumping into.

You take the elevator up to the lobby floor. Stepping out, you see the dozing form of Robert Fuller snoozing away at your desk. Your footfalls clack loudly in the emptiness of the lobby. Walking past him quickly, you go to the front doors. They open from your side, allowing you to go out. The doors lock behind you.

Past the heavy ornamental wooden doors separating the lobby from the outside world, you cross the driveway of Mission Friendship and stand in the grass field surrounding the entire colony. You blow out a breath. It's a little cold outside, so you see your breath fade away like a puff of smoke. Your instructions were to keep walking, and you do just that.

A motor whirs in the distance—far off at first. The seven moons light up the entire area around so you figure nothing can just sneak up on you out of nowhere. The motor sound is getting louder but you haven't seen a car or headlights flash anywhere. The sound is now almost right behind you. You turn, and coming over the top of the Mission is one of those airships you saw back at Solomon's Bay. This particular airship is maybe eighty feet long, and if it wasn't for the fact that there are ropes tying this ship to a blimp-like balloon that hovers above it, it would look just as at home on the ocean waves of the seventeenth century as it does floating in the air over the Mission. Two propeller engines are stapled to the back of the ship's body, pushing the machine along. The main body of the airship looks to be a relic from the great age of sail, except for its wheelhouse, which looks suspiciously like the front half of a flat-nosed bus from back on Earth that has been chopped and slapped onto the back part of the wooden superstructure. It's descending, the Coleman lanterns tied to its sides pouring direct light onto your face. A couple of cars—two old 1965 Ford Mustangs in rust and primer paint—hang from steel hooks suspended from large girders that project out the side of the airship. Their headlights have been kept on, providing more night-time illumination for the ship.

At first the tires settle onto the dirt, and then the entire ship itself sinks onto the grass. The words *S.B. Crue* are painted onto the side along with a logo that seems to be a drawing of a seal's skull.

You swallow a bit before you see a familiar face on the deck. It's Tek, the Ni-Perchta you know from the Benbow. You walk over to the airship, amazed. A slightly greenish glow emanates from the wood. It's very faint, but it's there. Tek picks you up telekinetically with his ori-baton and brings you on-board so quickly you barely register that you were just flung through the air. Immediately the ship ascends. In the distance you hear the sound of a European-style police siren.

Tek has retreated to the wheelhouse and sits behind the wheel, steering the ship to its unknown destination. All lights are off now except for one Coleman lantern hooked to the rope you grab near the ship's railing. You look over the railing and see the ground retreat away from you. A Mission Security car comes onto the scene a few minutes later.

CHAPTER ELEVEN:
THE TEMPLE OF KERN

Tek says nothing on the way over, not a single thing. Besides the breeze and the whir of the motor, there is no sound but the odd cry of an off-world bird passing near the airship. He seems to be following, from a few thousand feet up, a long black highway covered in reflective yellow Xs that span from shoulder to shoulder.

You see the city for the first time far in the distance, its lights blinking through the haze and the increasing darkness from the storm clouds overhead. It is obviously a futuristic city of some sort; a futuristic city in absolute ruin.

There is a burning between your shoulder blades; you are sure it is a warning that you are in someone's gun sights. Despite the feeling, you keep looking straight ahead and being afraid for your life while trying not to show it. Trusting a stranger is not your nature but something strings you along. A certain unknowable something.

Twenty-five minutes have passed since Tek picked you up on the front lawn of the Mission. The airship seems to be slowing down. You can see more now: decayed towers that hit the top of the clouds, a heap of broken buildings. A large sign covered with green reflector paint, like something you'd see over any freeway in America, states in English and Ni-Perchta hieroglyphics *SUPER SARGASSO-3 (Antediluvian Abandoned City)*. Another sign says: *Warning, Unlicensed Salvers Will Be Prosecuted by Ephors and*

Mission Security. Watch for Flash Storms AT ALL TIMES. The blue and white Venn diagram of the Network is stamped on one side of the sign.

You feel a chill as Tek lowers the ship back down to the ground, turning on the lights in all the lanterns and the two hanging Ford Mustangs.

"You go meet," he says as he steps out of the wheelhouse. "Goen Meet. Goen Meet."

You nod, just about understanding what he said, and step down the side via a metal ladder from the airship's deck, wondering why you couldn't have just used this before and not have been thrown on-board by Tek. As you step off the last rung and wipe your hands on your flight suit, you look back at Tek, who has immediately gone back inside the wheelhouse and taken off again, his ship drifting into the night. He yells something unintelligible to you as he motors the airship away.

"Oh, oh, oh..." you say, and think *what the hell*. You look to the disappearing airship and then back to the city. There is mostly stone and concrete rubble all around, but there are some actual buildings—little squat houses and pill box-shaped structures. Asphalt streets lead straight into this post-apocalypse. Octopus-like creatures, each covered by one blanket-like wing, stare at you through open places in the buildings, looking evil with dead black and white eyes but doing nothing except watching you pass. Bent street lights emit a ghoulish glow from their ancient bulbs. How they're still on years after the fall of the Antediluvian civilization is a mystery to you.

Guy Farson emerges from the shadows. Dressed in a gray and black jumpsuit with elbow and knee pads, a used riot gear helmet with visor, thick black rubber gloves and combat boots, he looks to you like a low-rent Ghostbuster. He raises his helmet's visor. "Sorry for the cloak and dagger shit but we had to make sure that a couple of Spitfires didn't come up behind you guys and put a few into the blimp. How'd you like that? A bit different from the usual back on Earth, right? Beats the hell out of driving on the four oh five, am I right?"

"It's so magical," Treena says in an odd, dead pan voice. "Mag-i-cal." She comes out of one shadow.

"Uh huh," you say. "I get a cool helmet, too?"

Winniefreddie, who is carrying a bunch of things in a rucksack, pulls out a crappy, banged up helmet and tosses it to you. She's emerged from the shadows as well and, like Treena, is dressed the same way as Guy. The two of them have yellow boxes strapped to their chests, the size of small microwaves, each with rubber handles and a large dial on top. A viewfinder sticks out of the top of each box.

"Smells like ass, so I suggest a shower afterwards," Winniefreddie says, gesturing to the helmet.

"Welcome to the night side of life, Sarah," Guy says. "We got a little and beautiful milk run of a mission to go onto—a search and retrieval at the locked up Temple of Kern in the southwest. You got your little book there, do you? Good. This is a good warm up for what we all should be doing together in the future."

Watching his surroundings carefully, Guy hands you a cheap Casio watch that you put on without hesitation. Treena hands you what she refers to as a folded up Sub-two thousand nine millimeter semi-automatic rifle. She's carrying one as well. Winniefreddie has a pump action sawed-off on her, and Guy has what looks like a bolt-action rifle sawed-off and made into a pistol. As you look on in confusion, Treena unfolds the carbine for you and shows you how to take the safety off. You instinctively know how to do this but your nerves make it harder than it should be.

This frightens you a bit but you bite your lip and just listen carefully. It's the first time you've ever held a gun in your life where a situation might arise causing you to have to use it for something other than target practice.

After strapping the gun across your shoulder, you take the book out of one of the zippered pockets in your flight suit. Treena and Winniefreddie start talking about the weather and flash storms in hushed tones. Each looks fearfully to the sky.

You can see that a set of pages has become illuminated in a pale green light; you flip to them. They're the map pages. There is a tiny, red flashing dot on a drawing of the city streets. Everything is labeled in Ni-Perchta hieroglyphics. The symbols seem to float off the page, and when your hand touches the characters, they change to English. The city you are in is next to a giant sea called the Super Sargasso Sea, and the city is next to something called the Sargasso region. As you walk forward a little, you see that the red dot moves just a tiny bit. You walk with the book in hand, and the red dot moves along with you.

Messing with the page, you find that you can zoom in and out of the map. The red dot is far away from three boxes flashing blue. One box is a city block listed in hieroglyphics only; another of the small blue boxes has no name next to it. The last one has the words *Temple of Kern* written on it in English.

"There's a Temple of Kern listed to the north," you mention to Guy, who nods and then whistles for Treena and Winniefreddie to stop gabbing and shut up. Without them talking, you hear nothing but a breeze and the sound of something falling off a building—like a piece of masonry that's chipped off and fallen down onto the street below.

"Just like that? Just like that I can…" Guy is looking at the book with no recognition.

"You can't see anything? Really?"

Guy shrugs. "Just that neat green light. So it actually says Temple of Kern?"

You bite your lip. "Yeah. In English. Quite the book I have."

"Quite the book," Guy agrees. "Alright ramblers, let's get rambling. Where to?"

You look at the book and point straight ahead. "Forward a city block, then right."

Guy jogs up ahead on point, and takes out his ori-baton. You pull yours clumsily, snapping it out.

"Stay behind me at least a hundred feet. Never bunch up, Sarah. You'll give potential toe-cutters easier targets and get us all killed and look like an asshole afterwards."

Feeling burdened and sweaty with your new gear on, and realizing that Winniefreddie was right about the helmet smelling bad, you walk after him, hand on your small rifle.

You finally arrive, after what must've been a mile, to sit down on an old crumbling stone bench inside some empty temple lobby. Dark statues with knocked-off heads tower above you from every angle, it seems, and a fountain still leaking water stands behind where you sit. A projection of a woman dressed in a thin, almost transparent black cloak, dancing under the seven moons, plays on the ceiling above you; a constant but quiet loop.

Everyone looks around anxiously.

"Sarah," Guy says. "If you see anything at all, the littlest shimmer or distortion, you'll tell us first thing, okay?"

You nod.

"Thank the good Lord you're here. I didn't feel like lugging this thing around in dark corridors and peeking into it every five seconds." Treena sets the yellow microwave box down with a clunk. So does Winniefreddie.

"What is that?"

"Schufelt ray. But you are going to be telling us all about the hologram traps, right?" Winniefreddie says. "Riiight?"

Guy shakes his head. "Pick those up. I still want you to peek into them now and again."

"What...what are you..." you ask desperately. "You guys are really throwing me for a loop. What traps?"

Guy pulls out what looks like a serrated floppy disk and presses a tiny tab that sticks out from the top end of the disk.

You sit inside that temple for another moment, waiting for the next step, but none of your friends are speaking. They're just watching the entire area. You start to walk away when the temple comes alive. Five ten-foot tall holograms of women in black cloaks tower above you. They chant something harshly as you stand there. Guy turns to you with a smile on his face.

"The defense key seems to work," he says. "The Old Man at Midnight knows his shit." He looks at the chanting holograms with amusement. "Antediluvians, God bless 'em. Now, these aren't the traps we're talking about, Sarah. We can all see these. "

"That hologram on the right looks like a young Demi Moore," Treena says, popping her bubblegum. "You ever seen *Blame it on Rio?* That's a disturbing ass movie with her in it. It's all about Michael Caine banging his friend's teenage daughter who tries to kill herself. It's all sorts of strange. But it's supposed to be a comedy," she continues, looking you up and down. "Are you trembling?"

"Oh," you say. The five tall holograms scream something and then disappear into whatever projector spat them forth. For just a passing moment there is a terrible image—a bearded head, fire flashing from its eyes, a half-man, half-snake creature with viper coils for the lower half of its armored body. The temple becomes empty again and the only sound is the wind passing through the crumbling stone and broken facade. You scream as the others look on in mute fascination at your behavior.

"Just the Storm King," Winniefreddie says, breathing heavily. "Jeez-us."

"You hear that?" Guy whispers.

You strain to listen, unsure what he is talking about until you hear the constant scratching sound, like a hundred hands scraping themselves against stone. Your stomach tightens. "What is that?"

Moments pass. Guy farts loudly. "Do you smell what The Rock is cooking?"

Treena smiles and stomps the stone floor. The scratching noise stops for a moment, then continues. "Antediluvians—the original people of this city. In a shelter underneath the floor. There'll be hundreds of those once-human vampire mummies below us. All those thousands-of-years-old creatures straining to get out, having spent centuries feeding on each other and going mad long ago after they ran out of fresh blood."

"We'd better get in and out quick in case the shelter seal breaks here. I'd say fifteen minutes," Guy says. He points to what looks like a set of carved stone doors that have opened in the back wall of the temple. He loads his sawed-off bolt-action gun with a few rounds and then lights a cigarette.

"Now, Sarah, we are the first to go into the temple, for, well, let's say a long time. What we need from you as our tetrachromat is to watch for a few, uh, anomalies."

"Anomalies?" You furrow your brow and lick your lips, unable to imagine just what he's talking about. "What anomalies?

"Examples, uh, any blinking lights, especially purple dots. If we step on one, it'll send out a bolt of lightning that can kill all of us. If you see a red circle that expands and contracts, that's a disintegrator, which means exactly what you think it means. It'll make you disappear if you step into it. If you see shimmering—like that sort of air shimmer you see on metal on hot afternoons—just scream "Shimmer!" and we'll all stand still. If anyone moves, we are dead, since it'll rush and burn us alive. It should go away after thirty seconds. There's also laughing ones—shadows that move in front of you and make a high-pitched laughing sound. You'll see 'em before us—they look like red outlines of people on the walls."

You breathe heavily, so nervous and scared now because of Guy's words. "Guy, I don't know about this."

He puts a hand on your shoulder and squeezes. "The girls still have the equipment. And we already turned off the security. This should be a piece of cake and what I said is just a precaution. Take a breath. Breathe deep."

You do that, smelling the must and decay of the place really deeply for the first time. "Okay. Okay, then."

Treena sneaks up to you and hands you a pill. "Have this. It's a treat," she says.

"What is it?" You swallow it with a gulp of water from Winniefreddie's canteen. "Some ancient super pill? Something to keep me nice and alert?"

Winniefreddie shakes her head. "Adderall. The law student's little helper. Enjoy!"

Guy takes out a small cylinder that has a wire connected to a thin box. It chirps a bit. He clips the assembly onto his jumpsuit and leaves the box on. "Geiger counter," he says. "If it starts banging away—run out."

"Radiation is spooky," Treena says.

You walk into the temple's interior with Guy moving slowly at the front. You still have the nervous shakes; that damn Adderall is not helping in the slightest. All it's done is to make you extremely wide awake and alert, and as you walk forward, you scan the entire area over and over, trying to keep everything in perspective and not miss a thing.

The walls are stone and have this sort of emergency light system that gives everything an eerie blue and orange hue, though much of the corridor is still covered in shadow. There is an unbelievably strong smell, a combination of cinnamon and rotting fruit. The walls display off-putting carvings and strange mosaics. Guy's Geiger counter beeps a little stronger but no one seems alarmed.

Your heartbeat and the footfalls of your companions echo through the temple's tall, wide corridor. Guy asks you to take a look at your book's map section. You look at it again. "Look for the correct passage to the donation room."

The map reveals that there is indeed something called a donation room, down the massive hall and upstairs to the left. You explain the directions and all follow.

"Good, otherwise we'd be wandering and wandering," Guy says. "These buildings can be such a maze."

You stare at the frescoes decorating the inside of the temple, amazed at their beauty and detail and the outlandish events each one depicts. In one the Storm King has the world under his feet, crushing cities of unbelievers in little mushroom clouds. Another is the view at street level of human being after human being with bright green eyes drinking the blood of babies and of regular human beings. Another image shows Ni-Perchta entertaining humans by slaughtering each other in crazed gladiator events.

One scene really catches your attention though: a depiction of a human woman fighting another human woman who looks exactly the same—same face, same features. An old man with three faces watches the fight in front of a castle, with a black beast or dog.

You and the others walk up a flight of marble stairs. Moonlight streams in from broken glass windows lining the corridor.

Red eyes flash in the darkness ahead and then disappear. A ghostly reddish form darts from one part of the hall to the other. You stumble for a second, pausing as Treena and Winniefreddie scan the area with their Schufelt rays.

"I just saw red eyes. Red eyes right there." Your friends unload their guns into the distance and drill bullet holes into the walls. You fire your carbine, too; there is a ricochet sound and then you feel something fly by your ear. You hear a snuffle of something and then a dragging noise.

"Shit," Treena says, reloading her gun. "Shit, shit. Snuffy."

"Oh lawds!" Winniefreddie says with a nervous giggle.

You look dumbfounded and lift up your visor. "The hell is Snuffy?"

Guy snaps out his telescoping ori-baton again and starts to envelop the whole area in front of him in a blast of flame, burning away some of the frescoes and destroying thousands-of-years-old art and furniture. The flames die out after a moment as if turned off by some unseen switch. A small spark still emits from the end of his baton.

"Mr. Snuffleupagus," Guy whispers.

"The hell did you just say?"

"You ever see Big Bird? Sesame Street? For years they said his imaginary friend wasn't really there, but then they found his nest or something. Same idea here—people thought it was just the imagination of a few hawks, but..."

You hear a long moan somewhere in the dark maze and your blood freezes. "Here we are, with a vicious creature with a stupid nickname." You hear a couple of odd mewling calls, like a cat that's been struck by a car. "Christ."

Guy flips your visor down before you can. A slight scattering of ash descends from the ceiling; more comes down with each snort and snuffle from the darkness. You almost scream when you see that your shadow on the wall is moving away without you.

"They tend to do that sometimes," Treena mentions casually, as if was the most common thing in the world.

"Spooky, huh?" Winniefreddie waddles ahead of you before she pulls you closer to Guy. Your shadow suddenly drops back to be with you, after pausing for a moment.

At the end of the corridor, Guy finds a box—a green, glowing box with handles, ancient and high tech-looking all at once. A million wires cover it, snaking around and going inside. A couple of human skeletons are near it; one bony hand still clutches one of the handles. Guy snaps the hand off.

"Stasis box. Must've been trying to bring it to the shelter inside." He checks the box and cracks his knuckles. "No lock."

The girls cover him as he pops open the lid ever so slightly, a green glow emanating from the crack. He smiles, lifting up a baton that had been left inside. It was definitely of the ancient style—silver, with a blue-green orichalcum stone in the shape of the Taurus zodiac sign embedded into the hilt.

"Animal control ori. Some other stuff. Sarah, we just found ourselves a nice little stasis box. Can hold anything in perfect condition forever and ever. Worth, jeez, a lot. Okay. Oh-kay. This is more than good enough. Forget the donation room—there could be more Snuffies here."

He picks up one end of the box and motions for you to pick up the other end. You grab it and then immediately drop it. Six of those vampire mummies that Jaime mentioned during your train trip charge you, coming out of nowhere and rushing the group with outstretched hands that have turned into claws from years of neglected fingernails. You scream and grab at your gun.

Winniefreddie opens up on two of them, shooting and setting them aflame with what you find out later to be dragon's breath rounds. The blasts from her shotgun are huge and long, almost like fireworks shooting out the end of the gun. Two of the mummies are blasted back and the rags of their ancient clothes set on fire, their glowing green eyes turning black. Treena and Guy cut down the rest in a barrage of deafening gunfire that makes your ears ring.

"Someone must've popped a shelter somewhere around here. Another co-op," Guy mutters in the lull of noise whilst he reloads.

You hear other moans from deep inside the temple and this odd scurrying sound. The Geiger beeps harshly for a moment, making your friends look around anxiously. Then it stops.

You and Guy run with the box, Treena and Winniefreddie behind you.

You look back and see that Winniefreddie appears to have changed shape—no longer a chubby girl, she's turned into quite a fit, attractive one in a slightly oversized jumpsuit.

You and your three friends get the hell out of the temple as fast as you can, passing the stone doors and the lobby where the holograms turn back on.

Guy clicks the safety key and the stone doors close behind you with a rumble. You hear one last snuffling sound before they shut, as if the creature was right behind you the entire time. Hieroglyphics flash along the back wall.

He thumbs the little tab on the serrated floppy disk again and the hieroglyphics disappear. "Damn security came on for full lock down. That would've been great."

The four of you stand there, breathing deeply. Winniefreddie is her old self again, making you think for a moment that you might have just hallucinated that last part about her morphing.

"Oh God," you say, doubling over. "Oh, God." Your three new friends look at you like that was one big nothing.

"Damn Snuffy got us good with his ashes," Guy says, looking over everyone's jumpsuits. "We gotta go back and zap 'em or else…"

"Oh, Jesus, don't mention that. That's crazy old man talk, that ain't reality. Don't tell me you've been raiding Treena's Adderall supply, Guy. Come on now," Winniefreddie says, growing upset. Guy says something you don't catch.

"Well, let him come and chase us. I don't care! I'd rather have that…"

"What?" you ask, taking off your helmet. "What?"

"Old wives' tale. Forget it," Guy says, meeting Winniefreddie's eyes.

You walk away from the temple into the cool night air and sit down under one of the street lights, jittery and frightened. You're sweating like a pig and your face is smeared with ash.

Winniefreddie speaks up. "Her time of the month or what?" Treena snorts a little in laughter.

Guy shakes his head and walks over. "Come on, this isn't normal, guys. Running into a ten thousand-year-old temple and fighting mummies and invisible monsters isn't the most normal activity. It shakes people up a bit."

Treena and Winniefreddie nod together in mock sadness.

Guy sits down next to you under the street light and offers you water from his canteen.

You feel a thumping in the ground.

"Oh God, are we on top of a Gug nest?" Winniefreddie says, looking down the empty and wrecked street.

Guy shakes his head and stands up slowly. "It shouldn't be. We're not next to open ground. Those things are huge but they can't, you know…"

Dark, man-like shapes, five of them, emerge from wherever they were hiding, wearing ski masks and black jackets. They attack you and your friends just as the thumping increases.

Guy fires at them with his rifle, hitting one of the shapes. One of the other attackers fires a steel arrow that punches through Guy's skull, killing him instantly.

Treena fires two shots, boom, boom. The gun sounds like a knife punching through cardboard. Red lightning shoots out from one of the figures and strikes her with such power that she flies backwards twenty feet, her jumpsuit singed and burning in places. Her eyes stare up towards the sky, unmoving. One leg has landed in a twisted jumble.

The ski-masked man-shapes march quickly towards you in a tight formation. Winniefreddie has taken off somewhere in the ruins, turning and shooting her gun once behind her without aiming.

As you run away, you are hit with a blast of lightning. You fall down behind the rubble of what remains of an old building. Barely able to crawl to a safe hiding place, half of your body numb, you try to scream but only a slight squeak of air gets past your lips. Moments pass. Your breathing calms and you have a death grip on your rifle. The ground continues to thump; you hear rumbling and shaking, too. Twenty freight trains couldn't make that same effect. Something is coming from below you.

You slowly regain feeling in your body, though everything hurts and tingles at the same time. You hear cries in Perchta and then someone shouting orders in an English accent. Someone out there is controlling your attackers. Someone else shouts "Mathias," and you wonder if that's the Englishman's name.

You peek your head out around the corner, leaning against a broken pillar for support.

It then emerges from the ground, all twenty feet of it. The thing breaks through the surface of the street in a cloud of dust and a spray of asphalt and concrete. It looks as sleek and black as a jaguar, with two red eyes as large as tires. The monster stands upright, like a person would. This thing—this twenty foot tall thing—has four claws. The thing has an overly large muscular arm on each side—as long as a street lamp—that ends in two shorter forearms. The sharp, wicked-looking claws drip with a sort of resin.

The head has a mouth slit not horizontally, like you or me, but vertically—straight up and down its face. Sharp, white teeth fill that maw. You don't bother to stick around, running as fast as you can, and trip and fall over some rubble, banging your knees hard against the ground. The sound of horns come from somewhere—a blast of strange sounds.

The thing is two hundred yards away, one hundred yards now, its massive legs working like black pistons knocking into the ground again and again. It gets so close you can smell it. Saliva dribbles out of its vertical mouth. Its right two forearms reach towards you, about to strike you like twin vipers, when there is a blast of hot air right above your head. A Ni-Perchta in cloak and steel armor dives into the path of the creature. Flames shoot out of this Ni-Perchta's hands, pouring out as if he has invisible twin flamethrowers. The creature yelps in pain, staggers backwards and falls onto its backside with a thump, its face aflame. It grabs the side of a building but inadvertently rips through it, falling with a crumble of stone onto one of its arms.

It gets up, only to have another Ni-Perchta fling a spear into its side. The creature grabs at the spear now lodged into its mammoth-sized rib cage with its two left forearms. The spear explodes, knocking the thing to its right. A huge red hole is left in the wake of the explosion, and the forearms on that side are reduced to mangled stumps. Another Ni-Perchta fires an AK-47, pouring shot after shot into the beast. Several rounds hit the side of its face and puncture one eye. A few empty, smoking brass casings fall near your head.

The flame-shooting Ni-Perchta puts out a hand in a stop motion and then clenches a white-gray fist. A bolt of lightning from the sky hits the creature in the back of the neck, driving it to its knees with an agonized wail. It falls down then, dead.

You breathe a sigh of relief. Then its corpse does something that is just insane in its grotesqueness. Its head detaches itself from its neck, cleanly separating from the massive dead body. Falling backwards, you land on your ass as the thing lurches towards you.

More gunfire erupts as the Ni-Perchta shoot the creature's head dead in a hail of automatic fire, finally killing it—you hope. The head lands next to you, and two inches from your face is one of its red tire-sized eyes, punctured and oozing, staring right into you. Blood trickles out of a hundred holes all over its face.

You stand up, shaking terribly. The Ni-Perchta who have saved you, the hunters or whatever they are, stand by and speak amongst themselves. You thank them in a mutter, dazed and shaken by what has happened, then walk away, breathing heavily. The mysterious figures that attacked you are gone. You slowly approach the bodies of Farson and Treena, calling out Winniefreddie's name. But before you reach them, your saviors scoop the bodies into sacks and carry them quickly away from the scene before you can say anything.

You watch in a state of mute shock, unable to think or speak at that moment.

You look at the box that the four of you retrieved from the temple. Not knowing what else to do, you decide to open it and see what was worth all this trouble. As you do, it bathes you in that eerie green glow. Inside are a few odd things—a couple of large, black metallic rings with blue and white orichalcum embedded into them, a good five pounds' worth of white orichalcum stones, cut into squares and refined, and a couple of bracers with ori that are shaded blue-orange attached. There are also triangular-shaped wine bottles and other goodies, candies you guess, and even cheeses wrapped in onion paper. A single pure silver baton with a blue and green glowing grip sits inside as well.

It starts to rain a little and you walk back inside the temple, dragging the box with you. The air becomes fragrant with that damp street smell.

You sit down on the box, hearing a commotion amongst the hunting party that came to your rescue. You thought they had left and wonder why they have come back.

There are strange tones, something not of this world, sounds that only the dead can hear, you crazily think. All around you there is a red circle that expands and contracts. It's being generated from a projector on the temple wall.

"Oh no," you whisper before you find yourself falling.

You fall from a great height, tumbling end over end over end towards a churning gray ocean. You crash into it hard enough to knock your breath away, then plunge ten feet under the waves. Struggling to the surface, you tread water for your life. The water is freezing. You accidentally unstrap your gun.

There are seven moons above you in the evening sky. The wind blows behind you, pushing you towards a distant shore, a beach enclosed by high rock cliffs.

Something large and traveling at an incredible speed whooshes over your head and crashes with a metallic crunch onto that beach.

The rusted-out hulks of boats and ships dot the sea all around you. It is full of this crazed wreckage—a liquid cemetery for things that once plowed through the oceans. There is no sign of life. Most of the decks are partially flooded or have capsized with only the barnacle-encrusted bottoms of their hulls above the waves. Life preservers, plastic bottles, Styrofoam McDonald's containers, and pieces of flotsam bob up and down next to you. There is a smell of salt and a chemical, bleach-like stink coming from the water.

CHAPTER TWELVE:
THE BURIAL OF THE DEAD

You swim for your life as hard as you can, letting the waves push you forward, trying to make it towards the distant shore. It is maybe a mile away. There are things in the water—it is clear enough to give you a sense of shape, of something alive and large. Really large.

There's a moan, and a giant gray and white splotched neck comes out of the ocean. A head the size of a Honda Civic is at the top of this neck. It has a mouth full of dagger-sized teeth and a tongue that ends in a thousand tentacles. Spidery eyes track your desperate movements. The head makes a chattering sound that is ugly and high-pitched, and then it returns to the sea.

After what seems to be half a lifetime, you end up on the green-colored pebble beach. You lay back, unable to think, too exhausted from the swim. The body of a young woman, face down, lies very close to where you are. She has long brunette hair, just like you. You blink once, twice, and fall into unconsciousness.

When you wake up, it is night, and the seven moons are out in full as well as every star in the universe. Someone has taken the body you were lying next to. Whatever has happened, the body is missing. Or maybe there was nothing there in the first place. You shake your head, not understanding, not knowing if it was even real.

Far off, you hear the sound of drums beating away and the playing of horns. Thunder rolls somewhere in the distance, over that sea full of debris. You are not alone under this alien sky.

A splash of seawater over your hair awakens you once more to the cool night. You lean forward. Your clothes are wet again.

You begin walking, more like staggering, forward. You turn back to where the sea is. That, at least, is real. You watch all the dead hulks floating out there under the light from each of the seven different moons. "Oh god," you moan, not knowing what to make of your surroundings. The high black rock cliffs, the sea of wreckage... It is a nightmare made real.

There is enough light that you can see where you are going very easily and avoid the accumulated debris from that rotten sea.

You yell out, "Hello! Hello! Anyone? Please, anyone?" There is no reply except for the constant crash of waves. It makes you question yourself. Are you alive? Dead? Or just dreaming? You sit down on your haunches for at least five minutes, trying to think up your next move.

The box from the temple has made it to the beach—you realize quite belatedly that the box was what you felt shoot over your head as you fell into the sea.

Looking down the beach, you see for the first time these black silhouettes—tall and dark, three of them, maybe a mile from where you are. They look human but their large size means they can't be. As you stare in their general direction, they fade away and are gone.

The Voice of the Four Winds book flickers with green light but does not seem to do anything more than that. You can't get it to work and hope to God it just needs time to dry.

You hear something crying off to your right, behind the wreckage of a fishing trawler. Carefully and slowly you walk behind the ship. There's a cat carrier there, and Slinks, the cat you left behind, is inside. Slinks, the cat you left at home in Long Beach. Slinks, who should definitely not be here in The Oberon.

You open it up and out he comes, unruffled and unperturbed, except for his constant meow. You hug him deeply, checking him for any scratches or injuries. By some miracle, he is here.

Holding his warm, little, furry body in your arms, you look out towards the moonlit coastline. "How-what are you doing here, Slinks? How did you get here?"

You put him back inside his cage, determined to ignore the absolute strangeness of his arrival. *Where in God's name?* you think—then clamp down on that thought, pushing it away and focusing instead on survival. A beached fishing ship is nearby and that part of your mind that is always struggling to keep you alive directs you towards it. You search through the wreck for things to keep you alive.

When you finish, you decide to do an inventory of things you already had and what you have salvaged from the beached fishing ship and from the stasis container. An ori-baton with a blue-green orichalcum stone embedded into the hilt—animal control ori, Guy had said. If there are wild animals hopefully you can control them and dissuade them from eating you. As many paper match packets as you could grab from the lounge of the empty fishing trawler, in order to start a fire. Slinks meows again in his travel cage.

You continue the inventory. Two good-sized plastic squeeze bottles full of water, again rescued from that trawler's wheelhouse. Six cans of chili con carne, plus a can opener. A tiny metal first aid box—color white—with antiseptic, Band-Aids, etc. You put everything into a gym bag you've also grabbed from the wreck.

One transistor radio. An old gray one, Sony, maybe from the '60s even, with a single silver antenna that you stretch out. It was on the floor of the small kitchen space of the fisher's lounge, so you grabbed it just in case. You push up the black *on* switch and move the volume dial up as well, hearing only a good squawk of static. As you move it across the FM dial, you get nothing but more static. You keep messing with the dial until you get to 100–101 FM.

Almost passing it completely, for a second you can hear some music faintly coming over the air. You try to readjust yourself on the sand, and as you do, you notice that if you take the radio and face it into a certain direction, the signal gets stronger; if you face it in another direction, it is weaker.

You turn the volume up as much as you can; some bouncy techno pop comes on.

A male announcer comes on with a very deep and cracked voice. Static crackles beneath every word spoken. "That was *Dream Machine*, Lazerhawk. The time is 10:32pm, Winkie Standard Time. You're listening to nonstop night-time music, the Old Man at Midnight, and you're listening because it's something else to listen to than Radio Oberon. The Midnight Special here's going for the record on how many hits off a bong one can do and still maintain a functional broadcast. See you in a second kids, hmmm?"

So you are definitely in The Oberon, or close enough to get a radio signal from Guy's contact. Considering the broadcasting range of a typical radio station, this is not completely reassuring. You could be twenty miles or two hundred miles from rescue. After multiple attempts, you light a fire with your matches.

As the fire flickers and the waves crash, you lie down on the sand in your flight suit, using your heavy rubber gloves as a pillow. Another pop song, that one from Drive, comes over the static-filled air.

I'm giving you a night call to tell you how I feel...
You doze off a little.
I'm gonna tell you something you don't want to hear...
You do not sleep, but only stare up at the stars. The constellations are so different, so jumbled up compared to what you saw on Earth. It's there, somewhere, you suppose, up in the middle of all that.

You realize you've dozed off when you suddenly feel the soft heat of a clouded, overcast sun on your face. Waking up, you see that the cliffs have become covered in those manta ray creatures that are busy chirping and chattering away at each other, hissing sometimes as well, like a flock of seagulls would on our world. You brush the sand off, take a swig of water from one of the water bottles, and then pour some into the little inside tray that hangs off the travel cage door for the cat. You eat some chili cold from the can, and give some to Slinks as well. He likes licking it off your salvaged spoon.

You are lost in thought when you hear the *Voice of the Four Winds* start to vibrate on the green sands. It's dry enough now, and as you flip eagerly to the map pages, you find that blinking red dot and see your location on an outline of the coast—you are directly on the beaches next to the Super Sargasso Sea, some three hundred kilometers from the Funeral Breaks/Star in the Mountain/Mission Friendship area.

Lines that you assume are for roads and rivers trail up and down the map. The roads are marked in a series of Xs, the rivers are marked by tiny images of running water. You decide to follow the river that dumps out into the Super Sargasso Sea. You remember something from a television survival program about how settlements are always next to running water. Maybe there is a settlement not marked on the map that is closer than your new hometown.

It is time to make some sort of a move forward.

Lifting the travel cage by one hand, you realize that it will be too bulky to carry down an entire beach. You need to be able to move as fast as you can.

You get on your knees, open up the cage, and let Slinks out. You breathe deeply, almost hyperventilating.

Slinks should not be—you push the thought out of your mind.

Using the ability to push and control from the orichalcum baton, you give him a nudge to run up ahead. You leave the cage behind on the sand, an empty, discarded container that will wait by the waves. You make sure to bring out what you can from the Temple of Kern box—

several orichalcum pieces, uncut, a wine bottle, a piece of cheese —and put it all into the gym bag.

After forty minutes you see it—the cliffs have a massive hole in them over a wide churning river that pours into the ocean. Daylight streams through it from the other side. A sandbar separates the edges of one cliff side from another. You and Slinks travel down the sandbar closest to you, underneath the cathedral-like ceiling of rock. There is a vast plain on the other open side of the cliffs with high grass blowing in the wind. Black storm clouds lie on the very far horizon; thunderheads as large as skyscrapers make their way across the distance.

The cavern must be over three hundred feet high, with heavy stalactites hanging from the top. A fine spray of water fills the air, perhaps from drops of moisture coming from that rock ceiling. Faint pictures decorate the rock surfaces. They are mosaic images, like the ones that they dug out of the ruins of Pompeii. Humans in robes and colorful tunics, cavorting or eating or kneeling to unknown idols, adorn certain areas of the cavern, and each image is tens of feet tall.

They are, in some cases, frightening—humans feasting on humans, some many times larger than their compatriots, with lightning coming from their hands and greenish eyes. Half-man, half-animal creatures are there as well, fighting and eating each other. There are old iron torch holders scattered all over the mammoth cavern, unlit but dirty with soot from frequent and presumably recent burnings.

As you and the cat make your way through that massive and long cavern, you see a massive lagoon that leads inward and perhaps onward. The sandbar ends a few yards ahead of you, and there isn't any way to cross without swimming.

Something titters and screeches in that cavern. It is a mad woman's laugh, a haunted asylum laugh. You freeze in place, Slinks near your side. His ears fold back and he bears his fangs. He crouches on the sand, ready to pounce.

You feel very cold all of a sudden. Voices whisper out from all corners.

"Sarah? Sarah?" A voice you were used to hearing when you were little beckons to you. "Oh, Sarah?"

"Rachael? Rach, is that you?"

Rachael Zur, née Orange, moves towards you, walking on water. She looks healthy, lively, like her picture on the cover of TIME. You hug for a long time and feel her warmth. There's a growing darkness in the grotto, every source of light dimming but not extinguished. Shadows grow from every corner. You look down, unable to look at her, unable to go anywhere, to retreat, to run away. There isn't a way to get across the water.

She grabs your hands and pulls you down onto the cold wet ground and smiles. "So whatever have you been up to, sis?" You smile but cannot respond. "You're in The Oberon now. You've been thrown out of Sargasso-3."

You can't raise your eyes from the cavern floor, ashamed of yourself. "I don't know why I wanted to come out here. I don't know why I left Mom, but I wanted to be somebody, and I wasn't going to be someone at home," you gush out.

Rachael looks at you with the countenance of a Buddha—serene and still. "You wanted to be successful, am I correct? Like me."

"Mom wouldn't stop talking about you, before you... died." Rachael wipes your tears with her shirt sleeve.

"Thanks."

"You wanted to come here and become as rich and famous as I was?"

"Yes," you confess.

"You wanted to be in *TIME Magazine* as I was?"

"Yes."

Rachael nods. "Then do what I would do. I made a fortune here—am I correct? I didn't share that, greed was my sin. How did I do that as a simple professor? When I was first here, this was a darker place. I planned my way out of any situation I was forced into, and..." You nod, swallowing.

"I'm sorry for your troubles here, Sarah. I am. I started all of it." She blinks her eyes three times, looking sad, and her eyes turn a deep green. "And I killed whoever, whatever, was in my way."

Shocked, you can't believe it.

"Mathias and Petty are mine. They are mine." A mist appears as a sandbar slowly emerges from the depths of the river. You and Slinks will be able to cross the lagoon after all.

"If you see me again, it won't be me," she says, as she disappears into the mist. "I have to go. He'll be here any moment." A pair of green eyes flashes in the mist.

Fear washes over you like a tide.

You grab Slinks, cross the sandbar, and run for at least a mile. When you can't run any more, you slow to a walk, walking forever, in a daze, without a real ounce of energy behind any footfall. The landscape is constant—high grass plains, the river churning next to you. At one point, you and the cat crest a series of hills, slipping on some of the jagged rocks that point out of the ground.

It is dusk, and you must've traveled fifteen or twenty miles. Maybe that's an exaggeration, but you are in decent shape, fantastic shape even, although you can feel blisters developing on the sides of your feet. The storm clouds you saw outside the cavern are still high and far away, though you can make out small flashes of white lightning in the distance.

When you can't take another step, you plop down on some grass and rest your head against your gym bag as a sort of half-assed pillow. Only the faintest glow of moonlight makes its way through the cloud coverage, and rain begins to fall from the storm that has finally caught up with you. A few drops hit your face, then more, and then more still, until it is coming down hard. Slinks curls up next to you, his warm and wet little body snuggling against your head.

You can't sleep and just lie in the grass as the rain pours down. There are no more of those umbrella-like trees around to give you shelter. You stare into the empty, hazy space ahead of you, not able to think or react to anything.

Soon you are soaking wet with and a sort of shaky chill runs through your veins. You try lying down again but can't with the rain hitting you in the face, so you sit up and pull Slinks into your lap. Thunder cracks incessantly, though you don't see any lightning strikes at this point. With every rumble Slinks shakes a little and you hold him tighter and tighter.

The storm passes after a few hours, leaving little rays of sunlight shooting out from the clouds. Lines of light spread across random spaces of ground, making small islands of light.

You hear something far off, a pop, pop sound. It's not the thunder rumbling but you can't tell what it is. The grasslands that are now a soggy mess still stretch out in every direction. Something like jeep tracks appear in the mud of the Sargasso Breaks.

A half hour passes as you follow the jeep tracks. You come upon a large and wide road, black, covered in bright yellow Xs. The vehicle tracks clearly lead right onto this road. It isn't made of any asphalt from Earth—it is a smooth, solid, jet-black block, with no lines or grooves or signs of potholing or deterioration. The hairs on your arms stand up a little, as if you are next to something giving off static electricity. Slinks growls. There's a hum coming from the road—something that you can feel in the back of your teeth. When you step onto it, all the yellow Xs light up and flash. They come on one after another. For at least a tenth of a mile you can see the road light up once you stand on it, but once you step away, the yellow Xs become dark again. After taking a deep breath, you start down the road, walking a little easier, and the fear subsides a little.

For about twenty minutes you walk down the highway until you see a fork in the road. You take out one of the water bottles, sip a little of the stale, warm water and consult the Voice of the Four Winds, which tells you that the right fork leads to Mission Friendship, which is still so many miles away.

You really want this to be over. You want to sleep somewhere that isn't out in the open, to be clean again, and maybe get the hell off this planet.

As you walk, you notice that your limbs feel lighter than they should. The road pushes you forward. Your feet, which no longer exactly hit the ground, slide forward, almost levitating a half an inch into the air. As you walk you feel like you are on a very, very slow airport people mover, though the ground doesn't seem to be moving at all.

A little later, a playing card, the ace of spades, slides towards you, and you pick it up. The back side of the card is like a tarot card, with a giant goat-faced devil on his throne, crowned with a pentagram; in one hand is a torch pointing downwards. Chained to his black throne is a nude Ni-Perchta woman, with gray skin, pointed ears and long platinum hair. A young, naked human man is chained to the throne as well. Both figures are holding hands. Embossed under the scene are the words *THE DEVIL, M AND P.* You drop the card, feeling dirty for having touched it.

A blanket of fear smothers your senses as you wonder what that card could possibly mean. Nothing but emptiness surrounds you for miles. There is this feeling of being watched, however. It feeds the fear you've had for so long and have been struggling so hard to knock down.

But even fear can't take away your hunger, and you take a moment to eat another can of chili con carne while sitting off to the side of the road, giving Slinks his fair share, too.

Chewing on the cold meat and beans calms you down somewhat. The desolate emptiness around you has no sound.

The Sargasso Breaks, this area you're stuck in, is beautiful, but you can't stand it anymore. The hills and the grasslands, the canyons...

The yellow Xs begin to light up again, though you are not touching the road. Fearing that a predator is coming, you look around for Slinks and panic. He has disappeared from sight. Your heart nearly bursts and you cry out for him several times, not able to see where he has gone despite it being so wide open that he could not have hidden anywhere.

A black DeSoto convertible with a cracked windshield glides towards you and honks. Unsure whether to wave or run away, you make no decision. You just stand there, shell-shocked.

An old man sits behind the wheel. He wears a black sweatband on his head and looks like a crazed Uncle Sam who has joined the hippies. He stops the car and gets out with an effort, standing with the help of a black cane. He slams the door and waves to you. "Good afternoon, there."

You nod and wave back. "A-after-noon." You can barely talk as your mind starts to check out on you.

"Was taking my afternoon drive, wasn't expecting someone like you, all alone out here." You nod again.

"I'm not alone, I had a, a-"

"Come on over, I'm no cobra."

You walk over, still looking for Slinks. Your impression of the old man changes. He looks like an old Abraham Lincoln—a dignified old hippie wearing a black leather biker jacket. Tall, too, way over six feet, maybe six foot five. "I work and live just moments away."

"No sir," you say, thinking that he has asked you a question, and walk back over to where you sat and look for Slinks. You try to mention it to this old man but the words just won't come out, and you start to cry again and hate yourself for it.

"Looks like you just fought a cougar and, uh, barely won." You turn and nod, looking around.

"Shouldn't be out here by yourself. Evil runs around these roads nowadays. Would you like a ride, hmmm? Are you with Solomon's House University?"

"N-no. And, y-yes I w-would l-like to go with you." You call out for Slinks three more times. The old man looks confused and perhaps slightly amused at the same time.

"I can't say no to people in need, I really can't. Not in my bloodstream, no ma'am." He walks over to the other side of the DeSoto and opens the door for you. You call out for Slinks one more time, finally giving up and climb in, brushing up against the cracked leather seat. The car stinks of cigarettes. "S-Sorry for ho-w- how I mu-must appear," you whisper.

The old man climbs in and heads back the way he came, looking forward through the cracked windshield. "No need for the apologies. The Sargasso Breaks is a hard place to be in, especially if you don't know it. I just had this urge to take a Sunday drive out here. I believe I had good fortune in finding you. There was a reason I went out my door today. Poor thing."

Sitting next to him, watching him light up a cigarette with a Zippo lighter, he looks very, very familiar to you, but you can't place him. "Do I know you?"

"Hmmm? Maybe. I made many motion pictures, until fairly recently, hmmm? I started at the top of Hollywood and worked my way down. Not too many people do that, hmmm? Go from leading man to just familiar face. But I did." He takes a drag of his cigarette. "Thank God I did."

His angular, gaunt face, the way he talks, that deep voice. You've seen *The Godfather,* and he looks like the police captain but that can't be right.

"John Hamilton," he says. He puts out one large and liver-spotted hand and does an awkward half shake, his left hand still on the wheel with a burning cigarette stuck between two fingers. "Just a wanderer."

You and he drive down the road for a bit, the yellow Xs lighting up as the car speeds down the highway. The evening is upon you and the clouds are now spread across the sky like ripped stretches of blackish cotton balls. It has started to rain again, a little drizzle coming down. A rainbow stretches over the eastern sky, away from The

Oberon's sun, and you feel that maybe now you can rest, regroup. Hopefully.

John Hamilton says nothing along the way and neither do you. The wind passing through your partially-opened window is the only soundtrack. You can see now that you are again following the river.

After a half hour, a small collection of warehouses appears on the riverbank, surrounded by a chain link fence topped with barbed wire. The warehouses are made of sheet metal and have a parking lot full of white pickup trucks with the Solomon's House University logo on their doors. A miniature trailer park with six different trailers is off to one side of the compound.

A bright red steel ship is anchored next to a pier at the distant end, looking like something that should be in a history book. There is what looks like a lighthouse built right into the middle of the ship.

Hamilton finally speaks. "McRoss Research Station. I'm the caretaker of the facility. The off-time overseer, if you will, for Solomon's House University. It's empty now, just me and the dog. Off season, you see. Will be on-season in a week, then I'll go."

Hamilton pulls the DeSoto up to the gate, gets out of the car slowly, and draws a key from his pocket to open the heavy duty lock. He pops it off, gets back into the car without closing the door, and pulls inside a few paces before jumping out again and locking the gate behind him.

He pulls the DeSoto up to where the pickup trucks are stationed, next to a dented yellow Karmann Ghia. Hamilton steps out of the car, and then opens up your door.

"My apartment, if such an abode deserves such a, uh, grandiose title, is the upstairs of this warehouse." With a nod, he indicates the warehouse next to you. A simple charcoal grill stands outside, as if a silent and useless guard. The lid hangs off one of its handles. "If you would like to come in. Hmmm? There's a shower and an extra guest bedroom if you are so inclined." As he opens one of the warehouse's side doors, a beat-up metal box, the size of a dinner table, with four peg legs and what seem to be cracked headlights for eyes, walks up from out of nowhere. It speaks with an electronic screech—a distorted mixture of different tones, sounding like a fax machine croaking out the tones from *Close Encounters of the Third Kind.*

You scream and the thing leaps backwards, almost cowering to the ground. The old man turns and with one improbably quick motion, produces a revolver from his jacket. "Hmmm? Oh! Maxie, you back off now, you hear? Disturbing our guests like that. Go on!"

The box shuffles away and then skips off on all fours. "What the hell?"

"Brain in a box, dear. The boys examined it before… it's a dog's brain in a robotic body. Absolute abomination, hmmm? Friendly though. Maxie—and I doubt that was his name— is a ten thousand-year-old cyborg, if we have to use such a term of fiction. There are more like him."

You turn to look at Hamilton but say nothing, and walk inside what seems to be an office hallway. Hamilton turns on the lights and fluorescents illuminate the linoleum path. "Nothing much to see here, until the three researchers arrive back from the university at Solomon's Bay. Nice group. They have regular day jobs with the Network. Some are at Mission Friendship."

Little offices filled with cabinets and desks hold dust-covered paperwork and once-used coffee mugs. Slim, gray Apple computers with dull, black monitors sit idle, encaged in strange metal boxes.

"Why are these caged?" you ask. There is a staleness in the air, a sort of dusty smell.

"Faraday cages. Otherwise these computers, hmmm? They'd just blow from the EMP we get randomly. Can't use too many electronics in The Oberon."

Passing through another door at the end of the hallway, you see a huge space filled with thick metal shelves; only a few boxes are stacked on them. You and he walk on the dirty concrete to where a little section has been built up. Around the side of this storage area, you walk up a set of creaking wooden stairs and into John Hamilton's apartment space.

Ceiling fans twirl lazily from the vaulted ceiling. The lights are turned on. If the DeSoto stunk of cigarettes, this place positively reeks of it.

There is an open cabinet with a single submachine gun in the bedroom; an open box of shells next to it, the little brass cartridges gleaming. There are a couple of ori-batons, one with a blue band painted around the hilt, another with an orange band. One has a blue and white rock in it, which vaguely reminds you of the Leo zodiac sign, a snake, while the other has a blue and orange rock whose two wavy watery lines seem to form the Aquarius symbol.

"Mi casa es su casa. It isn't much, but it allows the writer a place of reflection, a place to discuss anything with nobody."

Besides being covered in pictures of sailing ships and the sea, there is a large map of The Oberon.

"I n-need, I nee-d, goddammit, I can't speak." You pull at your hair for a second. "I need to get to Mission Friendship."

John Hamilton nods slowly. "You've got scratches around your neck and hands, look like you haven't had a decent meal in days, and were wandering around a wilderness as dangerous as the Serengeti. After a day's rest, hmm? We'll talk more."

You clean up and shower, and after an hour of waiting, throw on your clothes again, cleaned by the washer and dryer in the apartment. Walking through the corridor you went through earlier, you find Hamilton outside, smoking a pipe and enjoying the night air. He sits on a pool lounge chair, along with a boxy ghetto blaster. He offers to get you something to eat, but you refuse, not hungry in the slightest. You are confused as to why he is doing what he is doing, helping a complete stranger.

Moving the lounge chair forward with a scraping of asphalt, Hamilton puts the boxy radio on his lap with a groan, turns it on, and fiddles with the dials. He gestures for you to take a seat on an office chair.

He sits there listening. A female voice speaks, barely heard over the static. "For the benefit of Mr. Kite, there will be a show tonight."

There is a funky popping noise, then a sort of warbling of static comes in and out of the transmission. A message is read out over the frequency. "Wide unclasp the tables of their thoughts, these same thoughts people this little world..." It's Hamilton's voice.

The same message is repeated for at least the next minute before going into the regular "Old Man at Midnight" radio show.

"Checking on my day job, Miss Sarah. Always have to check. I produce it from an ancient transmitter sixteen miles away from here. You don't work for the Network, do you?"

As you stand there in a full Network uniform, you have to confirm that you do indeed work for the Network.

"A serious agent, hmmm? Sort that would report an old man for an unlawful broadcast?" You shake your head. "No, no, not in the slightest."

You hadn't noticed when you first came in, but there are street lights, four of them, near the yellow X highway, two on each side of the road. Just now they click on with an audible hum, giving off an orange light on the other side of the chain link fence you passed through. Beyond them lie the darkening canyons of the Sargasso Breaks. When the lights come on, part of your brain clicks on as well.

"Mr. Hamilton, I worked with Guy Farson. I think I have something to sell you." You swallow compulsively.

Hamilton turns with a smile. "Well, it's not my usual operating hours or my usual place of business, Miss Sarah, but I think I may be able to oblige. Have to make a living somehow here in this epic wilderness we are all caught in."

You retreat to the inside of the warehouse and bring back the gym bag you lugged miles across the Sargasso Breaks. You wonder how he knew your name but figure you must have introduced yourself.

"Did you liquidate the others?" Hamilton inquires casually.

"No, God no."

He looks you over and shakes his head. "I wouldn't have the guts to do that either, no matter how much money was involved. Were they all killed?"

The mechanical dog comes over slowly, interested in what is happening.

"No, I don't know about one. But the other two..." You re-tell what had happened to you in a flat, monotone voice.

He listens in silence, only agreeing and repeating parts to show that indeed he is listening and that he does care about this story.

You sit back on that office chair, sighing when you mention how you ended up here.

"I'm glad that little device came in handy, Miss, to shut off the security. Myself and Guy talked about that just a few days ago. My God." Hamilton scratches his chin. "That was an ejection field that hit you in the end. Non-lethal security but the physics and the reality bending behind it are above and beyond our rudimentary knowledge."

You open the gym bag, showing off the little goodies you've brought with you.

"I would have liked to have talked to Guy one more time. That goofy boy could always make me laugh." Hamilton looks over the items, counting under his breath, and stands up to look further into the bag.

"Such a shame. You said you heard an Englishman's voice giving orders? Is that what you said, Miss?" Hamilton stands there with both hands on his cane, licking his lips.

"Yes."

"Bad news, that. That was most likely Charles Mathias of the Mathias and Petty Gang."

A memory flickers in your head. *A wanted sign is pasted onto one of the pillars of the bridge. It says: WANTED— CHARLES MATHIAS, LEADER OF MATHIAS-PETTY GANG.* A hand-drawn and faded picture of a man with curly red hair has been Xeroxed onto the poster. *Convicted Murderer. 25 Million Dii-Yaa Reward, Alive or Dead, from Ephors of Kadath and the Bureau of Off-World Affairs.* A dragon-like symbol is stamped at the bottom of the poster.

"They're toe-cutters—cruel criminals. A mixed race gang. They attack salvagers mostly and human farms and stations." Hamilton glances at the chain link fence protecting McRoss Research Station.

Nothing is said for a good long time.

"I'm sorry about your friends. Well, I'll take everything in the bag here. I'm sorry, I'll have to pay you in Dii-Yaa."

You don't even really care about the money anymore. "Sure," you garble out.

Hamilton walks over to his DeSoto and pops open the trunk. He returns with stacks of red Oberon money.

"One million four hundred thousand Dii-Yaa." He hands you the stacks of cash. "You find this to be of a satisfactory nature, Miss?"

You feel all the cash in your hands and lick your lips. With fourteen Dii-Yaa to the dollar, it's one hundred thousand dollars you have in your hands.

"I'm the easiest crime boss you ever worked with." Hamilton smiles. He puffs on his pipe and returns to his lounge chair. "Smuggling is an interesting business." He sings a little. "And so very profitable..."

You can't sleep in the guest bedroom, you can only lie under stale sheets, stare up at the ceiling panels, and count the dots in the panels by the pale glow of the little Jiminy Cricket night light. Four white walls are your safeguard from the outside, thank God.

It feels so good to be in a real bed instead of sleeping in the open of the Breaks, though you miss Slinks terribly and worry about him. This is despite persistently ignoring the question of how Slinks even got to The Oberon in the first place or how you found your supposedly dead sister in that cave. There is real warmth under these covers, and even though every muscle cries out to relax, your brain keeps thinking, thinking, as you stare up into the nothing of those panels. Thirty-six dots you count on four panels, thirty-seven, thirty- eight now.

Something is crying outside the warehouse. You turn onto your side under the covers, your head still against the pillow, and listen. The old Mickey Mouse wind-up alarm clock reads 3:33 am. Your watch is broken, the Casio shorted out by the water.

"Help! Please!" the voice says, far away. Maxie, the brain in the box "dog" thing, cries out in horrible electronic tones, like a dial up connection with a constant slamming beep.

Your heart picks up its pace and your hands start to sweat. "J-John, John, do you hear that?" you call out to Mr. Hamilton.

From the other bedroom you hear John speak up after a rasping cough. "Yeah, I heard it." You hear him get off his bed with a squeak of bedsprings, and his clomping across the room.

"Pleaaaaaaase!" the voice calls out, much louder now, its sound almost reverberating off the metal warehouse walls. The sound of the dog-thing Maxie is now thumping through your bedroom walls. You slip on the flight suit, zip up, and put on your shoes.

As you walk out of the bedroom you see Hamilton in a blue and mangy-looking bathrobe and rabbit slippers. He has an ori-baton in his pocket, the one with the blue band, and is taking out a small stainless steel submachine gun from his dresser. There is a pipe in his mouth as if he is Sherlock Holmes on the case. His hands you a little snub-nosed .38, already loaded.

"Let's take a gander." He takes the pipe out of his mouth and sets it down. He leads the way, moving in a manner that belies his years. You notice he doesn't have his cane.

Hamilton opens the door that leads to the parking lot. A blast of cool air meets the two of you as you step outside. The four orange sodium street lights over that particular section of the yellow X highway light up the figure of a young woman who has both hands against the chain link fence. She cries out again in a voice that is so familiar to you. It is familiar because it is your voice.

It is a copy of you, an exact copy, wearing your flight suit. On the other side of the fence, is you, ragged-looking, gaunt, with holes in your clothes and cuts across your face and body. This other you grips the chain link fence, shaking it at the same time with a metallic scraping rattle.

"Please help! I'm so hungry. I've been walking for days! Please, God, help me." The voice is exact, no imitation, the exact same voice.

Hamilton stops in his tracks just a few yards away from the fence, though he still keeps the gun on the other you. Maxie bounces back and forth with an electronic sort of burble. His thin, metallic peg legs scrape and pound onto the pavement as he runs back and forth, intrigued by what is on the other side.

"What is this?" Hamilton whispers. The other you seems to finally notice you are hiding behind him.

"Who the hell is this? What is this? What is this?" the other you cries, shaking the fence, tears running down dirt-stained cheeks. "I need help! Please open up!"

Hamilton looks at you and swallows. "You don't have a twin sister, do you?" he whispers. You shake your head. Turning back to the other you, in a firm and loud voice, he says, "I don't know what this is about. Step away from the fence, slowly, and I will let you in at the gate entrance." He motions with his gun to the gate you passed through earlier, now locked.

The other you still tightly grips the fence, staring at you with increasingly glassy-looking eyes. There is a long pause.

"Who is that thing next to you? What is that thing? What is that thing? Tell me! Tell me now!" The other you backs away from the fence as if struck.

"This is Maxie. It's a machine," Hamilton says.

"Not that, it! It!" The other you points at you with one bloodied finger.

Your mouth moves, but no words come out at first. "I don't know who this is, Mr. Hamilton."

"What is this?" the other you hisses before launching herself onto the fence.

You know you will always be haunted by what happens next—the image of yourself climbing up the fence, scurrying like a spider to reach the top, and the inhuman wail that pours out of her lungs as she does so, a scream so loud and angry and terrified all at once. That scream will always make an appearance in your nightmares.

Hamilton uses the power of the ori-baton to push her off the fence. She lands on her back with a thud.

"Whoever you are, you need to please get a hold of yourself. I will not let you in without you..." Hamilton's voice shakes.

The other you takes less than a moment to get back onto her feet. Without another word she calmly and slowly walks forward and climbs the fence again, her face now expressionless.

Hamilton pushes her off again through telekinesis; she falls again with a hard crack. As she starts to get up again, Hamilton gives her a sharp mental push. She flies backwards as if yanked by an invisible bungee cord. She then tumbles across the width of the highway into the dust of the road's shoulder, flipping end over end.

"Enough! Do not attempt to climb this fence again or I will gun you down!" Hamilton ratchets the machine gun for effect.

Limping back across the highway, the other you again puts her hands onto the chain link fence, slowly gripping it with one hand, her face a mask of defiance against Hamilton's threat. Hidden in her other hand, she snaps an ori-baton that telescopes out and points the baton's end at Maxie; its peg legs stop the incessant stomping. Its distorted and ruined headlight-like eyes light up in little flashes, never staying fully on. A synthesizer squeal comes out, and the machine creature charges towards Hamilton.

In a second it rears up and thumps Hamilton down to the asphalt, knocking the machine gun out of his hands. The machine creature starts to pound into Hamilton's chest and face, meanwhile breaking the submachine gun in half. You can hear him groan, and there is the sick crack of a bone snapping.

You run back towards the door when the thing leaps off Hamilton and slams itself full force against the door, cracking it and popping off a hinge. You fall backwards and scramble up quickly, but you have left the ori-baton on the ground.

It turns with a sort of coughing snarl as you rear back and shoot the .38 twice. One of the shots knocks out one of its headlights in a crash of glass. The other shot shatters into the door frame behind Maxie, leaving a clean burnt hole in the middle of it.

A thin line of black and awful-smelling oil leaks from its side, and it sways back and forth for a moment, in a daze. Then it freezes completely; the one good headlight eye dies, and you think that might be it, but it comes alive again. The headlight eye flashes, and Maxie begins moving in jittery, awkward steps.

The other you has climbed the fence and is almost at the top. Hamilton is still lying on the ground, and his submachine gun is broken. He grabs the other you with his ori-baton, holding her in mid-air away from the fence, and puts out one liver-spotted hand that is flexing like a claw. "Shoot!" he cries, his voice blurred with pain. "Shoot!"

Still directing Maxie, the other you makes a pulling back motion. Maxie charges at you again and leaps, but you manage to dive out of the way, scraping your knee badly on the pavement, ripping a nice stretch of skin off and leaving a trail of blood. From the ground, you look through the fence line at the other you, who is floating in mid-air. The other you is an expressionless statue, no wires to be seen holding her up.

Without thinking, you aim the gun at her. Her figure directly lined up in your sights, you fire three times. You hit the other you in the leg first, then in the arm, and then in the chest. Hamilton drops her, and she flops onto the ground. Blood flows out in a little growing pool around the body, inching out and under the chain link fence.

The other you groans. One arm is caught under her body. She tries to get up twice. On the third attempt, the other you falls backwards, her head slamming into the yellow X highway with a hard crack.

You are breathing heavily and put the gun down onto the pavement. The smoking .38 rests in front of you, still hot. That fourth of July firework smell from the cordite makes you feel sick.

Dizzy, you dry heave a couple of times, then wipe your mouth with the back of your hand. Hamilton lies still on the ground. Maxie, still leaking a little of the black oil, walks around him, its body language conveying a sense of concern like a dog circling its wounded master. For a moment the boxy thing looks over at you and then makes a warbling siren sound.

"I'm okay, Maxie," Hamilton groans. "Sarah?" he says, looking up at the stars.

You kneel by his side. The old man's face is deeply bruised and purple. Maxie managed to smash in one of his front teeth.

"There's another ori-baton inside. It has an orange band. It's a healer one." He frowns. "I think...I think I could die out here." You stand up quickly, focusing on the shattered corridor door. When you try to open it, the door falls off its brass hinges and clangs onto the ground. You step over it and run back to Hamilton's apartment.

In the glass cabinet you find the ori-baton and run back out as fast as you can on your hurt leg and step over the remains of the door to the outside.

Pushing Maxie to the side, you kneel down next to Hamilton, who is breathing heavily.

"You know how to use ori?" he asks, his voice weak and barely audible over the cold wind that is now blowing.

"Barely."

"Oh, Christ," he says, his breathing labored.

"Well what the..." you say, near tears.

"Use it the same way you have used it before. Focus and concentrate, but think of, shit, think of positive things. Sounds stupid." Hamilton coughs in pain. "Put your hand on my chest...I'm nearly dead. You probably don't have a happy thought in you," he says with a grim smirk.

You grab the baton firmly, then gently put your hand over his chest. There is a sensation of warmth and connection that is as unreal and as fresh as it felt all those years ago with your sister, trying an ori-baton out before your mother ran out and...That is all the happy thought you need. Being with your family on your birthday.

There is a flash of green and a stream of greenish-white flecks come from the ori-baton and passes through Hamilton's chest. His bruises lighten. The smashed tooth returns to normal. There is such a loud sigh coming from him that you are afraid that somehow you've screwed this up, done too much of whatever it is, and killed him. But Hamilton sits straight up, holding his side.

"This was a bad night." You nod and laugh and cry a little, and then turn the baton to yourself, trying to heal your own leg. It doesn't work. There is a loud popping sound, and a tiny spiral of black smoke comes from the baton. That sense of connection is immediately lost.

"You can't do it on yourself. It makes a loop and burns out the ori, and then the baton is dead," Hamilton says, rubbing his face. "I'll help you in a second. And when something's dead, it's dead, hmmm?"

Hamilton and you sit up all night, exhausted but unable to sleep because of the attack. You're both jittery, anxious, on guard, so you sit on the tailgate of the white pickup truck and watch the stars, feeling the breeze blow in. Hamilton brings refreshments, and you pop a Solomon's cola, still cold and wet from being at the bottom of a cooler, pour the fizzing contents into a half-full glass of Jack Daniels, and mix the contents slowly by sticking your index finger into the drink.

"That's your third, Miss. You should pace yourself, hmmm?"

You keep drinking anyway. Hamilton coughs into his hand.

"I thinks you-I'll be o-okaay," you say, slurring your words ever so slightly. You look up to the stars again as it nears dawn. The orange sodium lights out on the highway click off. Every now and again you sneak a peek at the corpse that is still lying there.

"We b-b-better bury i-it," you blurt out.

Hamilton rubs his face and then blows out his whiskey-tinged breath. He looks much older than when the evening started. "Yeah."

He snaps out his ori-baton and heads for the gate. You get off the back of the truck and follow him. Taking out a key from his dirty, torn, and bloodstained bathrobe, he opens the gate. You take out the .38 again and check the cylinder before snapping it back into place to make sure you loaded it correctly.

You can't stop shaking. Your heart is racing; you feel as if you are going to throw up.

Looking both ways down the yellow X highway that lights up once you step onto it, you and Hamilton tiptoe over to the body.

The first rays of dawn creep over the Sargasso Breaks. Far down the road you see black silhouettes moving across the grass, just like those black shadows you saw at the beach. A moment later they fade away. You don't bother to tell Hamilton, who is focused elsewhere. You aren't even sure if they were real anyway, or just your imagination.

You look at the corpse. It is you, an exact version of you. There is a bullet hole in the chest and one in the leg. Blood is in your mouth and your eyes are open. You look closely and see that your pupils are dilated wide, strangely so. A bullet has nicked the ori-baton, you guess, as the hilt is smashed. A lone sneaker has fallen off.

It does not look like you are sleeping. You notice that during the fight one sneaker fell off, your sneaker fell off...

"I...I don't know what this is," you say quietly, almost to yourself. Hamilton has the good form to keep quiet.

You shudder. Hamilton starts to speak but you put up a hand; you check the back pocket of the flight suit. When you feel it there, you start hyperventilating, scared. What if you see...

There is a California Driver's License there, and you hand it over to Hamilton. "Please check who this..." You can't finish the sentence.

Hamilton takes the license in one hand, not releasing his grip on the ori-baton. His old, rheumy eyes scan the horizon, still waiting for the next wave of attack.

You are still kneeling next to the body. "Who was it?" you say, voice flat, emotionless.

"Miss Orange, we don't know who this is. This is the Sargasso Breaks, it's very different out here. The sort of place that's not the sort of place you might expect to conform with the laws of reality as we know it. That's why this research station was built, that's why the Solomon's House people come every winter to study."

You swallow. "Who was it?" Your voice sounds strangled. Hamilton says nothing, but flips the license over. He shows you who it was. Sarah Orange. The same picture you know you had taken at the Long Beach DMV. Sarah Orange. And now Sarah Orange is dead, and you are to bury her.

You sit back onto the yellow X highway, not saying a word. Hamilton speaks up quickly.

"No. We don't...we don't know what this means exactly, hmmm? This is a strange, horrifying thing but there have been stranger and more horrifying things that have happened ever since they opened the place. We settlers all know that..."

You get up and walk away, shoulders slumped.

Hamilton is quiet now, and with the exception of the chain slowly banging against the gated fence, making a metallic pinging sound, there is no sound for a long time. Maxie walks around the fence line, curious. Those metal peg legs thump the asphalt and scrape against it as he moves slowly, watching you two.

You bite down on your fist and scream, a loud, piercing scream. You can see yourself doing this, almost in a detached way. You feel so not alive and so not a part of reality that you are amazed at the strength of your own scream. Hamilton pays no attention.

Instead, he uses the ori-baton to make a series of clawing motions in the direction of the Sargasso grass and dirt on the other side of the highway. Hundreds of pounds of dirt are scraped away, as if by the hand of some angel, creating a cloud of thick, brown dust. The dirt is shifted, making a deep hole. Clumps of grass blow in the wind. A mound of soil grows to the side.

With great care, Hamilton lifts the body into the air without touching it, his orichalcum power doing all the work in a way that is so easy, it's disconcerting. There it hangs for a moment, suspended in space, like a wet and dripping ragdoll.

Concentrating hard and sweating a little, he gently points with his baton and lowers the body into the hole that's been clawed out of the planet's turf. With a simple shoving motion, all the soil that he dug out a few moments

ago topples over into the grave of the other you, covering that body for eternity.
 "It's over," Hamilton says.

CHAPTER THIRTEEN:
THE ROAD BACK TO MISSION FRIENDSHIP

You walk out of the living space and down the stairs, looking for Hamilton, who has disappeared on you. The two of you went back to sleep after the attack; you crashed on a couch in his bedroom and slept most of the day away, the guns and the batons still on your person.

"John?" you call out, disturbed Small, yellow bulbs behind iron cages that were dark the night before are lit all over McRoss, giving everything in the parking lot an ethereal glow.

The charcoal grill by the door has recently been lit and you see a wooden tray table with a couple of raw flank steaks on it. This isn't beef per se, but actually Afer steaks—Oberon cattle. You can tell by the almost wine-colored tone of the meat.

John watches the grasslands beyond the chain link fence from his lawn chair. His cane is between his knees and he seems to be lost in thought. A cigarette hangs from his mouth, a trail of smoke leaking out into the air above. The ghetto blaster next to him is tuned to Radio Oberon and not his Old Man at Midnight show. The volume is low, but in the silence surrounding you it is the loudest noise you can hear. The music stops.

"We interrupt this radio broadcast to update you on the special flash storm warning for the Sargasso Breaks.

Any and all persons within five kilometers of the center of Sargasso-3 must take immediate shelter underground. We repeat; this is a flash storm warning for the Sargasso Breaks region. Any persons within five kilometers of the center of City Quadling-3 must take immediate shelter underground..."

In the pockets of darkness around the station you see the "dog" creep about slowly, wandering to and fro with a slight limp.

"John?" you say, and he turns his head.

"Good to see you in a better condition than last night. Come, come, take a seat here. Watch the show that is about to unfold."

You sit down with a thump in that same office chair. There are little white flashes off in the distance, over the grasslands, like photos being taken by God. Though it is night, you see the sky turn a bluish-green, with white circles floating and rotating around the cloud cover, dancing with each other. Unearthly groans are carried forth and the wind picks up. You watch, feeling that the storm is both beautiful and terrifying at the same time.

"Would you like a cigarette, Miss?" Hamilton takes out a pack of Network cigarettes and offers one to you. You shake your head, watching the flash storm unfold. He tucks the cigarette pack back into his tweed jacket.

"I don't know what to do next." You drink another soda and Jack Daniels. It is so cool and refreshing, the bubbles tickling the back of your throat. "I should have started drinking a while ago. My friends always liked it."

Hamilton raises a gray eyebrow at that but lets it go. He takes a deep drag of his cigarette. "What we are dealing with is a series of strange events in your life, Miss Orange. Please let me know, from the first moment you arrived on this planet, what has happened to you."

You take a deep drink and say nothing. Part of your brain shuts off, locking your tongue. Anxiety wells up like a freshly struck oil well.

"I have to look to our dinner, Miss. Excuse me." With a couple of tries he finally gets out of his chair and prepares the steaks. He has strapped a gun belt on.

A few minutes later he brings you a plate with a rare hunk of steak and a steaming baked potato already sliced down the middle, loaded with butter and pepper. A little bit of blood oozes from the meat, soaking into the white of the potato and turning it purplish.

"It's Afer, so I hope you're not the allergic type. It's good and it'll pump you full of enough energy that you'll want to run a few miles after this."

You cut into it and eat—it is terrifically tender. The storm winds itself up with a sharp piercing wail and the sky to the west turns back to its normal pattern of stars. Hamilton is right—the meat has some sort of kick to it. All your fatigue and irritability start to fade away like a half-remembered dream.

You and he eat in silence, chewing away like a couple of barnyard cows, staring out past the fence line. The mound containing the corpse of the other you is hard not to stare at.

You get another drink from the cooler. You are beginning to feel, not relaxed, but mellow enough.

"You can go in the morning. I'll give you the Ghia. You'll have to drive it through Sargasso-3 in order to get to the Mission. I'll show you the route. I can pick it up at the Mission in a few weeks."

"I have a map." For some odd reason, you're terrified, fearful that Hamilton might ask about your book—the *Voice of the Four Winds*. He hasn't had a drop of alcohol since you got up, which is something you just assume is out of character for an old guy like him.

"Are you afraid of something else, Mr. Hamilton?" You bite your lip. "I'm sorry about last night."

Hamilton chokes out a false laugh. "No. Being as old as I am, you get over that sort of thing. At my age, everything is a near death experience. And don't be sorry. It's not like you planned that whole affair." He smiles a tight-lipped grin, raises himself up, and walks back to the ruined door. "In the morning. Oh, shit. Why am I telling a young girl like you to go three hundred klicks alone, especially after everything? I will go with you, of course, you needn't go alone."

You turn in your chair as he points out the dusty Karmann. "It should be just fine. I have to check a few things, but we can take off in the morning. That car runs the best. Should only be a few hours drive. Hell, it's the easiest drive in the world. I don't know why I said you should go alone."

He lifts his black cane and points it down the yellow X highway, opposite from the direction you came. "I've driven it more than a few times without incident." He laughs but then looks into the distance. You feel that he is becoming surer that his words are now ever so slightly absurd and that some other incident will soon come to you both.

"It's a good car, too. Got it off an oriental girl with an Irish last name."

You think to yourself for a simple second. "I wish I could just call somebody to get picked up out here. Why can't we call?"

Hamilton shakes his head. "Radio transmissions get blurred out over distances farther than two miles, something about EMP and something else. It blows out circuit boards, too. That's why you won't find any cars or trucks built past '81. I mean, look at this lot here."

Hamilton points to the Ghia.

"I could use my tower—it's been boosted with some of the ancient stuff," Hamilton says. "But it's not as if it's a private telephone. Anything I say is for public consumption."

You and he talk some more, but the reality is that you've decided to take off tonight, on your own. He said you could have the car, at first. It wouldn't be stealing. You down that Jack and soda, feeling unsteady on your feet, and you and John speak nothing of consequence until going to your separate beds.

You doze off and on during the night until the little alarm clock you wound up goes off with a ring that startles you. You grab the little thing and quickly shut it off, listening to see if John is up. His snores are labored and end with a sort of rasping cough. Your head hurts and your stomach feels like it is distended and bloated—your second hangover so far. You swing your legs over the side of the bed and then tiptoe out of the bedroom in your flight suit.

Looking around his little apartment space, you find a yellow pad and write Hamilton a message, telling him that you need to leave, that you don't want to put him through any further danger considering what your situation is, and that you will leave the car in the Mission parking lot. You apologize for leaving him behind. You sign it, S.

The first rays of light are coming in over the Sargasso Breaks as you walk out into the parking lot, your sneakered feet crunching asphalt. You have grabbed the .38 again along with the ori-baton that has a blue-white ori rock set into it that was made to look like the Leo snake astrology sign.

There's a set of binoculars on the seat of the Ghia, and you toss them into the back seat as you climb inside, along with your gym bag full of Dii-Yaa cash. As you release the parking brake, a little meow comes from behind you. You turn and find Slinks, somehow, some way, curled up in the back of Hamilton's car.

You are thunderstruck and horribly confused by his reappearance. You look at the chain link fence and back to Slinks. "How..." you start to say, and then Slinks meows again. You pick him up and hug him tight, thanking God he is back and somehow he found you. It is like one of those cheesy tabloid stories you always hear about a pet finding its master after ridiculous circumstances. You sit there for a good moment, and then put the little guy down.

You press Slinks to sit down on the passenger seat, where he watches you with such a great amount of kitty concern, his little face a constant O of amazement. Maxie the dog- robot watches with what you guess to be bewilderment, not making any true move to stop or sound the alarm, though its one good headlight eye flashes faster and faster as it sees what you are doing. Getting out of the car and taking a walk over to the gate, you open the lock and roll the car back onto the yellow X highway without turning on the engine. After a brief pushing match with Maxie to get it back behind the gate, you lock the gate and scramble back inside the car. The engine starts after a couple of stuttering tries and you drive to the highway. You think of leaving the gate key behind when Hamilton calls out to you, and you stop the car. He walks over and leans his large frame into the window. How he got past the gate you do not know.

"Look," you start before he quiets you.

"You earned this," he says, his voice slightly accented and strange sounding. He hands over a small black ring with a little orange rectangle on its top. "You earned this. Press on the rectangle there at the top of the ring, and you can turn invisible for thirty seconds at a time. It recharges after two minutes. This can occur only at night. Only after the sun sets. It'll protect you. You passed the test; you earned it."

His face changes into Scratch's for a just a moment, and then returns to normal. "Be seeing you."

He walks back inside the station. "There's a storm coming, Miss! I'll blow it off course for you."

Hamilton levitates several feet above the ground. His arms are outstretched, and his eyes have now taken the strong appearance of almost pure white light. Lightning comes from his chest, eyes and hands, and bounces across the entire sky.

He descends to the ground, and then sits down on the asphalt.

He looks up at the sky, staring.

You slip the ring onto your finger without a second thought and leave.

After the first hour on the road, you start to feel a little more relaxed, a little more comfortable with your surroundings. The car's engine, sounding decidedly like a lawnmower, runs and runs and you feel increasingly sleepy. The long yellow X highway flashes on and on, running over the next hill and beyond. Thick and dark clouds stream across the sun-filled sky, casting long shadows onto the grasslands. They seem to be rushing away from you.

The second hour you see some shapes pass in and out of the clouds, up and down, right to left. You stop the car at the side of the road, leaving the engine on, and look out at the shapes, making out that the things have sort of sails on them—not airships per se, but something like the airships. You grab the binoculars.

Looking out again, you see that there are actually people flying through the clouds.

You focus on the one that is going up and down and flipping around a dark cloud embankment that blocks part of the early morning sunlight. A guy is on this modified windsurfer thing. It has the surfboard and the plastic sail. Two other sails slightly turn towards the ground projected from the side of the surfboard, like wings. A large metal cylinder with wires sticking out of it and glowing a light green is attached to the back of the surfboard. The person on it is tied with a sort of cable and wears a backpack.

Drops of rain fall against your bare skin. You see lights behind these flying people, like the lights of city skyscrapers blinking through the haze. Sargasso-3 is not that far off.

It is then that you notice smoke in the distance, a black column of it streaming into the air. You think you smell the stink of spilled gasoline on the wind. Unsure, you get back into the car and drive for a couple of minutes, rounding the top of a hill until you can see a Network police cruiser burning, the engine blown. You get out again and walk gingerly forward, looking every which way to see if anyone is still around, if the attackers are still nearby, ready to pounce on you. Your heart starts that sick beat and your stomach begins to cramp. Tarot cards are sprayed all over the place, maybe thirty or fifty of them thrown about, some gently flipping over in the wind. Those damn M and P cards showing the Devil, and the man and the woman who are chained to the Devil's throne.

The bloodied and burned bodies of two young men lie on the side of the road. One is face down, the other has been shot in the arm and chest. His body leans against the burning police cruiser.

You know who these two are. Robert Fuller and Tadeo Marcelino, the Counters that escorted you on your first day.

You look at the cards scattered around the road, some of them slowly moving away from where they were dumped.

A scene plays in your head, a movie you watched on video a long time ago at your friend's house when you were not supposed to.

"*Hey Captain, what's that?*" Lance says in Apocalypse Now.

"*Death Card,*" Martin Sheen says.

"*What?*" Lance says.

"*Death Card. Lets Charlie know who did this,*" Martin Sheen says.

You run back to the car, navigate carefully around the destruction then hit the gas as hard as you can, making Slinks hiss and cry out from the sudden maneuver. You keep moving then peg the gas pedal to the floor again. Slinks is thrown against the car door, and after recovering his bearings, he glares at you as he washes his paw.

Ten minutes further down the highway you come up to an overturned motorcycle. There are a thousand pieces of debris scattered all over the highway, little pieces of chrome and bits of glass from the windscreen. The motorcycle's rider must be nearby and may need immediate help. You think of turning around but your sense of simple human responsibility blocks you. Someone must've been hurt. Blood is spread all over the highway. As you look around for the injured driver, you can see that the debris is drifting away towards the right shoulder. They wink out of existence in tiny flashes.

You speed up again to pass the scene. Right then and there what you fear the most happens. There is a small explosion under the car, a metallic crack and bang loud enough to hurt your ears. You've run over some sort of mine or explosive trap and the left rear tire is shredded. The car glides to a stop, and you pound on the steering wheel before looking over your shoulder, figuring any second that whatever killed those people is just around the corner, waiting to finish you. But nothing else happens. The trap went off, your car is dead, but you and Slinks are still alive.

After looking around again for wherever the motorcycle rider must have crash-landed, you climb out carefully and look up and down that deserted road. The yellow Xs have stopped flashing. You have your pistol in your hand, ready to go. As you stand there, watching, searching, an overwhelming feeling of dread comes over you. You need to get out of there right now. But then your knee explodes into a thousand needlepoints of pain. You never heard a shot, never saw a flash, never saw anything. You just feel the pain as your body drops to the ground, and scream as you realize your shredded leg now hangs off your body. Something pulls you forward and you crawl towards the shoulder, not thinking of what to do next other than just to get off the damn road.

That's when you see the two of them stand up from the high grass fifty yards away, a young man and a woman. She's a Ni-Perchta in a scuffed up black leather jacket with a full helmet on, visor down—the only way you can tell she is Ni-Perchta is by her photo negative skin color and the long strands of platinum hair falling out of the helmet. She puts out her hand and your pistol floats towards her.

You think you recognize Mathias from the wanted poster, but a demonic-looking red and yellow mask covers the lower half of his face. He's carrying something that looks like a sawed-off M-16 with a flashlight for a barrel and a black cord plugged into a metallic backpack. He wears a revolver like a cowboy, strapped to his thigh.

"Tall for a girl, ain't she? Long streak of piss for a woman, I am right or am I sorry to be wrong?" Mathias says, his cockney accent slightly muffled by his mask. His eyes glow a deep green for a second, then turn to blue. He hangs up his sawed-off M-16 by hooking it into the metallic box on his back. You recognize that voice from where your co-op was ambushed.

The Ni-Perchta woman nods, and then uses an ori-baton to lift a couple of hidden Kawasaki motorcycles out of the grass and onto the highway. You moan and continue to crawl towards the shoulder, knowing that this is the end. These are killers, and they're going to laugh and joke around and then murder you. You can feel the bullet thumping through your skull before the shot is even fired. Fear engulfs you. You just want it to be all over. Slinks runs past you and disappears into the high grass.

The two walk forward, the young man grabbing the Ni-Perchta woman by the hand, like a lover would. You try to stand up on your good left leg but you fall over again, sweating, desperate to get out of this, wanting to be somewhere, anywhere but here.

Mathias speaks again. "Looks like one of those bugs you step on in the street doesn't she? You just manage to crush the one half and the other half is still moving forward like nothing goddamn well happened. Sort of an insect with half of the life squished out, ain't she? Sort of desperate, ain't she, Miss Jenny Petty?"

The Ni-Perchta woman nods, taking off her helmet. She's beautiful of course, even with those surreal skin tones. However, one eye is whitened and blind looking, scarred deeply.

"Stop crawling around like that," Mathias says to you, as fast as he can spit out the words. "Stop crawling around like that, you ain't a bug, you're a woman, for crissake. Be a woman."

You feel yourself lifted off the ground and slammed back onto the side of the Karmann Ghia. You don't even see Mathias flick his ori-baton with his wrist—seemingly he just thought it and it happened.

You watch the two of them and try to hang on to the car like a drowning man trying to cling to a life preserver. There's a fire in your leg. It is horrible to look at—a blackened, cauterized, and still slightly bloody mess where your knee is supposed to be.

"Cat got your tongue and gotcha by the short 'airs, is that right? Sarah Oooooooooorange?" Mathias says, frightening you with his knowledge of exactly who you are.

The Ni-Perchta raises one hand, palm outward and towards you. It sparks like an electrical outlet on the fritz. There is a slight white glow around the periphery of her eyes.

Mathias takes out a long-barreled six shooter from an inside pocket of the old school army jacket he is wearing. "You see, girl, I could've burned you where you stood. I could've shot you from cover and sprayed the fried contents of that skull of yours six ways from Sunday. But I am not a dog. I do my thing straight up, you understand me? Me and Miss Jenny Petty here, we are upstanding people." He turns to his Ni-Perchta girlfriend, who watches you with a sort of ugly, earnest intensity, almost perversely sexual. "Keep 'er covered, lovely."

He walks up to you and actually gives you the six-gun. "I wouldn't try raisin' that shooter. Miss Jenny Petty here has an 'air trigger personality, you know that?" He backs away slowly, fifteen paces. Miss Jenny Petty looks very nervous now, like Mathias is doing something very unexpected.

"You've wasted a lot of our time, Sarah Oooooorange. Funny meeting you out 'ere." He takes out a cigarette from a tarnished silver case, snaps his fingers and a small flame seems to come out of his thumb. With this he lights the cigarette, takes a puff through the hole in his mask, and puts the case away.

"You know my name is Sarah..."

"Sarah, Sarah, Sarah..." Mathias grins.

"Oh. God," you croak out, tears filling your eyes. Your chest heaves up and down as you hyperventilate, and your whole body is sweating. Your hands feel so weak and the gun is too heavy.

The Ni-Perchta woman, Jenny, blinks quickly.

"I'm Charlie Mathias and this is Miss Jenny oh so Petty. Well, look, Sarah Orange, this is 'ow we are going to do this. I ain't a coward and I ain't one to give somebody no chance, alright? I challenge you, girl, for being in our road. So you've got that six-gun there—that's a Smith and Wesson New Model No. 3 I just gave you. A very particular one. The very particular gun that killed Jesse James. I figured if I get killed one day, which will probably be very soon considering what's happened to the rest of us, I'd like to go out with the same weapon, right? 'Cept I won't be stupid enough trying to dust off a picture and have some ponce shoot me in the back of me head, right? This is going to be an old fashioned, 'igh noon show down." Mathias clips his ori-baton back to his studded belt.

Then, moving at a horrifically fast speed, he draws the pistol strapped to his thigh and takes a shot at you, blasting out the driver side window with an explosion of glass that rains down onto the highway. You scream. In the same motion, he puts the gun back into its black leather holster.

"But you gotta be faster than that," he says, and tosses his cigarette away.

You start sobbing and then begging. "P-please, j-j-just let me g-go."

"I-I c-c-can't. Now on three. And on the three now, not on the two." He puffs out the last tobacco smoke as he speaks.

The Ni-Perchta woman looks now as if she is ready to say something, but can't.

"Oh, and..." Mathias draws again and shoots you in the right arm. The sound of the gun firing rolls like thunder. You drop your own gun onto the highway. A large ribbon of blood flows down your arm, but no pain, which makes your heart pound away in terror. You can smell the gunpowder and your own skin burning. "Left handed, too. Robert Ford shot ol' Jesse with his left, okay there?" He brays with laughter, sounding like a donkey. The Ni-Perchta girl looks absolutely shocked at his behavior, a part of your brain idly notices.

You are mentally screaming as you try to balance and pick up the gun, which starts to float up to your hand. Your mind has become a white slate with only pain running through it. Your life plays out like a silent film reel. You see everything up to this point and you think of the tarot cards, of waking up on the beach, Sargasso-3...

You grab the gun and manage to pull the hammer back with your thumb. You keep the barrel pointed to the ground.

"Alright, then, this one will be right between the eyes, so don't worry. One." You try to ready yourself to outdraw him and kill him first.

"Two." His fingers dance alongside his holster. "P-please," you say out loud, your eyes raised to the sky.

"Three!" Mathias draws and shoots you twice in the belly, dropping you to the ground. Hot lead perforates your sternum, giving you pain that is so intensely hot that you wish you were already dead. Gasping for air, you feel very, very cold. Realization washes over you. You are bleeding out. Dying. So far away from everyone and everything you love.

Petty walks towards you and you have time to wonder if she's going to shoot you, too. When she raises her baton, you close your eyes, positive that the end has come. But then, in the moment before your death you find yourself fully healed. Sick to your stomach, but healed.

Mathias kneels down and grabs his gun, jamming it back into its holster as you cough and hack. "You're lucky whose sister you are," he whispers. "You understand? You get me? This is a lesson, nothing more, nothing less. You spread the word to all your other parasite friends—especially the Network men. This is Not. Their. Planet. Don't go into the old cities. Don't bother the Ni-Perchta. Just leave." Mathias slaps you on your rear, hard. "What I just did was just a light spanking."

The two of them jump onto their cycles and drive off.

You stand up slowly, shakily, and then promptly collapse. You are still covered in your own blood. You stand and fall back down again. When you try again, your legs slip out from under you, so you rest your head against the car door, trying to slow your breathing.

While you rest, one of those skysurfers descend to the road. Stepping away from the machine is a woman—one you are not expecting to see at all. Saki, your office mate, takes off her motorcycle helmet and comes over with a confused smile on her face.

"Nani mo wakaranai," she says in Japanese. "Are you alright?" she asks in English, looking at the destruction of your car and your own bloodied state. She licks her lips, looking everywhere for some sign of threat.

You don't even know what to say at this point. "I want to go. Let's go back to the Mission," is all you manage to spit out. You have the presence of mind, though, to grab the money that Mathias and Petty didn't take. You also pick up your gun from the road.

"I'll take you to Mission Security." Saki leads you to what she calls a Tri-Skysurfer, which floats a couple of feet off the ground, the wind buffeting it to and fro. She takes a piece of blue-white orichalcum from a small box and stuffs it into a slot in the cylinder section of the surfer, you guess in order to power it up. "You good for this, Sarah?"

Saki seems to be more herself when she is explaining what the Tri-Skysurfer is—the windsurfer-like contraption with the cylinder, green wires, and pulsing light. It has three plastic windsurfer sails, two of the sails jutting out from the sides of the overly large surfboard, and a spring pogo stick contraption under the surfboard's bottom.

You both hop on and Saki ties herself to a leash that is connected to the main windsurfer sail, and then ties you to her. She hands you a black parachute case to put on.

You don't say a word for a while as Saki continues to nervously explain what she is doing.

"Why were you out here?" you finally ask.

"Nani?" she replies.

"Why were you..."

"Just skysurfing. It's our week off, you know? What were you doing out here?"

"Weekend stuff," you mutter as the wind blows your hair into your face. The surfboard section of the Tri-Skysurfer sinks lower to the ground with both your and Saki's weight on it, low enough for the pogo stick-like part to touch the ground. "I need to talk to the police."

"Hold on to me tight," Saki says and then jumps up and down on the surfboard, slamming the pogo stick part into the road. The Tri-Skysurfer then bounces high up into the air, soaring a hundred feet so quickly that your ears pop. You scream out loud as you shoot upwards. You swear you can feel the moisture of the clouds as you pass overhead; the air is a little thin. "Oh my," you say.

Saki leans forward and to the side, catching and playing with the air currents to move at a frightening pace. She uses the controls to flex and stretch the two side sails.

As you zoom through the air, you see a massive machine in the distance. Antediluvian of course, an old technological monster from a time no one remembers. It's an octopus-like thing with a slight white and green glow around its struts and girders. There are giant wheels and serrated blades stretching out from all sides, with flashing lights emanating from hundreds of control towers. It is literally eating the soil in all directions, barely moving but always moving forward. It leaves a deep, giant track of destroyed land in its wake for what seems to be tens of miles.

Smoke pours from multiple beams and the sound of rumbling and crunching is loud even at your far distance. It stands thirty stories high, at least. The blue and white Venn diagram is plastered all over the thing.

"Gulag machine. If you ever wonder why some Ni-Perchta don't like us people, that's reason number two hundred thirty-nine," Saki says very loudly, ending it with what you guess to be a Japanese curse.

She turns and zooms towards it. You are descending now, the Tri- Skysurfer rattling. Saki pulls a lever and brakes a little as the two side sails flip forward, slowing your speed. Ni-Perchta workers are sweating and toiling away at the soil below, looking for anything orichalcum, you suppose, an army of miners filling all sides of the machine, working away at the soil it has ripped through. They look half-dead, almost skeletal.

"There should be a Mission Security team..." At that moment a black Ford Mustang drops out of the sky in front of your Tri-Skysurfer, just missing you and Saki and hitting the side of the Gulag machine with a crunch and a bang that results in a fireball. An alarm sounds off in the distance, this shrill, annoying warble you can hear over the wind as you and Saki fly away from the mining machine. You catch a glimpse of the Ni-Perchta miners running in every direction.

You look over your shoulder to see the *S.B. Crue* floating over your head. You don't see who is in the wheelhouse, but someone just tried to drop a Ford Mustang on your head, and the Tri-Sky is being pulled towards the *S.B. Crue* by Tek as he aims a baton at you. There is a shotgun in his other hand. Two other Ni-Perchta, dressed in traditional cloaks and armed with what look like tridents or three-pronged spears, are with him. You hold on tightly and close your eyes as the Tri-Sky crashes into the deck of the ship with such force that it knocks the air out of you. When you try to get up, you realize that you are still stuck to the mast of the Tri-Sky, tied to it. Poor Saki has been knocked unconscious.

You already have your pistol out. As you squirm and try to get the damn leash off, you fire into the air, making Tek duck intuitively and fire off a shotgun blast that tears into one of the Tri-Sky sails. A trident is thrown in your direction, cutting the leash, and you instinctively crawl backwards as Tek raises his shotgun again. Before he can shoot you, you fire your pistol, hitting him square in the jaw and blowing his greenish-colored brains out. Tek's muscles jerk in a death spasm and he fires his gun into the Ni-Perchta next to him, shooting his companion in the chest and making him fall forward, dropping his spear.

You turn and quickly shoot the last Ni-Perchta, the one who threw his spear first. He rushes at you and jumps on top of you, trying to strangle you with his bare hands. You smell his breath and look right into his eyes as you shoot him three times, emptying your gun into his chest. Covered in his blood, you gasp for air as his hands stiffen at first, and then relax.

Rolling the body off, you stand up, ready to fall over, ready to heave. You slowly come to the realization that no one is flying the ship. Then something else hits you across the face like a wet slap—you are victorious yet again. You have survived the last few fights you have participated in. You laugh a little, then cry, and then try hard to cheer yourself up as you look over the dead bodies of the Ni-Perchta you have just defeated.

Saki is still unconscious.

You look out over the bloody deck of the *S.B. Crue* and say softly to yourself, "This has been quite the last forty-eight hours." You laugh.

In the wheelhouse, you study the controls—a steering wheel, a gas pedal on the floor, a simple looking radio set, and some sort of lever that you can push up and down.

Wiping some of the Ni-Perchta blood off your hands and onto your flight suit, you play with the controls a little, but you're afraid to really do anything with them.

When Saki moans, you call out to her. "Saki? Saki, are you awake? You okay, Saki?"

She stands up and mutters in Japanese. Then she takes off her helmet and surveys the utter carnage. She walks over to you, rubbing her face. "What happened?"

"Oh, I killed those Ni-Perchta that tried to drop a Ford on us. They pulled us on deck, knocked us out, blam, blam, here we are, and I'm the winner yet again." You smile crazily. "I'm the winner and you got to drive this thing back."

"Airship," Saki says. "I know this airship." She looks around. "I can drive this, I think. Oh God, this is the *S.B. Crue*?"

"Oh, I know, right?" you say, laughing a bit. "I swear this wasn't in the job description—maybe it was in yours. I didn't think we'd be doing something like this at all. Not in the slightest, but you know, you know, God opens one door after closing another and it's our time to shine!"

Saki tells you to get out of the driver's seat. As you do, you notice a set of keys hanging from a hook above the controls and grab them. You wonder what they open and jam then in your pocket, figuring they might come in handy. Saki takes the wheel and drives away.

Later she helps you throw the bodies overboard.

CHAPTER FOURTEEN:
THE NEW NORMAL

You and Saki manage to land the airship in a field somewhere to the southwest of the Benbow Inn. A gust of wind takes you a little off course and drives the ship into the ground a bit, ruining the rudder and making it tough for Saki to maintain control, but she figures out how to deflate the balloon. You end up leave the ship there in the middle of a green meadow like a discarded toy.

Saki mutters a lot of things in Japanese that you don't understand, making you a bit uncomfortable and worried. Your adrenaline is still providing energy.

You walk over to the dark and quiet Benbow, checking the outside of this old Ni-Perchta building turned into a semi-modern pub. You take out the keys you found hanging in the wheelhouse of the *Crue* and open the front doors of the inn.

During the journey you have been blurting out your entire story to Saki, who listens carefully and without judgment. You continue your tale in the Benbow. Saki simply pours herself a drink behind the counter and continues to listen intently.

You keep talking as you wash your face and the top part of your chest with a rag and then clean your hands over and over again with antibacterial soap.

Saki nods and listens, nods and listens, and then finally states, "You want to keep drinking?"

You put out your hands. "Why didn't you say something earlier?"

You look at the open front doors of the Benbow and decide to lock them. "Just in case." You also look around to reload your gun. When Saki isn't looking, your hand shakes terribly and your eyes begin to water.

You and Saki sit at the bar for a long time, unable to say much more. Saki gets more red- faced with every drink, her accent becoming thicker as time passes. It gets cold since you haven't lit a fire.

"I'm a nighthawk, too. For a living. Sometimes with the Tokyo Sex Whale girls. And someone else," Saki finally says, looking you over. "I've never had what happened to you happen to me. I would just go out on the Tri-Sky..."

"Oh," you say, sipping your beer. It's nearly empty so you head to the bar to refill it and find a bottle of Treena's pills just sitting there, practically begging to be taken. You slip them into your pocket, grab another beer and sit back down next to Saki. "Oh," you continue. "So it is a crazy ass story? Huh? Was it completely nuts? I got to tell you it's screwing with my head a little..."

Saki puts out a hand. "I don't think we should report it to Mission Security. Fuller and Marcelino play it by the book, but that Botha, he blackmails you something bad. The Bureau agent, Alexandros, I don't know him but I wouldn't trust him. Dee, the Mission Manager, is mentally retarded."

"Fuller and Marcelino are dead. I saw them out there, out on the yellow X highway," you say, and then start laughing again. "Dead as Dillinger!"

Saki's face grows long. "Wow."

"That's what I said! Shit!" You reach into your pocket to take out an orange prescription pill bottle that is in Treena's name you found on the bar's counter; you examine it for a long time.

Pills were always something that could get you past some of those feelings you'd had in the past; guilt, sadness, embarrassment, whatever it was, those little orange pill bottles you used to steal from your mother's medicine cabinet provided those tidy little treats that helped make something deeper than physical pain go away. Temporarily, of course. All too temporarily.

Pills were a guest of the house that couldn't stay long. You wish the bottle you have was full of the Vicodin your mother had on her, but you think it might just do, if used incorrectly. "Say, what happens when I crush one of these and snort it? Is it awesome?"

"You're able to concentrate better, feel high, then get jittery and crash something pretty awful," Saki tells you in a deadpan voice. You ignore her, and with your beer bottle, smash one of the pills onto the counter. You make it into a little line, and then snort it all at once with a plastic straw.

"Ohhhhhhh, booooy, that is college, my friend." Your mind surfs through that high. The rush allows you to start forgetting, for a moment, what has happened. You laugh a little too long, rubbing your nose constantly.

Saki rubs your shoulder. "I'm sorry about what happened. I've known people who have died out there. I knew that co-op."

"Barely knew 'em!" you muster out. "Barely knew 'em! Isn't that crazy? First time up to bat out there... And pfft! Do people actually die like that? Without warning? Without even a chance? Does that happen, Saki? I mean Guy Farson, he got it." You make a trigger pulling gesture to your head.

Saki looks crushed for a moment. "Guy Farson was out there, too? I thought he was..."

"Yes."

She holds a hand to her mouth. "I knew he'd end up like that one day. I didn't know so soon... I thought he wasn't going..." There's a long silence. To your surprise Saki tears up and stares off into space. She smells her own long black hair for a second and frowns, sobbing a little. "Unfortunate, unfortunate... Am I saying my rs and ls right?"

You nod.

"Unfortunately," she says with more confidence, and takes a deep breath. "Tomorrow, we have to go back to work."

You look shocked at this prospect. "What? What? We had seven days."

"It's been seven days, Sarah. Christmas off-time is gone."

You try to figure out how much time has passed. "No. I was—wait, it was Christmas. Holy shit. I say we call in."

Something bangs on the front doors of the Benbow. You take out your gun and Saki snaps out her ori-baton. A spark of electricity shoots out of its end.

"Let's go through the Nemo and get out," you whisper. "Let's go." Saki puts up a finger to her lips, telling you to shush.

"Open the damn door or I'll blow it open! I hear you in there!" Winniefreddie cries. "One, two, screw you!"

The doors open with a blast, revealing a dirty, disheveled, and angry Winniefreddie. She walks in with her ori-baton out, looking ready to hurt anyone in her way. "Oh it's you all. Was that a set-up, or what?" she says with a chuckle, and then collapses.

You watch as she changes back into that beautiful young girl in an oversized jumpsuit you thought you saw when you and the co-op were running away from the Snuffies in the temple.

Before you can figure out what to do with her, she wakes up and after clicking a button on a small ori-baton tied to her belt, changes back again.

"I like being this way and I'm lucky enough to pull it off," she says sheepishly. "Long story." She doesn't speak for a long time and neither you nor Saki press her. You light a fire in the fireplace and give her a blanket you found in one of the back rooms.

You do another line despite Saki telling you to stop it.

"Winniefreddie, this is Saki. She's the other SSR."

"We know each other. What a set-up, huh, what a goddamn set up. You know, I knew Guy since, like forever, and Treena, my sister, before that even..."

You snicker a little, but then shut up, horrified at yourself. Saki turns to you, wide- eyed. Winniefreddie looks a bit unhinged and unable to take in what just happened. Her eyes are always wide.

"Guy Farson and your sister were killed by Mathias and Petty."

"Guy Farson and my sister were really killed by Tek, too. I know that. Tek shot at me when I tried to get to the rendezvous. I thought it was you at first but I heard you guys through the windows..." What she says makes you wonder how long she was listening before you even knew she was there.

"The natives, you can't trust 'em at all. You can't. You just can't. You just can't. We should have just dropped napalm on their villages one by one, killed 'em all, cleared 'em out, then moved in," she says bitterly.

You think of the Ni-Perchta who saved you from that creature out there but do not speak of it, seeing the distress in Winniefreddie's puffy face.

"Mathias and Petty are like a political gang. It's not what the Network says they are, Sarah. They are not just, you know, toe cutters, they have a political edge to them. They want the settlers and the Network people to move on out." Winniefreddie starts to sob quietly.

"Mathias is human," Saki says after an eternity.

Winniefreddie rubs her red eyes before speaking. "Well, I guess he figures he's one of the enlightened ones. Unlike us. Us, you can just gun us down like nothing because we're exploiters..."

"They killed our Mission Counters," you say. "Blew 'em up. Had their weird tarot cards, those weird things, all over the scene."

"Botha?" Winniefreddie asks, hopefully. "Please tell me Botha ate it?" She sniffs.

"Nope, the young ones," you state with a sigh. "I want to go home."

"How'd you make it out, Sarah? I got to the Sargasso Free Zone and got a ride," Winniefreddie says. "I had to give a couple of hand jobs to get back here. Double barreled like Kristen Stewart in that movie."

You and Saki look at each other.

"Kidding! Just one hand job," Winniefreddie says, laughing a little, then sobbing deeply. "Nothing like that, actually. Nice people gave me a ride."

You go over and give her a hug.

"Tek set us up. You can't trust any of 'em anymore. Maybe this whole thing is going down. Maybe we all need to get off this planet. How'd you get out, Sarah?" she asks again, with a sort of weird intensity.

You fill her in as much as you can, omitting certain, important, things.

The three of you go through the Nemo Gate and get back into Mission Friendship, only to find that there is no one there except an inebriated Botha, who pulls out his ori-baton when you walk into the lobby. A rocket launcher, several ammunition magazines, and a pile of grenades are all neatly stacked up on your desk, where he sits, his dull red eyes following you as you walk to the elevators. He points the end of the baton at you as you walk by. A sniper rifle and another ori-baton filled with other orichalcum bits sits at Saki's desk.

"Nobody here but us chickens!" he says, nonsensically. The three of you watch him watch you until you're inside the elevator and the doors close.

When you get back to your apartment, you instinctively pile all the furniture against the front door. Since you are still hopped up on that Adderall shit, you take the first watch.

Winniefreddie leaves in the morning, going back to her apartment on the fourth floor.

The next day is a bitch. You and Saki both wear sunglasses, completely hung over and sickened by the adventure you have just been through.

The most disturbing thing to you both as you sit behind your computers is the overwhelming sense of normality at play. Dee makes a joke about you two having a "fun" Christmas. The Bureau agent, Alexandros, asks how your Christmas break was and talks about his kid, who you don't care about, for twenty minutes. You state in reply to Alexandros that you were shot multiple times and almost drowned in the Super Sargasso Sea before that. He laughs long and hard and pats your shoulder with one manicured hand. "Oh, you. What a jokester!" he says.

The miners and the managers and all the independents come and go out of their apartments as they please. You get phone calls about noise complaints from apartment 616, and you even talk about renewing an apartment lease for 212 without issue.

You leave and go to the bathroom every half hour to sneak a little line of Adderall, just to keep your energy up.

For lunch, you eat at Subway, being very polite to the Ni-Perchta girl behind the counter and explaining to her very slowly what you want on your sandwich as she doesn't know English that well. When she accidentally puts on provolone, you ignore it and let it go. "This." You take out a couple of Dii-Yaa bills. "This tip."

"No tit," she responds.

"No, *tip*. You keep. You keep tip." You hand her the bills.

"Oh-oh, okay. Okay."

Jittery and sick, you try to eat but barely get a mouthful down. The events of the last couple of days stick with you. You clench and unclench your fingers in nervous motions, which you watch with an almost clinical detachment, and hum the *Fresh Prince of Bel-Air* theme. Saki tells you that your lunch hour is up and that people can hear you singing. You ask her how she is doing and she simply says, "Not good."

NIGHTHAWKS AT THE MISSION

The day ends with someone complaining to you about a dog barking up on the sixth floor, which you dutifully note in the system. You and Saki clock out for the day only to hear Alexandros and Dee calling you to come into Dee's office.

You both wander in, too exhausted to think. Alexandros closes the door behind you.

"Guys, we just have to have a little meeting, a little strategy meeting," Dee says. "I've been informed by the Chief of Security, our Mr. Botha, that our two other Mission Security members, Robert and Tadeo, have been transferred to another Mission for the time being. For a time."

You and Saki say nothing about this, though Alexandros looks at you both very closely and seems to scrutinize your faces. He hasn't shaved for at least a couple of days, and his eyes have thick bags under them. Dee seems to be buying whatever Botha has told her.

"The Bureau will be sending over around forty of the Ni-Perchta security forces. The Witch-Lord will send an Ephor and his apprentice on over as well to coordinate with us," Alexandros says. "If anyone should ask, please inform them that these security forces are here to help rebuild part of the railway and not because of any general security concerns. Some people might think there is a security problem that's really not there at all. People easily panic," he says with confidence.

"Is there a security problem?" you ask.

Dee and Alexandros laugh at you. "No, no, of course not. It's very routine, you know. Helps the security forces get to know the area. To get the lay of the land, so to speak. No real security threat here whatsoever. We wouldn't want a panic and people shipping back to Earth," Dee says.

"What about Mathias and the lady, Petty?" Saki asks innocently.

Dee licks her lips compulsively. "What about them? They haven't been seen around here since, oh..."

Alexandros laughs so loud it makes you jump. "Mathias...he's long away from here."

"Well, guys, I don't want to hold up your evening at all," Dee says. "Please, please, enjoy. Get some rest after your time off. Looks like you two need it! All that partying, huh? God, I wish I was young and fit like you two."

You both say goodbye and leave the glass-enclosed office. As you wait by the elevators, you see that Ernesto and Te-La-Calles, the Ni-Perchta foreman, are replacing the glass in the offices with glass out of a box marked *Bulletproof.* Ernesto is cursing at Te-La-Calles in Spanish as the Ni-Perchta almost drops a glass sheet onto the tiled floor.

Alexandros takes out his gun and gives it to Dee, who puts it in her purse while looking around to see if anyone's spotted her doing so. You look away before they see you.

Upstairs, you take a long, hot shower and put on a fresh flight suit. You wait until about midnight before you venture upstairs, where the lobby is now swarming with Ni-Perchta security forces in traditional metal armor and cloaks. Armed with spears, bows and arrows, and rifles, they sit around the food court and the lobby as an armed camp, whispering to each other. You hide your gun in a side pocket and keep the ori-baton collapsed and in your right hand. The Ephor Dwelka Storma is there as well, sleeping on a cot set up in the lobby. His snores echo through the space.

A couple of Ni-Perchta walk over to you and you hold up a key. "Benbow, Benbow owner. Have to check, uh, beer levels. Beer. Beeeeer," you pronounce carefully.

One of the Ni-Perchta smirks and in perfect English replies, "Yeah, sure thing."

They wave you through.

You open the doors to the Benbow and step through the Nemo Gate into the abandoned bar. Looking around, you stalk out the front doors of the place and into the green countryside outside. The land is softly caressed by the light of two of the seven moons. The other moons have disappeared as they do during this part of the cycle, they say.

You walk to the idle *S.B. Crue* and climb on-board, listening for a moment before you climb the last rung of the metal ladder that leads to the deck. Your heart skips a beat as you hear an owl, or some other creature, cry out in the dark.

Taking out a flashlight, you walk over to the small compartment where you put the gym bag full of Dii-Yaa money, take it out slowly, drag it across the deck and unzip it.

"Well," you say, looking up at the stars. "Coming home soon enough." You laugh a little. "Goodbye stars, goodnight moon, I'll be home again so very sooooon..."

With the gym bag over your shoulder you climb back down the ladder and into the Benbow. "Goddamn planet," you mutter.

"Yeah, yeah, that's true," Winniefreddie says, revealing her true form as she steps out of the shadows. It's her of course, exactly her, but a fit and firm version of herself. "Yeah, that's really true. Wanna duel?" Winniefreddie says this so evenly, so nonchalantly.

She cracks her knuckles. "I'm serious, you wanna duel? You didn't tell me about that. You told me everything except that." She points to the money.

You don't know what to say at first, your mouth moving a little but no words coming out. "Look, Winnie, I had to drag all that crap through everything. I had to bring it out of the sea, walk it miles back, find Hamilton," you nervously explain. "I'm sorry, I didn't want to share. I was going to leave."

"I just lost my goddamn sister and you're going to tell me you had more work to do and you deserve the whole share?" Winniefreddie says quite simply, as if remarking on the weather. She then snaps her ori-baton out and extends it.

"Here. Here, I'm sorry, I just wanted to go back home with something. I wasn't thinking." You open the gym bag and pull out the money. "I'm sorry. I should have told you I got the cash."

A solemn look comes over Winniefreddie's face. "Think I'm stupid? You were probably in it with Tek as well."

Fear turns to anger. "If I was with Tek, why are you still here? I could have blown you away last night. Just like that. I could have ended—"

Winniefreddie interrupts. "Saki was there. You probably didn't want to chance it with her there. No more complications for you. I know what kind of girl you are." She takes off her glasses and puts them into her jacket pocket. "You're a simpering little bitch who doesn't have the guts to do all the shit work yourself."

You swallow, watching her intently.

"Do you know about duels out here? Did they tell you about that? Why did you think you could just waltz right past the security forces downstairs?" She smiles. "Just a bunch of dumb Winkies, huh?"

Fear has kick-started the adrenaline in your body. "They thought—"

"Oh, please. They're ignorant but they aren't stupid. I told the Ephor I wanted to duel with you and to let you come on in. I'm giving you something you didn't give Guy or Treena or me—a chance to fight back. Can you do that? I don't think you can."

You snap out your baton, not knowing really what to do next. Winniefreddie lifts her own baton and telekinetically snaps yours out of your hands.

"I'm not going to hurt you, Sarah. I really won't. Unless you accept the challenge. I'm fair. Unlike you. But if you don't accept the challenge, then that's fine. I'll just walk back and tell the Ephor and the Ni-Perchta. And you'll be branded a coward and an outlaw by their laws and be hunted down like an animal."

"Good god, fine," you croak out.

"Where do you want to do it then? Here? Inside Sargasso-3? Where do you want to die?"

"Let's get this over with. Here. Here and now. I want you to know I had nothing to do with—"

Winniefreddie picks up your ori-baton and throws it back to you. "It's on, then."

You snap out the baton. Winniefreddie watches you intently. With as quick a motion as you can possibly muster, you take out the pistol and fire three times. She rolls out of the way and from both of her hands shoot out these two white, snake-like, ugly and fearsome looking creatures about seven feet tall. They have black shark eyes and stand on two long legs with white, razor-sharp claws. You've never seen anything like this before—the creatures just appeared out of her hands. A psychotic magic trick? They rush at you with such speed.

You shoot at them but miss. You drop the gun onto the ground in a panic as you have no more bullets. You suddenly remember the strange ring that Hamilton gave you and press the rectangle on it.

The world grows silent and dim. The creatures keep rushing at you but you roll away from them. They cannot follow you now as your whole body has disappeared into invisibility. They look around, hissing and snapping their jaws.

Winniefreddie looks frightened and pulls out her own pistol. She fires twice into the air in front of her. "Where did that bitch go?" she spits out.

You take out your ori-baton and swing it like a baseball bat, not doing anything special, just slamming Winniefreddie in the face with it. She is knocked hard to the ground. You walk over to her and kick her twice in the face. "I didn't set up your sister! I didn't set up your sister! I didn't set up your sister!" you scream, kicking and kicking her. The snake creatures disappear into smoke.

You wrench her pistol out of her hand and fire twice into her, killing her instantly. The sounds of the world return to normal. You look around to see if anyone has come by or heard anything. The gun is hot to the touch now, still smoking, and you throw it on top of dead Winniefreddie.

No one comes in the still night. You are all by yourself under the stars, with a dead Winniefreddie. You feel numb and almost like you can see yourself outside of yourself.

You feel for your crucifix and then remember it's gone. You wonder if Winniefreddie deserved what happened to her and your conscience answers no.

You walk back into the Benbow, pour yourself a beer, drain it, pour another one, drain it, pour another one... The guilt stains you and you feel you can never wash it away.

You take out your ori-baton, and just like you saw Hamilton do for that doppelganger who attacked you out in the Sargasso, you do for Winniefreddie, except you dispose of her by telekinetically dragging her body hundreds of yards away from the Benbow itself and throwing her into the river. Using the ori-baton takes so much concentration to "feel" what you are picking up that it leaves you drained. After a short rest, you take all the cash from the gym bag and burn it in the Benbow's fireplace, telling yourself that the cash has an innocent person's blood staining every note. Winniefreddie did not have to die. You should have said something.

Around dawn you walk back into the Mission. The Ephor, Dwelka, is awake now and watches you with interest, unblinking as you wait next to the elevator. The Ni-Perchta that are awake cheer three times in succession. They beat their shields and chests in unison, again three times in succession. Storma walks over to you.

"Her death has been noted in our logs." He bows slightly, perfunctorily, and walks away.

With two hours of sleep and another rail of Adderall, you make it back into work. Saki looks better and more relaxed than yesterday and she takes most of the internal phone calls for the day.

The security forces hang about like the watchful sentries they are. They look at you at times and make comments amongst themselves, comments you can't begin to decipher, but you know they're about you. The Benbow stays closed all day, and some residents complain to you about it. The security forces make them a little nervous, too. "I'm sorry. I have to ask the owners of the Benbow," you state, but the residents just wish to complain and complain, it seems.

A lonely older man who describes himself as an ex-pilot and independent miner won't stop talking to you and Saki. He sits at your desk for a good hour. You immediately forget his name after he leaves—Jim or Tim something. He hangs around the lobby, blathering about politics, the weather, flash storms, ori-reactors, and other rambles.

That night you go up to the fifteenth floor, and wearing a complimentary swimsuit, do a few laps around the pool. Bern is there, naked of course, which makes it extremely uncomfortable at times.

Saki jumps into the pool and swims up to you in a sort of awkward dog paddle. Her hair is covered by a bathing cap. When she sees the concave ass of Bern getting out of the water, she wrinkles her nose and immediately turns to you. "So you talked to that Winniefreddie girl?"

"She shot herself last night. Her sister is dead."

Saki treads water next to you.

"Well! Can't take the heat, stay out of the oven, right?" she says sadly. You squint your eyes at her. "Yep."

"Sorry," she says. "You..."

You nod. "I told the Ephor, Storma."

She nods slowly. "There are so many screwed up things about living off-world." You both float in silence for a few moments before she continues the conversation. "So what will happen with the airship and the Benbow?"

The flash of memory reminding you that you just disposed of Winniefreddie outside the Benbow blows through your mind. "I don't..." You start to cry a little so you dunk your head under the water. "Wait, don't you care about what I just said to you? She's dead. She's dead and you just want to talk."

Saki stares at you. "I know."

"You used to do it by yourself? Salvage work?" you say, sniffling.

Saki shrugs. "Boring, though. And not enough money for it to be worthwhile. It was interesting at first. Sort of oddly su-sur—"

"Surreal?" you say.

She smiles. "I was going to say surprisingly screwed up, and peaceful, too. Depending on what building you hit up in Sargasso-3."

You and Saki get out of the pool and hit the hot tub after Bern leaves. You sit there in the tub for a long while, dozing off a little.

"Hey, you ever smoke marijuana cigarettes? Reefer?" She pronounces it "leefer."

"Reefer," you say back to her.

"Yeah, that's what I said."

"Yes." You blink a few times, about to pass out. "Yeah, yeah, that sounds great," you continue. "So tired." You both get out of the pool and dry off just enough that you won't be tracking water all over the place.

You stand in the elevator, eyes down, and hit the stop button. "She challenged me to a duel. She thought I was holding out money from her. Please don't tell anyone," you say, not looking at Saki.

"Did you?" she asks coolly.

You shake your head. "Damn fool thought I was but, I wasn't..." You compose yourself before continuing. "Ask the Ephor, it was a legal duel and she challenged me. Whatever a legal duel is, we did it. Goddamn girl."

"How do I know you're telling the truth?" she asks quietly. "That you weren't holding out money on her?"

You laugh. "You don't. But if I had the kind of money to fight a duel over, I'd be long gone from here, don't you think? Please don't tell anyone." You hit the floor button again.

Saki sighs. "All right. All right then. Winniefreddie is... was not thinking things through. What a world we live in."

"Please don't tell anyone," you beg.
Saki says she won't.
You beg a god you barely believe in anymore she doesn't.

Saki's apartment is decorated in a mixture of Japanese war flags, Bob Marley posters, and tatami mats. Pictures of Japan and Route 66 line one wall, making for an eclectic mosaic of photographs. There are tens of pictures of Saki in front of random American landmarks giving the peace sign. A couple of pictures of her and Guy, one with them kissing each other.

She's up on the fifth floor with a halfway decent view of the countryside and the nearby village of the Funeral Breaks. You can almost see the Benbow Inn, you think.

Back to wearing your flight suit, you wait on a soft leather couch until Saki comes out in a light kimono robe with a bong that's as big as she is. She's gone back to her normal self without a word.

"Sweet Jesus," you say.

Saki starts it up, ready to take the first hit. "Yoshi yaruzo!" she says.

You lean forward, smelling the herb burning, and take a hit. You immediately cough.

"Drugs. Drugs to forget." Saki nods. "Drugs to forget."

"I don't think I ever want to get out there again," you say, off-handedly.

Saki looks at you in confusion. "What do you mean?" She takes a hit so long and hard that her eyes turn red. "Whatcha mean, oh jelly bean?"

"There's a lot of death out there. You know? Past... out of...past the Mission. Death, death, and death. I want to get past all that."

"But out there, that's where the money is. So they say."

"You ever think that there should be a better way of living than this? Than just scrounging around to try to get a few bucks?" You hit the bong again, making yourself a bit cross-eyed. "What did you do? Lace this? Oh god..."

"No. This is it and we just have to deal with it," Saki says. "Death shouldn't be a bother so much. Everyone has to do it. That shouldn't hold you back."

"Why'd you come out here, Saki?"

Saki looks off to the side. "Money. In Japan there's no really poor people, but there's not a chance to really get rich either. You?"

You nod. "Trying to get money, too. In America there's a few rich and a lot of people who used to be middle class now becoming poorer. I want to get money."

Saki sits next to you on the couch. "Want to listen to the radio?"

You say yes, feeling absolutely swept away by the pot and by the nice swim in the Mission pool. Saki gets up again and flips on her old radio set. It's getting late, and she manages to find the Old Man at Midnight, who is playing a selection of newer stuff Radio Oberon won't play. Something smooth and mellow lifts itself out of the radio, filtering through the air and bouncing across the four walls of Saki's small apartment home. Her robe hikes up a little bit, showing one of her firm thighs. You even get a glimpse of one her breasts accidentally as she turns to the side.

"I'm really, really tired," you whisper. "I'm so tired of all of this. I would really like to go home."

"You don't have to go back downstairs right away." Saki misinterprets and gives you a hug. "You my new smoke out buddy!"

You stare into her deep brown eyes, getting lost for a moment, not feeling aware of your surroundings, feeling lost in that micro-sea of brown... Something stirs inside you. You want to be comforted, to be next to her and for some sort of desperate release. Your clothes feel overwarm and itchy. An instinct takes over as if you were with Tyler again.

You kiss her, deeply.

Saki looks shocked, frightened a little. "Nani?" You blink and draw away from her.

You walk out to her balcony, frightened yourself. Saki doesn't follow you or say anything for a good while. Breathing in the fresh air wakes you up a little bit.

Saki stands up, smoothing out her robe. "I think you better go."

You leave, thunderstruck at what just occurred.

Back in your basement apartment, you sit down on the couch, still trying to wrap your head around what happened upstairs with Saki. The guilt you feel for kissing her.

You don't think you have been more embarrassed and ashamed of yourself in your life, but kissing another woman makes you realize that anyone who would really have disapproved of it, or maybe would have mocked you for it, are all gone. Anyone who would ask any questions about your behavior is long gone. The void welcomes you.

Your father is dead. Your mother is dead to you. Your old neighbors and those people in school, they are long gone. Fact of the matter is, they are actually, in all seriousness, millions of miles away.

You lie down on the couch and pass out for at least an hour before you hear your phone ring. You pick it up, expecting Saki's voice. You even ask if it is Saki.

"No, this isn't Saki. This is Guy Farson. I'm here. At the Benbow."

You hang up, unsure.

You take your gun and your baton with you. On the elevator ride up, you fidget. Your palms sweat terribly. Your stomach tightens itself into knots. You tell yourself that this isn't something you've just hallucinated, this isn't just the residue of all the pills, the pot, and the booze you've plowed through. No, his voice was real. Guy Farson appears to be alive.

You exit the elevator and walk to the Benbow, opening its doors slowly, scanning every corner with your gun out. You walk through the Nemo Gate and appear inside a warm Benbow Inn. Guy Farson stands behind the counter and Treena Page sits on the other side.

"Well, here we are," Guy says, putting a toothpick into his mouth. "You want to take a seat for a second?" Both of them are drinking Tokyo Sex Whale. Both are alive and healthy looking.

"Where's Winniefreddie?" Guy asks. "Did she get out?"

"She didn't make it," you respond. "She..." You shrug your shoulders. You can't continue.

Treena blows out her breath. A tear rolls down her cheek and she walks away from the bar without another word and sits down at an empty table behind you.

"Did you get out with the stuff?" Guy asks.

"Halfway. Mathias and Petty stole the money," you answer back. You scan both of their features. They have on the same jumpsuits as that fateful night—bloody, muddy, and torn in places. "How?" you ask. You look at both of them. "How are you still alive?"

"A Ni-Perchta hunting party. They were, uh, hunting a Gug in the area," Treena turns back to you and says with a sniffle.

"Kept us alive. Healed Treena in ten minutes, took me three days with the damn arrow piece. They just kept doing different things—over three days and three nights." Guy rubs his nose. "Those Ni-Perchta...I don't get it, some are real barbarians, some are gentlemen. They need to put signs around their necks so we can determine that a bit easier."

Guy drinks some more. "Goddamn Tek. Talk about needing a sign."

"Goddamn natives," Treena says. "Can't trust 'em at all. Well, most of 'em, not like the hunting party ones..."

Saki enters through the Nemo Gate behind you, dressed in a Network-issued flight suit.

"Saki-san," Guy says with a wry grin.

"She's, she's my..." you start to say. Saki looks at you in mute surprise.

"Co-worker, I know. Biggest stoner this side of Jamaica, that I know of. And my long time girl..."

Saki looks at him for a long time, checking to see if he is all right. They kiss deeply, almost making out in front of you. Guy looks at you for a moment, as if feeling guilty. He tells her he is okay.

"You both smell like weed. Did she see that bong that's the size of my dick?" Guy asks crudely.

"Hai. You guys need anything?"

"Just money, and all the pain pills you got. You know we spent our last dollar just getting the airship fueled?" Treena says with a harsh laugh. "New sister, too. I'll kill whoever killed...Whichever one did it, I'll nail their ass to the wall. I'll obliterate them and their effing families, and I won't stop until the bastard drowns in their own blood. I won't stop and I'll just keep coming and coming until they are dead." Treena throws a bottle against the wall, shattering it into a million pieces.

"You're goddamn right! We should hunt whoever it is and just execute them then and there! Kill 'em all!" you scream. "Kill 'em all!"

A long silence follows your outburst.

"Okay, okay," Guy says, putting his hand on your elbow. "All quiet now."

CHAPTER FIFTEEN:
SHOWDOWN AT MISSION FRIENDSHIP (THE NEW NORMAL, PART TWO)

Guy and Treena keep to themselves at the Benbow, the doors open, the place up and running. The next day you help them put a cover over the airship. What happened at the temple is too much for any one of you, and it'll take a while for you to get back out there and nighthawk.

For the next two weeks, Saki and you go to work as always, trying to make the settlers happy and keep Mission Friendship operating. Ernesto, the maintenance supervisor, invites the two of you for drinks over at the maintenance shop—ice-cold Coronas—during lunch, which you share with the other Mexican workers and the Ni-Perchta helpers on the rooftop of the Mission. You realize at this point that you have sunk into a sort of daily and understandable routine. No one talks about the temple and Sargasso-3.

At night you meet with Saki at her apartment with what's left of the Tokyo Sex Whale co-op, and jointly smoke out of that monster bong. She seems to be ignoring what happened that one night when you kissed her. You enjoy the relaxation the green brings you; it's a bit different from the Adderall shit you pop. Guy sleeps at Saki's apartment all the time.

One night you listen to the album *Nighthawks at the Diner* at high volume until you fall asleep on a balcony chair. Guy brought the vinyl over. With the pot, the cool night air, and Tom Waits rambling over a jazzy set, you are relaxed.

Papers are drawn making you an official member of the co-op, which you present to Jake Alexandros, the Bureau agent. He accepts them without a word, though you sense an odd hostility. Dee takes you into the office and speaks on behalf of The Network by stating that she hopes that you signing on with a co-op does not distract in any way from your duties at the Mission and that you do not work directly in "that place," meaning the Benbow.

Tim, the lonely ex-pilot and independent miner who now constantly talks your ear off, says that Mathias and Petty are still heard to be lurking out there. Supposedly they killed a co-op of five near the boat quays four nights before. He says he feels better with the security forces surrounding the Mission at night. "They're a bunch of kooks, that Mathias and Petty. You don't know where they are or where they can hit you. I don't know why the Network just doesn't stomp them out." He lights his second cigarette after putting the first one out in a Styrofoam cup.

You nod and say nothing. Then, much to your disbelief, in walks Charles Mathias. Someone you never wanted—or expected—to see again. You hit a small red button on your desk, setting off a blaring fire alarm that pierces your ears. Saki stands up and looks at you in desperation. Security rushes into the lobby, their inexperience and confusion showing. These are not professional soldiers.

Mathias waves to you as he snaps out his ori-baton. "I'm sorry, Miss Orange, would there be an Ephor by the name of Dwelka Storma here?" he says through his evil half-mask. This time the mask is black instead of red, though still with those off-putting yellow jaws.

Botha walks out of a side office with his gun drawn, only to have it telekinetically ripped out of his hands and thrown onto the floor in a crunch. Alexandros and Dee watch from their offices, seemingly petrified.

"Dwelka Storma, step on down! I challenge you!" Mathias yells over the sirens. He points his baton at your desk, telekinetically picks it up and slams it against a siren light, knocking out the alarm system.

Storma walks out, a walking tank of a Ni-Perchta man in his ridged and black armor. He snaps out his staff.

"I challenge you to a duel! You and your best men!" Mathias shouts again.

Storma nods. Three Ni-Perchta, including his apprentice in similar black and ridged body armor, step out into the large lobby. The few residents caught in the lobby rush to the elevator.

Tim, your talkative friend, doesn't make it in time and just stands there, caught up in the middle of everything and punching the elevator button over and over again.

"You have wronged me by simply existing! I invoke the custom of the duel right here, right now, and I challenge the four of you!" Mathias repeats it in Perchta, in case anyone cannot understand.

Storma tilts his head and takes out his sword. "Challenge accepted."

Mathias draws his pistol just a second afterwards, emptying a clip into one of the four Ni- Perchta who stand in front of him, making him fly backwards and down the hall. The first to die is the Ephor's apprentice. He still has his sword in one hand. He dies leaving a bloody trail, eyes still open.

One of the other Ni-Perchta, a short one in a blue Army surplus uniform, instead of the usual armor and cloak look, fires his submachine gun, pouring out gunfire in a quick mean burst that thumps the air. The shots bounce off some sort of energy shield Mathias has around him and he retaliates by shooting a burst of red flames into the gun, making it explode in a series of pops as if a group of firecrackers have been set off inside the magazine. The explosion kills the Ni-Perchta.

Without even focusing on them, Mathias forces the other two Ni-Perchta to slam into each other so hard that you are sure you can hear their ribs and skulls break from the impact.

Suddenly, Storma transforms into this eight foot tall, whiter-than-white version of the creature that attacked you down by the temple, complete with the two forearms on each arm and the zipper-like mouth. You can hear his bones pop as he changes, his skin stretching to make this new thing. The Storma creature jumps at Mathias with a frightening slash of one of his arms, a slash that crackles with static electricity. Mathias is knocked to the floor once, twice, three times, his personal energy shield flashing orange. He desperately draws his other gun, and fanning the hammer back, shoots into the creature multiple times with some oddly powerful rounds that explode like cannon fire, dropping Dwelka to the floor. The creature stands up again quickly, bleeding white blood but not slowing for a moment. Then, all at once, the wounds explode with powerful detonations that continue to pop for a good minute, reducing the creature to ragged ruin.

Dwelka slowly transforms to his original shape and lies dying on the floor, his chest and arms shredded.

The smell of gunfire fills the entire lobby as well as that awful burnt pork-like smell of charred bodies.

Mathias's half-mask is cracked and hangs off his face. He adjusts it slowly, as if in pain.

The other Ni-Perchta stand there in groups, not moving, not saying anything.

"Hello again, Sarah." Mathias's eyes shift from a deep green to blue.

Tim, who is standing there in absolute silence and shock, watches as Mathias takes a single cigarette out from the pack sticking out of Tim's jumpsuit pocket, and then lights it by snapping his fingers together to produce a flame—no lighter is needed since he is holding his ori-baton in his other hand.

"Cheers. I won't see you, or you, or you around, right?" He points to several Ni-Perchta. "Sarah, I should really..." Mathias claps once. "I should really smack you down, but you know why that's not happening."

He heads for the front doors, then turns. "I see any of you pigs still scurrying about, I'll burn the whole Mission down around your ears."

The elevator door finally opens, and Tim rushes inside.

"Somebody...somebody call the medics and get out the equipment! Now!" Jake Alexandros yells, stepping out of his office in a panic. Wellington, the doctor you met earlier, rushes out from his office with a couple of ori-batons covered in several blue-orange orichalcum stones. He starts the healing process on the nearest dead Ni-Perchta—Storma. With green flecks coming out of the end of the baton, life returns to the Ephor.

Saki grabs the other baton from him without a word and starts to revive Storma's apprentices. With white flashes of light coming from both sets of their eyes, they come slowly back to life, coughing and jerking.

Without warning, Mathias returns, holding a small device that spins in his hand like a top. "No healing today, folks, sorry!"

He tosses the spinning top into the high vaulted ceiling of the lobby. The thing blows and creates an incredibly thick cloud of choking purple gas and ash. Your lungs burn and your eyes water something terrible. The apprentice who was being healed drops back dead to the floor. Storma, however, makes it out of there with Wellington's help. You rush over, too, and all three of you enter the Nemo Gate back into the Benbow.

Minutes later, after the gas has cleared, you return to the lobby to see the exodus. Jake Alexandros looks too stunned to try to pull back the crowds of people who are getting into their vehicles. By nightfall, you and Saki count that half of the residential apartments are now empty.

"The damn security forces just stood there!" one of the residents yells as he walks through the lobby.

"What the hell is the Network doing?" cries another. "The Winkies don't care if you live or die. It's time to go! The portal is only open for another week."

"You know that the Ni-Perchta security cops could've swarmed him," the usually naked Bern, clothed now, complains. "But they didn't."

"Not their way of doing things. It was a duel," Saki says.

"Well, you know, sometimes cultures need to grow the hell up," Bern says. "I'll be in the pool."

Hastily stuffed suitcases and crying children are being led out in constant droves. More Ni-Perchta security forces arrive by dusk but it seems useless. Bern, and surprisingly Tim, state that they are in for the long haul. "No cheap ass cockney son of a bitch is going to make me move, no sir," Tim says strongly, though his hand shakes every time he takes a puff on his cigarette.

At five o'clock, you stand with Saki in Dee's office and realize that her desk is cleared out and the framed picture of her kid is gone.

"She took off," you say.

Saki rolls her eyes. "Wow."

There is a note on Dee's desk. It reads: "This place is done. You should leave, too. Dee."

Jake arrives and snatches the note. "Ignore that. There will be no evacuation." You and Saki shout questions after him but he leaves you to shout orders at the Ni-Perchta scattered around the lobby.

Ephor Storma walks towards your office. "The men will stay here to protect the Mission, but I am no longer in charge of them. I lost that right when I lost the duel to Mathias. There is a security forces lieutenant." He points out a single Ni-Perchta, skinny, very young and very weak-looking in an Army surplus uniform dyed blue. "He is in charge of our fellows here." To your astonishment, Storma takes off his body armor and leaves it in a clump on the floor.

More and more Ni-Perchta security forces show up during the next day and fortify the Mission as well as they can, dragging sandbags into the lobby.

Storma walks out in his tunic, pausing in the doorway to stare at the sky for a long moment.

"And so Moses walked the desert for forty days and forty nights, exiled by Pharaoh... Banished from his people..." you say in an oddly deep voice. Saki looks at you in wonder.

"Sorry. I did a couple rails of Adderall while this was all blowing over..."

Botha arrives back in the lobby in full body armor and loading an M-16. He orders Ernesto and the maintenance crew to bring in fans to blow out some of the lingering tear gas. Ernesto asks if you are okay. You tell him, yes, yes you are, and ask if he is going to stay.

"Wherever you go, it's something nowadays," Ernesto says. "Always, you know, something. You can go to the World Trade Center in New York back in 2001 and that was the safest place in the world—until September 11th. You can go to this place I used to go to—this shopping center in Seal Beach, California."

"I didn't know you lived around the Long Beach area." You wonder why so many people like you are all from the same part of California. The odds have to be ridiculous.

"Sí. You remember Seal Beach, right? The hair salon that got shot up?" You do.

"Crazy guy just bam, bam, bam, shot it up, killed a bunch of women. No place is safe. Life ain't safe," Ernesto says. "People are crazy everywhere..."

You and Saki don't show up for work the next day and Jake and Botha don't even bother to call you on it. You spend the day at the Benbow, talking things over with Guy and Treena.

"Are we leaving?" Saki asks Guy.

He walks over to his small humidor case made out of cherry wood. After taking out a cigar and lighting it with his ori-baton, he shakes his head. "Less people, more opportunity. More opportunity for all of us. Sargasso-3 is going to be wide open at night now. People are afraid just to go out during the daytime."

The Inn, surprisingly, is doing well—those who have decided to stick out it despite Mathias's attack are now drinking their anxieties away.

"Best thing to happen to the Benbow," Treena says. "So much money it's not even funny." She holds up the extra Dii-Yaa. "Too bad about Winniefreddie not being around for this." She bites her lip.

The new normal continues right up until the portal's official closing date. The toughest who have stayed living at the Mission seem simply resigned to the closure of the only way back to Earth. They still follow their daily routines, heading to their independent mines and the few salvaging jobs left, albeit under the armed guard of the security forces. Mission Security long-range patrols go out as well, their old, European-style police car sirens echoing in the night. Mathias' and Petty's gang disappear back into rumor and innuendo, though no one feels truly safe.

You give your official two weeks resignation notice to Botha, who is the last true Network representative onsite, besides Ernesto and Saki. As the Benbow has picked up business enough to warrant your presence, you leave the Network.

You move into Saki's apartment as a roommate, crashing on the couch as Guy stays over many nights. You hear them through the wall at night and cover your ears with your pillow.

The Mission starts to suffer. There is no food court operating anymore; Subway and McDonald's have been boarded up. The security forces make the lobby seem more like a military barracks. The pool has turned a disturbing green color, though the hot tub is still functioning. The gym has been turned into a room for the security forces to sleep in.

Ernesto and the other maintenance crew members barely show up to do their jobs anymore and respond with open contempt to those around them, especially the more mouthy residents of the Mission tower. Payment from the Network comes erratically, if at all. You and Saki used to be paid every day, now for Saki it's every other day, or once a week. Oddly, you get paid daily until your last day.

You tend the bar at the Benbow. You still wear your old Network flight suit but you've ripped off the Network logo and replaced it with a logo you made yourself. It states *S.B. Crue* and has that seal skull design of the downed airship.

At night you smoke cigars on the patio of the Benbow Inn with Guy and Saki and discuss all sorts of things. Guy tends to become the philosopher after the third beer of the night. You discuss matters such as communism, Las Vegas, gay rights, and whether or not advanced aliens would invade à la *Independence Day* by bombing the shit out of everything or like *V: the Mini Series* where they would slowly take over.

One night, as it gets cooler out, Guy, you, and Saki watch as a flight of Spitfires— maybe sixteen of those old World War Two planes—pass through the night. Their engines boom across the fields, and their silhouettes are obvious in the moonlit sky.

"Spitfires," Guy says. "Hunting illegal airships. They'll blow up illegal salvagers at night-time but they won't fly out to protect regular people in the daytime. Funny world, huh? Shows the Network's priorities. They could just...I don't know."

He nods over at the yellow Karmann Ghia. A week ago, with one last and very dangerous run of the *S.B. Crue*, you picked the car up and have since worked with Guy to repair it. It's the first time you've ever worked on a car before, and Guy is very patient with you, despite you almost dropping the car on his head once when you were not paying attention.

"The Old Man at Midnight ever mention his car?" Saki smokes a joint and blows out rings of smoke.

You shrug as Treena comes out with her own beer. "Wrote a letter about it. I guess it's mine for the moment," you say. You received a letter from a Ni-Perchta messenger a few days ago from Hamilton. He said you can keep the car until he needed it again.

A bug zaps itself on a green electrical bug zapper next to Guy's head. "Hmmmm..." Guy says.

"Hmmm what?"

He shrugs. "Just saying hmmmm. Wanna go nighthawking again, girls? It'd be fun and interesting."

Before you get a chance to even answer, Treena shakes her head over and over. "I'm not leaving here for all the tea in Asia, Guy. I am not. The chances of dying out there I figure to be exponentially high."

He blows out a smoke ring from a cigar he's just lit. "Exponentially high? How do you figure that? It's not like you can just google something like that, you know. Not here, not ever. Puh-leaze, Treena."

She blinks a few times. "I'd rather not. I have a general feeling of dying horrifically out there. Like a dog. Toe cutters, wild animals, Gugs, unknown traps—why we ever did it in the first place is ridiculous in retrospect. Short-sighted."

You sort of nod. "I agree."

Guy raises his hands. "So no one is going. We have a golden opportunity to grab some low hanging fruit here and you guys...I mean, most of the legitimate people took off. No one's heard from Mathias and Petty since the lobby thing. We won't be able to drag a lot away, though. With the *S.B. Crue*'s rudder being screwed up we burn through a thousand dollars' worth of fuel every flying hour. But by car we can grab that, you know, low hanging—"

"No, no, I said I agree with Treena. I do, about dying like a dog. But I'll go out there, Guy."

He puts out a hand for a high five. "Okay, then! I don't like your suicidal impulse at all, but that's better than... Who else can we rope in? Saki?"

"We can't do any major runs. The *S.B. Crue* is too expensive to operate, with the fuel and the repairs, so it's going to be so boring." Saki wrinkles her nose. "I am not down."

"Can you just go out with us a little so I can train newbie here?" Guy nods at you. "Please?" He turns to you. "We never really got you up and running."

Treena rolls her eyes. "Have fun with a gruesome death. I have no plans to go out there to that desolation ever again."

With your Tokyo Sex Whale jumpsuit, elbow and knee pads on and your ori-baton outfitted with several different types of ori, you take a little trip out to Sargasso-3. Your group has taken the yellow Karmann Ghia out for a spin, filling it up at a late night Ni-Perchta-run petrol station. It's the best car for gas mileage, and considering that, off- world, gas is basically twelve dollars a liter, this is a good deal. Guy smokes a cigar the whole way, making you a little ill. You are stuck in the back, and Saki is driving.

"You don't know anything about orichalcum, do you? Just a guess," Guy says, as you head down the yellow X highway at a very high speed. "That's a dangerous thing not to know out here in the wastes. Very dangerous. I'll teach you what I know, as if you are a child."

You nod, a little annoyed. "I just try to think of what I know from TV and movies."

"Saki, stop the car," Guy tells her. He turns around in his seat. "Get out." You both climb out. Saki puts her seat back and throws the radio on. She brings a book—Stephen King's *The Stand* in Japanese—out from the glove compartment and flips to a random page. She straps a miner's flashlight to her head so she can read easily.

"What's she doing?" you ask, looking back as you put on a helmet.

"Just in case we have to get out fast for any reason," Guy says. "Come on, we got a little bit of a walk to do. Saki?" He turns back to her. "Three honks for trouble, okay, honey?"

Saki gets angry. "I am reading now! Yes, thank you! I haven't had a chance to read outside in a long time..."

"Read outside?" you ask.

Guy shrugs. "Saki's a little strange." He and Saki kiss, making you feel odd and queasy.

Saki slaps Guy hard on the cheek and revs the engine. "One hit of the gas and I leave your ass!"

Two minutes into your walk, Guy speaks again in low tones. "You know, I thought of it, visualized, pondered it, and here you are—the product of the universe and my thoughts. I always wanted to be around a smart, tough girl with a sort of minor superpower."

You are unsure of what to say to that. "Oh well, that's cool," you finally say, and jump over a pothole the size of a dinner table. Neon lights on an ancient building across the street flash and fizzle with sparks.

It is quiet again, your shoes crunching along the broken street. You pass by six decaying bodies laid out by a rusting old pickup truck and an old Volkswagen Bug. The Bug has been spray painted with an M and a P. Nailed to the side of the pickup, you count thirteen of those tarot cards with the man and the Ni-Perchta woman chained to the Devil. "Lightning doesn't strike twice in the same spot," Guy says.

"This wasn't lightning."

Guy points to what used to be an open-air bathing place. Broken benches and an overflowing pool easily the size of a lake are all that is of left of the grand complex. A broken holographic display plays advertisements, including images of nearly nude men and women frolicking under the sun, being served by others with gray skin who wear odd, Greek chorus-like masks. There are also black robotic things scurrying back and forth, serving the people.

"See that?" Guy asks. "Depraved and decadent and overall messed up reminder of the past. Men and women together like that. A sick civilization used to live in these cities—at first human but then vampire. The Antediluvian people lived here in Sargasso-3—just as evil as the people before the flood were. They were wiped out by a metaphorical flood before the time of Christ; some think nuclear or biological or both. There's an awful lot of radioactive bullshit around.

"According to this professor I once heard talk, they gave up the worship of the original High Three Gods—Ak, Kern, and Bo—for what you saw earlier, that bearded face creature—the Storm King—and became, well, evil, making themselves semi-immortal, enslaving the Ni-Perchta, manipulating their bodies and drinking Ni-Perchta and human blood to keep their lives going and going. You ever hear of Bevan's disease?"

You know what it is but ask for an additional explanation anyway. "There are three types. Type three Bevan's—this disease is actually what the ancients did to themselves on purpose in order to extend their lives. It's human-made. You can live forever if you are lucky enough to grab it. But the poor type ones or twos die quickly or become insane. No one knows why so few are lucky. They don't talk about that on Earth, do they?" Guy's face turns hard.

"No, no, they don't."

"All the type threes have to do is just drink a blood pack once a week. No big deal. Just guzzle three quarts—it's so gross when you think about it now. But if you get type three, you can live forever and stay young just by drinking blood packs."

He keeps going. "Type twos die feral and insane in three weeks, usually chewing their fingers off before they die. Type ones just drop dead—splat. So don't take the mummy lottery—if you get bit, you'll more than likely die horribly."

"Are we sure Saki is okay?" you ask, looking back at the Karmann Ghia.

"I asked her three times if she was cool with this. She's just Saki. That's all. She zigs when you think she is going to zag," Guy says. "I know, right? Her staying in the car? But she likes to be out here sometimes, even at night."

"You see something else there, poolside?" Guy points out another thing, changing the subject. It's a giant U shape that has been spray painted in white on the side of a broken marble wall. Under it is a glowing and vibrating machine—perhaps a vending machine at one time. A picture of the Milky Way plays across the side of it. There is another painted symbol under the giant U shape—two straight lines separated by a squiggly line. "A nighthawk sign. Says it's safe to camp here but don't drink the water. We can set up camp, based on a stranger's spray paint. Isn't that interesting?"

You study the marks, remembering that you've seen one like that before on the bridge your first night at the Mission.

Guy walks forward through the pool complex and stands next to a modern plastic lawn chair. There's a makeshift fire pit full of dead black coals.

"Our little camp." Guy takes off his visored helmet and tosses it onto the lawn chair. He snaps out his ori-baton, smiles and lifts you up off the ground telekinetically with the baton. You float in the air like a mote of dust, your heart beating quickly. You keep going higher and higher and higher to the point that you are nearly three hundred feet up until he finally lowers you. You're feeling queasy and ready to throw up. "Sorry, the look on your face..."

You kick him straight in the balls; he drops to his knees.

"Oh, come on. Some, some goddamn levity. Shit." He tosses you his baton. "Heal my balls." He holds himself, bending at the waist and trying to suck in air. You shake your head as you use your baton to heal Guy's you-know-what's.

"Look, I also did that for a point. This isn't a game out here, Missy! You need to know how to use it at least to a point of some proficiency. Or else someone's going to just pick you up like that and drop you off the side of one of these very tall buildings."

He straightens up. "I should have trained you properly from the get go. I don't know if it would have helped you by the temple. But it may have made you a little more comfortable. Sorry, schoolgirl. That was my mistake."

He shows you his baton. "See this? Typical orichalcum baton, usually made in Singapore. Usually covered in metal. It's got a little battery inside like a wristwatch. That's all the charge you need."

You nod, biting your tongue. You already knew this.

"I have a good amount on mine. Here, look, the Network cut up the stones like zodiac signs. See, Leo, for telekinesis." He points to the stone shaped like a snake. "Sagittarius, for fire control." One long finger points to an arrow-shaped stone. "Libra, electrical control. Aquarius for healing, and Cancer—which I don't have here—for random transformation of the body and for shapeshifting. That type of stone, the shapeshifting, is expensive and very hard to use. The only one who could do that day in and day out was Winniefreddie. You have to have a weird focus for this stuff."

You nod.

"You have two—the Leo and the Sagittarius—those are good standard orichalcum to start with, the most basic and most useful, most common outside the mines. Now to me they all look like blue stones." He grabs your baton and looks at the stones embedded into it. "But they don't to you, do they?"

You shake your head. "Leo is actually blue and whitish, the other is a bluish-yellow. To me."

He nods and steps to the side. "I want you to spray out a jet of flame, a gust of it, straight ahead. Feel the power inside that baton and think of heat."

You put out the ori-baton strapped to your belt and think of a great flame. A little spark comes out of your hand, just a little ball of flame that shoots into the water of the overflowing pool.

Guy shakes his head. "No, not like that. Here, let me show you."

Part of you suddenly becomes enraged. Perhaps it is frustration; perhaps it is just the journey so far. For a moment you think of torching Mathias, that laughing murderer who tortured you by the Ghia.

A jet of flame as powerful as something from a flamethrower comes out of your hand and goes spraying across the water in a sixty-foot arc. The flames reflect off the stillness of the green water. Guy jumps back.

"Like that?" you say. "I said I could be good with this stuff." A little bit of flame still dances at the end of your fingers, but not hurting you in any way, and you blow it out. Part of your mind whispers, *Beginner's luck*, making you feel small once again.

Guy claps his hands, the sound echoing throughout the empty pool area. "Very good. What about the other? Telekinesis? Can you work with that in the same way as you did the flames? I've seen people working with orichalcum for five years—ex-Green Berets, SAS—who couldn't pull off that little trick."

He points to a fallen girder that straddles the overflowing pool area. "Pick it up. Try to imagine the texture of that girder, its roughness, its absolute weight, and focus."

You stare at your sneakers, trying to focus. "Give me a moment. Never something that, you know..."

Guy claps his hands together quickly. "In real life you don't have a goddamn moment! Just do it, ya dumb bitch!"

His outburst startles you but you point the ori-baton, telekinetically reaching out to touch the girder. You try to use the same focus you did last time. In five seconds, you lift a steel girder that probably weighs two thousand pounds and is fifty yards long off the ground. "What do you think?"

Guy stares. "Sorry to get crazy there. You know my point."

You feel the girder, actually *feel* it in your own mind, really exploring its rough texture and rusted-over parts. Then you throw it right into the holographic display of the old ancient world, shattering the sickening replay of the men and women and those poor slaves in those hideous masks. The girder sticks into the middle of the holographic display panel, and a few sparks shoot out the side.

Guy zips up his jumpsuit a little. "It's getting cool out." It is, too—the clouds are thick and ghostly, hovering overhead in the moonlight. It seems possible a night-time rainstorm is coming through. He stares at the girder now stuck inside the building. The display is emitting a torrential rain of sparks.

For the next few hours, you practice what you can with Guy. He gives you tips on how to focus as he attempts to distract you at the same time, shooting his bolt-action gun into the air or crumbling a part of the complex onto itself so all you can hear are falling buildings. He tosses you up and down into the air in the most ridiculous goddamn ways in order to throw off your thought process. You can command fire and you can telekinetically lift and throw things—including Guy at one point.

You are a natural, you come to believe—a sort of freak.

NIGHTHAWKS AT THE MISSION

Before you know it, it is getting lighter out, and Guy calls out time just as you are moving a vending machine and throwing it a hundred yards into the pool area where it explodes with a bang.

You return to the Karmann Ghia to find a sleeping Saki. Then she pulls out a pistol without opening her eyes and points it in your general direction. "Gotcha," she says.

"Just drive us on home, girl. Please. And thanks for waiting," Guy says.

A few nights later it's just you and Guy doing a nighthawk run. Saki has work, of course, and can't be out gallivanting around the dead city of Sargasso-3 like you and Guy can. She says it's boring, which you know is definitely not true, at least for you. Treena says she wants to stay at the Benbow.

You take a leisurely route to the east of the super-sized city, passing a Mission Security car that immediately pulls you over to the side of the road with a flashing of its blue and red lights. A harsh, cold wind blows out from over the grasslands, chilling you and Guy as he rolls down the window of the Ghia.

You are greeted by a flashlight in your eyes. "No flying the *S.B. Crue* today, Guy?" the young officer asks. He's got a similar uniform to Botha but it looks more rugged and lived in. Oddly, the other officer is looking up at the moons or the stars, ignoring you.

"Nah, just a midnight drive." Guy takes out his wallet and gives the long range patrol man fourteen hundred Dii-Yaa. The Mission Security man winks at you. "Thanks for the donation to our Widows and Orphans Fund."

The Counter leans into the car. "No one has heard anything about Mathias and Petty out here in a long time; be careful though." He then slaps the car's roof. "Alright, have a better one!"

Guy puts the Ghia in gear and floors it. "This little piece of pussy got some engine on her! This ain't natural!"

"Holy God, you're crude," you say, as Guy flattens the gas pedal. You rush to the lights and the wreckage of the old city with old school devilish speed. The land flies by as Guy pushes the Ghia to top speed. After a while of making it through the city, you park.

Guy and you step out of the car inside a building that is blown out and easily accessible to the street outside. "Okay, special eyes, keep a look out." Guy jogs up ahead, switching his Geiger counter on; it beeps lightly. "I'm trusting you with my life, so don't go full retard on me out here, okay?" You shuffle over a lot of rubble and wreckage. Modern graffiti paints some of the old buildings. A giant Sean Connery glares at you in black and white paint. Underneath him someone has written *So A Man Walks Into A Bar With A Monkey. I Forget The Rest of the Joke But Your Mother is A Whore.*

Another building has some sort of philosophical writing on it: *Real Eyes Realize Real Lies.* One building with its top half cut off and lying on the ground is covered in a picture of a cat with a watermelon. Another crumbling skyscraper is painted in an amazing array of bright crayon colors, and in red letters it says over and over: *God is Love* and *Eat Dead Pork Rinds, Eat Dead Pigs.*

People—humans, of course—have been all over this place, and quite recently. That makes you feel a little bit better, but the emptiness of the ruins, the great no-sound that is at play at here, frightens you.

"Cool," you sarcastically whip out.

Guy, up ahead of you, turns. "Graffiti Alley. This is all picked over pretty well but there's something I wanted to check."

You stand there for a good long moment, looking over everything. Guy is far ahead, so you hurry after him. He points to the sky, and you hide behind a pillar. A large Network airship that looks like a modern freighter hooked to a massive steel blimp scans the cityscape with floodlights that dart in every direction. Loudspeakers blare out, "Illegal salvage activities will not be tolerated. Trespassers will be prosecuted," in English, Spanish, and Japanese.

After the airship has passed on, you scramble over a piece of fallen skyscraper. Your hands are scratched and your knees scraped as you struggle to get over it. At the top of the ruin, you sit down and watch Guy slide down the side, helping him get down with the telekinetic ori. You look at your surroundings—this valley of broken stone and mortar. Though there are some vines creeping into the abandoned city, amazingly they have not turned this whole area into some sort of overgrown garden. The flash storms, you guess, keep some of the vegetation down, though you idly wonder how all the creatures you have seen manage to get through those storms. Must burrow or hide, you guess; something in their biology tells 'em to take off.

You think you can hear a jackhammer at work but you can't tell from where in that canyon of structures.

A white circle with two arrows is spray painted on the side of what looks like a Greek temple; a temple where all the statues have four arms and long tails and are missing their heads. There is also a spray painted rectangle with a single dot in the middle. You push yourself off the bench and walk forward.

You then slip down the side of the fallen skyscraper, carefully sliding as much as you can, scraping your ass a little as you do so. Guy helps you down with his ori. He stops by what could have been a large office building made out of glass. The ruined shell, all the broken windows twinkling in the moonlight, partially obscures a massive machine. A couple of miles away you see this massive digging machine at work. It looks like the marriage between a couple of dock cranes, like you would see at a port somewhere on Earth, and a massive buzz saw/scooper. The whole thing is propelled by a series of treads the size of your old apartment back home. It is knocking over a couple of buildings and digging out the remains with the metal ripper at the front. The noise grows and becomes terrible. The simple white-with-red-sun flag of Japan flies from its control tower.

Guy leans over to you. "This is good! Jap the Ripper will block out the sound of any gunfire that may go on."

"That's not cool!" you say.

"What? The gunfire or what I said?" Guy frowns, screaming back his answer over the noise of the machine.

"'Jap the Ripper'. It's not very cool!"

Guy makes a jerking off motion. You slap his arm hard. "No duh! I didn't name it. Yes, it's offensive, I'm not going to argue that. It's horribly racist. But that's what everyone calls it. Especially the stupid goddamn Winkies. The fourteenth century people don't know any better."

He snaps out his baton. "You see that building over there?" He points to what looks like a large metal box with yellow and black zigzag marks on it. "The Network set up a half-assed subway system in this sector. See that?" He points to a hand-painted sign next to what looks like set of rusted metal stairs on top of old marble stairs that descend below the street. The sign has a rectangle painted on it with two circles along its bottom edge; it looks like a little train. You nod.

Guy looks at his watch. "Five minutes. Okay."

You and Guy descend the metal stairs with a quick clang and stand inside what was once the Antediluvian world's equivalent of a subway system. Cast off to the far side of the platform, you see clear, long, and plastic-looking monorail cars, God knows how many years old, their clear cockpits covered in still glowing and twinkling lights. You can barely make them out in the gloom, as the space is only lit by gas camping lanterns and torches. The monorail cars are shoved off to the other side of the marble platform, stacked up like forgotten toys stuffed into an old chest. Separating those cars from you are three metal tracks leading past the marble platform and into the black gloom of the large subway tunnel. A wooden sandwich board marks this platform as *Atlantic City* and *Designated Flash Storm Shelter.*

Within a minute of standing there, an old NYC subway car pulls up with a screech, its headlights heralding its arrival from the opposite tunnel. The blue and white Venn diagram of the Network is painted onto one side, masking the old NYC graffiti that still adorns every spare space of the subway car.

The car is driven by a girl, maybe even your age, and she says nothing as you get on-board. A large man, maybe three hundred pounds, with long, scraggly, black hair and a full goatee, black shirt and black shorts, sits next to the young girl. The man sucks on a candy and holds an automatic shotgun between his knees.

According to a poster on one wall of the subway, it's forty Dii-Yaa for co-ops, fifty-six for independent operators. Guy puts his index finger up to his lips and mouths the word "Bugged," pointing to the ceiling of the subway car.

The driver flips on a record player. An old blues record scratches out a tune.

Bright lights, big city, gone to my baby's head...

Whoa, bright light, an' big city, gone to my baby's head...

You get to the first subway stop (*Thunder Road; Radiation High*) and a man in a full radiation suit along with a thick lead-covered case comes on-board and sits down on another plastic molded seat. Guy nods in his direction, and the radiation suit man gives a little salute. An ori-baton and a red tag attached to the outside of his suit mark him as a *Registered Salvager*. When he gets off at a stop called *The River*, he drops his Dii-Yaa into a goldfish bowl, next to the girl, that's half full of money.

Two minutes later you make it to your stop (*Nebraska*) without incident. The conductor hands Guy a long receipt and you step back into the light. Another one of the Wanted by Ni-Perchta posters for Charles Mathias is pasted up here, though someone has written *Good Luck, Love*

Charlie on it in marker. You wonder if Charles had indeed autographed it.

Farther away from the subway car, Guy speaks in a whisper. "Okay, the Wookie guarding the subway car back there is Sicko Steve from Santa Barbara. He works for the Rhodesians out of the Free Zone. He's Mr. Conductor on this subway track with that Gwen Stefani wannabe, and he finds all the best lines on salvage." You march up the stairs and into the moonlight of this open sector of the city. Guy straps the empty black backpack on without a moment's hesitation.

You listen, keeping your eyes on everything around you, and take an Adderall pill out of the bottle you snagged from Treena a while ago and dry swallow it.

"Woooo! Okay," you say.

Guy grabs your wrist and looks at the prescription bottle. "Okay, Hunter S. Thompson. Keep up with me."

It is nearly three o'clock in the morning when you come upon the star at one end of a wide boulevard. When Guy mentioned it before, you hadn't really bothered to ask him what it meant, figuring it was self-explanatory—which of course, it is.

Over thirty stories tall, this is a glass and steel building in the shape of a star. Its mid-section is like a glass bowl and its points, which are dissimilar in size and length, stretch upward and outwards. It's not as big as Star in the Mountain, but this is still a monster of a building.

A few points have broken off and taken out what looks like a city block. The rest, however, seem to be in good condition. There's an odd red light around it, barely there, but definitely not just a simple reflection of moonlight. A concrete statue the size of a house stands in front of it—a four-armed man with two heads. Someone has drawn a white rectangle with a big white dot in the middle of it on the statue along with a diamond with a line coming out of the top.

"A star like this could hold up to five thousand people, if not more, so it could be an effing zombie town in there," Guy says. "You see those signs? They mean 'danger' and 'defend yourself'. You notice anything?"

You squint your eyes, really taking the place in. "It's red."

"What's..." Guy pipes in.

"It's got the color, I mean, this glowing..."

Guy takes out his baton. "Okay, well, that's not good. You're sensing the security system being on." As you walk towards it, he whispers to you. "That huge bastard back there told me a while ago there's a new hole in the side of the building. Jap the Ripper weakened one side of it and it must've collapsed later."

All around you lay emptiness and destruction. Roads and buildings have been chewed up and spat out as gravel and small chunks of rubble.

"Normal Network salvagers have already picked the area clean, 'cept for our little secret opening. You see that, Sarah? It looks like something caved in the side there, probably after they cleaned out the block."

You look at him. "Saki is our friend and let's respect her culture."

"What? Because I called that machine Jap the Ripper? I respect her culture. I go down on her all the time. I don't know how to respect her culture more. Look, I love Japan. Japan is the coolest nation on Earth beside America, so don't look at me like I'm the racist here." He shakes his head and descends what looks like a pile of gravel leading into a giant black hole inside the star. With the moons blocked out by the rest of the star, it's like looking into one giant black mouth. "Japanese the Ripper took out some sort of support and this caved right in."

You follow after him, descending, making small avalanches of gravel with every footfall.

"Stars can't be broken into usually, but it looks like this one has been."

Guy takes out a flare gun strapped to his thigh and shoots it into the empty, black hole, illuminating what looks like a large lobby with a very high ceiling. The flare sticks to the high ceiling, revealing creatures hanging upside down inside. They're the octopus-like animals with those odd single wings like blankets draped over them. Guy fires another flare to get more light and barely misses hitting one of them. The animals aren't disturbed in the slightest.

The opening leads into what was once a shopping mall. Murals of people shaking hands or drinking or kissing line the walls. Inside this lobby there are small, box-like buildings that may once have contained buyers and sellers.

"You see anything, Sarah?" Guy asks. "That Superman vision working?"

You shake your head slowly. At the bottom of the gravel hill, you step onto the stone floor of the lobby and start breathing heavily, scared of this musty place that you can barely make out, even with the flares burning.

What you first think are rocks on the floor turn out to be human skulls. "Huh." Guy kicks one away like a soccer ball.

You and he walk through this shopping mall. You constantly scan around you to see if anything is lurking. A few neon lights and fluorescent light poles come on as you walk around, giving you a little more light to operate with, but not enough.

With the lighting system disjointedly popping on, disturbing shadows play out against the great walls of the star. Guy walks into one of the small buildings. Inside are strange glass tubes, each containing a skeleton. "Now that's just odd," you say.

A creepy hologram starts to play. A half-naked and beautiful woman with green eyes, wearing a white towel, busily sucks on the neck of a young girl in a Greek chorus-like mask in a way that is sexual and definitely depraved. The masked girl is dying during the scene, and then is dropped on the floor like a discarded soda can. You trip and fall backwards, and the hologram stops for a moment. The woman in the white towel then speaks; you see noticeable fangs amongst her teeth. She asks you questions in a language you can't understand—an odd, almost musical language. The hologram stutters and then disappears in a puff of smoke that comes out of the wall.

"The Wookie was right," Guy says. "Civilian shopping area. Let's see what we can nab here." He steps away from the building while you take a few deep breaths. He takes off his backpack and peeks into doorways, backpack in hand. Other odd holograms go off randomly, even more disturbing than the first one you saw. One you swear is trying to sell you human flesh; another is some sort of sexual advertisement.

Guy ignores them and finds what he was looking for. "Oh yes, yes, yes..." Something that looks like a large refrigerator is propped against the wall, and glows. Guy opens it like he's about to take out a cold beer. Inside are row after row of small gray tubes lined up on white racks.

"Oh! My! God!" he says, taking the gray tubes off the racks and stuffing as many as he can into his backpack. "Shit, yes!"

"What is that?" you ask as you hear something snuffle and groan in the dark around you.

Guy's celebratory mood dampens. He lifts the visor off his helmet, looking towards where the snuffle came from. He pops on his flashlight, smacking it a couple of times since the batteries seem to be loose or weak.

Seeing nothing, Guy goes back to what he was saying. "Syn-Simulator." He holds up a gray tube with what looks like a metallic mouth at its top end. "You can shoot yourself up with this and be off in a dream world for what feels like a good three hours, but in real time is about five minutes. A perfect, unmatched little dream world that feels one hundred percent real in all ways. Like a lucid dream. You ever had one of those? It's the dopest dope on anyone's block."

He looks at the tubes in fascination. "It's also horribly addictive and as illegal as shit. People start burning out their synapses on this crap. Back in Las Vegas you could sell these things for three, four hundred bucks a pop right on the street. Nevada still keeps it legal." Guy smiles and slaps you on the ass. "Wooo!"

You hear that snuffle again. "Goddamn Snuffy. Why do they always...?"

Guy snaps out his ori-baton. "Let's move out."

Returning through the open mall you listen hard, looking for anything moving. All you hear is the wind outside that makes an eerie sort of howl and your own sneakers beating against the tile floor. You take out your own flashlight and see that there is a large hall to your left leading further into the base of the star.

"Turn yours off, you'll probably see his outline easier," Guy commands. He flips off his flashlight as well. "Our lights attracted him. That's good, though."

You look at Guy like he's gone batshit insane. "What? You want him to lay in wait?"

"The light drives 'em fu—" Guy can't finish his words. A pair of red eyes rushes up to you. You spin and with your mind send a jet of flame shooting out of the ori-baton, igniting the creature and showing its true form—a scaly, disgusting-looking ape-like thing with octopus tentacles coming out of its foaming mouth.

"Oh Christ!" you yell, setting the thing aflame before it can slash you in half with its claws. It jumps backwards with a growl so loud it hurts your ears. Guy opens up with his bolt-action gun, sending shot after shot into the creature by quickly turning the bolt back and forth. Loud and large blasts come out of the muzzle of Guy's gun. The thing stumbles backwards and turns to run away, trying to disappear back into the darkness.

As it does so, Guy takes out a grenade that you didn't even know he had on him. You watch as he lets the limping thing get farther and farther away before hurling the grenade after it, like someone doing shot put. You hear a clink as the bomb bounces on the tiles and then an explosion that makes your ears ring. An orange ball of flame destroys the creature, reducing it to ruin.

"Goddamn right," Guy says, wiping his mouth. "Well. I didn't even see that thing."

He takes out his flashlight again and heads towards the still-burning corpse of the infamous Snuffleupagus. As you reach the smoldering creature, you're amazed at its odd simian/lizard-like shape and overwhelmed by its skunk-like smell that you hadn't noticed before.

"It's dead," Guy says, looking it over in the beam of his flashlight. "It gives off that stink when it dies. It's officially dead." One of its tentacles twitches, making you take out your own rifle to pop it so it stops moving. "There are usually one per level in these buildings, so we should be okay." He sounds like he's talking to himself more than you.

"Eww," you say. "Sooo freakin' weird." You are in a long, dark corridor of the star. "Where we going? Maybe we should just leave. I mean, how much money do you have on you now with those gray tube things?"

Guy touches your empty backpack. "We ain't leaving until we fill up your little backpack. Come on, this has been so far so good."

A couple of red sparks shoot out of the corridor ahead, and then a bolt of red lightning stretches from one side of the corridor to the other. Static electricity builds around you, making the hair on the back of your neck stand up. Guy is suddenly pulled towards the ceiling some seventy feet up in the air.

"Shit," Guy swears. "Don't move."

You hear the crackle of electricity. "Oh." You stop in place.

"We triggered a catcher," Guy says slowly, his face smooshed up against the ceiling. It doesn't look like there is anything holding him up—he is seemingly just pressed against the ceiling by an invisible force. "Oh, this is scary."

"I can bring you down." You point your ori-baton at him in order to telekinetically drag him back to the floor.

"Stop! Stop, don't you do that, it'll fry me. I'm supposed to be caught and to wait for the ancient police to show up and pull me down. If you use ori around here..."

Guy coughs. "If you use ori, it'll fry me, so please don't." A loud announcement in some strange language that sounds similar to Perchta but isn't starts to ring out over everything.

"I can't move either so what the shit am I supposed to do?" you say, trying to speak over the freaky announcement.

"It's okay to move now."

"Why now?" you ask.

"Shut up and let me think." You move forward a bit. "The system will think you're just another customer and not an accomplice running away from the scene." He lets out a breath. "Last time this happened, Winniefreddie found a controller station a couple hundred yards up the way. It should look like a giant orange iPad thing on the wall. You touch it so it glows blue instead of red, and the system should be turned off. I think."

"So, I got to walk in the dark by myself, oh Christ. You know, Guy, I thought I had you figured to be a veteran and expert about these things. So far you've been shot in the face with an arrow and caught by a Star Trek trap." You pop another pill. "I wanna go home. I wanna go home." You realize that you have not been thinking much lately, but rather just going with the flow about everything—even into this scary, late night activity. You've been just drifting along, a subconscious death wish pulsing in the back of your brain.

Farther away from Guy you drop to your haunches, crying a little, shaking and jittering all at the same time. "Goddamn it." You take a deep breath and then throw off your helmet, tossing it away since it's so damn hot on your head. It bounces against one of the tall blank walls with a slight bonk. You take out the Voice of the Four Winds and consult it before walking further.

Stepping through one section of the hall that looks solid but isn't, you see in the near dark a glowing red panel against an interior wall. You walk up to it, hearing it speak that not- quite-Perchta language in repetitive tones.

It flashes repeatedly with Antediluvian hieroglyphics. Not knowing what to do, you simply put your palm against the panel. It stops flashing red and turns to a more subdued blue. You hear Guy scream somewhere and say, "Oh shit!" at the top of his lungs. You bite your hand in fear, thinking you might have just killed him.

There's no sound for quite a while, and you fear you'll have to walk back by yourself. You head through the invisible wall again and come back into the corridor.

"I'm perfectly alright," Guy says. "No thanks to you. Some warning would've been great, Sarah Orange."

You sigh with relief, only to see farther down the corridor a few flashlights swirling in the pitch-black of the star's interior. Someone else is here.

You take out your rifle in a hurry. It could be Mathias and Petty and their people. Guy sits on the star's floor with his helmet off.

"What the hell, girl? No warning? You could cry out," he says in an increasingly high-pitched voice, his eyes looking up to the ceiling and back to you as if to say "Look how far that drop is."

"Shh." You hear voices coming from the far end.

"What the hell," Guy whines. "Do you realize I had to telekinetically push off ..."

"Shut up for once and just listen," you tell him.

Flashlight beams dart out of the hallway ahead, probing into the darkness.

"Who?" Guy asks, trying to stand but unable. You shake your head. "Who got here before us?"

"Come on," you say.

Guy points to his ankle. "I landed funny, heal me, come on."

You can see the bone. "Holy God," you mutter.

Guy shakes his head and points. "Heal it! Come on, now, heal it!"

You point your baton right at the wound. Green flecks stream out as usual, fixing the broken ankle. You help him to his feet so you two can run but the flashlight beams are on you. You can't see who's behind them. One nasal voice says, "That a Network uniform?"

Four flashlight beams converge on your face. "You Counters?" the nasal voice says again.

"Sorry Officer, but this star was just open. We have our paperwork. We know it's after operating hours, but you see…" You cross your arms to cover the little *S.B. Crue* patch that you slapped over the Network flight suit.

"Is that so? What do you think, Officer? What do you make of this situation?"

Guy looks at you if you've just gone crazy, but quickly recovers. "Well, I don't know boys, this seems like… well… We got a whole squad at the front looking for you fellas. We better radio this in." Guy is careful to stay behind you so they don't get a good look at his uniform.

The one with the nasal voice puts down his flashlight. "Oh, oh!" You see the shadowy outline of a bearded man, probably around your age. "Here." He takes an object out of his denim jacket and tosses it to you. "We didn't find it off a dead hawk or nothing. Honest to god, ma'am, that guy back there's been dead."

You and Guy look at each other for a moment, confused. It's a glowing purple square he's thrown to you, the size of an iPhone. You touch one part of it accidentally as you are turning it over to look at it, and it turns a bright orange. Suddenly your body feels very heavy and sluggish. You press it again, and it turns a brighter shade of purple. Suddenly you feel as light as a feather. Messing with the device makes you think that it must change the gravity around you somehow.

"Grav-Mod?" Guy says, confirming your thoughts.

One of the men curses under his breath and seems to reach for his pocket. "These assholes ain't Counters."

You immediately point your gun at them on instinct. So does Guy.

The other three men put down their flashlights and hold up their hands. "You're messing with the Love and Terror Kings, girl."

"What's that, asshole, your Girl Scout club?" Guy says. "What else you boys got on you? Move a goddamn inch and I'll put one in your skulls."

They toss over another couple of those purple squares, which you throw into your backpack. "Ten four, Officer," you say.

You back slowly down the corridor, watching the men carefully. You can see now that they wear denim jackets with some sort of motorcycle club patch on their chest pockets; they also have gas masks hanging from their necks.

"Okay, okay." Guy backs up. One of the men makes the wrong move, and Guy puts one into him with a blast, and then turns to run as everyone scatters. Gunfire rings out through the corridor as you take off, running with Guy as fast as you can back through the lobby. Guy tosses another grenade, which blows behind you with a loud bang. You hear someone scream.

"Ha ha, fuckers!" he yells.

You take out one of the squares Guy called a Grav-Mod and make it a bright purple. Suddenly you and Guy are able to run much easier than you ever could before. You run up the hillside of gravel like it is nothing and keep running all the way back to where you started. You meet the subway car again at one of the Network subway stations after a tense and long ten minutes.

You jump back into the Ghia, laughing. Guy's eyes are watering from all of it. "Are you nuts? You totally just rolled with that asshole's comment! 'Isn't that right, Officer?' He must've just thought your Network uniform...What a moron!" He starts up the Ghia with an uncharacteristic roar.

You hold your stomach and can feel your face turning red. "What is that, your Girl Scout club?" you spit out, repeating Guy's words.

Guy just shakes his head. "You ever see *The Sopranos?* There was this same situation, so I just threw out that comment. Same situation! God, what morons. You know I wanted to be a biker when I was little, but I never had the balls. Now, God, if that's who you hang with in off-world's biggest biker gang..." Guy keeps laughing and you do, too, before you start crying.

Guy looks at you, confused. "What's...What I do?"

You shake your head. "I don't know. I don't know, Guy. I never want to do that ever again. I really don't. I hate going out there. It's so scary. We could have died back there."

Guy puts an arm around you. "But we didn't."

You stare out the passenger window, looking at the ruins all around you. "I never should have left Earth."

Guy doesn't say anything for a long time but just gives you a hug. "I try not to think about it," he says weakly. "I..." He doesn't complete his sentence but just holds you. He kisses your cheek lightly once and then twice. "I always got a thrill out of it," he adds, honestly.

You look at him. "This whole thing's insane."

He nods sheepishly, and then looks you directly in the eyes. "I know."

You and he kiss deeply. You blush a little afterwards, then you kiss him again, this time tasting him, your tongues meeting together. "Let's go home," you say. He ignores you. You make out with him more and he starts to unzip your flight suit, all the way to your crotch. Still kissing you fully, he slides one hand into your panties. Soon you are doing everything short of making love. When you are done, you zip up. So does Guy.

Guy turns the car around and flips the radio to Radio Oberon. You are back at the Benbow before dawn.

You sleep on the couch during the day while Saki's at work. When you feel something fluttering on top of you, you wake up to see thousands of Dii-Yaa mixed in with regular US dollars covering you and the sofa. Guy has just opened a suitcase stuffed full of cash and dropped it right onto your face.

"What the heck is this?" You sit up and grab clumps of cash. Guy does a happy dance.

"Guess how much that is? How much do you think that is? Come on, girl, guess. How much you think that is? The Rhodesian Mafia came through big time!" He snaps his fingers, dancing around Saki's apartment. "You ever notice Saki is doing the same pose in all these pictures?" Guy mentions, looking at Saki's pictures. "Saki is awesome."

You hold the money in your hands and do a quick count. "With the regular cash and the Dii-Yaa money, it's about sixty-three thousand, two hundred eighty-five dollars. Not counting what fell under the couch."

Guy stops dancing. "How'd you do that?" he asks, looking at you bug-eyed. "I had to count that shit slowly and use an abacus in the Free Zone to come up with that number. How'd you do that?"

"Just good with numbers, that's all. Good God, do you really make this kind of cash?"

Guy shrugs. "Mostly less, sometimes more. We only go out when we need to score some cash. And only when it's good tips. We're kind of juiced in here with my contacts being excellent. We know how to get the best scores."

"Why would you keep going out? I mean, it was a hundred thousand last time. I know, split four ways, but still..."

Guy sits down next you and takes away the clumps of cash he just dropped on you. "Well, we all have our spending habits. When the portal opens up back to Earth during the summer solstice, Winniefreddie and Treena go traveling around the world. *Did* travel around the world, I guess. I have my houses in Quadling and in Cuba."

You stare at him, shocked. "In Cuba?"

Guy nods. "Me and the Castro brothers." He twists two of his fingers together. "Tight. I have Oberon citizenship, not US. You should look into it. Freakin' awesome and I'm not paying jack for shit in taxes."

"Does Saki have money?" you ask. "She used to go out..."

Guy nods. "She does. Her family has an Afer station, a ranch not that far from here. She stays as an SSR so she can get her slot into Solomon's House University."

You remember that briefly you wanted to go to Solomon's House University and become a xenoarchaeologist, like your sister, but you just gave that up like it was nothing. You look back and realize you didn't even make a conscious decision. You think of the cave and meeting your sister there, and wonder if that meeting was real or the start of your mental destruction.

"What money can be made." You look at it, pleased. "Unlike the USA."

"Unlike the USA nowadays, yeah. Now it's all Mitt Romney-Ivy League-Walmart exec types who've sucked up all the money," Guy says. "I miss having my USA citizenship, dumb as it sounds. But the USA..." He makes his hand into a little airplane and pretends to crash it right into the ground while making a humming noise.

"You have a house in the Quadling?"

He nods. "Magician's Hideaway. Paid cash for it. You know, I think it's time we took a little cruise down that way. You and me. Saki will be away for a little while and then she'll come down..." He looks at you intently. You put up a hand to his handsome features, a little rough with stubble right now because of the late night you both had. He isn't what you would call movie star handsome but there's a nice symmetry to his face, a boyishness and a ruggedness mixed together.

"That'd be nice." You kiss him. "I like you, Guy."

Guy smiles. "I'm going to collapse now. It's been a long day."

Later that night you get stoned with Saki while Guy is asleep on her bed, and listen to the radio. She gives you a glass of wine from one of those odd triangular bottles that you know to be Antediluvian in origin, and you disjointedly talk together.

"I'm going to my father's house out near Sargasso-3, on the north side, for a little vacation," she says.

"Sweet, sweet..." You blow out some rich smoke. "That's a thing to be done, vacations... I thought your... wait, I thought your parents were out in Osaka? You said that somewhere..."

"No, we used to live in Osaka," Saki says. "So sorry."

"Can I come with? I'd like to meet your family."

Saki looks at you funny. "Sure. But right now, well, no, that's...that's something to think about for the future, you coming by."

"I'm actually thinking about doing a trip to Quadling," you bring up, thinking of something you and Guy had talked about at the gym a while ago.

"How are you going to get down there?"

"Mono-train. You want to use the Ghia?" you ask her, anticipating her.

"Yes, could I?"

You lean forward, rubbing your hands together. "Me and Guy just fixed it. It runs like a charm. How much?"

"How much what?"

"Never mind," you say. "Forget it, just take it."

"Are you feeling okay?"

"How do you not get effed up on this stuff?"

"Japanese strength."

"Can I keep your cool war flags and Bob Marley stuff? It really ties the room together," you ask.

Saki frowns. "No, because I'm coming back. Me and Guy will be in Quadling soon."

"You have no idea how much that helps me, Saki-san." You take your flute of wine and walk out. "I'll be at the Benbow, drinking Maker's Mark, cranberry vodka, Maker's Mark, cranberry vodka. What, what..." you sing.

You get to the Benbow despite the elevator having a few problems; first it keeps stopping at the wrong floors, then when it gets to the lobby, the doors only open part way. The security forces are entertaining themselves by roasting an animal or something inside the lobby, filling the large vaulted space with the rich, fragrant smoke of whatever is being spit-roasted.

"Oh, that's nice." You also see that your computer and Saki's have gone missing. You laugh at this and head for the Benbow. Guy is there, laughing at your inebriation. You pop another Adderall. "Shouldn't you stop?"

"Aren't you asleep upstairs?" you ask the Guy hallucination, who disappears into thin air.

You laugh and walk outside, watching the beginning of a regular, old-fashioned thunderstorm play out in the west.

You wake up on the patio of the Benbow, apparently having passed out the night before, with a blanket on top of you. Saki is starting up the Ghia.

"You leaving?" you slur.

"Yes," Saki says. "I'll see you."

You roll your eyes. "Well, bye," you say, finding a half-emptied beer to drink out of. "Loved your sushi." You wink at her. "That's, that sounds sort of weird to say. To a girl."

Saki frowns and drives off, leaving a trail of dust behind her.

"Goodbye and good luck." You give the retreating car the finger. "Can I have your boyfriend to myself, now? Got to get going, myself. Bottoms up." You pop another pill and then another one. Your heart starts to beat faster and faster and then skips a beat or two. You collapse into the dirt.

You feel yourself floating in space, loose and lost in the middle of nothing. It's a scary feeling; it's something you've never felt before. You sail away towards something— a bright light, you think, or maybe a tunnel.

NIGHTHAWKS AT THE MISSION

SARAH'S DREAM OF AN OFF-WORLD RANCH AT MIDNIGHT

Four shapes emerge out of the dark, prepared to murder under an alien sky. Their movements are careful and slow as the four look upon the long white ranch house far off in the distance and the woods to the side of it. The location is a twenty minute drive from Sargasso-3.

A cold wind blows on that night, carrying a trail of dead leaves off the solitary oak tree under which the figures stand, and chilling them despite their heavy black coats and sweaters. Gingerly, the four cross into the woods as a distinct monorail whistle echoes from somewhere far off. The white forms of seven moons peer down from high above in the star-filled sky.

A couple of them stop, turn their heads, and listen as they go through the woods. In either direction there is nothing but the solitary road cutting through the countryside and the ranch house itself, a few gas lamplights glittering from it in the night air. The road itself is strange, a blacker than black pavement covered in large yellow Xs that stretch from shoulder to shoulder.

The four walk through the woods carefully, as quietly as they can. One turns his head, thinking for a moment that he heard a metallic click just as the monorail whistle blew. He dismisses the thought and keeps walking.

The ringleader looks down at his digital Casio watch. It is 11:59 am. Then it shorts out, going completely off.

NIGHTHAWKS AT THE MISSION

"Hold up one minute, the storm's just hit. We have to..." the man begins, his voice barely heard over the wind.

There is a slight rumble of thunder, perhaps the beginning of a storm coming out of the Sargasso Breaks, perhaps something else. Dry lightning plays out against the western skies, illuminating at times a flock of luminescent manta ray-like creatures, their tendrils drifting behind them in the wind as they make their way back to the Super Sargasso coast for the winter.

Away from the woods, an old Japanese man, a teenage Japanese boy, and a Japanese man with an age in-between the two, sit on the white ranch house's porch, watching the display in the sky from the comfort of a rocking bench and a patio chair. A single gas lamp on the patio is emitting a weak, ghostly light, illuminating the three.

The old man sits next to an extinguished gas lamp; a two-headed dragonfly suddenly lands on it. The dragonfly is the size of a small bird. The teenager turns his head and watches it fly away into the night, passing the blue pickup truck parked outside the large home.

"That was a ridiculously large bug, Dad," the teenager says in Japanese, shaking his head. He zips his denim jacket up a little bit tighter.

The dad shakes his head. "Not as big as the one your mother married." He starts scratching the receding hairline under his white cowboy hat.

The grandfather croaks out a laugh and shakes his head, becoming very serious. "No need to talk about that, Katsuo. You know that."

Katsuo smiles to himself and turns the radio up a notch. The wind picks up. The teenager asks, "So this is, uh, safe, right? Where we are?"

Katsuo nods. "Safe as safe can be. It's all light and noise here, with some wind. Inside the city though, psht, you just disappear. Just vanish like a puff of smoke when it happens. Storms come out of ol' malfunctioning reactors in the city centers."

Coming from the radio is a Led Zeppelin song:

If it keeps on rainin', the levee's goin' to break If it keeps on rainin', the levee's goin' to break
When the levee breaks I'll have no place to stay. Mean old levee taught me to weep and moan...

A bald-headed white man, tall and muscular and with reflective aviator shades on, opens up the front door of the house and stomps down its wooden steps, almost walking into the radio. A ring of keys jingles in his large hand.

He has on a large backpack with one shoulder strap around his arm. "That Led Zeppelin playing again, Katsuo-san? Radio Oberon finally allowing 'onest rock 'n' roll to play all the time now?" the bald-headed man says with a working-class English accent. He walks past the truck and circles around the house towards the back.

"You going somewhere, Sunglasses-san?" the old man asks in English, gently taking out his pipe again for a light.

The man with the sunglasses on nods his head quickly. "Left some stuff behind in storage. Be back in fifteen."

Katsuo Sr., the middle-aged man, raises his eyebrow. "Don't want to hang back here for a second? It is going to be happening any minute now."

The man with the sunglasses shakes his head. "Oh, it's nothing too exciting. A light show for a few minutes and then it's back to listening to the frogs mate."

The old man chortles. "You can listen to this for a while, Billy-san." The old man farts.

The man with the sunglasses snorts. "Working with you is always a privilege, sir. I'll be back. Jeremy should be here in a few." With a few extra steps he disappears into the dark beyond the house.

Katsuo Sr. and Katsuo Jr. laugh for a good minute, tears streaming from Katsuo Jr.'s eyes. The middle-aged Katsuo Sr. picks up the glass of whiskey on the armrest of his chair and takes a sip. "Oh, Grandpa," he says in English, wiping his eyes.

Sure that he is clear of the ranch house, the man in the sunglasses puts both straps of the backpack onto his shoulders and takes off at a full sprint towards the road with the reflective yellow Xs on it. In that still moment, he can almost hear the approaching sounds of a horse at full gallop, somewhere off in the distance. If he had stayed, he could have seen the man with a goatee charging along on his black horse.

The Led Zeppelin song is interrupted as the radio cuts out into an eerie emergency band drone.

The announcer, a woman with a crisp English accent, comes on. "We interrupt this radio broadcast to update you on the special flash storm warning for the Super Sargasso region. Any and all persons within five kilometers of the center of the Sargasso-3 Antediluvian city must take immediate shelter. We repeat, this is a flash storm warning for the Super Sargasso region. Any persons within five kilometers of the center of Sargasso-3 must take immediate shelter..."

The storm starts. The black sky filled with several moons, begins to be covered in a fast movement of clouds. The wind gathers strength and there is a terrible droning and echoing sound throughout the countryside. The ground begins to shake so much that it rattles the glass of Scotch off the armrest and knocks it to the deck floor, shattering it. No one can actually hear the glass break over the now ringing and discordant warning sirens going off and the roar of the sky itself. The sky then lights up, red, then blue, then red again, and then turns into an almost fiery orange.

The teenage son stands up and walks out into the yard, watching the fantastic display. A ring of white circles spreads over the horizon and swirls in and out of the clouds. A chain of circles forms and shoots downwards and upwards from the sky and back to the ground.

The teenage son loses his footing for a moment due to the wind, stumbling to the side. Green lightning shoots out in all directions now and again. For moments at a time the entire world seems to light up in white flashes as bright as millions of flashbulbs popping at the same time.

As the son turns back to his father and grandfather, he yells out, "Wow! This is... wow!" However, he sees then that his father and grandfather are now standing up with a look of concern on their faces.

The four figures come out of the nearby woods as the storm continues to play out, ski masks over their faces. The sky turns a deep bluish-green and becomes incredibly thick with clouds. The white circles begin to join together, split apart, and join together again. The circles become blue. A sound like a thousand groaning screams comes forth from the sky.

Jake Alexandros comes forward and yells to be heard over the flash storm that is still ripping across the sky.

"Where is Billy Knochen?" Alexandros shouts out. Katsuo Jr. runs back to Katsuo Sr., who turns off the radio that is just issuing static. Katsuo Sr. looks to his own father, who speaks first. "Billy Knochen? I do not know anyone by that name!"

Alexandros looks to his friends for a moment. "Last chance, friend! Billy Knochen. Bald head, wearing sunglasses, Englishman. Been working with you for the last two months!"

Katsuo Sr. speaks up. "Don't know anyone by that name. Now, please, let us-"

Katsuo Sr. is immediately lifted off his feet by some unknown force. Alexandros has simply stretched out his ori-baton and pointed it at Katsuo Sr., then makes a motion as if yanking the baton back.

Katsuo Sr. is thrust forward violently, his body crashing through a beam holding up the roof of the ranch house over the deck floor. He is then thrown through the windshield of the pickup truck parked outside, shattering it, and is reduced to a ragged and bloody clump.

"You want this to happen to you or the boy, old man? We want Billy Knochen."

A man with a goatee appears from the side, a rifle in hand. It's the ranch hand, Jeremy. He fires off the first shot which strikes one of the masked people in the chest, knocking him back. The man's black horse bolts off, frightened by the storm and the shot, galloping away as fast as it can.

Jeremy pulls the bolt back and fires again, grazing the right side of Alexandros's head, making him instinctively slap his hand against his head and fall down awkwardly. As Alexandros falls, his left forearm bashes against a sharply edged rock and a puff of green smoke comes from his sleeve. He pulls out his own small semi-automatic and returns fire erratically, spent shells spitting out the side of the gun.

Certain clouds above begin to dip downwards as if ready to emit a giant funnel. The clouds become purple again. The wind is at its strongest now, rattling the windows in the ranch house, and the flashes of white become more and more frequent. They are lasting longer.

The grandfather and Katsuo Jr. rush inside the house as fast as they can. The teenager cries, "Jeremy! Get away from here! Run!"

One of the masked people changes from a human assassin with a ski mask to a strange, five foot tall giant mantis that's flashing bright white with large, jagged jaws and serrated legs. He changes seamlessly, as if the original human being is winked out of existence. The insect jumps forward, knocking Jeremy backwards and fatally stabbing him in the chest with both of its long front legs. It then chops him in half with its jaws, tossing his torso down the road. The man reappears in one white snap of noise, takes off his ski mask and reveals himself to be Botha, his arms and face bloody.

Alexandros rips off his ski mask; a thin line of blood trickles down the side of his head. He rushes forward, enraged, Botha behind him. Alexandros kicks open the ranch house's front door, screaming at the top of his lungs. "Knochen! Give him up!"

They rush up the stairs to find the boy and his grandfather.

Outside, Dee has her ski mask off. She grabs the right arm of the now prone and very dead Dr. Wellington Cartwright. A green light begins to glow around both their bodies; flecks of green come from Dee's arm and into Wellington's body. His ski mask-covered head starts to change a little and becomes distorted. After a still moment, Cartwright's dead eyes flash white, once, twice, and then three times, and he begins to cough horribly. Cartwright then leans forward and takes off the ski mask, inhaling deeply.

At the top of the stairs is the old Japanese man with a double-barreled shotgun he has just loaded. Alexandros makes a fist and both shells in the shotgun explode, killing the grandfather in a burst of flame and shrapnel. The wall behind the grandfather, proudly displaying pictures of the family's home here and in Osaka, is covered in blood and the striped wallpaper is scorched. The house begins to shake more than ever, with a rattle that hurts the ears of the assassins and the boy they are after.

Botha spots the boy going out a bathroom window. He stretches out his ori-baton and a single green lightning bolt shoots from it, making a thunderous sound, burning through the walls and shattering the glass in the mirror, but ultimately missing the boy, who manages to climb down a drainpipe outside the window and run off into the countryside as fast as he possibly can.

Before leaving the homestead, Katsuo Jr. runs up next to a long pole with a blue police light at the top of it. There is a small red button under a plastic cover that is marked *Emergency Only—Will Call Ephors/MS/Security Forces*.

The boy presses the button and the blue police light begins to flash. Two seconds afterwards, a series of flares shoot up from different locations around the entire farm— blue, green, and red ones— lighting up the entire area.

The boy manages to get a small distance away but Cartwright is watching. After a long pause, Cartwright decides to act. Slamming the ground with his own ori-baton, there is a harsh and sudden crack far away. Dee and

Cartwright can see only in shadow that the boy is now impaled on a sharp, thin stalagmite that has erupted from the ground.

Dee looks away. "Oh, man."

Alexandros and Botha meet the other two outside. Alexandros calls out to them. "Did you see Knochen? Where is that bas-"

Botha, who sees the silent blue flashing light, makes a throat slashing gesture. "We gotta go! An Ephor could be here any moment! We gotta go and we gotta go now!"

Alexandros looks terrified. "We can't end this. We have to find-"

The storm stops. There is now utter stillness. The clouds begin to disperse. Stars once hidden begin to shine again. A dog barks in the distance and a crow caws back.

The four begin to run away from the house. Alexandros can speak now without yelling but does so anyway. "You three take off. I'll take another moment! If he's here, he's by himself, and I'll take 'im!"

Botha and the other two nod and without another second passing, disappear completely into the night, only leaving behind them the dull sound of some very far-off thunder and an overwhelming smell of ozone. Where they were once standing they leave only their footprints in the dirt.

Alexandros, by himself now, looks around the outside of the ranch house, searching for any sign of life or activity. He moves as far away as he can from the home.

"Knochen!" he screams. "Knochen! Show yourself! Show yourself now! You've got ten seconds! Ten damn seconds before I obliterate the house!"

After a frustrated wait that seems to take much longer than ten seconds, Alexandros makes a slicing gesture with the ori-baton. The truck that he threw Katsuo Sr. into lifts up into the air and crashes into the roof. Then it drops through the home's first and second floors. Alexandros then makes a pull down gesture with both hands on the baton and the truck explodes, setting the home ablaze.

Standing around, gazing at the house like a feral animal, he thinks he hears something in the distance. A click, or something metallic dropping onto the roadway.

Alexandros stands still and closes his eyes. There is a flash of green around him and then nothing. Again he tries, and again a flash of green, and then nothing.

Pulling up one sleeve, he displays a metal arm-guard that goes from wrist to halfway up his forearm.

Alexandros inspects the arm-guard, and to his mute horror, sees that the blue stone, shaped like the zodiac symbol of Scorpio, is scratched and broken in two.

Without hesitation, Alexandros runs to the road, his lungs burning, his body aching from the exhausting battle he has already pulled off. The highway itself is flashing, pulsing with yellow neon lights that clearly mark out every X.

After a few moments, Alexandros sees that there is a simple vehicle speeding down the lone black highway marked by the yellow Xs, its lights on. It is a Karmann Ghia—a yellow, slightly rusted compact car coming at full throttle; a machine used by its driver in a current fit of abject terror after seeing the burning of her family's home.

He takes out his pistol and runs into the middle of the road, holding up one hand. The car does not slide to a nervous, screeching stop but rather charges forward, fully enveloping Alexandros in its headlights.

"Stop! Stop!"

He fires three shots into it as the car comes towards him; one shot punching into its front bumper, the other passing through the windshield, and another into the left side of its young driver, a woman by the name of Saki Tetsuhara.

The car slows to a stop in the middle of the road. Alexandros charges towards it. He sees Saki clutching her side. Her face is a horrible mask of pain and fear. "What the fu-"

After a brief moment of eye contact, Alexandros grabs the door handle. If he had been listening, he might have heard Saki say "Please", whilst looking at him through her brown, watery eyes.

"Get over! Get out of the f-" he yanks the door open and pushes Saki violently into the passenger seat, sitting down in a small pool of her lifeblood. She screams for help as Alexandros jams one sneaker-covered foot onto the gas. He turns the car around in a wide U-turn, driving over the shoulder and back in the same direction that Saki just came from. He switches the headlights off.

Out of the darkness comes a tall, beautiful woman who seems to slither forth from the night, her immaculate figure dressed in a dusty black coat. She watches as the Karmann Ghia flies by, easily seen in the light of the seven moons shining overhead and the flames erupting from the ranch house. The woman closes her eyes. The Ghia crunches to a stop, throwing Alexandros forward and cracking his nose against the steering wheel with a short, sharp snap. Saki is knocked briefly unconscious as her head slams against the windshield, cracking it.

The tall woman walks casually over to the stopped Ghia, her features faintly illuminated. Alexandros sees her through the rolled down driver's side window and his eyes become wide with fear.

In under a moment, Alexandros and the driver's side door are yanked from the car in a screech of metal and screams, and flown nearly thirty feet before being deposited back onto the shoulder of the road. The neon yellow Xs stop flashing.

Alexandros, his left arm broken and a few ribs cracked, straightens up and in terror shoots at the woman whose face is stretched and contorted in a hideous death mask grin.

Saki regains consciousness and stumbles away from the vehicle after opening the door that is now slippery with her own blood. She begins a pitiful pattern of falling and getting up again as she moves down the road.

The beautiful woman picks Alexandros up by his neck. He shoots her twice before noticing there is no effect.

The beautiful woman, in a clear voice with a hint of metallic buzz under her words, speaks as he gives up struggling. "Quite a bad mistake you've made here. Why couldn't you wait?" She loosens her grip on Alexandros's neck.

Alexandros drops to the ground, his pupils dilating, becoming as wide and as black as the night sky. His voice takes a drugged, lethargic tone. He sits up on his knees. "I don't know where he is..."

The beautiful woman squeezes his neck again and then lets go.

Alexandros speaks after a moment, struggling for breath. "I don't know... Please, the Ephors or someone else will be here shortly. We need to go..."

The beautiful woman studies him for a moment. She puts out one hand, now a deep blood-red. She lifts his limp form, then sets him ablaze and tosses him forward. As Alexandros falls back to the dirt one last time, burning alive in that horrible fire, he shoots once more into the air, his gun making an audible clicking sound as he runs out of rounds.

He dies in agony, flailing around on the cold dirt as a literal human torch while the beautiful woman stands by and watches, her face devoid of emotion.

Saki does not die right away. She struggles to move forward on the ground, crawling, and then collapsing finally. She tastes her own blood in her mouth as she weakly cries for help. She clutches her side, feeling herself go numb. A blank, stupid terror rips her rational mind, tearing it into unresponsive threads. She recognizes the feeling of coming oblivion and of a fright so ugly. Saki feels her life leaving her.

When her head hits the dirt, she hears the single bell that tolls for all God's creatures and becomes conscious of an uncompromising darkness surrounding her. Saki feels reality rip away. As she dies on the side of the road, she thinks only, *this shouldn't have happened, this shouldn't have happened...* A thousand tarot cards emblazoned with the Devil on his throne holding a torch downwards, his goat head crowned by a pentagram, fly past her in a whirlwind, reviving her. She manages to grab one that's stopped on her body, seeing its awful design up close. *THE DEVIL, M AND P,* it reads.

As she is in the dark, alone, and in another place far from herself, Saki thinks she hears the other woman say, "And over the world, nor stop, nor stay, the winds of the Storm King go out on their way..."

You awaken in an unfamiliar spot, with an IV in your arm and your chest feeling as if it is stuffed with cotton and glass. You think about your dream as the seven moons send light through your hospital window. Was that a dream, or was it somehow real? When you try to finger the IV, your hand only moves a few inches before it stops abruptly. How did you get handcuffed to your bed? You cry a little, frightened and alone, as the realization comes to you that Rachael Zur, the woman in the dusty black coat, as pale and as dead as corpse—your sister was the woman in the dusty black coat. You pray that night, crossing yourself and begging Christ that the dream was not true. You think of how you met your sister in that cave a lifetime ago but always thought the incident was a lie your mind made up, a fragment of a dark imagination like Slinks's unexplained appearance and disappearance. You don't dare dwell on the meaning of that little period of time when you wandered back from the coast, as it would hint that perhaps you are not healthy and not whole and that your mind is a broken instrument that can no longer be relied on. You forgave yourself for your downfall and you moved on to forget about the cave. You pray that the dream is not real.

CHAPTER SIXTEEN:
LAST NIGHT AT MISSION FRIENDSHIP

The next time you wake up, Dr. Cartwright is standing over you. He takes out a flashlight and checks your pupils.

"How do you feel?" His face is kind and reserved. He wears a white doctor's jacket with his ID sticking out.

You respond with a cough. "Where am I?"

"Back inside the Mission."

The Ni-Perchta lieutenant from the security forces is standing to the side, watching you closely. You're wearing a medical gown. An IV pumps something into your arm. "Shit," you whisper.

"You seem to have had a reaction to certain, ah, medication you've been using." Cartwright indicates the nervous, blue-uniformed Ni-Perchta. "The Lieutenant here found you. You collapsed outside the inn."

The lieutenant comes over and unlocks your handcuffs. "You were angry," he says.

"Was I poisoned?"

"By yourself," Dr. Cartwright says coldly. "Drug tests came up positive on many different, uh, matters. We'll discuss further in forty-eight hours."

How you got into the lobby remains a mystery to you. You remember the dream, of course, that strange dream of your sister, the man on fire, Dr. Cartwright...

"You were near death. Actually, past that. You had a heart attack," Dr. Cartwright says, looking over at a calendar that shows a picture of Solomon's Bay lit up at night and of Solomon House University's main building floating in the air.

Seventeen days are crossed out. The calendar shows the month of February, 2013.

"What day is it?" Your stomach feels tight and cramped; a drowsy feeling fills up your head at the same time.

"February Seventeenth. You've been out for two weeks. We thought about giving you a med-evac back to Solomon's Bay, but that was overruled by the new Bureau agent," Cartwright says, with a bit of disgust.

"Who? What happened to Alexandros?" you ask.

"Oh, Jake? Transferred to Mission Passages in the North. There's been a problem there. They burned half of the Mission down. Some of the security forces rioted. I guess things are getting worse near the remote tablelands and Bear Center. We have a new agent—a Mr. James Farson."

"Farson?" you ask.

Cartwright nods. "Apparently a cousin or something to a certain Guy Farson."

You nod, seeing Dr. Cartwright closely as if for the first time. There's a look of hesitation on his face. He pats your arm.

"Get some rest."

You nod, trying to get comfortable with the hard, sterile pillow of the hospital bed. At night you wake up again, the seven moons once more streaming through the windows of the clinic. You breathe deeply, awakening from dreams that boil in the back of your brain. You think of the cave and Slinks and of what may have happened to Saki.

There's a shadow in the corner of the room; it's man-shaped. You can barely make out who it is until it's nearly on top of you.

Saki whispers something into your ear. "My family is dead, Sarah." She looks around the room to see if anyone is coming. Her eyes are wild, red, and crazy.

You prop yourself up on your elbows.

"I think Mathias has people inside the Network. Jake Alexandros was with them, then was killed in front of me by someone I don't know. But these masked people took the body away..." Saki says, whispering further. "They killed my family, Sarah," she repeats. "They were after one of the ranch hands. Uh, a Billy Knochen. I managed to bring our ranch hand back to life. A man named Jeremy. He told me."

"God," you say. You get out of bed and look in a white cabinet next to it. A Network flight suit and your underwear are in it, and your sneakers are on the floor.

Saki shakes terribly. "I'm leaving. But Mathias has agents inside the Network." She sits down in a plastic chair next to your bed. She holds up a tarot card in the moonlight as proof.

"These were all over the road."

You look over the tarot card, sickened by touching it. You hold Saki tightly and kiss her on the cheek.

"Please, where is Guy? Where are they?" Saki asks.

"Did a woman save you, Saki?" you ask quietly, petting the back of her hair, comforting her.

Saki looks at you curiously, pushing you away. "Yes, yes, a woman did. She was traveling up the yellow X road. Saved me from Alexandros but I think she..."

You zip up your flight suit. "I know."

Saki gets out of her chair quickly and pulls out what had been Alexandros's gun. "How do you know?" She sticks the gun in your ribs and cocks the hammer. "How do you know?"

You stare right at her. "I just do. I've been here in a coma, Saki, please." Her eyes flicker to the calendar and the chart. "Please let me explain..."

She seems to relax a bit, gun still pointed at you, and sits back down.

A burst of submachine gun fire blasts through the clinic. The Ni-Perchta lieutenant blows Saki away, shooting her several times in the chest and once in the head. She lies there bleeding on the floor; the gun she had in her hand drops.

"Oh no!" you scream. "Oh no, oh no!"

One of the other Ni-Perchta security forces, this one in traditional armor, drags you away from the scene as another one takes out an ori-baton and tries to heal Saki. It seems to be working a little. Her eyes flash white, the green flecks go into her body, and her wounds are healed. But it doesn't take. The lieutenant, young and scared, speaks up in broken English. "It do that. It do that if she been healed early in the past. If in the past, it does not heal right. It does not heal right."

They try over and over, and Saki's eyes start to flutter but never fully open. The Ni-Perchta lieutenant listens to her chest. "I think..." He stops. "Her heart is beating slightly." You thank God for that.

Twenty minutes later and down the hall, you wait for James Farson, the new agent from the Bureau of Off-World Affairs to arrive. When he does, he sits with you in his office, as Saki's blood still dries on your shirt.

Farson, who looks sort of like Guy but unlike Guy, speaks with a Jersey accent, takes out a cigarette and lights it. "I need to take your statement on what happened in there."

You sit there silent, licking your lips. "She was upset. She wanted to show me the gun but your security forces..."

"They see a woman pointing a gun and they shoot. I'd say that was an appropriate response. I'm sorry to hear that she's comatose. Did she mention anything else about the attack on her family's farm?" he asks. "We'll send out a patrol. All stations have to report in once every two weeks."

"So, Jake, he was transferred?" You nervously tap a series of patterns on your knee with your left hand.

James raises an eyebrow. "The whole Oberon is going through a period of transition. So they're moving people around like chess pieces. The Ni-Perchta are rioting in the north. The Witch-Lord just sits on his hands. Look, I'm not a newspaper. Read up on it, and read between the lines of what's reported. And so I guess Jake is transferred. Central Services in Solomon's transmits the orders. I don't ask the details behind said orders."

You nod.

"The doctor tells me you had high levels of Adderall and cannabis in your system. Adderall you do not have a prescription for, and cannabis, well... You're banned from the Mission grounds. You no longer work for the Network, and you're banned from any future employment with the Network. You step back on Mission grounds, you'll do three years in a Witch-Lord dungeon."

You call him something that starts with a c and ends with sucker.

"Keep it up, Miss, and I'll ban all the residents here from the Benbow. I might still do that when the new Mission Manager gets here."

"Who's left to ban? Half the Mission's departed," you state. "We'll be lucky to make it until the summer solstice. Mathias and Petty and God knows who else are gonna get us all killed."

James ignores you and signals for the trigger happy lieutenant to come over and escort you out. You stare at him for a long time. "Winkie bastard..."

The radio is on in the background as Guy sips a whiskey and listens to your story about Saki, his eyes red and watery. The fireplace roars and a regular storm is picking up somewhere out in the Breaks. The wind batters the windows every once in a while. Your suitcases are strewn around the bar because of James Farson's permanent eviction order.

Guy is very upset about Saki's condition; so is Treena. Guy seems like he is going to cry. "Poor Saki's family. Poor Saki," he says with genuine sadness. He then repeats that same phrase with genuine anger. "Oh, God."

"They didn't trace the Adderall you jacked to me, did they?" Treena asks. "You shouldn't be doing it to begin with. It's a vital tool for concentration, and I should have never lent you any or looked the other way on your addiction and theft. I felt bad for you and I should have said something. It's not some, some toy for clubbing and staying up listening to badly-produced techno."

Guy nods and then sighs. "My uncle is such a dick. I can't believe he's out here. Rule-crazy dick. One time when I was fourteen he saw me drinking a beer with my friend Steve and told my dad. What a faggot. I'm sorry, we are related but it's not a, uh, friendly relationship." Guy rubs your arm.

You shrug and say in an almost dead monotone, "They've got armed guards outside the Benbow now with strict orders not to, you know..." You take a sip of beer and put it down, pushing it aside. You work up the courage to say, "Guys—can we talk outside?"

The wind is really picking up and you hear the first splattering of rain against the Benbow windows.

Guy rolls his eyes, sniffling. "Oh yeah, sure. Let's go out in a freakin' thunderstorm. Can't this wait, girl?"

"No. I want to discuss things about the *S.B. Crue*. To get it flying again so we can take it to Quadling," you insist. Treena gets the hint and tugs on Guy's shirt. The three of you walk outside, and you lead them out as far from the Benbow as you can, like you are walking to where the *S.B. Crue* awaits.

Lightning plays out in the fields around you, and drops of rain blast through every once in a while.

"Saki told me that Dr. Cartwright, Dee, the old Mission Manager, and Botha work for Mathias and Petty. So did Jake."

Guy strains to hear what you are saying, so you have to repeat yourself. Treena grabs both of your arms and leads you to the *S.B. Crue*. You all crawl on-board, under the tarp that's been placed over the ship.

As the rain pitter-patters all over the tarp, you tell the others what she said.

"It's all true." You make yourself believe it as you tell a heavily modified version of your story to Guy and Treena. You know she was helped by a woman, your sister; you know that she said Jake was there, and that she had Jake's gun. The dream was too real and the evidence is there. It frightens you deeply.

You talk about how they had on ski masks and those black coats—just like outside the temple.

"But, why didn't they just wipe us out like they wanted to?" Treena asks. "I mean, they wanted to kill us. They killed Winniefreddie, right?" She starts to cry. "Oh God."

You don't correct her on this.

"Why wouldn't they just do it here?" Guy asks, pulling out another cigar.

"Why don't you put that away for once?" you snap. He ignores you and lights up.

"I don't know why! I don't...they...they're maniacs!" you bluster out. "Who knows what's in their heads?"

Guy takes a long puff of his cigar and blows out a ring of smoke. "I know what's going to be next in their heads. Doctor and Botha's heads, anyways." He takes out a small pistol and racks back the slide. "It sort of makes sense, Network people working with Mathias. I mean, how else can they knock down people and know where they are in such wide open spaces? The weaponry that Mathias carries..."

"You, Treena, and me, on the roof. The *Crue* is still fueled up right now when it comes to the ori, so we can at least fly it on over and take off again in a hurry. We can jump down onto the roof. I don't think I've seen anyone up there in the lounge...This is ugly, isn't it?"

You nod. "We need a plan. We need to really think about this."

Guy nods. "Well, we need a plan, but we're doing it tonight, okay guys? It's a regular storm out there, meaning they can't scramble Spitfires out to burn us out of the sky.

And we don't know if they know we know about them. We gotta move tonight."

"What if we tell your uncle?" you ask Guy.

Guy licks his lips, thinking. "Who can we trust? I haven't seen him in years, Sarah. I don't know. I mean, I thought Dee was just this corporate twit, Botha this racist, and the doctor, as well, just this, nothing. But if they're in it together, who can we trust? Besides, the Network will just place them under arrest and they could just get out again. Them dying is safer for all of us. We need to make some people dead tonight. Poor Saki's family. Murdering bastards, goddamn..." He bites his lip. "After I say goodbye to Saki in the clinic, we'll get together. After I say goodbye." He looks at you. Despite how bad you feel for Saki, you do not like that Guy will say anything to her again.

You and Treena leap onto the rooftop of the Mission, your ori-batons out. Guy hovers above in the *S.B. Crue*, but it's blowing this way and that through the winds of the strengthening storm. You help Treena tie a cable from the *S.B. Crue* to a pillar so the ship won't just blow away in the wind.

Guy says good luck as the three of you get into the half-working elevator car. You hit the button for each floor that your targets are on—seventeen and nineteen. With your full nighthawk gear on, you're ready for battle. Ski masks cover your faces, the *S.B. Crue* label on your flight suit removed.

Treena puts away her glasses and mutters a small prayer as you descend in the elevator. Guy blinks rapidly. Each of you switches on an old school walkie-talkie that looks like it came from the Second World War and hook it onto your belt. "Signal when you get to the apartment. They should be asleep so just blast through the door, like we talked about. Just keep blasting."

You and Treena nod. "What about Cartwright's wife?" you ask, thinking about your target and remembering his wife from the bonfire ceremony that seems centuries ago. The other target, Botha, lives alone.

"Guilty," Guy says, just with one word. "You know what I mean?"

Treena nods. "I'll be there, too." She squeezes your hand.

You shake your head. "We don't know that."

Guy and Treena look at you with eyes that are dead, dead for just a moment. "Oh, we know."

You sweat profusely, almost soaking your Network flight suit. "Christ," you moan.

"You okay, Sarah? Shit. She's not up for this," Guy says, holding you for a second.

"I'll be fine. I'll be fine," you mutter.

The elevator doors open onto nineteen. Guy steps out, snapping his ori- baton. "See you on the roof." He walks down the hall, looking at apartment numbers.

The doors close and you lower to seventeen with Treena. When they open again, you and Treena step out and immediately spot the Cartwrights' apartment at the end of the hall—1719. A little choo choo train with their name written on it is nailed to the door.

You check your synchronized Casio watches. It's 2:58 in the morning. When 3:00 hits, that's when you'll burst through. You wait outside the door, ready to destroy whatever is inside that apartment.

You squeeze each other's hands. Your watch turns to 3:00. Treena blows the door off its hinges with one snap of her ori-baton's telekinesis power and throws it clear across the apartment. It explodes through a plate glass window.

You walk into the apartment, shooting everywhere you can, spraying shots left and right. Treena sprays out a jet of flame that torches pictures, couches, and chairs. She even snaps off a lightning blast that destroys the bedroom door and throws it, blackened and charred, against the other side of the room.

Loud bangs and an explosion from a couple of floors up rattle the walls—the loud thump of a grenade blowing. Glass shatters and you can see through the window a little bit of flaming debris that must have ejected out of the apartment on nineteen where Guy is. Fiery fragments float down.

You search everywhere, using your own baton to throw the Cartwrights' bed against the wall. You scream something primal and then talk into that large walkie-talkie. "Nothing," you say.

As you and Treena leave, absolutely disappointed, the fire alarm goes off. People are shouting and a couple of apartment doors open randomly. Tim spots you with a look of absolute wonderment on his face. Residents look at you in shock as you climb back into the elevator—which now won't work because of the fire alarms going off. You sprint awkwardly past the residents again without saying a word.

Sprinklers turn on as well, dousing everyone. You and Treena charge into a stairwell and rush up the stairs as fast you can. You meet Guy on nineteen, who looks as confused as you are, and continue running upstairs to the observation lounge, where the wind is still blowing and the rain is coming down more and more. Guy climbs the cable in a second and then uses the ori-baton to telekinetically lift both you of you on-board. Treena runs into the wheelhouse, and the *S.B. Crue* with the screwed-up rudder takes off into the storm.

"God, we almost had them," Guy says, disappointed. You rub your chest for a moment, trying to calm your breathing. The wind and the rain hit you across the face in a stinging tide. "But we'll have them one day."

Treena sets off towards the Quadling region to the far south as Guy takes you inside the wheelhouse.. No one says anything for a long time before switching on The

Old Man at Midnight, who's playing an Alex Clare song, *Too Close.*

You feel shaky and ask if there is a bathroom on-board. Guy starts to tell you but you fall over in a heap, your chest burning. You pass out again.

NIGHTHAWKS AT THE MISSION

CHAPTER SEVENTEEN:
THE MAGICIAN'S HIGHWAY

You think you can hear waves crashing somewhere far off. It is quiet except for the steady beat of footsteps coming down the hall and then away again. You are in a small bedroom with white walls, wooden floors, and a window without glass that looks out over a deep blue sea.

There is a strange feeling inside you—no calm, no sense of peace, but a sense of numbness, of unfeeling, of emotions being checked into a corner. You feel as if every bit of you has been dipped into Novocain. You can almost feel terror, almost feel unhappiness, almost feel angry—but these are oddly distant feelings, feelings that can be heard coming from one room over, like terrible music being heard through a thick wall.

You look over and see that there is a small radio, something that looks like it is from the forties, next to your bed. With your right hand you turn it on, and the same cultured and feminine voice that had narrated the beginning of Morgan Freeman's monologue on the Queen Mary speaks: "...to Quadling region. Here at this southern-most part of The Oberon off-world settlements, you may visit the outskirts of the ancient Antediluvian city, Quadling-1, witness the annual gathering of the Baleen dragons in the Quadling Sea, and explore the mystery of the Arc Waters and the beauty of the Baths of Urncalles, a two thousand-year-old bath palace thirteen stories high containing a collection of a thousand rooms, ten thousand shrines, and two hundred thousand statues, all carved into a natural land bridge extending a mile and a half across the Quadling Sea. This is situated above the Telaknives Chimes, the largest wind chimes in the universe. All provided to you by the Network and the Bureau of Off-World Affairs."

Then an excited male voice delivers an advertisement for Brettie Pies. You turn the knob until you hear some old rock 'n' roll. Radio Oberon.

You turn over in the bed, wearing oversized pajamas. "Mom?" you say to the room, coming out of a slight daze. The door opens and Guy walks in, drying off a cool bottle of that Soviet insignia beer, and singing as he sees you. "My love is in league with the freeway, its passion will ride, as the cities fly by..."

"What am I doing here?" you say.

Guy hands you a water, which you immediately put down. "And the tail-lights dissolve, in the coming of night, and the questions in thousands take flight..."

You blink twice.

"Welcome to the Quadling," he says. "Sorry, I am three beers deep already."

You come out of the bedroom wearing a black T-shirt and jeans, a couple of sizes too big for you, grabbed out of one of Guy's wooden dressers. It is morning still, a bright sunny morning with a couple of moons hanging ghost-like in the sky.

The house is small and stands on a little rock of an island, along with an obsidian Nemo Gate. It's a small Gate, big enough for only one person to step through. The entire house is composed of white walls with a thatched roof set upon it, and sits under the shade of two large palm trees.

The house itself is three large rooms, all open to the elements most of the time. There are heavy metal storm shutters that can be dragged down and heavy bamboo blinds, outside and inside the windows respectively.

There is a large porch section with a swing bench covered in leather cushions, set up to give a perfect view of the Quadling. In front of you is the wide, great, deep blue Quadling Sea, marked by a couple of gray rocks the size of skyscrapers, along with a smattering of others.

On the small platform with the personal Nemo Gate is a winding and crooked wooden staircase that descends right into the clear sea. A steady wind blows from the beach far ahead of you. A crude, hand-painted sign on the platform reads: *The Magician's Hideaway.*

Off to the south you see the beaches of the Quadling and what you guess is Stonetown, judging by the rock walls outlining the city. It has a mixture of rundown towers made of rough gray and orange stone, thatched wooden houses, and other, noticeably human-style, constructions.

Part of Stonetown extends into the sea. Its wooden boardwalk and dock are filled with normal fishing boats and abnormal wooden ships with red triangle sails. The other half of the city retreats farther inland to allow for a large area of white sand beaches. A red stone land bridge stretches from the far western edge of the beach into the dark, cobalt waters of the sea. It's half a mile long. One section of the land bridge has to be the Urncalles, the red and white stone baths, thirteen stories high, a thousand rooms, according to the radio. The mass of the much-talked-about Arc Waters hangs suspended above it like a permanent watery rainbow. Airships dart about in the sky above.

You blink rapidly. "Oh. Wow. All the homes like this?"

Guy smiles. "No, just mine. Just mine."

You watch the waves roll in. "Where's the *Crue*?" you ask.

"Treena has it down at the docks. She's holed up at the baths and will stay nights over there," Guy says. "We might be wanted for questioning back in the Sargasso region. Our names haven't been on the radio but everything else—all the other info—has. Your name came up as a person of interest."

You sigh. "Should we be worried? Should I?"

Guy laughs. "They aren't good about tracking down criminals, not out of their regional jurisdiction. I mean, The Oberon is twice the size of Australia, so I don't blame 'em. It's a lot of ground to cover. Still, though, I wouldn't be talking about our identity to the Counters openly. If there's a Network Liberty Marshal around, now, that could be an issue. We ripped off the logo on the *S.B. Crue* before we landed."

Guy rubs his eyes as if they are itchy. "Right, then," he says, stepping inside his house. He comes back with a cigar, cuts the tip and lights it. "I don't think we'll be able to get back to Earth any time soon."

Guy wanders back inside to sit on a brown Chesterfield sofa; you follow. A picture of him and Saki hangs on the wall—fishing together somewhere back on Earth.

"So you know nothing more about what's happened, where those..."

Guy's mouth moves as if to say something, but nothing comes out at first. "No."

"You know nothing, is that right?" you say, desperate for information.

"No, I don't, Sarah. I wish I did."

"So you know nothing."

He puts his cigar onto an ashtray, his face giving away not a single emotion. "I know nothing. You know, it sure is sounding like a *Hogan's Heroes* episode in here."

You walk down to the platform with the Nemo Gate. You can feel Guy's eyes on the back of your head as you sit down on the platform and stick your bare feet into the warm water. It helps you relax.

Guy gets up and you can hear his footsteps come behind you on the wooden planks. He sits down next to you, not saying anything.

"What are you thinking?" you ask, staring out at the sea.

He chews on his bottom lip. "Nothing, I guess." He laughs a little. You lean back and close your eyes, listening to the chain of the swing as it rocks back and forth in the wind.

"I'm losing my mind," you whisper. "I killed myself out there in the Sargasso, did you know that? A clone or something. I have a witness though. Maybe it was me. I saw my dead sister out by the coast." Your eyes flick to his face and to the floor, unsure of what he will say. "Maybe it was really me that died."

Guy is good enough not to say anything.

"What should I do now? What should we do now?" you ask. "What will we do tomorrow? What I will do tomorrow?" you continue to ask, your anxiety coming through loud and clear. You don't bother to look over to where he is; you could be speaking to the sea.

He rubs his nose as if he has allergies that are bothering him. "The hot water at ten. And if it rains, a closed car at four. And we shall play a game of chess, pressing lidless eyes and waiting for a knock on the door..."

You look at him, confused.

"Just quoting the only poem I like," he says with a sad smile. "And Saki liked. I hope my girl's okay. I've paid off the guards there to look out for Saki. Back at the Mission. I'll know if anything comes up." You stare at the sea, not saying a word.

You walk out into the street to reveal yourself. It had been literally a four-hour-long process at the salon in Stonetown's human quarter. Guy smokes a cigar and reads TIME Magazine while sipping on a Coke from a plastic cup at this little outside cafe. It will soon be dusk. He looks at you very strangely; he puts down the magazine that discusses the rise of orichalcum attacks in the USA.

"See! Ta-da!" you say, accidentally bumping the table and knocking the Coke onto the magazine. A Ni-Perchta shop owner nearby laughs.

Guy ignores it as he looks you over. "Interesting look, there," he says. "So you bleached the shit out of your hair to make it blonde and cut it short. And straightened it." He stands up. "And you got heavy black eye shadow, whore lashes, fake eyebrows, pink lipstick."

You catch a glimpse of yourself in the mirror hanging on the food stall; you look radically different in a tight black blouse and tight blue jeans.

"I look like a stripper," you say, and almost start to cry. You really don't know what you were thinking. "You said we might be fugitives and I thought..."

"Well, it's not a bad idea, honey," he says. "I mean, I should do something like that, too. Probably. I think you overreacted a little, but I don't think you look like a stripper. Slack-jawed swamp donkey was my first choice. You look like a lot of fun now."

You stroll through the Cydonia Quarter, the mostly human part of Stonetown. Most of the buildings on both sides are rough stone towers, some painted white, some painted blue, and most look like they are about to collapse, with years of weathering and water stains covering their sides. Wooden balconies strapped to the sides of these buildings, along with ironwork galleries, break the monotony of the stone, along with the colorful tiled rooftops. There are a few normal-looking houses like those row houses in San Francisco. American, Greek, and green and white flags that you find out are Rhodesian, hang from every spare balcony. You've never even heard of Rhodesia. Guy tells you it is the old name for a white supremacist country in Africa that got liberated later and became modern Zimbabwe. Rhodesia was the old name of the white government and whites from Zimbabwe, and some of them still call themselves Rhodesians. After Zimbabwe's big economic crisis, most of the remaining whites fled and came to The Oberon over the years. Most are legitimate, law-abiding people, but the Rhodesian Mafia, the guys who run the smuggling operations, are definitely not. It's also the source of the large amount of cash you and Guy have on hand.

Humans stroll about among the potted plants and palm trees that are next to every building. Street vendors, human only in this part of town, are everywhere, selling Greek food like gyro sandwiches, Souvlaki shish-kabobs, moussaka, calamari, and even those trilobite things that definitely are not a Greek delicacy. You are getting very hungry and Guy, who is now acting like a bonafide boyfriend, is picking things up for you to eat.

"Is Treena okay?" you ask.

He nods. "She just wanted some time alone. Not catching those people... She's very bothered. It was her sister, Sarah. She doesn't want a funeral for Winniefreddie, she's that screwed up about it." He hands you a plate of food.

You nod. "We need to get revenge for her death."

You sit on a curb with a pile of plates full of different foods, munching away. Crowds of people pass by as you eat like a maniac, stuffing yourself to the point that you'll need help to get up. You start with that good and fresh gyro meat and fried calamari that is perfect with a cocktail sauce, and you finish up with baklava that really makes your day. To have real food after days of almost nothing but IV fluids refreshes you.

"Not a bad place to end up," you tell Guy.

A young couple walks by, holding hands. You do the same with Guy after a while.

A couple of Counters in their neat leather uniforms pass by, chatting and smoking, and you see one Mission Security officer drinking openly.

That night, as large bonfires burn across the beach that looks out to the red land bridge and the Baths of Urncalles, you sit on warm, white sand as the tide rolls in.

"Well then..." Guy says.

"I want to get hammered, bad," you say.

Guy pushes some white sand forward with the heel of his shoe. "You mean get drunk, right?" he says, sounding sheepish. "Sarah, you think that's a good idea?"

"Alcohol would be nice." You stand up and brush off your jeans that still have the tag attached.

"Okay, 'cause, yep, let's go," he says, laughing awkwardly. He yanks the tag off your jeans.

You and Guy walk to a brick building covered in purple ivy that has one of those green and white Rhodesian flags prominently displayed outside. Ni-Perchta town guards stand ready to pick up feisty drunks. They carry wooden shields and batons, ready to inflict some order if need be.

A gust of wind blows the pub sign that juts out from the side of the building. It states that this is *The Rhodie Bar*. A picture of a trooper in green shorts, shirt, and hat with a beer mug in one hand and an M-16 in the other is engraved into the wooden frame.

"What is this place?"

Guy shrugs, cracking his knuckles. "The Rhodie Bar. Only real bar in the Cydonia. It's nothing like the places at Solomon's Bay, but still..." He opens the circular door with its iron ring handle. Pool tables are in the back, and a stone stairway leads up to the second story. The place is full of wooden booths and has a long stainless steel bar.

Most prominent are the Rhodesian flags from the colonial era to the time of Independence, draped behind the bar, along with a plaque saying: *ALCOHOL IS ILLEGAL WITHOUT A PERSONAL LIQUOR LICENSE—WITCH-LORD LAW* in English and Greek. Dark but homey, the place has that rich smell of years of beer being spilled and of eggs—there is a large clear glass jar of deviled eggs sitting in the middle of the bar. This reminds you of another bar you've been in.

The place is rocking out, a jukebox thumping away. No gas lamps in this place; it is all electrical.

A lone brunette girl smokes a cigarette behind the counter and a Ni-Perchta male with one side of his face heavily scarred wears an apron. They serve drinks alongside a gaggle of human girl waitresses in black slacks and tops. The full house appears to be made up of college kids along with the locals. The Ni-Perchta's platinum hair is tied up in a ponytail, and he wears a Pink Floyd *Dark Side of the Moon* T-shirt.

"What's up, Guy?" the brunette says as you and Guy stroll up. You can barely hear her over the music. An odd accent colors her words. This very attractive girl must be missing her right eye, since it is permanently closed and has a punched in, flat look.

Guy shrugs. "Just doing what I do, Kayla. We need some drinks here."

"One, two, two." You miscount as you and Guy down your fifth shot of tequila. Your tongue is starting to go numb so you sip your water. Guy's doing a little better, although to your double vision both of his faces are wearing sunglasses that are quite askew. Why he is wearing his white-framed Ray Bans now, at night and indoors, you have no idea.

It is getting late, and you and he have a pile of shot glasses and beer pints lined up on the table. You still have a lot of energy, though your head does not seem to be connecting very well with your body. You chew on a plate of what looks like seaweed, which it is basically, from the Quadling Sea. It's supposed to keep your system healthy and functioning, and it tastes like pure salt.

"I like not paying for shrinks," you say, realizing one word was wrong in that sentence. "Something's not wrong with that s-something tings, wrong with that sentence." You try to keep one eyelid open with your fingers. "I like not...using money... for shrinks." You frown. "Whatever."

Guy straightens his sunglasses. "What you go smend-spend your money on, kid? You got nearly a lot in there, honey, from the job, but what if you get more? I know what

NIGHTHAWKS AT THE MISSION

I would spend on, true shit, I know what I would spend on, not something stupid." He downs the last of his fourth beer. "Look, this is what I would spend my money on, girl, this is what I spend...are you listening?"

You feel like passing out but you straighten up.

"Two birds. One a parrot and one an eagle. That's first. I'd buy 'em and release 'em because there needs to be some kindness in this world, you know. If someone was selling these birds that wouldn't be right, and releasing them would be an omen. Let me tell you a couple of three things, like Phil Leotardo would say. First would be a Maserati—a kick the shit out of everything else car, few years behind the market, something that if you saw it rolling up you'd go, 'Ho-ho, look at this guy! He's a money-making machine. A triple-M mother-shut your mouth man.' Next would be like some restaurant out in Hollywood that's only open four hours a day, and celebrities just got to gravitate to it, you know, like magnets, like a hot ass magnet for hot ass people. And B, the original demo tapes to Bruce Springsteen's *Nebraska*. You know that album he did in his closet back in '82 that's just songs about killing cops? You dig the boss, right, who doesn't dig the boss? That's history, my friend, it belongs in a museum," Guy finishes.

"I'd get a Hassermati car, too. I knew a guy with a Hassermati," you say. "Like that effer right there." You see someone who looks like Tyler heading your way.

"Oh shit," you say, recognizing who it is. It's Jaime Van Zandt, your husband once upon a time. Not Tyler. He waves. He looks sunburned and his hair is a lot longer than you remember. He's grown a patchy beard.

"Holy wow! I just came in here because of all the history. My god, Sarah? Is that you? I can't recognize...but I love it," Jaime says, sitting next to you in the booth. "Can you believe how far south we've gone?"

Guy snarls a little, like a threatened dog. "Who's you, friend?"

Jaime puts out a hand. "Uh, Van Zandt. Jaime Van Zandt. I was—well I guess am—Sarah's hubby here. Legally, not, uh, spiritually. God, I was worried about you with the Mission and all. I read stuff in the Network Morning Star. All those stories about Sargasso. I wandered through the Sargasso a bit before coming down this way," he plods on, sipping a little from his cranberry juice as he does so. "Sarah, you want to hear something nutty? Just damn screwy, really?"

You twist your head and yell out, "Hit me with your best shot. Fire away!"

He looks at Guy, clamming up. "Guy's cool as shit," you say.

"You know Mathias and Petty, those crazy people? They're attacking people out there, right?" Jaime continues. "I know something about them." He calls you both in closer. "I know their real identities, or, well, I guess, their fake identities that they use as cover." Jaime swallows. "You remember those people on the monorail? Boston, and, uh, Love?"

You think to yourself for a long moment, sobering up.

"That's them. That's them in disguise. I even know where they are all the time. They were at the boat quays, but now they are at a place called McRoss Research. I hitched a ride out there once with a couple of Solomon's House guys and saw that Boston and Love— Mathias and Petty—were living there as caretakers along with some other people who are supposed to work for the university."

Jaime smiles for a long time as you and Guy sit there in silence. All the air seems to be sucked out of the room.

"How do you know all this, Jaime? And why," you grab Jaime's collar, "why doesn't the Network know about this?"

Guy spreads his hands open. "Yeah, shit man, really..."

Jaime looks at you both. "Have you seen the people who work as Counters? Or the Ephors? Really? Would you trust 'em not to tell Mathias and Petty first about me? I saw one walking around with a beer. They take bribes. It'd be like reporting a drug lord in Mexico to the Mexican police. Forget that! I found out by accident, hiking through the Sargasso. I got, frankly, well, lost, and saw them change shape from Mathias and Petty to Boston and Love as they were talking to some people after they..." Jaime looks away. "After they killed them. That's why I'm so far south here now. They still operate under those personas. I met 'em one time afterwards." He looks like he wants to cry, and abruptly changes the subject. "I've got some great sketches of all the areas around here."

"That's why we're here, too. Not the sketches. You know..." you say.

Jaime sips the last of his cranberry juice. "Sorry, it was screwed up. I'm staying across the street at the Pegasus House if you want to stop by. Got some really great sketches about life in The Oberon." He walks away, and you watch him go to the bar, pay, and then wave back to you. He looks very upset.

"Huh," you say.

"It's a god-late hour here, you know. It's that hour and that time when you gotta go do some shit. Come on, killer." Guy stands up and immediately trips over his own two feet, almost landing on another table. The other people there laugh. He picks up one of their beers and takes it with him as he makes his way back to the bar and Kayla. You follow him, swaying slightly.

"What Jaime said, man, oh, man..." Guy drinks the last of the beer. "Kayla, it's time, it's time, it's Vader time, time, time..."

Kayla bends down to the safe, opens it, and withdraws a shiny metallic card with serrated teeth at its end. It is labeled: *Guy's Home.*

She says something in Perchta and the Ni-Perchta helper grunts back, continuing to wash dishes.

"Night, Cal. Always love your bar, here," Guy says, waving to the Ni-Perchta bartender.

Holding the key in one hand, Kayla walks out from behind the counter and leads you upstairs.

"Kayla, I like free drinks," you say, in all seriousness.

"Anything for Guy Farson," she mockingly says.

Guy makes a trigger motion with his fingers. "Uh-huh."

She opens up an almost empty room with four stone walls. Inside is a pile of empty cardboard boxes, empty beer bottles, and a Nemo Gate.

The three of you walk up to the portal. Kayla puts the metallic card into what looks like a dragon's mouth sticking out of one side of the Gate. It pops into the Gate's side for a second and then ejects with a thunk. "It's programmed for your place, Guy."

There is a crackling sound and you can feel static electricity building up.

"Good night, nighting, nighting, nighting..." Kayla says in a singsong voice. Then she bows and sweeps her hands towards the portal.

"After you, Madam," Guy says to you.

Hesitant as always, you step forward and once again have that particular sense of stars exploding and watching a white ring grow and grow. A moment later you are standing on Guy's very small island, the wind blowing steadily from the beach far ahead of you.

"Right," you say, not sure at all what to make of this little turn of events.

Guy materializes a moment after you and removes the serrated metal key from the end of his Nemo Gate, shutting it off. He chuckles. "And a-what and a-who now? A house inside a bar? I love my house and rare, programmable Nemo Gate."

"We can catch and kill Mathias and Petty," you say, suddenly a little more sober.

Guy high fives you hard. "Burn 'em down. Get 'em back for Saki and her family," he says evenly, his face showing no expression. He walks away towards his bathroom, leaving you alone outside.

You listen to the waves crash against the island for a long while, not saying a word as you sit on the swinging bench with Guy. You just look up at the stars, reflecting on where you are after so many days. What you have just been through. These thoughts jolt you into the shallow end of sobriety.

"We'll get 'em," you say. Chill winds blow, cooling you off in the humid night air.

Guy nods as you swing back and forth. "I was always a fan of this world over the other one. Don't know why. Even with all the monsters," he says, as if anticipating your thoughts. "Everybody's talkin' about me, I don't hear a word they're saying..." Guy sings off-key.

You take off your shirt and throw it to the side of the platform leading into the sea, feeling drunk and horny and over-heated at the same time. You kick off your shoes, take off your jeans, and dive into the warm sea, backstroking out a little bit.

"I like this, Guy!" you yell, only to barely make out that Guy has passed out on the swing, his sunglasses half off. You tread water for a while, enjoying your swim under the moonlight.

After you don't know how much time, you crawl out and walk up to Guy. You kiss him on the mouth as he is passed out, laugh a little to yourself, and then decide to sit down on the bench and go to sleep next to him. But he wakes up and sees you there, soaking wet and in just your bra and panties. He doesn't say anything but takes his stupid sunglasses off. He kisses you, first on the mouth, then on your neck. His strong hands slowly take down your bra straps, exposing you further to the warm night-time air. You make love for the first time under the stars.

You awake the next day, hung over, naked in bed together. You realize that you just gave your virginity up to a man you are not married to. Saving yourself for marriage, that last boundary you had set for yourself, was shredded last night. You feel a little empty afterwards for having done so. You betrayed something about your old self and you can never go back to the way things were. Like every other unpleasant thought, you shut this thought far away before your conscience speaks. You do not know if you truly love Guy enough for this to have happened.

Guy says he has something that is the perfect hangover cure for the both of you. The Baths of Urncalles. Just around the corner, he says, on the red stone land bridge that juts out and over the Quadling Sea, so you make the journey, looking dirty and disheveled, both now wearing white-framed sunglasses and sipping water bottles like crazy.

A set of double doors reveals a circular stairway of rock leading into the baths. Strange Antediluvian hieroglyphics line the wall, ones that look to the uninitiated eye like nonsensical circles and long lines. The stairway is gloomy with only a few little white orbs for light. An odd booming noise echoes throughout the stairwell. You both walk up, Guy trying to convince you to try out one of those trilobite things. "It's just like a giant lobster tail. It's good, honest injun," he tells you.

"I already had one as a sandwich. It's good but it's weird, man," you reply.

You head up floor by floor until you get to a roped-off area that cuts you off from going further. The rope has a red warning sign on it written in English, Greek, and Perchta: *Danger, Do Not Enter!*

"This is cool. You'll like this, believe you me. This will be a good early birthday present for you."

When you slowly open a set of double doors on your right, you find yourself in a courtyard area open to both blue skies and what looks like a giant pool of water suspended up in the sky. High red rock walls and ancient Egyptian-style pillars surround the courtyard. In the middle is a huge statue of a creature sitting in the lotus position. It looks like a smaller copy of the giant statue that is in Solomon's Bay. Like the giant statue, it has two faces: one angry, one calm. It holds with one hand a lightning bolt and the other hand has seven stone balls forever floating above the palm, representing the permanent moons. A crown of demonic-looking skulls rests on its brow.

"Welcome to the Baths, Missy Orange. But this isn't even the best part yet."

The deep waters of the pool change color from black to white to red to gold and then to blue. Life-sized statues of the Gug creature you ran into and of Ni-Perchta warriors dot the yard. Each of the large Ni-Perchta warriors has a spear that shoots red and blue laser lights into the atmosphere high above, changing the color of the giant pool of water hanging in the sky from a bright blue to a dusky red, and then back again. The Arc Waters that hang in the sky must be the size of six or seven football fields, and they must be at least two hundred feet up.

A few rich American kids are laughing and horsing around with each other, sitting on towels near the courtyard pool. Somewhere there is a boom box piping in Radio Oberon. "Not working must be fun," you say.

Guy laughs a little. "We can work towards that."

You and Guy come upon a massive hallway with statues of two-headed men and of otherwise normal-looking women with fangs for teeth. The ceiling stretches upward, the vaulted roof and tiled floor separated by a hundred feet of air. You feel like you are in one of those documentaries about the Vatican due to the Urncalles' ancient and positively Greco-Roman look. Farther along is a corridor where purple water travels quickly upward on a slant with nothing supporting its trajectory, just open air.

A few young men and women in bathing suits and equipped with those ring-shaped life preservers are jumping into the pool and shooting upwards, disappearing into some area beyond in a rush of ever continuing water. A Ni-Perchta man, tall and imposing, guards the entrance to the water arc with a whistle tied around his neck.

"Go get changed," Guy says, dishing out a ton of Dii-Yaa. "They got complimentary stuff inside for you." He points to two nearby locker rooms with a male or female logo on each stone door.

You take the cash and remark, "I'll pay you back. You're being too generous."

"I know."

After changing, you jump into the Arc Waters wearing a black one-piece bathing suit and a smile. Holding onto the preserver, you shoot up through the waters, going quickly into the air until you hit the top end of the water arc that hangs suspended in the sky. You slip into the life preserver ring and start swimming. The giant pool, literally hanging in mid-air, gives an incredible view of the whole area. The water is cool but warm enough.

Guy pops up next to you, putting himself through his life preserver. He put his sunglasses back on after holding them in his hands. His toned body is easy and pleasant to look at. He's attractive enough to be in Hollywood as a second string leading man—he wouldn't be the hottest celebrity in the world but one that could carry a decent fan base.

Maybe twenty or thirty feet below you can see the pool and the courtyard. Off to the south you see the beaches of Stonetown.

You and Guy swim aimlessly across the Arc Waters as they change in color from black to purple to red, and reach the other side. There are more than a few floating islands made of barrels scattered around the waters, and lifeguard towers manned by both human and Ni-Perchta watching to see if anyone is about to drown. Some of the barrel areas are pretty large—big enough to hold a couple of picnic tables along with snack stands.

You swim to the outer edge of the pool, afraid at first that you will simply topple over the edge, but when you see a couple of swimmers holding on to an invisible wall, you go up to it. Guy keeps next to you, quite relaxed.

It is morning still, a bright sunny morning. A couple of moons hang indistinct in the southern sky. Just then you hear a murmur in the air from some of the other swimmers and then some gasps.

Coming out of the west is a herd of Baleen dragons, the multi-ton creatures that are colored a dull grey-green with oversized, toothless jaws. They have wingspans up to forty feet. Their spiked leathery wings beat against the air with a rhythmic thumping, and they call out to each other with sounds like whale song.

Flying just above the great sea, they lower their heads just under the waves, sucking in water and then letting it flow out from their mouths. The water trickles back into the sea in little streams, along with a few fish filtered out from their jaws. They ignore the small crowds on the nearby beach. These dragons are not meat eaters or vicious carnivores, so you have heard. Having never seen one before, but knowing what is described in books, you guess that the people aren't really in danger.

A few of the dragons stop and stand in a shallow part of the sea close to the beach, dunking their heads into the water and then out again. You watch in amazement, hearing nothing but the dragons chattering to each other. The other swimmers watch, astonished.

Guy laughs. "That time of the year again. Damn, look at these guys."

A lifeguard calls out to one of the other swimmers. "Don't worry, they're harmless, just like to eat shrimp."

Guy motions to you. "You want something to eat? We can swim up to one of those little islands there." He points to one of the floating barrel areas that has a wooden snack shack on it.

"Yes, starving."

He starts off for one of the shacks marked *Eggs up in the Air*. You tread water with the life preserver around you, looking out at everything, feeling mildly content. Then you follow Guy over to the shack, pulling yourself up onto the platform, and sit down at one of the picnic tables. Guy pays for the food with money out of a clear plastic pouch tied around his wrist. You eat in near silence on that beautiful morning, enjoying the sunshine and everything around you.

You open up the conversation with a random question. "Guy, I just thought of something."

"Noh?" he says with a mouthful of eggs. He leans back, scratching one of his nipples.

"Mathias and Petty," is all you say. "What Jaime said."

Guy raises an eyebrow. "I was there." You laugh a little.

He takes off his glasses, focusing on you very intensely and setting his fork down. "What do you want to talk about, Sarah?"

"One big cash out," you say. "You've seen the wanted posters—millions in Dii-Yaa. Those people want us dead. They killed Saki's family, and we know where they are now. They won't expect us to come swooping in." A cool wind blows in. "We all want them dead. For poor Saki's family, Saki herself. If she doesn't pull out of the, you know. And for Winniefreddie. All these innocent people. But at the same time, Guy..."

Guy bites his lip, thinking, and then leans forward. "There's still a big X factor over all of this, Sarah."

"What?" you whisper.

He looks off to the west. "You realize how dangerous these people are, don't you?"

You frown. "No, I really don't," you say sarcastically.

"The portal between Earth and The Oberon opens in June. We—me, you, Treena, Saki—could just take our money and go. Before anything else weird or bad happens. Stop being so effing greedy."

"You walk around without a gun in hand. I don't see you worried."

He points to the very normal-looking digital, and presumably waterproof, watch that you now notice him wearing. "Specially made, Sarah. Get it? You won't ever see me take off this watch, okay? It's got a little slice of T-K orichalcum in it."

"Alright, alright," you say, turning to your eggs and concentrating on eating for a while.

"You ever had a near death experience, Guy? I mean, yes, you did. You remember what it's like almost to head into...into nothing?" You shiver a little, still wet from the Arc Waters.

Guy looks a little angry. "I had an arrow shot through my face. So the answer is yes."

"You remember why you were scared, Guy? Do you remember why?" You look across the still waters. "Because at that moment when you are about to die, you realize, all at once, that you haven't done much with what time you've had. And there'll be nothing afterwards. You will be canceled out forever. Washed away by the flood."

Guy clears his throat. "Yeah, sure."

"What if we get all that money from doing you-know-what to Mathias and Petty, and we take that money and figure out a way to put it to good use. Then we can make sure that the next time we see death we do have a life worth reflecting on. Besides killing them for what they did to Saki and her family. Otherwise, there's just a ticking clock."

Guy pushes his food away. A Ni-Perchta girl, around ten years old, picks up the plate and takes it back to the shack. The human owner barks something harsh at her and hits her lightly upside the head with the back of his meaty hand.

"Let me think about it," Guy says, standing up and leaving a tip from his plastic pouch. His voice is cold as he says this, and he leaves you there at the picnic table. You call out in front of everyone on the barrel island, "You're not scared, are you?" A couple of people glance in your direction.

With preserver in hand, Guy jumps off the side and into the water again with a splash, swimming away from you and all the way to the invisible wall at the far end of the Arc Waters.

You can see him thinking, looking out over the wall and then back to you. A constant frown decorates his face. You grab your life preserver and jump back into the water to swim over to him. You say a moment later, "I honestly am sorry. That was just mean."

"Surrender, Sarah Orange! Surrender, Guy Farson!" strange, modulated voices, loud as thunder, cry out like a chorus from Hell.

Three people wrapped in black cloaks fly across the sky, arms out, legs spread apart as if standing. A device across each of their belts emits a red glow. They don't seem to know where you two are at first, so you swim forward as casually as you can. The fliers attract the notice of some of the Baleen dragons on the other side of the Urncalles.

"Surrender, Sarah Orange! Surrender, Guy Farson!" the voices continue to yell.

Guy curses under his breath. "Keep going to the wall. I can figure out somethin'."

You swim towards the invisible wall, as apprehensive and frightened as Guy is.

The fliers then yell something in Perchta so loudly that you think your eardrums will burst. A great white light pours out from each flier into the waters, sending a slow shockwave that freezes people in place.

The men, women, and children who were swimming now stare emptily, frozen as if dead. Some of the swimmers are face down in the water. One of the fliers peels off to flip them over using telekinesis, so that they won't drown. You don't know what to make of that.

You feel for the invisible wall and pull yourself out of the water, leaving the life preserver behind just as the shockwave crashes forward. But Guy is too late and is struck by it, freezing into place. You stand seemingly on nothing at all, though it feels solid under your feet. You hold up your hands and cry out, "Alright, alright, don't hurt anyone! We're here!" It is at least a couple of hundred feet down to the Quadling Sea below. You already feel like you're standing on thin air on the non-existent wall, and it makes your head swim.

The three fliers converge, and you feel yourself being picked up and lifted straight into the air. You curse yourself for being a fool. Guy is picked up by another flier, his drooping body dripping water as he is hauled up.

Then one of the Baleen dragons, perhaps attracted by the noise and the commotion, swoops in out of nowhere, its wings beating the air, and knocks two fliers out of position. The two of them spin around like propellers. The dragon isn't aggressive, just a curious and completely oversized beast seeing what the commotion is.

You fall backwards onto the invisible wall, hitting your back and almost going off the wide edge.

The fliers motion for the dragon to go away, but it doesn't. One of the frustrated fliers sprays fire into the dragon's face, trying to make it move along faster, while another flier shoots bolts of white electricity at it. The creature hisses in pain as it tries to back off. All they've done is anger it, and it knocks into one flier with its giant head. The flier goes down into the Arc Waters with a splash. As it hits the water, the swimmers become unfrozen all at once, screaming and crying with fear. Guy wakes up and tries to re-orient himself. The other fliers decide to keep fighting the dragon that is now calling out in a singsong rumble to its kin. They fly in to protect him. One flier only just avoids being swatted with the wave of a giant dragon wing. There are now five dragons swooping around the Arc Waters, terrifying everyone who is there.

One flier manages to shoot off what looks like a small meteor from his ori-baton and hits one of the dragons in the wing, which is left partially shredded as if it's been popped by a shotgun blast. The dragon keeps flying forward but is sinking in the air little by little. It tries to glide to the sea below by diving between the Arc Waters and the Urncalles.

You watch in fright, lying on the invisible wall. Guy grabs your hand and pulls you up with a jerk.

The fliers are driving the dragons away; soon they will re-focus on you and Guy.

An incredible kaleidoscope of light erupts around one flier, who transforms into a giant, white, hydra-like monster, ready to fight off the dragons. Each one of its spiked serpent heads covered in thousands of white scales bites one dragon on its neck with needle-like teeth.

The wounded dragon flies maybe ten feet under the Arc Waters and above the baths. In two seconds it will be directly underneath you and Guy. It is in agony and looks to be descending into the Quadling Sea below.

"Grab onto that dragon!" you say, pointing to the dragon angling between the land bridge and the Arc Waters. *Roll the dice, Sarah,* you think. Guy understands; he extends out a small radio antenna from his watch. You take a deep breath, say the Hail Mary, and grab his arm. You look into the sky that is such a bright blue and think to yourself, *there could be worse ways to die. And on uglier, less scenic days.*

You two jump off the ledge, and Guy screams. You are falling faster and faster. You feel the wind fly through your hair. You *know* that the most likely thing to happen to you is that you are going to die, and crazily, you think that if you survive this then your future is going to get better and better because this is the worst thing you have ever been through.

You fall end over end, a limp creature, crashing towards the water at high speed. There is no life reflection, just the conscious thought that you are falling forever.

And then Guy's watch pays off. With the telekinesis power of the device, he grabs onto the dragon's remaining functional wing just as it's diving back towards the Quadling Sea. You grab onto a protruding bone, or whatever is sticking out of its side. In five seconds you're both knocked off, but the dragon is losing so much altitude that instead of falling two hundred feet, you roll off and hit the sea from a somewhat more reasonable twenty feet.

You crash into the water as loosely as a drunk flying from his unbuckled car seat into the night air, closely followed by Guy. You go under the water, deep under, and hear nothing but the rush of water past your ears. There is no breath inside your lungs; all the air was sucked out by the impact. Panic sets in at the volume of water above you, and you almost black out as you swim upwards. As you break the surface, you suck air like a dying fish, and unable to move forward, rely on the waves to push you towards the empty beach. It is a good five minutes before you touch land again. Guy swims next to you.

The wounded dragon is in the sea, sitting low in the deep water and crying out, its dinosaur growling echoing throughout the scene.

Above you, five dragons circle the top of the Arc Waters, calling out to each other in their whale song and roaring in pain as they fight against the fliers. The white serpent creature is putting up a hell of a fight, but then it suddenly disappears. You think you see the flier it had once been get knocked backwards through the air before re-orienting himself. The three fliers then flee the scene, booming back to wherever they came from.

Your body hurts badly and you shake like a leaf, but you stand up and walk towards one of the Stonetown gates. Guy hugs you. "You, holy, holy, good god," he keeps saying. He stares wide-eyed at the whole scene. "Still alive." Then he throws up, right onto the sand.

Treena runs over to you. She has on way too much sunblock and wears a big floppy sun hat. "Well! I thought it had something to do with you two," she says. Her own ori- baton is out. "Goodness. Nice look, Sarah."

"Good to see you," you say, before dry heaving a little. "Christ. Eggs and all that."

Guy sits down, as white as the sand he is sitting on. "Bastards need to be shut down. I think it's time we collect that reward money for them."

Treena breathes heavily. "You sure it's them?"

"What the hell do you think? They want us for some reason. First they wanted to murder us, now they want to capture and then murder us. Who else would it be, Treena?"

She blinks a few times and watches the dragons as they leave Quadling.

CHAPTER EIGHTEEN:
DEATH BY WATER

You sit down with Jaime and Guy to talk over Jaime's story one more time. "They're working at McRoss Research Station. That's all they said."

Jaime asks if you are in trouble or need anything, and you tell him no as the three of you sit at a rooftop bar in Stonetown. No one else is there. The Ni-Perchta bartender left after you paid him to.

Jaime asks to come with you. "We're old friends, aren't we? A little more than that in some ways? If you are in trouble..."

You and Guy lay out everything that's happened so far and let Jaime make an informed decision, which he does.

"*Well*, I mean they're gonna attack ya, so you better give 'em a quick short sharp shock, so they don't do it again?" You look at him carefully, feeling very paranoid and very open to attack right at this moment. The great wide open sky is all around you, making you feel insecure.

"Back to McRoss Station, then." Jaime takes out his sketch pad, showing off an elaborate drawing of it. "They just got back up to full operation."

"You know the Old Man at Midnight?" you ask.

"The pirate radio guy?" Jaime asks, scratching his head. "No, why?"

"He was an...not an overseer, uh, a whatcha call it? Caretaker, during the off months," you reply, sipping on your lemonade.

Jaime shakes his head. "I didn't see him there. Just Boston and Love. There were three other people stopping by, uh, three Network people. They said they were going to go back around this time. They were nervous, jumpy people. I got a weird vibe off them, and I just lied and gave them a totally different name as I left. I got there on this Triumph bike I inherited, a nice little—"

Guy shushes him. "That's good." He looks at you. "You ever shot a gun before, Jaime?"

Jaime leans forward. "I was really hoping you would ask me that," he whispers.

You nod and look to Guy, who immediately stands up, whips out his ori-baton and puts it right next to Jaime's neck.

"What was the one thing you told me before you left that night at Mission Friendship?" You look around at the other rooftops to see if anyone has spotted you.

Jaime squints and thinks long and hard. "This isn't Earth, this is a cool situation." He seems not the least bit worried, like he is enjoying this a little bit too much. He winks at you. "Alright, Cutie McCutes."

You exhale deeply. Guy puts his baton away. "Sorry, dude. Me and Sarah had a suspicion. You might be somebody else. I mean you show up and then they show up. Must be something else, then. Something tracking us."

A thought dawns on you, something that has been nagging you for a little while now.

Down at the docks, you and Jaime, Treena and Guy sit in the wheelhouse of the *S.B. Crue*. Even though the sun is falling down in the west, the air is humid and you wipe your neck with a cool towel. An evening rain comes down, despite the almost sunny skies.

The frustration builds up as you continue to play this game of pretend. The constant trickle of rainwater into the sea behind you grates on your nerves.

"We gotta flush these people out into the open," you say abruptly, and hope you don't sound insincere.

"I say we forget about it and run," Treena says, oddly and flatly.

Guy, looking around the wheelhouse with suspicion, states, "The Old Man at Midnight will meet us a couple of minutes away from McRoss. Just a few minutes down the road. We make the deal there. We still got so many leftovers from the star job."

You nod hesitantly. "When?"

"Six days from now. Talked to him through his contact here in Stonetown at The Rhodie Bar. We gotta pick up the stuff, you and me, girlie." Guy points to you. "And bring it on over. Treena, you have to..."

You talk basically nonsense for the next five minutes and then leave, getting off the hovering airship and walking back onto the dock. Guy follows you after a couple of minutes. The bogus plan you rambled off should be believable to whoever is listening.

"Has to be, right? They had to have bugged the ship back when Tek was driving it. Something Antediluvian, right? Weird bugging device?" you whisper to Guy.

Guy puts his hands around your waist. "You're completely right. Gotta be. How else can they be onto us, unless Treena is selling us out."

You shake your head, looking down.

"I doubt it. I mean, they...with her sister..." Guy says.

Jaime comes out of the ship, looking around the docks. "Crazy. Crazy, crazy world we live in. Told you it'd be an adventure, Sarah," he says, punching your arm lightly.

"Alright, Treena will drop off the Ghia," Guy indicates the car which is currently hanging by a cable next to the extra Ford Mustang, "a little way down the road."

"You think they bugged the Ghia, too?" you ask. James Farson handed you back the keys to the Ghia the day you were expelled from the Mission.

Guy shakes his head. "If they did, we'd have been hit again, right? When we went out to the star that night?"

"Right."

Jaime asks if you want to get something to eat and both of you refuse, too sick to even think about eating a single thing.

You drive the Ghia for almost nine hours, going right down the yellow X highway back to the Sargasso region. Guy sits in the passenger seat, smoking a cigar. You pass around the city, avoiding the wreckage of that once mighty place. No one says anything during the long drive, even when you take out one of the spare gas cans and fill up the tank again.

Guy takes a piss out in the grasslands as you wait.

With your ori-baton, you heat up a can of clam chowder to share while sitting next to each other on the hood of the Ghia. Guy can't stop talking, mentioning places and things he has done around the area. He keeps a nervous wave of chatter going.

"Okay, let's visualize this. This is something I do before any one of these big salvage ops. We shoot Mathias and Petty and potentially get a ton of money for doing it—the Witch-Lord has a huge reward on their heads. What will you do with the money if we survive this?"

You stare at him, wondering if he really wants to have this conversation. "I...I never thought about it, actually," you say, truly stumped for a moment.

"We could potentially be sharing a million by the end of the month and you have no idea what you'd do with it?" Guy says with a hysterical and nervous laugh. Then he stops laughing. "Should we just call it off?"

"No, I just..." You look up at the sky, thinking about it. "I've always had this, uh, dream, too, besides all the material stuff." You shut up, really thinking. "When my dad and my brother were killed in a car accident, I kind of went into a shutdown mode for a month. I stopped speaking. My mother finally sent me to a doctor, and I got some help and some pills. My sister had died a year before, and it just made my head feel like it was full of noise. A thought came to me. A giant one that just stays flashing in my brain."

Guy takes off his new white-framed sunglasses, setting them down as he listens to you.

"What's happened out here is emphasizing this thought, too, this dream. The thought is I don't want to waste one hour on doing something for somebody else, working some b.s. nine to five job, day in, day out, for twenty years, getting fired, getting rehired, scrounging around for work. If we get a lot of money here, we've bought our freedom, permanently. Forever. No one controls us anymore. No more bosses. No more lost time. We don't have much life to begin with, so why in God's name are we wasting our lives on all this crap that doesn't matter in the end? I don't want to work in an office or anything, and if I can murder a couple of murderers that hurt our friend Saki to do so..." You wipe the tears away from your eyes. "You probably wanted a fun answer."

Guy smiles. "Yes. I was visualizing a silver Maserati GranTurismo Sport convertible, and a home in San Francisco. I just like that city a lot. Is that gay?"

You start to laugh, wiping the tears away at the same time. Guy puts a hand on your shoulder. "I like that, too," you say, kissing him again. "You taste like clam chowder." Guy laughs a little. You think of Saki and their relationship and you feel a sort of hate build up against yourself. You are kissing someone else's boyfriend. You are no better than Tyler's girls back home. You smile despite the pain you feel inside.

Guy takes over the drive from here on in. You pray silently the whole way back to the Sargasso region, and your stomach clenches when you see the green reflector sign stating that the turn off for Mission Friendship is coming up. Guy turns in the opposite direction, towards where McRoss should be, and drives into the dry and weathered grasslands and the broken canyon-scape of the Sargasso Breaks.

"I think we're getting too close now. We need to park so we can sneak up on it," Guy says, the wind from his open window smothering some of his words.

He drives the Ghia deep into the thick grasslands, finally stopping with a few scrapes. You gather everything up and jump out.

"We'd better start moving away from the station, come around to the south. Otherwise, if they're coming by air, they'll see us." Guy straps on the bulletproof vest he bought in Stonetown and gives you a yellow belt with a golden electrical box hooked into it. You realize what it is—a shield belt.

"Forget about it," he says as you to try to reject it. "It was the last one they had. I wish we could get more. You only get a few shots before it breaks down. It's older than the pyramids. You know it's on when your skin feels a little stretched. That bastard Mathias has one, too. Probably a better one. They aren't reliable. I'm sorry, but it's better than having a real vest."

You and he clomp through the grasslands in the dark, keeping your bearings by the small compass on Guy's watch, barely talking and barely acknowledging the other's presence. You're able to see where you're going as the seven moons are out in full, each one of them providing more than enough light to walk by. A Network van drives by along the yellow X highway, a big blue and white one with extra metal welded to it. It passes at full speed.

About an hour into your walk, you hear music playing, maybe Pink Floyd or some other psychedelic rock stuff. The music thumps through the landscape, probably the best neighborhood in the universe to play music this loud and for this long. Then you see the station.

McRoss is lit up under a mix of orange sodium lights and regular light bulbs behind iron cages. The lighthouse ship is still there, docked on the river, its light shining over the wasteland.

Guy motions for you to get down and to follow what he does: army-crawl in the high grass, keeping low and out of sight. Your nose itches like crazy, smelling the fragrant brush that you are crawling through.

"Neat looking boat," Guy whispers and you nod, your head throbbing with all the adrenaline.

"We have to...wait, look." Guy brings out binoculars, kneeling and raising himself just above the grass. Three dark figures stand behind the chain link fence, next to a barbecue that glows orange from heated coals. Their shadows are long in the orange light of the station. Guy puts the binoculars to your eyes. The three figures each have a beer in their hand, and the van you saw driving by is there with its doors open.

"People you recognize?" Guys says, sarcastically.

You do. Three figures from your dream and waking life. Oscar Botha, Dee Ricco, and Dr. Wellington Cartwright.

They are talking and laughing. Guns are strapped to their chests and ori-batons armed with little orichalcum stones are lashed to their hips. They each wear thin, blue jackets that say *Solomon's House University* on the back in gold letters.

"Gotta be our fan club," Guy whispers. "Three guys—three attackers over the Arc Waters, right? Gotta be."

"God, I hate the Network," you say. "They really need to do background checks on people. I got my job in four hours."

Guy blows out his breath. "They must've got our little false signals out of Stonetown, then. Your plan seems to be working, kid. Arrogant asses, too. Look at that—playing music, sipping beers..."

As you watch them standing around, enjoying their beers behind the chain link fence, you feel nothing but hate for them, true hate. These people are the face of Guy's attempted murder. They killed Saki's family. You swallow compulsively when you realize you are very scared of them now.

"Don't be nervous. It'll be like pulling out a tooth—a lot of pain and fright and then it's over in a second," Guy says, a little too quickly. He takes out his sawed off rifle with a pistol grip and slowly pulls back the bolt with a snick, brushing away some of the grass from his face. "And then I guess you feel numb afterwards." He pats you on the back. "That probably didn't cheer you up any." He mutters a prayer under his breath and crosses himself.

"I didn't know you were Catholic." He kisses you. "Ever do this before?" you ask.

He shakes his head after a moment.

"They look a little too comfortable, don't they, Guy? I mean, how can they just be...?" You shake your head. Those aren't people on the other side of that chain link fence, just nightmares in human form. The dream has become reality again, right in front of you. You clench your palms so hard your nails dig in, leaving little bloody crescents.

Guy scopes out the situation with the binoculars. "Mathias and Petty must be tracking the *Crue* in Stonetown. They'll rush back here once they realize it's stuck on autopilot heading...well, wherever."

Guy rolls his eyes over to you. "Must be it. We rush them right now, throw 'em down. Blitzkrieg their asses."

You nod. "Yeah. Yeah. Okay, then...we wait. Let 'em get comfortable, really see if it's the three of them. They're drinking and barbecuing, right? Everyone who's there should be around in the open or will be in the next few minutes. They seem pretty nonchalant. We hit 'em after the beer hits them," you say.

Guy scratches his nose. "Maybe. We'll wait. Let's try to take them alive, then. We can kill 'em after we torture them. I want some damn answers. I want to know where Mathias and Petty are right now... We'll wait," he says with a sigh, readjusting his body armor. "Oh Lord, we will wait." He looks up to the sky and makes a circling gesture.

For an hour you sit in the high grass, watching the three of them go back and forth, eating and drinking, their actions so normal and so trivial that you wonder if this is really the terror of the Sargasso or an evening in the park in your old hometown on Earth. Guy nearly hyperventilates next to you; you can almost hear his heart thudding.

To you, these moments are something like going in front of the class before doing your five-minute speech on Kennedy, or when you were asked to do the Pledge of Allegiance. It's a performance anxiety, not a fear of death. That isn't there. You are just afraid to screw up somehow and screw up badly. But the dream, the dream keeps replaying in your head, and you see their faces. You see your sister's face as well.

The music coming from their radio has a funky, reggae beat and reverberates through the night. The three monsters relax on lawn chairs. Each of them had two or three beers. They're fed and full of beer.

"Let's do this, girl," Guy says, his voice a little higher than normal

"On three?" you say.

"No." Guy licks his lips. "Just fire for effect into the air. It'll scare 'em. You got dragon's breath rounds, right? That's the shells." He pulls back the bolt on that bolt-action sawed-off rifle/pistol that he has. You have Winniefreddie's shotgun with you, for practicality and for irony.

Guy takes off in a charge across the grasslands. You rush forward to keep up with him. He yells as loud as he can—it is scary, intense, frightening. A mad man's scream. He crosses the yellow X highway in a full sprint and then, waving his ori-baton, rips out the chain link fence and throws it to the side. It makes a fierce screech as it is ripped out of its posts.

You fire the shotgun repeatedly, the bursts of flame lighting up the night sky, the booms shattering the stillness of the night.

The three bastards are still trying to get out of their lawn chairs when Guy using his baton telekinetically tosses the smoldering barbecue at Dee. She falls back with a scream, brushing off the hot coals as fast as she can, burning her hands and dropping the pistol she was quick enough to draw.

Treena jumps down from the sky and lands directly on top of the van. Her Tri-Skysurfer lands with a crash on one of the other buildings. She's laughing as she waves her rifle around.

"Freeze! Freeze!" Guy says, covering them with his sawed-off rifle. "First asshole to move gets his brains blown out!"

The three have their hands up now. Dee Ricco, your former boss, is crouched on the concrete next to the orange coals and ash that flew out of the barbecue, her face dirty with soot and reddening from burns. "Alright, alright, alright..." she says repeatedly. Botha is on the ground next to her, his own hands up.

"Where's Mathias?" you cry, terrified about where the outlaw is at that moment. "Where is he?" You fire the shotgun into the air and six feet of flame shoots out of the barrel.

Cartwright, who fell over backwards in his lawn chair, still has his beer bottle in his hand. He slowly puts it down. "Mathias? What are you talking about, Sarah?"

You walk over to him and put the barrel right into his face. "Don't use my name. I know you," you say. "I know your true face."

Cartwright starts to speak before the door into the warehouse of McRoss Research opens to reveal his wife. She has her own assault rifle pointed at you.

"Put it down, Sarah," she says, her voice quavering. "Please."

You look a little bit too long in her direction, the barrel of your gun shifting to her, and Cartwright pounces on you. He throws you backwards, making you fall hard on your back and skitter down the yellow X highway. Your gun unloads into one wall of the warehouse. The doctor's wife turns and fires wildly into the air, her burst of rifle fire making a savage popping sound in the night. Her shots hit you several times, knocking out your energy shield in just moments—five straight shots right into you bounce off because of your shield belt's energy. Her gun jams. She then kicks the door closed.

Botha engulfs Treena in flames, the ori-baton in his left hand spewing out a jet of flame and fuel, while the gun in his right hand fires shots into her bulletproof vest. Then, with his ori- power, he flips the van over onto her, crushing her under its heavy weight.

Guy shoots Dee in the head, the bullet cutting through her and depositing in the wall behind her. The shot pushes her backwards, but not before she engulfs Guy in flames. He falls back in a scream, and drops and rolls to put the fire out. Then, with his own telekinesis powers, Guy slams Botha into the side of the van with a hard crack, knocking him out.

Still on your back, you shoot out a powerful burst of green lightning that misses Cartwright by an inch, but makes him duck his head as he tries to pull his gun out. You leap to your feet, quicker than you have ever been in your life, thanks to the Grav-Mod.

"Come on, you son of a bitch!" you yell, drawing your revolver and firing quickly. But you miss all six shots, the gun dry firing on the last pull of the trigger.

Cartwright empties his clip in your direction as he fires from the ground. One shot pierces the edge of your ear, making you fall to the ground and drop the revolver. Blood runs down the side of your face as you pull out your small semi-automatic.

Cartwright is quick enough to telekinetically throw the lawn chair and what is left of the barbecue set right at you with his baton, trying to knock you back. He reloads quickly.

You manage to roll out of the way, though part of the barbecue hits your left leg hard.

You pump the trigger of the little gun as many times as you can, and the third shot catches him in the eye, right through his glasses. The doctor twitches and then lies still, blood running out the back of his head.

Botha gets up, still reeling from slamming into the van. You get him in your sights and pull the trigger, but there is nothing left except a dry click.

You look over at Guy, who is sitting on the ground. The left side of his face is pale; the right is bruised and burnt. His right eye is bloody and lifeless. He holds his limp right arm. The leather from his jacket has melted into his skin.

"Well," he says, coughing. "Well. Go get him, Tiger. I'm just going to walk over here." He flips the van telekinetically over with his ori-baton and shuffles over to Treena, stooping to heal her smashed figure.

"Treena's here. I'll be good." Guy coughs and winces in pain. Treena's eyes start to flash, and she wakes up with a nasty and bloody cough.

You reload the revolver, put away the small gun and start a limping jog forward, heading for Botha. As you round the side of one of the warehouse buildings, you can hear the shuffling noise of Botha trying to make a getaway. You catch a glimpse of Cartwright's wife running with the assault rifle and try to pick up some speed, despite the pain in your leg. As you get closer, you gun her down without a second thought.

Finally, you find Botha as he runs through a chain link gate at the back of the station. It leads to a grassy bank of the fast-flowing river that pours out to the Super Sargasso. The lighthouse ship is in its dock a few hundred yards ahead; its flashing and swirling light stretches out across the empty grasslands.

You fire into the air, one loud shot, and Botha stops in his tracks and turns. He puts up his arms. "Okay! Okay, I'm done! I'm done here. I'm done here!"

You advance past the open gate, keeping your gun on him. The river gurgles in front of you, its current slower than it was when you were wandering out here, alone. Botha backs up, positioning himself right next to the flowing river.

"I don't want any more of this," Botha says. "I just want to go back to South Africa." Botha drops his baton to the ground. "I don't want to die. I just did what I had to because I didn't want this place to end up how my country ended up years ago. I'm sorry. I am sorry. But if we hadn't done what we did... People shouldn't be here, colonizing this place. We don't need to export our shit, you realize that, right, Sarah? If we do, thousands of Ni-Perchta will be enslaved and die, and for what? For big companies? For Wall Street? What in Christ's name are we doing here? I'm sorry for all who have died, but there is a reason why that needs to happen. We never did it for money!"

You can't say anything in response. Pity grips you. Botha turns as he sees you hesitate and dives into the river. You watch him swim across, the current pushing him forward a little. Botha is a strong swimmer, and he is making a good distance.

You take a bead on his head, putting the sight over his skull.

You fire once, and his body sinks beneath the waves, disappearing under the reflection of the seven moons above.

You holster your pistol and sink to the ground, right on the riverbank. You sit there for a good while.

Eventually Guy calls your name, and you limp back over to where he is.

NIGHTHAWKS AT THE MISSION

CHAPTER NINETEEN:
WHAT THE THUNDER SAID

Guy, Treena, and you help each other that night, fixing injuries with the orichalcum you have on hand, reducing your physical wounds to nothing though unfortunately leaving the emotional wounds fresh and tender and biting you still. You all hold each other for a moment.

"Been through a lot together in the last few days," Guy says to the both of you, looking pretty deeply into your eyes. "You alright?"

The three of you sit outside in front of the ruined part of the station. The bodies have been thrown into the river, unceremoniously, by Guy. You personally disposed of the doctor's wife. You think of what happened to Winniefreddie briefly as the scene reminds you of her demise.

Treena finds a couple lawn chairs, covered in dust, in the back storage room, along with an old radio. You and your friends are quiet, shaky, and unable to speak more than a few sentences to each other. Everyone looks as if their eyelids have been peeled back a tad, and darkness encircles all of your eyes.

"—update you on the special flash storm warning for the Sargasso region. Any and all persons within five kilometers of the center of Sargasso-3 must take immediate shelter underground. We repeat, this is a flash storm warning for the Sargasso region. Any persons within five kilometers of the center of City Sargasso-3 must take shelter underground... The storm is expected to commence in two to three hours..." the radio announcer says.

It is nearly three o'clock in the morning. Treena, Guy, and you are sleeping outside, waiting in the cool night air for Jaime to come. You're holding your shotgun in hand, and Guy has his hand stuffed down his pants like Al Bundy. You awake when you hear a hum. You nudge Guy with your foot.

"Guy. Guy, wake up." The hum is a little louder now; the air is still and windless. Guy wakes up with a belch.

"Waz up?" he says.

Barely visible in the night sky is Saki's old Tri-Skysurfer, which lands nearby. "Jaime's back."

He comes out of the darkness, looking mystified. "Holy shit," he says, seeing the blood and the destruction all around. "You three kids alright? Everything's all done here, yeah?" He surveys the damage, then tosses you your special little ring. "It worked great. If anyone is following the *Crue*, they never saw me get off."

You put it on your finger. "No Mathias and Petty," you tell him, disappointed. "We searched the damn station. Nothing, nada." Guy and Treena nod.

Jaime shakes his head. "Well, at least—"

On the highway behind him, the yellow Xs pulse in the late night air, silently but constantly flashing that neon yellow.

"Something coming this way," Treena says, following your gaze. "See how it's flashing fast? Something very quick is coming this way. I can't tell how far off—they could be flashing for something miles away. The road can be sensitive this far out from all civilization."

"Something wicked this way comes..." Guy says.

Suddenly you hear laughter right behind you.

"Actually, Mr. Farson, something wicked is right here." Charles Mathias's eyes flash green for a second as he steps out from the shadows and into the orange-bathed night. There is a low crack of sound as Jenny Petty emerges from blue whiffs of smoke that carry the scent of ozone throughout the air.

Mathias has that odd-looking M-16-meets-flashlight gun in both hands, Petty a mean-looking and stubby orichalcum baton. Armored Ni-Perchta, armed with swords and bows and arrows, surround you on all sides. Mathias calls something out in Perchta and laughs.

He looks at you with those scary, oddly flashing green eyes above his weird red half-mask with the yellow jaws. "Your sister is quite the woman—and I use that present tense very appropriately. She's declared herself the true Witch-Lord. These are her warriors."

"It is prophecy, they say." Mathias nods to Petty. "Which I believe as well." He takes his mask off, revealing himself to be Boston. "This is the fourth time we've met..." he says in Boston's voice, before returning to his true form. "I'm sorry we had to meet this way again."

He calls out to the Ni-Perchta, who open fire with their ori-batons and arrows, slaughtering all of your companions. You stand there surrounded by the lifeless and bloodied bodies of your friends, and fall to the ground, so shocked you don't know what to do, what to say. Your mind slams shut and becomes a white void.

"Thanks for getting everyone together for us. And for taking care of the others back there. Poor people had their covers blown somehow. Poor friends of ours," Petty says.

"Your sister really loves you, you know that?" Mathias says almost tenderly, without the usual brutishness in his voice. "You'll come with us to meet her."

The mention of your sister makes you think of meeting her in the cave and the memory snaps you back to reality. So the meeting in the cave *was* real. She lives. She was there when Saki's family was murdered.

The presence of the Ni-Perchta reminds you of something else. The savage custom they have. The Oberon custom. You stand up slowly, and reach deep into yourself for something a little more. Just as Petty comes over to grab you, you speak up.

"I challenge you!" you call out. "I challenge you to a duel, Mathias, right here, right now!" You don't even know what you are saying at this point. All you know is that everything you have been through, experienced, and fought for in the last few days cries out against you just standing there and letting this vampire take you to her, your living sister. The ghosts of a thousand recent, painful memories all roar out against it.

Mathias turns very slowly, a smirk on his face. The Ni-Perchta watch from the sides, all weapons pointing at you as you rush towards him.

"I challenge you. Over what you've taken from me. From all of us. I don't have to follow you anywhere, you fucking murderer." A simple coldness comes over you, powerful and enticing. It wells up inside. You repeat the word you think is for duel again and again in Perchta, hoping the watching crowd understands. You heard the word in the aftermath of Mathias's attack on the lobby and you are pretty sure of its meaning.

Mathias walks over to you, and, inches away from your face, speaks quickly in low tones. "You know, your sister, our people...we aren't doing this for the money. Do you understand that? Your sister is the most honest woman I know. The best of all of us. All the people we've set up to be killed, the salvagers, the station managers, the Counters, it's murder, we know that. But we are only murdering the exploiters of this world. We're trying to stop the colonization here. The oppression. The collective will to turn this place into another Africa. We don't kill unless we need to. We could have burned the Mission to the ground and killed everyone there. Our people have lived inside for months; we could have conducted a massacre but didn't. We even allowed you and your friends to live. We just applied pressure, and managed to get four thousand people packing to Perth and Long Beach."

"We are principled," Mathias continues, again sounding nothing like himself. "We just want the exploiters to go home. You don't need to do this. We don't need more blood on our hands."

You look at Mathias. "You won't have."

Mathias cocks his head, as if listening to something. "I refuse your challenge." He walks away. The Ni-Perchta stare at him from all sides, their red eyes fixed on him.

"I challenge you again," you say, loudly. The Ni-Perchta speak amongst themselves. Mathias exchanges a look of regret with Petty.

One of the Ni-Perchta calls out, a sort of anguished shout or question. Others join in, crying out to Mathias. They turn their weapons on him. To your surprise, one of the Ni-Perchta even hands you Winniefreddie's shotgun.

"Then I have to face you," he says with a frown, looking at the Ni- Perchta. He puts on his odd and demonic-looking half-mask. "I cannot refuse you again. Otherwise I will be branded a coward, and my life and belongings would be forfeit according to the custom. Sarah, you cannot beat me. This is your death if you keep at this. I'm sorry."

You rack Winniefreddie's shotgun, and Mathias nods. You stand ten yards away from each other, on a yellow X. "I'll make it quick," he promises. One hand inches towards the inside of his blue leather jacket.

You pull your shotgun barrel upwards and fire, then immediately hit your invisibility ring. Mathias moves with such speed that the gun blast misses him, only a few bits of flame hitting his side. He throws a knife at you, striking you despite being invisible. The six inch stiletto hits you in the right side, so sharp and sudden you can't feel a thing at first. Warm blood trickles down your side, and when the wave of pain hits you, you play it up as something more to lure him in. You become visible again, then disappear and reappear again. The ring must have been damaged, and you know you can't count on it anymore, so you drop to your knees, releasing your shotgun. Mathias walks over, pistol out.

"Yield, Sarah Orange."

You snap out your ori-baton and telekinetically slam him against the yellow X road, hard. He drops his pistol.

You stand up quickly and jump out of the way as he shoots out twin bolts of lightning. Pulling out your reloaded small semi-automatic, you shoot six times. The first five bullets slam into Mathias's energy shield and knock him back a few steps. But the sixth shot hits him in the stomach as the shield fails. You then strike with a blast of lightning that pushes him far down the highway. Your stomach turns when you smell his hair burning.

Mathias holds his stomach, and you see something you didn't expect—a glimmer of fear flashes behind green eyes that turn back to blue. Then the glimmer is gone, and the lack of emotion is back.

Petty intervenes, shooting her own submachine gun at you, getting off a blast that barely misses. A Ni-Perchta warrior grabs her and punches her twice in the stomach, dropping her to her knees. The Ni-Perchta are enraged. They rush over en masse and restrain Petty by slapping and striking her.

"I didn't ask for her to interfere! Hold!" Mathias manages to exclaim, putting his hands up as if it is time out in a basketball game. Then he clips a little box onto his shield belt, and you wonder if he is recharging it.

"Come on!" you say, feeling your blood thumping its way through your head and heart; pure hate fills you. You can taste them. You pull out your revolver, pain rippling down your side from the stiletto still in you, just as Mathias changes into a creature—a sixteen foot white creature with tentacles coming out of its face. He's become a hellish half-lizard, half-octopus killing machine with webbed feet and a long, almost fish-like tail.

Some Ni-Perchta scurry away from the horror coming down the highway. Treena screams, startling you badly. She's been playing dead; she limps quickly away from the scene.

You fire at the creature but the shots are completely blocked by the new energy shield. Petty is still being restrained; she's fighting and cursing at the Ni-Perchta, and you aim your baton and drag her out of their arms and towards you. Her petite frame slams into you, and you accidentally touch the bracer she has on.

You both appear somewhere in Sargasso-3, the empty and dead city. The windy necropolis is lit by multiple moons. Miss Jenny oh so Petty pulls your hair, but you rip out the stiletto from your side with a scream and stab her in the throat. She crumples to the broken asphalt, flips onto her side and disappears in a crackle of static and thunder. A small grenade with the pin still in it falls off her belt before she teleports. You are alone in the wastes, still bleeding.

A sick display of holograms dance across the buildings. Human and Ni-Perchta gladiators fight in the street with orichalcum powers and swords.

You sit on a curb, reload your gun and put it away. You snatch up Petty's grenade with trembling, bloody and sticky fingers.

The tentacle monster formerly known as Mathias appears a second later, and you pull the pin and chuck the grenade, which blows with such force that you feel a thousand tiny needles and a hot wind slam into you. The blast shreds the tentacles off the creature's face and blows out his energy shield. He changes back into his human self and ducks into the open lobby of a massive temple guarded by a headless statue that holds a book in one hand and a globe in the other. Within seconds, Mathias comes back out healed and ready, and throws a fireball at you. It explodes only a few feet away and envelops the side of one of the ancient buildings in blue flames. You shoot a bolt of lightning his way, burning a mark in the marble pillar next to him.

You limp-run away from the scene, shooting back at him. A rumbling sensation blankets you, and something like groans or cries come from the sky. Discordant warning alarms echo throughout the empty streets. The sky light ups, red, then blue, then red again, and then turns a fiery orange.

"Oh no." You check your Casio watch, the one Guy gave you. It is dead, completely blank. You look for shelter. Rings of blue and white dance all around the city, some coming out of the sky and some going into the sky, over and over.

"I don't mind the storm, Orange! I can leave any time! Can you?" Mathias cries out, his voice barely audible over the sounds of the flash storm. Green lightning shoots in all directions, and the feeling of static electricity is overwhelming. The air pressure thickens all around you.

You look around, searching for shelter. The sky is now full of clouds that look like dipping funnels, and flashes of white come from all sides. You see what the phrase "flash storm" truly means—white cascades of energy shoot from vortices that appear and disappear all over. Plant life disappears in a second. A tree vanishes when zapped by one of the downward energy blasts, leaving only brown earth behind. Purple rings occasionally shoot out from the sides of the white, downward energy blasts and bounce off the buildings.

The only shelter anywhere around is the temple and possibly an empty skyscraper's lobby across from it. You have no choice but to get back to the temple and finish Mathias off. Taking a deep breath and holding your side, you summon all your strength and energy and run back to the square just outside the temple.

Mathias comes out next to that headless statue. You pull it down with your ori-baton. The sixty-foot behemoth smashes onto the ground, barely missing Mathias, who runs across the street, just barely avoiding the downward energy blasts. He constantly looks up to the sky, dodging this way and that, trying desperately to survive.

He shoots back at you again and again, the slide of his pistol blowing back and forth, brass casings shooting out. The rumbling increases, like a thousand voices crying out. You can barely hear the gunshots, but you feel them pass by your head.

You follow him into the street, hoping desperately not to be vaporized into nothingness. You throw your own ball of lightning at Mathias, something you didn't even know you could do, and barely miss him. It scorches what is left of the façade of the skyscraper Mathias is heading into. You feel wildly excited for having pulled this off. Your entire body tingles with fire and electricity. You send another lightning ball at Mathias. It misses, but hits a window above him. Glass blows out and rains down as sharp little daggers that pierce his body. As he stumbles backwards, you whip out your pistol and shoot him four times in the chest. He falls onto the lobby floor.

"God!" he cries. He's ghostly pale as his blood drains away. He tries to stand, but only manages to prop himself up on one elbow. He spits out blood. When he sees you, he kicks his legs out as if trying to scurry backwards like a crab.

The storm rages behind you; the energy introduces itself into every corner of the empty lobby. A huge, vault-like door sits in the middle. A nighthawk sign is spray painted on it. A rectangle with a dot in it.

"Yield!" you say, sick of people dying.

Mathias makes a throwing gesture and telekinetically, with a scream of metal, rips the vault door off its hinges, then throws the entire door at you. You dive to the ground, but not before part of it tears a chunk out of your back. It crashes out into the street with a clang.

Mathias, suddenly looking healthier, gets to his feet and limps towards the street. It is then that you see the evil flood that charges its way out of the darkness of the shelter. Tens of those disgusting once-humans with green eyes burning bright as coals, their clothes hanging like limp rags around their emaciated white bodies, rush out. The mummies slash the air with long, claw-like fingernails, their bloodshot, yellow, and encrusted eyes blinking rapidly. Several swarm Mathias.

The rest of the Antediluvian people barrel at you as a horrid wave, their revolting smell threatening to suffocate you. They tear at you, hands grasping your throat and legs. You push some of them back with a gust of flames, and manage to pull out your baton and throw several across the lobby, slamming that mass of undead flesh into a glass partition that bursts with the weight of their bodies.

You shoot a couple in the head, reloading as fast as you can. You floor another group, giving them a mental push with your baton that knocks their weakened frames to the floor with a crunch.

More mummies grab your neck, slashing you with their dirty, jagged fingernails. One bites you—luckily the bite doesn't pierce your leather jacket, it just pinches your shoulder blade.

Mathias shoots out a blast of lightning from the front of the lobby and kills a swarm of those creatures. It also hits your arm, the one that is holding the gun, and numbs it. You drop to the side, gun and baton flopping out of your hands—you are paralyzed. The mummies turn and flee; it seems a fear mechanism has clicked in their heads. They run into the street, falling over each other, only to be vaporized by the increased tempo of the flash storm's energy, leaving behind only rags that float in the air.

You try to move but your muscles won't respond.

Taking out a small pistol from the back of his jeans, Mathias runs over to you in order to deliver the final blow. He is five steps away, four steps, and lifts his pistol so slowly, it seems, and points it at your head. Your eyes catch his—green eyes that threaten to drown your consciousness—and you feel yourself slipping away. Fighting back with everything you have, you grab your ori-baton with one awkward and painful effort and manage to bend his arm back by just using your mind, without a single noticeable gesture of your ori-baton, in a way you can never fully explain.

You are still telekinetically twisting his arm back, and in another quick thought rip one of the bracers off his arm with a snap and toss it across the room. Your ori-baton has not moved once.

Mathias is frightened, maybe for only the second time in this man's life. You look at him, feeling something you couldn't imagine—pity. You smother the thought and make him pull the trigger on himself by telekinetically jamming his finger back onto the trigger. He shoots at point blank range with a full clip of shells, hitting his upper chest and throat.

You then telekinetically throw him clear across the street, near the temple steps. His half- mask comes off. He tries to stand again, but falls down the temple steps.

Mathias heals, amazingly quickly, and stands up, eyes flashing, revealing fully extended fangs. As he moves towards you, a white blast of energy slams down, vaporizing him. You can hear him scream, faintly, as if from far away. The flash storm moves in in full swing, its changes of light and energy rings dancing over every single square inch of that dead city.

When the storm dissipates, the feeling comes back into your body and you grab Mathias's bracer, his ornate ori-baton, and even his little half-mask. You put on his bracer and return to McRoss Station in a flash of light. All it takes is a simple thought about the location. When you arrive, Guy and Jaime are being carried out on stretchers, IVs attached to their arms. Treena stands by, enclosed by a blanket. She is handcuffed and sitting on a curb, still covered in Jaime's blood. A pack of Mission Security long range patrol cars are parked nearby, their lights flashing in the gloom. The bodies of Ni-Perchta warriors, machine-gunned and ori-attacked, line the highway. You even spot Petty's body amongst the massacre. The few warriors who survived are in handcuffs.

James Farson, your local agent from the Bureau of Off-World Affairs, walks out of the darkness as the rest of the Counters notice you and raise their guns. He doesn't say anything. You toss him Mathias's half-mask and sit down on the road, ready to pass out from the blood you've

NIGHTHAWKS AT THE MISSION

lost from the stabbing and all the energy you used to survive this final battle.

EPILOGUE

James Farson does the right thing and gets you a partial reward. Mathias's death is "unconfirmed," screwing you out of a lot of money. Eight hundred and seventy-five thousand dollars still comes your way—nothing to sniff at, but nothing to go home in triumph with either in your own twisted reasoning. You are, however, well known as the girl who shot Charles Mathias and you have achieved a level of fame bordering on celebrity.

The Mission is restored to its former self after the summer solstice, with a new line-up of settlers coming in. Subway and McDonald's return to the food court, bigger and better than before.

Guy, Jaime, and Saki come out of their induced comas around the same time; Guy first, then Jaime, then finally Saki, weak and thin. Besides a little discomfort, all are none the worse for wear, though poor Saki's memory of the last few weeks is patchy at best. Guy had to be the one to tell her that her family had been killed. You're thankful that she's forgotten quite a bit more than that.

Bad dreams seem to be the only remaining issue. Treena holds a funeral for Winniefreddie that is only between her and, to your surprise, a Ni-Perchta priest. They symbolically throw Winniefreddie's ashes into the same river you dumped her body in, which unnerves you. A terrible guilt wells up inside you, but you never tell Treena.

You often sit with Guy and Saki on the patio of the Benbow, taking in the sunsets, drinking cold, home-made beer. Saki and Guy are together; you are not with him, except in secret where you make love whenever you can. Guy professes that you are his best friend and that Saki is the love of his life. You have decided to accept that. They sit next to each other most nights, holding hands and watching the sun fall away.

You ponder the relationship you have with your new friends on lonely nights on your penthouse balcony. You are the richest person in the Mission, and what Dee said you could never have is now yours. A lovely and large penthouse.

Jaime stops by every now and again, crashing in one of the extra bedrooms, showing you sketches. He asks for nothing in return.

Despite the end of Mathias, there is no security stand-down. Ni-Perchta security forces at the Mission have been replaced with hired guns from the United States. They treat you with forced courtesy and the Ni-Perchta like rabid dogs.

The bad days of the "Mathias Terror" are used to scare brand-new settlers during drunken late hours at the Benbow, now a true inn. Another level has been added to the place, with rooms for those visiting from other Missions and Ni-Perchta cities. You are required to keep it "a separate development," meaning your liquor-providing license will be revoked if you allow Ni-Perchta guests. In the late hours, you find yourself thinking that there is some truth to what Mathias said.

More settlers have come, more arrogant than the last and more vicious in their dealings with the Ni-Perchta. There are no more Ni-Perchta helpers on site at the Mission, having been banned for security reasons due to a new agreement with the Witch-Lord. The walled village of the Funeral Breaks is closed to them, the previous inhabitants scattered. Moondog Street still stands in the emptiness of the village. The bars and the strip clubs could not be closed.

The Funeral Breaks is to become a new Mission, Mission Pathways, for human settlers only. The closing of the village strikes you strangely—you feel sad and bewildered for those Ni-Perchta you barely met. Even the coven that gave you that gift long ago seems to have re-settled somewhere in the tablelands up north and you don't see them for a while.

When you drift off to sleep, you think of your sister waiting out there, somewhere in the deep darkness of The Oberon, waiting, biding her time, like a viper curled up in a deep hole for the winter. You can't believe she's alive and behind so much carefully executed misery. You say nothing to the others about her though they ask.

You and your friends sometimes drive out to Sargasso-3, just to do something, especially on warm and pleasant nights. You recovered the *Crue*, lost in the Sargasso Breaks up until a few weeks ago, and sometimes you take that out as well, your friends aboard. You pay for the rudder to be repaired and for it to be de-bugged by off-duty techs, and your friends sincerely thank you.

One time, having set the airship on auto over the Quadling Sea, you drink a little too much. "Do you think Mathias ever had a point?" you ask Guy, referring to what's happening to The Oberon, the ugly changes being made.

Guy doesn't hear you over the wind and just grins. "What?" He's holding Saki's waist. You think of discussing you and Guy with Saki, but they are happy with each other. You give Saki the blessing of being kept ignorant about the man she loves, which is something you wish someone had done for you. The lie is better than the truth.

One day, near dusk, as your friends are out doing something else, the little Ni-Perchta children you "bought" a while ago show up at the Benbow when it is empty of all customers. You follow them to the green hills outside, where other Ni-Perchta are waiting—it's the coven you met on your first night out in the Super Sargasso region.

NIGHTHAWKS AT THE MISSION

They are passing through the area, traveling to somewhere called Thi-Herku, a group of hills far off. One of the Ni-Perchta greets you—the tall male you saw out on the hill who gathered up the children that day. He talks to you for a bit, stating in good English that the coven are migrating back this way for a little while and that they want to thank you for your kindness to the children and for releasing them. He invites you to their temporary camp a mile away.

That night, you sit at their campfire and eat with them. You talk to members of the coven through the kind translator who speaks for you.

After the meal, one Ni-Perchta adds war paint to your face. It has some meaning you are not fully sure of. The translator says that you are part of their coven now, and that you are the Finder of Lost Children besides being a Force-Fire. You are moved by this, moved by their simplicity, their friendliness towards you, and their humor. They ask you why the city Ni-Perchta and humans have such a love of money and things. After a moment of bitter reflection upon seeing how you have ended up, you shrug. "I don't think we know any better," you tell them.

You apologize about the Network forcing them to move this way and that. The translator, speaking for the chief, says that it cannot be helped and that you are welcome to join them wherever the winds push them.

You stay the night, awakening at dawn. The translator tells you something you weren't expecting. He says that he is worried for your "kind" and for the city Ni-Perchta as well. He asks you to go with them. "There are other humans who have stayed with us before and will stay with us again," he says.

You thank him but decline to go, and watch them drive off into the distance, their wagons and cars and trucks disappearing over the horizon. The children and the translator wave to you as they go off into the wilderness.

To the annoyance of your friends and customers, you leave the war paint on your face for the next day, finally washing it off with reluctance.

Stepping out under the red skies and tiptoeing past the puddles and overflowing pond that was hit by today's earlier maintenance storm, you head for the *Crue* parked outside the slightly improved Benbow Inn. You've just remembered that you left your wallet in there.

There is a man standing next to your old covered wagon decoration, its side painted with the words *Sargasso-3 or Bust*. You put that decoration up with the permission of the other co-op members, though Treena thought it was gay. A couple of scarecrows sit inside the wagon, their insipid smiles aimed at the green countryside all around you.

The man standing there has a goatee and wears a Hawaiian shirt. He's in his fifties, balding, with slightly stooped shoulders and large as a bear. He stares out over the empty, green landscape. A crappy Volkswagen is parked next to where he stands, its front trunk punched in a little. It has a funny-looking blue and white circular license plate—the new license plate that the Witch-Lord and the Network require all vehicles to have. A regular Nevada plate is bolted next to it.

"Very peaceful out here, you know? Sort of an oasis away from it all." The man points to the sky. "Look at those clouds parting there. Nasty old maintenance storm just took off—pew, pew, pew—in every direction, you see that?" He laughs like a little kid. You watch him, curious.

"Had such a desire to come out here, too, you know? I forget if I saw it on the Internet, or I heard about you, something. You get much company out here?"

Guy, who you guess is returning from the other side of the *Crue*, interrupts. Saki is with him. "Sometimes, with the new rooms we put in. Bit slow lately because the portal is closing soon," he says.

"Well, this is better than the Mandalay for what I want. Jeez. Nice place. Nice place. Quiet. You got a room for rent?" The man then takes out an orange prescription bottle from his pants pocket and dry swallows a couple of pills. "Heart's been acting up."

"Uh, yeah, we got a few," you say. You and Guy look at each other in concern about this stranger. Something is off but you can't put your finger on it.

"Good stuff. Look, I'm just a simple guy—you got burgers and beers here, right?" You and Guy both nod.

"You can call me, uh, Will Kosti. I'm a writer." He puts forward a big, beefy, gnarled hand and you shake it, and so does Guy. He is wearing two watches, one on each wrist.

Will reaches into his pocket, taking out a wad of Dii-Yaa, regular cash, and a couple of funny gold coins.

"That's five hundred bucks and a couple of Krugers—I haven't had a chance to swap it out. Just let me know, girlie, when I've worked through that." He smiles, showing off a gold tooth in one corner of his mouth. "No registration, that alright?"

His jovial demeanor has changed; he has become angry and commanding at the same time.

"No registration and no Network report. You cool with dat?" He smiles again. "Used to work out here years ago for these, uh, foreigners, and I can't stand all this new bureaucracy. I'm glad to be back in The Oberon. It's a place to make a killing in, you know?"

ABOUT THE AUTHOR

Forbes West was born and raised in Chicago, Illinois and graduated with a Master's Degree in Political Science from California State University, Long Beach. He currently lives and works mostly in San Francisco, CA and owns a home in Ojima, Japan- a village five hours south of Tokyo by car that is in the foothills of Mt. Fuji.

Web: http://offworldnetwork.thirdscribe.com/
Twitter: https://twitter.com/Forbes_West
Facebook: https://www.facebook.com/forbes.west

NIGHTHAWKS AT THE MISSION

LAST MEAL
BY JASON ANSPACH

I'm in a Network apartment overlooking Solomon's Bay. It isn't mine. And even though I'm a thief—I've come to terms with that fact—I have no intention of stealing anything. Honest, I've never cased the place or been here in my life.

Mike brought me here. That's not his real name. I don't know what his real name is. Only that he's a guy who works for the guy I need to work for if I'm ever going to do something with my life.

Before me is an array of delicacies taken from the Oberon or somehow smuggled here from earth. Stuff I'd never even think about eating if I weren't acutely aware that this could be my last meal. Caviar and real lobster, along with a fat trilobite, freshly caught. Filet mignon, probably from an earth cow, not those weird six horned abominations. Every fixing I could want and a few I'd never want. If it weren't for the fact that everything before me was kept inside resealable plastic containers, the banquet would easily pass for something served at Chez five-star or whatever other upscale restaurant I've never been to.

But I'm not hungry.

So I stare at the kitchen table and the mess of belongings on the floor owned by whoever rents this apartment. Mike unceremoniously swept it clear with his arm, like a field commander determined to lay out a map and turn the tide of battle, sending a framed picture of the cute renters, some flowers, and an old radio crashing to the floor. Then he unzipped an insulated foam bag, the type your Mom would use to keep her casserole warm on the way to a potluck and starts setting out eats that cost more than I make in a month. Legally, that is. I'm only counting what the Network pays me.

Mike is staring at me, waiting for me to tuck in. "You should eat that. Could be your last meal," he growls. Every word he's spoken to me since he picked me up outside the Benbow Inn has been rough and coarse. That's why I call him Mike. Have you seen *Breaking Bad*? Mike Airman...Ehrmantraut? The old guy? This is him. His twin or inspiration, at least. Bald, all business, looks like he's taken a few for the boss and dished out a whole lot more.

"I, uh, I guess I'm not that hungry."

Mike rolls his eyes with an exasperated sigh. Kids today. "You mean to tell me I spent the better part of the last three days getting all this, making these arrangements," he sweeps his hand around the apartment we just broke into, "and now you're not hungry?"

"Did you...did you bring the burrito?" I ask, raising my pitch with each syllable so the word "burrito" becomes an apology in itself.

"That microwave 7-Elevengarbage? Yeah. I thought it was a joke when I read the list, but I found one. Cost more than the caviar."

Mike pulls a still frozen burrito out of his pocket, sealed in red cellophane with a smiling cartoon man in a sombrero giving a final wink at you before he settles in for a siesta as he leans against the logo on the packaging.

Red Hot Beef and Cheese.

I haven't had one in ages. Used to live off them in college and now, with death looking

me straight in the eyes like a gunslinger on the opposite side of a dusty old western street, the burrito is all I want.

But, alas, no microwave. Nobody has a microwave.

"But, no microwave," I say, hoping that Mike knows a way.

Mike sighs and pulls out an ori wand. I've seen this kind before. Well, stolen it.

You see, living in the Oberon is pretty much a dead end situation if you're on the straight and narrow. I could be—was—a corporate drone back on earth. I didn't expect to be one here. But that's what all the recruitment videos never tell you. You make good money, but it all goes back to the Network. So you sail through the portal with delusions of wealth and self-betterment and end up in a lousy rat race only without the Netflix to take your mind off of it. Unless you cut corners. Become a Nighthawk. Or, steal from the Nighthawks—or Dayhawks, I'm not picky—before the Network gets a chance to steal the salvage for itself.

And that's what I do.

The only way to get ahead in this brave new world is to start out rich enough that you can afford to get further ahead, or to break the law and do it on your own. So people get to Oberon and disappear, salvaging without claim or authority. I take what those people find and sell it to the fences before they have the chance to do the same.

And I'm not the only one.

Hawks carry shotguns for more than just the dusty Antediluvian vampire people out there.

Is what I do wrong? Eh, everything on this entire planet is wrong. It's different here, man. I'd never do this on earth. And I'd never do what's coming next.

Breaking Bad opens my burrito and tosses the wrapper onto the floor in a crumpled ball that starts expanding the moment it hits the floor, like one of those cheap glowworm fireworks from Independence Day. He readies his ori wand like a conductor about to lead the orchestra.

"Just like back home," I say, repeating the instructions I left with the fence who ran the note back to Mike's boss. My future boss, if I live through orientation.

Mike stops and cocks his head, his face signaling impatience. "Any other special instructions? Hold the peppers?"

"I like peppers."

He mutters something about punk kids as the ori stones light up. He touches each corner with the wand and I can smell the D-grade beef heating, juices mixing in that salty, saturated fat laden cocoon of a flour tortilla. This stuff will kill you, but so will the rest of my day.

My mouth is watering.

"Here." Mike tosses the burrito unceremoniously onto a paper plate and then makes his way over to a window, allowing me to eat in privacy. I'm thankful. It creeps me out when someone just stares at my while I chew. It's rude.

I bite into a corner of cholesterol packed goodness, and instantly the taste buds on the front of my tongue are burned away. The layer of skin on the roof of my mouth feels like I've just gargled brimstone. The burrito's temperature is roughly that of molten glass.

Perfect.

I squeeze the center of the burrito towards the top and can feel the ice crystals crunching between my teeth. A microwaved burrito, properly cooked, is always still a little bit frozen in the middle. Part of the charm. Mike did wonders with that orichalcum. Really top notch.

Mike is looking through parted blinds out at the sky, watching the weather. I push a mound of beef and beans to one side of my mouth and ask, "Why do I have to do this again?"

"You know why," Mike growls back at me. His answer is dismissive, like he's told me a hundred times before. His concentration remains fixed on the clouds and impending weather.

But he's not wrong. I *do* know why.

A while back I stole a book along with some choice pieces of Antediluvian tech from a nighthawk who didn't know enough to tell when he was being followed...or to keep his finds close, even when nature calls. I could tell right away that this stuff was going to set me up for weeks. Maybe even get me flush with enough Dii-Yaa to throw a nice party for myself. Eat some smuggled convenience store snacks. Live the good life, you know?

So I left for home—Solomon's Bay—to find a fence with enough cash on hand to help me lead everyone at the Benbow Inn in a rendition of *C.R.E.A.M.* I should've known something was up from the way the fence's eyes widened and then narrowed into conspiratorial slits. He told me he had to go in the back to find something out about this book.

"Don't worry," he said, "it's definitely worth a lot. I just need to see how much."

Honest guy, I thought. Honor among thieves and all that. So I waited for five minutes. And then five more. And then The Boss himself, The Don of the Oberon, comes in from the back with the fence, dusting off his hands and regarding the squalor of the fence's basement shanty with obvious distaste.

I'd never seen him before, but I knew it was him.

In any society you're going to have the straight shooters, working for a living. Let's call these people the suckers who get stuck in the long, slow corporate funeral. That was *almost* me. And then you have the risk takers, willing to face the consequences of swinging for the fences for the chance to make it big. But these guys are still playing by the rules for the most part. Now, I'm an opportunist. I take what fate drops in front of me. I left behind me whether fate's fortunes fit in the arbitrary rules of society two months after arriving in the Oberon. But some people see bigger opportunities, and The Boss is just that sort of person. Think *Sopranos* or *The Godfather*. Here's a guy who turns what I do into a business and is rolling in Dii-Yaa because of it.

The Boss picks up my book and stuffs into a lining in his coat. He doesn't ask permission and I know better than to open my mouth.

With a straight face, The Boss said, "I'm going to take this. It belongs to me. I sent nighthawks out looking for it, but you've brought it to me first." He sounds like Marlon Brando, but I'm pretty sure that's an act. No one really sounds like Brando. "I'm grateful for that. Charlie here," he gestures at the fence, whose name is Charlie (who knew?), "says you've got a knack for taking things from under people's noses. He shared a list of what you've had him fence, and I admit, it's impressive. Now, I'm not going to pay you for what I already owned. But I am going to *reward* you with an opportunity to work for me. You understand what that means?"

I nod. This was too good to be true. I mean, this was it. This is how to get ahead, how to become something more than worker bee or a petty thief stealing just enough to pay rent and buy non-Network beer. This was bigger than money. This was being *someone* in a sea of *nobodies*.

"Good. And you understand what's expected?"

I nod again. I'd heard the stories. Literally do or die.

"You understand, working for me will *make* you on the Oberon, but I don't hire anyone who isn't willing to die for me. Think of that as a... prerequisite. Go to the Benbow Inn every day at noon and wait there for a half hour. When the time is right, my guy will pick you up. Capisce?"

"Capisce."

"Now if there's nothing else..." The Boss turns to leave.

"Last meal."

He turns, appraising me with an arched eyebrow even as Charlie the fence swears and backs up.

"What's that?" The Boss asked.

"Last meal. I know I've got to put my life on the line to get this job. I figure maybe I can get a nice last meal, like the guys on death row back home."

A wide and almost warm smile stretches across The Boss' face. "Give Charlie a list."

And that was it. Mike shows up today and I'm eating my burrito. Ate my burrito. It's gone and now my stomach feels sick and I don't know if it's the red hot beef or what comes next.

"Time to go," Mike says, sensing that I'm done.

I stand up and look around at the mess that's been made of the kitchen. "Shouldn't we clean this up before whoever owns this place gets back?"

"Leave it," Mike says as he passes by me on his way to the door. "One of my guys will clean up."

I start to follow, but stop to remove my wallet. There's a wad of Dii-Yaa from the fence. Maybe Mike's guys will clean this place up without a trace of our ever being here, but I feel bad about using whoever's home this is. Taking advantage of them while they're gone.

Ironic, I know.

I open up a cabinet and stuff the cash behind a white bag of Network branded flour. If I don't make it, I won't need it. And if I do, that stack will be like pocket change. Anyhow, I'm guessing the saps who rent this place could use it. Anyone trying to make a go of things on The Oberon would if they're playing it straight. Playing the fool.

We move down the stairs toward an underground parking garage. "Did you ever have to take the test?" I ask him.

"No." Mike looks straight ahead the whole time, though his voice sounds as if he's disgusted by the question. "My loyalty isn't in question. I proved my worth long before we expanded into The Oberon. You're a different story."

"Just wondering."

"Huh."

The parking garage is dark, just a few lights barely keeping the shadows relegated to corners. I see a small crowd—maybe five people—gathered around a white armored car straight from the seventies. It still says "BRINKS" on the side.

"Did you prepare a last meal for all these people, too?"

"No."

"Guess they should have asked?"

"You were the only one *dumb* enough to ask for a favor. Be happy I didn't shoot you instead of feed you."

Mike walks in front of me, a slight limp in his gait but at a surprisingly fast pace. The lights in the garage begin to flicker and dim, and I hear the familiar tonal warning that a storm is inbound. The too perfect voice of a woman comes on, warning everyone to find shelter. A speech I'm so used to hearing that I usually block it out instinctively. But not this time.

The others make room for Mike and he swings open the back of the armored car. "Everybody in."

We all comply and I make my way to the front. There's nothing inside but plate metal lining the walls, ceiling, and floor. Just a little rust showing between the seams. I'm standing next to a wiry guy with a terribly thin mustache. I've seen him before. What did he do again? I don't remember. He's trembling and looks like he has the flu. Can't blame him. Who's to say any of us will survive? Who's to say this isn't how The Boss takes care of people that chance into his business?

But I can't *just* be a thief. So I take a deep breath and try to settle myself. Questioning the wisdom of a red hot beef gut bomb.

Mike hops into the back of the security car last of all, closing the door behind him. He makes his way to the back, splitting Sickly and me like Moses parting the Red Sea. He pounds a fist against the steel mesh partition. "Let's go."

The engine comes to life and the armored car begins to pull away, causing everyone inside to take an extra step to catch their balance, hands shooting out to steady themselves on the metal walls.

We drive. Fast but not too fast. Not like we're excessively speeding, tires squealing and all. I don't know. Maybe it just feels fast from being in the back. I can see the swirling gray from the flash storm through the two small windows on the back of the vehicle. A colossal bolt of Oberon lighting explodes into view, sending the two who stand nearest to the window back into the small crowd behind them.

Those things will vaporize you. And we have to go right out into the middle of it.

Someone in the center of the pack loses whatever he ate for lunch. A wet splat hits the ground and the air instantly fills with the stench of vomit. A space opens around the mess, as if it were enchanted by some magical circle of protection. I look over to Mike and Sickly. Mike rolls his eyes while Sickly swallows and swallows.

My stomach isn't feeling so hot, either. The internal temperature of the car is rising, and a wreath of sweat is building up around my collar, pasting it to my neck and trapping my body heat. I almost feel a sense of relief when the armored car stops, sending us lurching. Someone plants a sneaker into the puke and slip slides, saved from falling on the floor by a Good Samaritan standing nearby.

"Out," Mike orders, the commanding growl leaving no room for disobedience. "Head straight for the other car. Make it inside and you're in."

A guy and a girl up front undo the latch to the doors and swing them open. A rush of stormy, ozone smelling air whooshes in, and I'm happy for the cool it brings and the fresher air.

Eager, either to die or make a good first impression, the two in the front burst out of the vehicle and begin sprinting for another armored car parked five hundred or so yards away, back doors open. It's like those movies where the boats unload the troops to storm the beaches of Normandy. It's terrifying but thrilling, too.

The middle of our column halts as another terrific blaze of light descends to the earth, engulfing the lead runner, a guy wearing a Members Only jacket, and leaving absolutely no trace of him. The girl outside continues to sprint, darting awkwardly as if she can juke the lightning.

Seeing all of this, those of us inside halt. Mike pulls an H&K MK 23 and points it at the four of us left. "Out. You might die out there but you damn sure will if you try to stay in here."

With nowhere else to go, we start to hop out and take off into the storm. The first girl out reaches the van, and this seems to kindle hope in those who live. Legs pump, but the storm is getting angrier.

Sickly and I are the last in the van. I'm at the opening and Sickly is in the back, shaking, crying and talking to himself while Mike stares daggers at him. "Leave now," he says, and I don't know if he's talking to me or Sickly.

The pale faced man—what did he do? A counterfeiter, I think—won't budge. Mike nonchalantly raises his weapon.

"Whoa, whoa, c'mon man!" I shout and then implore Sickly, "Let's go, pal!"

Mike points the gun at me, obviously angered by my interruption. I shut my eyes tight, expecting to feel a bullet rip into me for being too slow out the door. A few seconds pass.

Nothing.

I open my eyes and see Mike, gun down at his side, pointed to the floor, looking at me as he shakes his head. "Let me give you a little piece of advice: This ain't earth."

"O-okay," I stutter.

Sickly is still whimpering. Mike grabs him viciously by the neck, twisting one of his thin arms behind his back. He drags Sickly to the opened doors and tosses him outside on his chin like a barfly who got too drunk and lippy for his own good.

I see Sickly squirm and crawl, like he's going to try to make it back inside the armored car. Suddenly the hairs on my legs stand on end, and Sickly is vaporized just outside the door. Mike and I dive to the back of the van instinctively, heaving breaths at the close call as wisps of smoke mark Sickly's final resting place.

Mike looks over at me and swallows. "Get out. And then walk. Don't run. And when you get to other van, you remember what I said. You listen to me, and you'll do all right, kid."

I nod and hop down. "Thanks," I say, without the faintest idea of whether that was an appropriate response.

I turn into the wind and walk, straining against the gusts. Ahead, I can see that the girl runner is still alone in the van. The two who jumped out before me are still running. Maybe two hundred yards away from safety.

I'm going to die.

But I listen. I keep walking even though every part of me is screaming to get moving, to get out of danger immediately.

Above, a swirling mass of angry clouds churns. The pair in front of me are running like wild dogs pursuing a fox. I see a soft whitish-blue light form at their feet, then between their legs, building with every stride.

A blinding flash sears my eyes. I shut them tight but can still see the image of the lightning bolt in the dark behind my eyelids. I flutter my eyes open and blink, still walking, the last person still outside and alive.

There's a scorch mark where the runners used to be and I can make out the toe of a shoe, a shell top from a pair of Adidas Superstars.

The storm rages.

I keep walking.

The lightning flashes somewhere, a little more distant.

I keep walking.

I can't *just* be a thief. I can't be just another cog in the machine.

I keep walking.

ABOUT THE AUTHOR

Jason Anspach is best known for his acclaimed humorous paranormal noire series, *'til Death*. Living with his family in the Pacific Northwest, Jason is also the co-host of the *Literary Outlaws* podcast and a regular with Forbes West on the *Sci-Fi Writers Playing Old School D&D* gaming show. Visit JasonAnspach.com to see more of his work.

OH DIYOS IN THE OBERON
BY TODD BARSELOW

Oh diyos, bakit ako ginagawa ito? Oh god, why am I doing this?

This is the persistent thought that runs through Bong Boy Cagayan's mind as he boards the small boat which will carry him through the Nemo Gate and into the unknown, into The Oberon. The place where he'll make his fortune. The place where he'll be able to earn enough to provide for his family for their entire lifetimes—all thirteen of them. His parents, three grandparents, three brothers, and five sisters. They are all depending on him now. Well, not literally, but hopes are high that their lives will become easier once he starts rolling in the Dii-Yaa...

He leaves today, but his journey began two months ago when he found the Network flyer while scavenging for scrap metal at a construction site down the road from his parents' home. No telling how that flyer found its way to the Philippines. The best Bong can tell, resettlement in The Oberon is an American thing, or at least a North American thing, even though the Nemo Gate is on this side of the world.

The call to the Network number on the flyer isn't a good one. He finds out he's not qualified for official resettlement—no experience in anything considered valuable over there; no money to invest in a new or existing business venture; not even a simple college degree in Hotel Restaurant Management he could parlay into a front desk position or even a busboy job at a mission somewhere. Disappointed, but having already made up his mind that this is the opportunity he *cannot miss*, he begins devising a plan to pass through the Nemo Gate when it opens two months hence.

At his parents' and grandparents' insistence, Bong goes to speak with the local parish priest who immediately assails him with tales of the devils that live in The Oberon and the risk of possession he runs if he goes there. Even knowing the trouble it will eventually cause him, Bong proceeds post haste to tell the priest to fuck off with all his devil bullshit—blessing be damned. He's not buying it. People have been going there for what, forty, fifty years now? If there were devils there surely they would have come through the gate and destroyed the earth by now, or enslaved all of humanity like the priests insist will happen when the world ends, right? Well fuck that. His world isn't ending, it's just goddamned beginning—finally.

Bong manages to beg, borrow, and steal enough to get from Digos City in the southern part of the country all the way to Shepherd's Point, New Zealand. From there he will secure passage onward to the Nemo Gate itself. He's going in illegally, but he's sure he'll find work. He's young—just nineteen—relatively intelligent, in good shape, capable of doing just about anything with even the smallest amount of training. Something in his gut is telling him he'll be just fine, better than just fine. He's going to be super-fucking-fantastic. He's going to be a king in The Oberon.

Fallout from the fuckery with the priest isn't as bad as he imagines it will be. His mother merely shakes her head while his father smiles ruefully and claps him on the back. "Boy, I've wanted to speak my mind to that priest for years now. You have done it for me, and for that I thank you. Your journey will be blessed with or without that bastard's consent." His mother gasps at this but says nothing. And that's it. No more is said about it, reinforcing Bong's internal feeling he's making the right choice.

The weeks leading up to departure see Bong Boy Cagayan spending lots of time in the neighborhood internet café, researching and learning all he can about The Oberon and its denizens as well as the Nighthawks who pillage it. He has determined he wants to be a Nighthawk, one who strikes it rich on every outing into the void, into the vast unknown wildernesses. He will be a *trailblazer*. No one before or after him will find more riches, more wealth buried in the ground or deep within the recesses of the antiquated structures left behind by...whoever they were. This is his destiny.

Oh diyos, bakit ako ginagawa ito? Oh god, why am I doing this?

Bong Boy is on the bangka, the small rickety boat that shouldn't be this far out at sea, much less about to go through the massive Nemo Gate into an unknown world. Second thoughts—fuck that, third, fourth, fifth, and even sixth thoughts—are flashing like lightning through his brain. He's made a terrible mistake. He knows no one in The Oberon. If nothing else, he's probably going to starve to death, or die of exposure. He doesn't even have a place to stay.

The bigger boat that has towed him this close to the gate cuts the rope tethering them together, and Bong is truly on his own for the first time in his life. He cranks the outboard engine—momentarily panicking when it doesn't catch right away; he'd be truly well and fucked if it doesn't start—and heads towards the coordinates he's been assured are the location of the gate. Even without the directions, he'd be hard pressed to miss the Nemo Gate—it is *massive,* so massive he's almost sure it will just suck him in, bangka and all, and spit him out on the other side in a billion pieces. Besides that, there's a whole flotilla of other vessels awaiting transport to the other side. Panic almost grips him again before he realizes that there are so many vessels here there's no way any sort of authority or law enforcement from the Network could be checking them all for valid paperwork to cross into The Oberon.

While contemplating this, Bong begins to see the gate glowing, softly at first, growing gradually brighter and brighter until it's like staring at the sun almost. The vessels in the front that he can see begin to disappear across the event horizon by the dozen or more. This is it. Once you're in, you're in for good. Or for at least as long as you can survive. Or at least until the gate opens again. He's motoring on toward his destiny, filled with thoughts of promise, even hope, when he feels the bangka lurch and almost flip. He struggles to hang on, to not get tossed into the sea.

A yacht filled with what appear to be drunken, rich, white people has clipped him without even noticing. Well, almost no one aboard notices. One bikini-clad bottle-blonde rips her top of and shakes her tits at Bong, laughing all the while. He's furious and frightened, yet at the same time more aroused than he's ever been in his life—until he realizes he's sinking. The bottle-blonde must have belatedly realized this, too, because she strips her bottoms off and proceeds to shake her ass at him as well, in farewell he supposes. If he's to die here, now, before ever reaching the Promise Land, he sure would have loved to fuck that one, at least once.

As hope begins to abandon him, along with thoughts of ever being with a woman again, he hears someone call out to him. He spots the boat hailing him; they're beckoning him to take the life preserver ring with the rope attached that's just been tossed aboard the bangka. Hazily, he gets the ring around himself and hops overboard to be pulled onto the other boat which has chosen to have mercy on him. He imagines he will now be escorted back to land, back to face charges on one thing or another related to his illegal attempt to enter The Oberon.

Instead, he's introduced to Timkin Potomac, Nighthawk extraordinaire, and his two-person crew, Jala Garrison and Gary Jordan. Technically, they're all Nighthawks, but Timkin is the leader so he claims the title for himself and Bong doesn't argue.

"This here stunning specimen of the female form is Jala Garrison, but you can call her JG. And that over there, the, uh, not-so-fine specimen of a man—"

"Hey, fuck off, Potomac!" Gary Jordan says.

"—is Gary Jordan, but you can call him GJ."

"Uh, JG and GJ. That's, uh, going to be a bit confusing I think, but I'll try to remember. I'm Bong Boy Cagayan from—"

"Bong Boy! That's one helluva name, kid! I like, I like it. We like to partake of the holy herb on occasion in this crew so I think you'll fit in just fine, just fine indeed," Timkin Potomac says.

"Nice to meet you, Bong Boy," Jala chimes in. "You can call me Jala. No need for the initials. Timkin is just fucking with you."

"Yeah, kid, just call me Gary, okay? No need for no complicated shit. Welcome aboard. We seen how those fucks on that yacht did ya and couldn't very well let you drown out here, this close to The Oberon. We took a quick vote and decided to pull you onboard and carry yous across with us. Yous good with that?"

"Well, I mean, yeah, fuck yeah. I don't want to die by drowning. Worst way to go, I've heard," Bong says.

"Fuck that, BB. There's a lot worse ways to go, especially where we're going. You even know *anything* about The Oberon?" Timkin asks. "And before we go any further, I want to make a few things clear, you dig?"

"Uh, yeah. Okay. What's the deal?" Bong asks.

"For starters, you can call me Tim or Kin or Potomac. You can even call me Timkin, but don't you ever, *fucking ever*, call me fucking Timkin Potomac. You got that? That's cause for immediate expulsion from our group of wandering, wondering, gathering travelers. That full name is reserved for one single person in the entirety of existence, besides myself of course. Me dear old mum, Matilda. She's the light of me life, the—"

"Timkin, enough already. The guy's just about been killed and you want to fuck about with him. There's time for that later. Let him catch a breather and regroup his head, man. He's got a lot to wrap his brain around just now, yeah?"

"Okay, okay. The beautiful vixen calls it like it is once again. My apologies, BB. I can't resist a good ribbing when the opportunity presents itself. You can call me whatever the fuck you like, yeah? I like BB so that's what I'm gonna call you. Any objections?"

"It's okay by me. My grandfather calls me that when—"

"You trying to call me old you little sonofa—"

"Jesus fucking christ, Potomac, give it a goddamned fucking rest already," Gary fairly screams.

"No, no, of course I didn't mean you're old or—"

"Can it, BB. Just fucking with you again. You have my sincerest apologies."

Wondering if he's made a horrible mistake, he accepts a dry towel from Gary and a can of beer from Jala.

"Okay, back to the serious business, BB. You attached to a team already? You got people waiting for you on the other side there?"

"I, I don't. No one I know has ever gone to The Oberon. I've had friends and family migrate to just about every place on earth you can imagine, but I'm the first to go off-world. I'm going to be the first to strike it rich."

"HA! We'll see about that, then Bong Boy. When we took our little vote earlier about whether to let you drown or not, we also included a little caveat about whether or not to let you join the team as an apprentice. This depended on what kind of person you turned out to be in the first ten or fifteen minutes. We're going on twenty minutes now and I think we've probably all come to the same conclusion." Jala and Gary both nod. "Looks like you're the newest apprentice for the Frack Rats. That's what we call ourselves. This is a provisional decision, of course. Still have to run it by the wifey when we get to the other side and all. She's the other half of the legit business we got going in The Oberon. And yes, we are legit...sort of. We're a licensed business, the wife and me, and Gary and Jala are our employed 'consultants'."

"I, wow. Thanks so much, I guess. I—"

"You *fucking guess*? What the fuck is wrong with you, kid? We're giving you the golden life on a silver fucking platter and *you guess*? Are you fuckin—"

"I'm in! I'm in, goddamnit! I'm in! I'm not good at talking. I think faster than the words come out. Shit. Yes, thank you. I'm in. I want this. I want this more than anything ever in the world. I will work hard and do what I'm told. I'm a fast learner so you won't have to tell me stuff a whole bunch of times. I—"

"Relax, Bong. You're good. We could tell the minute you stepped on the boat, or were dragged on I guess you'd say," Jala says. "Here, light up this joint and relax for a minute, yeah? You're about to see some shit that's going to blow your mind, man. And if you've got a phone, which I guess if you do it's already shot to shit from your little dip in the drink, you might want to turn it off and take out the battery. It's gonna get fried as we go through the gate in a few minutes if you don't."

"No phone. I read not to bring any electronic devices. All my stuff—" Bong realizes in that instant that every possession he had in the world—this one or that one through the gate—was on his boat. "Oh fuck! Oh, shit fuck! My stuff! Oh diyos, what am I—"

"Whoa, whoa. Hold on a minute, guy. You're fine. You're gonna be okay. We got you. You're with us now and—"

"But I have absolutely *nothing* now! All my shit was on that boat!"

"We've got you covered, BB. We have contingency funds set aside for shit like this. You're one of us now, so when you start earning you'll chip into that contingency fund, too. Consider this an early payday for you. We'll get you outfitted with the stuff you need, no sweat compadre," Timkin says.

Bong wants to be filled with disbelief, but he can tell by the look on Timkin's face, and Jala and Gary's, that this is serious, it's for real. They aren't just fucking with him. He's landed with a real-deal, bona fide Nighthawk crew. He sits back, takes a huge, lung-busting hit from the joint he's been bogarting, and watches as they pass through the Nemo Gate into The Oberon.

Less than twenty-four hours after entering The Oberon and Bong Boy finds himself in the thick of it. It's everything he'd imagined and more. So much more.

His first outing with the Frack Rats sees him earn more in four hours than he could have ever hoped to earn in a lifetime in the Philippines. And, according to Jala, it's a meager haul by their standards. BB keeps a bit of cash for himself and chips into the contingency fund to pay back what was fronted to him. The rest of the loot he forwards to his parents from the Network Banking Center at Mission Friendship. Even with the exchange rate and fees imposed, his mom and dad will have enough money to retire now, if they like, and Bong Boy feels really good about that.

Second trip into the void, well that's a different story all together.

As they're prepping for another run, Bong Boy takes a quiet moment to say a prayer, to speak to his ancestors and ask them for guidance and good fortune. His quiet interlude of reflection is abruptly smashed when Timkin barges in.

"The fuck you doing on your knees in here, BB? You praying over here? Thought you weren't the religious type, what with telling the priest to fuck off and all that."

"I'm not religious, really. Just talking to my ancestors, asking for guidance is all."

"No offense, but you don't need no guidance from the ancestors, BB. We got gadgets galore for that shit. Tell you what, though. You hear a good word from the other side about a stash, you be sure to let me know, you hear?"

"Yeah, of course. I mean I won't hear anything because I'm not crazy, but yeah. I'll keep my ears open."

"You do that. Now get your shit together. We've got some actual actionable intelligence to look into. We move out in fifteen." With that, Timkin storms out of the room, shouting for Jala and Gary to get their shit together, too.

True to his word, Timkin is waiting in the truck, a beat up F-350 extended cab with some wild looking modifications, within fifteen minutes. One of those modifications is the foghorn he's leaning onto to get them all outside.

All piled into the truck with their gear stowed in the back under the camper top, the Frack Rats light two joints and hit the road, destination unknown as far as Bong Boy is concerned. Nobody'd bothered to answer his query as to where they were going next.

An hour and a half on the yellow arrow highway, traveling just a hair shy of 150mph the whole time, and Timkin slams on the brakes, sending the truck into a fishtail that Bong Boy is sure will end in death for them all.

Back in control, Timkin takes a left off the highway and onto an overgrown but rutted track leading towards what BB could only describe as a temple of some sort. With Gary and Jala grumbling and bitching respectively at Timkin's driving prowess, BB begins to imagine, even speculate about what kind of treasure they're about to find.

"Timkin, what the fuck are we doing here? We checked this shithole months ago and barely found enough junk to buy lunch," Jala says to murmured agreements from Gary.

"Just hold your horses, y'all. The wifey got it on good authority that we missed some serious shit last time we were here." He pulls out a crudely drawn map on what looks like a shitty napkin from the Benbow Inn. "She was lifting a snifter with Reba, that kooky chick what works at that place over there by the Benbow, and they got to talking about this and that and the other thing. Well, it came up that Reba'd heard talk from her husband's brother's cousin or something that there's some hot ticket items still pinging inside this here temple. The cousin's husbands' brother or whatever was testing out a piece of tech he found and it went ape-shit crazy."

"What's that got to do with us and why we're here? He must've gotten anything of value that we missed out by now, right?" Gary says.

"That's the thing," Timkin says with a gleam in his eyes. "The shit-poke fucker fell down, and get this shit, *he twisted his fucking ankle so he had to leave.* You ever hear any bullshit like that before?"

"Must've been one hell of a twist," Jala says.

"Yeah, that seems pretty fucked up," Bong Boy says. He's getting a sick feeling in the pit of his stomach now. "How well does your wifey know this Reba lady?"

"Knows her well enough, Sonny Jack me boyo. This might be our golden ticket. The reason we didn't find the cache before is that it's underground."

"Hold up just a damn minute, Potomac. We checked this place top to bottom with the ori-radar-dogadgetmakickey. We didn't find any spots underground. Far as we could tell, if I'm remembering rightly, is that it's sitting on a solid base of rock. Seems like I recall you making a joke about that. Something about 'the rock of ages' or some such nonsense," Gary says.

"Yeah, that's right. You were singing that old hymn and we had to throw shit at you to get you to stop. Then you got all pissy and wouldn't speak to us," Jala says.

"What? Me get pissy? No fuckin' way, hotlips. You must be rememberin' it all wrong," Timkin protests. "Can we just focus on the present for a goddamned minute anyway? I got this here map of exactly where this underground cache is. We go in, scope it out, pull what we can, and split the take with the brother's husband's cousin or whatever. Thing is, we can shortchange this fucker and he'll never know the difference. He never actually laid eyes on any of it. We're gonna come out covered in gold on this one, guys. I'm fuckin' tellin' you!"

"You've had some bad ideas in the past, Timkin, and this ranks right up there with them, but I'm feeling your enthusiasm a little bit and I'm gonna roll with it," Jala says after a minute.

"I'm in, too," Gary replies grudgingly. "You've yet to lead me too far astray, Potomac. I just don't like you springing this kind of shit on us. We're supposed to be partners and—"

"Now who's getting all whiny and pissy! Ha! You're worse than a bitch, Gary! No offense intended to our beautimous—"

"Stuff up your ass, Potomac," Jala says with more than a little hint of a smile.

Bong Boy is still feeling queasy but seeing and hearing the banter is easing him off somewhat. He's not keen on getting too excited in case the lead doesn't pan out. If it's as big a score as Timkin thinks it is, he might be able to retire after two days on the job...

Once they're geared up they head inside the temple. Timkin leads them towards the back left corner of the structure where, he says, they will find the equivalent of Tutankhamen's fortune. Less than half way there, an ominous feeling descends upon them like a ton of bricks. Bong Boy is sure he's going to be physically ill. He's going to upchuck his breakfast all over Gary's back. Man, the hell he's going to catch for that.

"It's a fuckin' ambush!" Gary yells as he unslings the rifle he's carrying over his shoulder. A millisecond later they're enveloped in a blinding flash of light.

There's some sporadic gunfire, Bong Boy thinks, but that's about all his fried brain has time to process. His eyes blink open and closed, intermittent pictures burning onto his retinas before being shunted into his mind. He sees first Gary, then Jala. He never sees Timkin Potomac again. With his last fleeting thought, he knows he's dying. At least it's Jala's beautiful eyes and luscious lips that are sending him off into eternity and whatever awaits him.

"I'm going to kill them all. This won't go unanswered. That kid didn't need to die for this...this stupid fucking bullshit," Timkin Potomac rages.

"If I'd have given him the shield like I should have, the energy blast wouldn't have killed him. This is my fault, Timkin," Jala says.

"The fuck it is, Jala. We had no way of knowing it was gonna play out like it did. How something so petty ended up so fucking brutal. No way we could have known. None of us," Gary says.

Reba, Timkin's old lady's source, pissed at some perceived slight, had arranged for her husband's cousin to ambush the Frack Rats to rob them. She'd teach that uppity bitch. She sure would.

The perceived slight? Timkin's wife hadn't laughed at one of Reba's shitty jokes months ago. She stewed and let it fester, and in her small-minded way, plotted revenge.

What should have been the equivalent of a relatively harmless joke in which Timkin, Gary, and Jala simply lost some of their stuff, turned into a death knell for one Bong Boy Cagayan, Filipino entrepreneur turned freshly minted Nighthawk.

No blood was ever spilled as a result of BB's death, but the Frack Rats went on to make life a living hell for

Reba and her kin, so much so that three months later the whole lot of them left The Oberon all together. Rumor has it that Reba's husband ended up putting a good sized knife through her neck just before inserting a small piece of hot lead into his own brain.

Jala made it a point to send money to Bong Boy's family every month. Little did she know that Timkin and Gary did the same. While BB didn't live to see it, his family ended up living the life of comfort and luxury he'd always envisioned being able to provide for them.

ABOUT THE AUTHOR

Todd Barselow is best known for his work as an editor who specializes in assisting independently publishing authors. He is also known for his role as Senior Editor at Imajin Books, a small Canadian publishing house whose books are widely read and enjoyed around the world.

Todd is the owner and publisher of Auspicious Apparatus Press which produces quality fiction in e-book, paperback, and audiobook formats.

He is a frequent contributor to Anne Rice's Official Facebook page and is known as a Pillar of the Page there with numerous instances of recognition by Anne herself.

Todd lives in Davao City, Philippines, with his wife and their flock of lovely little budgie birds—Max and Sherlock, Charlie and Sandy, Watson and Aly, baby budgie Poppy, and five other as-yet-to-be-named baby budgies..

THE LAST LAUGH AT THE END OF THE WORLD
BY FENTON COOPER

I was angry about how I couldn't get a goddamn beer in this Mission.

It was nearly one-thirty in the morning here in The Oberon on some mid-summer night's eve. I'd been off-world for months and I was making my rounds in The Network, working the bars and the Missions, you know, doing my thing, talking my jokes and my bullshit to the orichalcum miners and the Network settlers and this night I was breaking my vow not to drink and now I wanted a goddamn beer. I'd been on the wagon, straight and narrow, for the whole tour and I wanted a cold one on this cold night.

A Budweiser. This was American territory, sort of anyway, and goddammit I wanted an American drink.

To give you some background, I was at this Mission, Mission Hazelden, way out there in Mau-Mau Ni Perchta Land, and there's already been things going down. Matthias was just ten hours away. That sounds like a lot of fucking time and space between me and the Terrorist in Chief, but believe me brother, that ain't. In ten hours they can come up in their souped up cars or their airships right down the Yellow X freeway and they'll be dissecting you through supernatural means before they want to have dinner. Ten hours was nothing. And there they were out there, ready to come up, or so everyone said.

NIGHTHAWKS AT THE MISSION

I told Howie, my assistant, I wanted a Budweiser and he looked at me sort of cross eyed.

"Jim, you've been clean and sober for months now. Come on. What set you off? What are you doing, buddy?"

We were at the top floor lounge of the Hazelden, where I had just done a set. Looking out at the glens and valleys here in the north of The Oberon, the Burzee region they called it, you could see green fields under the light of the multiple moons, the clean and clear rivers, and one of those Antediluvian Stars slammed down on the ground like a forgotten Christmas ornament.

The lounge was run by Japs from Osaka and they tolerated our coffee drinking and late night conversations for days, but I'd had enough coffee. I needed something real to get my night over with. I had been telling jokes since ten-thirty—terrible puns, local color sort of humor, that sort of shit. Telling jokes was terrible when I was sober but the small crowds lapped it up. I had promised my wife when I left Earth that I'd be sober on tour, but fuck it, she's millions of miles away. I don't know nobody that can maintain a watch on me from that far away

And Howie, my long haired hippie assistant, he ain't telling shit about shit about this.

He went over to one of the Japanese girls and brought back a pitcher of the Cold Gold. I didn't honestly think they would have it. Most of the ads around the lounge were for Kirin and Jap whiskies. But they did have Budweiser—on contract from The Network.

"Oh thank Christ. Thought I was going to have a stroke," I said, looking over the pitcher. A couple of ice-cold glass schooners were provided by the lovely Japanese girl who disappeared back into the darkened recesses of the lounge. Roy Orbison was playing from a jukebox and though I was still working off the adrenaline from the set I just did, making Ni-Perchta jokes and how stupid the bureaucracy was out here in The Oberon, I could finally feel I was relaxing like a real man. First time in a long time. Reno seemed like a fading dream to me.

"How you feel, boss?" Howie said, drinking from a schooner he had just filled for himself. I had just put my lips to the cold glass and sucked half of the Budweiser down without a blink. I felt good now. I felt like I was at home, in my own house, with my own supply, enjoying life, despite the dumbass tuxedo I was wearing that was part of my, I don't know, some shtick. My old boss, Jimmy Wentworth, he used to dress in a tuxedo for his one-liner Rodney Dangerfield-type comedy and I had copied him.

I was millions of miles away in potentially hostile territory. The Ni-Perchta around here had been getting, well, active, probably jazzed up because of the attacks in the south. A bit too active, from what the word was amongst the ori-miners, the supervisor class looking down at their Ni-Perchta peons. Mission Security and the Bureau were watching them, according to the drunks who came to my show. I was told to be careful leaving the Mission. Take a long rifle and an ori-baton that can do some damage, go in pairs, never out after dark. Not that I wanted to go out anywhere until my next gig at another Mission, which I should have been updated about over a week ago. The Network hasn't said a goddamn thing.

"What is that, a village out there?" I said. I pointed through the double paned wide windows at the lights at the edge of some foothills in front of us. Probably just a couple of miles away.

"Ni-Perchta place. They work in the mines for the Network and then go home there. That's their place," Howie remarked.

"Fucking winkies, huh? Look at that. Looks like a shitty model village you'd find under a Christmas tree at a retirement home... Sometimes, when I see that sort of stuff, it freaks me out. They do live in the past."

"Really they do, boss." He sipped his schooner. He was happy I wasn't harassing him about this stupid no drink policy I had been trying to maintain while on tour. But I was off the wagon now and I was no longer enforcing my own rules. I was relaxing. My wife was on Earth, after all. Not here amongst the stars.

I turned my head. "Miss? I need another pitcher. I just know it." She agreed and turned around back to the bar at the other end of the room.

"I'm not going to bed sober," I said to Howie. Howie shook his head.

"Go hard or go home?" He chuckled.

"Fuck it. You and me don't work until tomorrow night. I'm getting blitzed, brother. I don't want to be sober on another planet. That's a fool's game. Let's enjoy, man. I mean how much do these pitchers cost? A few dollars? The Network is overpaying me—us—on this comedy tour ten times what I'd—we'd—get in Reno."

Howie smiled and took out his pack of American Spirits. He gestured for me to have one. I slipped a cigarette out of its blue pack.

"I thought you had quit smoking," I said to him. He smiled at me, pushing back his black-rimmed glasses.

"Please, boss. We all got to maintain off-world." He lit up his cigarette. I took his lighter and lit my own. It was a beautiful night. You could see all the moons of The Oberon coming through the windows. The stars as well. The place was dark enough we could barely make out our own reflections in the double paned glass.

"You think America is going to annex the place, you know, pull a Hawaii on this place? You heard some of the miners talking, just like I did," Howie said abruptly. He was not political, not the current events type. I stared at him.

"How the hell should I know? Do I look like a Congressman? And besides, Americans can't just grab the place, you know. They got other people from other countries might say something. I mean look at our hosts here." I gestured back to the girls speaking Japanese and laughing at each other about something.

"Them and the Greeks and the Russians and those crackers from Zimbabwe. They might say something about Uncle Sam gobbling this all up for himself." I poured another round into my glass schooner, which was sweating and defrosting on our table, leaving droplets of water everywhere.

"Yeah, right."

"Yeah right." I took a deep, long drag of the American Spirit. "I don't smoke often but when I do I fucking love it."

"They wouldn't though? Maybe put in troops or something?" Howie said.

"Since when did you become the political type? Who cares? That's for the Winkie natives out there." I pointed out the window, towards the lights of the village. "Who gives a shit? If this becomes true American territory, that's out of my hands. The government changes, I'm still the same, right? That's America."

Howie shifted in his seat. "I don't know. I guess being out here has made me think about things."

"You think too much. Just think about sound levels and if I'm getting paid so I can pay you, my good and dear friend. You're with Jackie Corsen. Jackie Corsen is the one act that people still like out here. Not these Blink 182 cover bands or the Shakespearean theater companies boring the shit out of high school drop outs. Not those women acts with their vulgarity. I come up with funny shit, you help me out, we are good." I sipped my beer. I had been sweaty since the set and working the crowd, making my jokes. Having something so cold and relaxing—damn this was a good life.

"Come on, Jackie, you don't mean that, do you? You don't think about life out here? I mean people back in America would be weirded out. The magic, the cities, the Ni-Perchta, the whatever. I mean, what is this place? We came over here on the Queen and we get promised all of this stuff and yeah we are making good money, but wow."

I sipped my beer, listening to him. He hardly ever spoke more than a few sentences on tour and all of a sudden he's Al Gore doing holier-than-thou philosophy with the Harvard libs.

"Yeah, wow. We get paid ten times more than usual to tell miners lame jokes about the company that's paying us in the first place while they stuff themselves on cheap steaks and local beers. Yeah, it's terrible."

Howie was silent.

"Look, Howie, you're young, I'm forty-eight. I got a wife and a kid with M.S. at home. I don't, well I should say, I can't share your concerns. Yeah, is it colonialism and all that? Or empire building? Yeah, sure. I mean look at us here at this Mission. We got Jap broads serving us ice cold beer in a nice and comfortable lounge and look down there—the Ni-Perchta are working 19 hours a day living like Russian serfs. I wish I could change the world, my man, but I'm too old. I need to just take it as it is, you know? We make our money and we vaya con dios back to the good old USA when the Nemo Gate pops back up during the next solstice...

"Look, Jackie Sr., my old man, he came from Yu-go-fucking-Slavia. Okay? He didn't have the opportunities like I did. And you know what? He didn't even agree about what the USA was. He hated a lot of what the USA was and he didn't like the, you know, poor people on the street corners, or how inner city kids get shat on, stuff like that. He grew up a Commie. But he knew that in the end, all his personal feelings aside, he's trying to do his best for his family in the system already setup. And there's nothing more we can do. Unless you want to be some asshole and help the Ni-Perchta build their revolution. Like that Matthias fuckwit."

We stared out the window, sipping our drinks. At the table next to us sat man with a sort of D.A. haircut, large tie, late forties maybe even early fifties. Looked weathered and tough. He ordered a straight Hibiki from the waitresses, and sat quietly, watching the outside world. They gave him a double, straight, in a highball glass. He sipped it.

We didn't say anything to him. He spoke first.

"Where you gents from? America?" he said. He spoke with a friendly American accent himself, like a blue-collar guy shooting the breeze at a local dive bar after a shift at the factory.

"America. The land of the very unfit and sort of free," I said. He chuckled at that.

"Max Holt." He stood up with his whiskey and sat down at our table, uninvited. He rubbed his lined forehead.

"Jackie Corsen. This is my assistant and boy Friday, Howie Bic." I put out a hand. He refused to shake it.

"Sorry, I might have a cold, I don't want you to get it." I let my hand drop.

"Incredible," he said to himself, staring out the window. "The End of the World."

"Excuse me?" I said, looking at Howie. Howie shifted in his seat, uncomfortable.

"You were doing some good comedy. I was watching at the back of the room. You were playing it right at the end of the world, or the edge of the known universe. Comedy at the edge." He sipped his drink and leaned forward. "Do you know that?"

"We're far north," I said.

"I'm serious. Here we are, right now, this is the furthest Mission settlement in The Oberon. You go twenty miles past that little shitty village, past the Star there, and its nothing except mountains and snow and Ni-Perchta villages and a few asshole prospectors in some little co-ops. We don't know anything really past the mountains there. They've had explorers out there, but they don't come back after the three hundred mile line. They just don't.

"We sent fifty armed men out there to check the trails, and all we know is the Yellow X ends, and nothing else begins. They sent planes out there, scout planes, and there are some cities out there, Antediluvian, but that's it. They got to turn around because of fuel. But this is the last real place in the universe. This bar here, staring out at the peasants below. The edge of the everything. It's sort of thrilling looking out there."

"Yeah, sure. That's crazy," I said. I've been listening to enough bullshit stories out of the miners to know better. I know this was the North, the Burzee. Don't try to scare me. I had this feeling of being on edge already. This is The Oberon. This ain't Earth. There was always a lingering feeling you were about to fall off a cliff when you were off-world. Maybe it was for me only, I don't know. You felt out of place, and yeah, you should. It's another goddamn planet.

"Yeah, could be something strange—stranger out there. " I sipped my now slightly warmer beer, feeling uncomfortable.

"Look at that," he said. He pointed out the window.

There was something going on at the village. Like we could see torches being lit. Figures in the dark. The sound of drums.

"They having a get together?" I said. "Festival season?"

"That ain't no get together," Max said. He stood up, took off his tie and slapped it down on the table.

"Better pack your shit. I've seen this before."

"Why are they lighting torches?" I asked. "That's torches right?"

"Yeah, and it's not for a barbecue, asshole." He stood up and rushed over to the Japanese waitresses talking. He said something to them in Japanese and they picked up the house phone in order to call Security.

"Doesn't security know?" I said, my voice getting a bit higher. "About whatever you are talking about?"

I could see more and more torches lighting up in the distance. Had to be a lot of them out there. They were forming lines.

"I mean, doesn't security know they can do something down there?"

"I've been on The Oberon since the Morgan discovery. That's a lot of years off-world. In all of my days in the off-world business, and that's no small amount of days, I've seen little uprisings here and there. They haven't burned a Mission since '97, but when they did they came as one big crowd right in the middle of the night just like that one gathering out there. Just overwhelmed the staff, tortured the residents to death, buried them all by scattering their pieces out in the forests around here. The Network used Spitfires and old Korean War jets to blast them into submission and the Witch-Lord burned the survivors to death in dungeons. Betcha never heard of that on *Dateline*, now have you, Mr. Comedian? Full on 300 humans killed, 3,000 Ni-Perchta."

Howie shook his head.

"Call me Jackie," I said in a whisper. My balls were slowly retreating into my body it seemed.

"You see a crowd like that? At night? They don't like to get up in the middle of the night unless they got some bad business ahead of them. They're about to go hard in the paint," Max remarked.

The alarms for the Mission started to sound. It was different, not a warbling sort, but a constant pounding noise. "Attention! Seek shelter immediately! Close doors and windows! Shut off heat, ventilation, and air conditioners! Seek shelter immediately!"

"How much security we got here?" I said, my heart racing. I was thinking about my family now. Little visions of them danced just in front of my eyes.

"There's about ten guys, really only two worth a damn. There's an Ephor squad around the other glen. You better hope they come else or we got to start saying prayers—"

There was a strong smell of something sweet in the air. Like bananas mixed with some sort of pungent rum.

"What the hell is that?" I got out.

Max's eyes and mine met. He then dived under his table. The girls who had been serving us did the same behind the counter. Howie did, too, but then he reached out and grabbed my suit leg and dragged me down just as the first explosion rocked the Mission. It was like a car had slammed into the building and the lights flickered and then there was a hard boom that hurt my ears. Then there were three more of those hard booms and the sound of glass shattering and screams from somewhere.

I crawled out from the table after the last boom, looking for an exit. I saw a green exit sign just behind me. The smell of bananas and rum was all over.

Max Holt stood up, ripping his jacket off. "Goddamn sweet gun! The fuckers dug up a sweet gun! Sons of bitches!"

"The hell is a fucking sweet gun?!" I turned and saw Howie crawl out from under the table, looking like he was shaken up a bit. But he was maintaining better than me.

Max took off his belt a telescoping ori-baton and snapped it fully out. "You fuckers got a fight, you hear me you Winkie assholes!"

Through the shattered remains of the glass we had been looking out, we could hear the chants of the Ni-Perchta as the torch carrying mob made its march towards the Mission. There were a lot of them out there.

"Bastards!" Max straightened out his arm, holding the ori-baton horizontal like a magic wand, and his eyes glowed green. From whatever dimension or ether, a large glowing white crab appeared behind the mob in a flash of lightning. It was slashing its claws this way and that, chopping some of them in half. They began to strike it with lightning from their own batons or with a few gunshots and the white ori-creature reared back in pain before attacking the mob again.

"Holy Jesus motherfuck," I said. Max's eyes returned to normal.

"Try that! I've been here twenty years, assholes! I know your secrets! I've been trained by Ephors!" he screamed at the top of his lungs. "I'm here, bastards! I'm here! Come and deal with Max Holt!"

I saw Howie was right behind him. There was a sudden shimmering all over him and he turned into somebody I had never met before—a bald headed and very pale man, skinnier then even the skinny Howie ever was.

"Free the planet!" he cried and then he stabbed Max in the side with some sort of butterfly knife he had produced out of his jeans pocket.

Max looked stunned and dropped his baton. I grabbed the glass pitcher on the table and swung it at the Now Not Howie's head, shattering it. Glass and beer sprayed everywhere just as another hard boom slammed into the building, knocking us all off our feet.

When I looked around, I saw Max on top of Not Howie. He had stabbed Not Howie right in the throat. Not Howie stared at the ceiling blank-eyed, not moving.

"Goddamn that hurt," Max said, his face very pale and his voice shaky. He turned the baton onto himself and flecks of green flowed into his body. The nasty gouge wound on his side healed right before my eyes.

"I've seen that on T.V.," was the only thing I could say.

"So he was the spy. I knew it was somebody here selling secrets to agitators but goddamn—" He turned and saw that the white ori-crab had disappeared and the mob was beginning to regroup below.

"My assistant was—wait, what?" I whispered. I grabbed the other pitcher and began drinking the Budweiser direct. Oh god it tasted good.

"Yeah, it fucking happens around here. People change into things and people into other people. It's The Oberon," Max said, shaking his head.

"Goddamn mutt ruined my shirt."

He took a deep breath and held out his ori-baton. A storm began to come from nowhere. Clouds began to form and lightning began to strike from random locations. The wind blew strong, tossing some of the Ni-Perchta to the side.

"That's it for the baton at the moment. That's too much." He put his baton back onto his belt and took out a small semi-automatic.

"Where's the girls?" he asked.

I turned around. They were nowhere in sight.

"Gone girls gone," I said.

"Jesus. Come on, funny man." We took off towards the exit. He got ahead of me and kicked the door open and I ran behind him. We ran down the stairs, avoiding the elevators. Other people were in the stairwells, screaming and crying, trying to get out. Their feet were clanging against the steel steps.

"Traffic jam," Max said, turning to me as we were stuck behind miners and their families trying to get through to the levels below. We were stuck behind a wall of crying and screaming people. He looked over my shoulder and to where a large white rectangular sign said **FLOOR 27**.

"Almost out of this goddamn death trap." Max pushed aside some people and I followed behind him into a hallway that had the apartment homes there in the Mission. I could hear now the chanting coming from outside, ungodly loud. The Mob was close. It sounded like Zulus on acid just outside. The noise was becoming stronger and stronger, despite the wind and the thunderstorm cracking left and right. Flashes of light were coming from the hallway windows.

"I thought they'd be more scared off by the storm. Jesus. They got something pushing them out there," Max said, looking around. Doors were flung open and it was apparent the apartments had been vacated in quite a hurry. The alarm was blaring and the same "Seek shelter immediately!" statement was banging out over and over again.

"What's your plan, superman?" I said in a huff. "How we getting out of here?"

"That mob is going to massacre the shit out of those people running for the exits. They're dead." Max was looking around for something in the walls.

"What are you looking for? A fucking fire extinguisher?" I said, taking off my bowtie and throwing it to the ground and popping off my collar button. "Goddamn Winkies."

Max spotted something funny about the wall. He touched the wall and a few lights started to shine, as if coming from the other side of the painted surface.

"Yep. Knew it. Bolt hole gate. I knew it."

He touched one of the lights, which turned from green to purple. The next light he touched turned from purple to green. The wall began to open a hole about the size of the door, revealing a steel lined closet with a small Nemo Gate inside.

"What is this bullshit?" I said.

"Bolt hole for the bosses, my funny valentine. You're too far down the ladder to enjoy this fine shit. They don't tell people about it because, well, you might not defend the Mission otherwise. Right?"

The chants were getting louder now. I swallowed. We listened to them for a moment and the storm outside.

"Jesus—hey, look, man, I'm going back to the stairwell and I'm grabbing people to get them out, man—"

He pointed his gun at my chest, all nonchalant like.

"It's not a regular Nemo. It's one built in Singapore. It's only got enough of a charge on it for two high-ranking executives to bolt. This is the lucky 27th floor and this is the only Nemo Gate in this whole fucking place I know about and that's highly classified shit. Now I'm feeling awfully bad about those people, but we are fucking out of—" He stopped, and looked behind me. His eyes were wide.

There was a little blonde haired girl, in her pajamas, holding a big red Clifford the dog plush doll missing an eye.

"Jesus," I muttered. "Come here, baby! Come on over here!"

She started to tentatively walk forward. I turned to Max. "Come on. She gets a ticket, man."

Max nodded. "You! Get your ass over here!"

She stopped in place, staring at us, tears filling her eyes.

"Fucking goddamn idiot parents left her here." Max walked over to her and grabbed her roughly by the arm. She started screaming

"Come on!" he roared at her. He looked at me and then at the Nemo Gate. I turned my gaze to it as well. Salvation was ten feet away.

"You take one step towards that fucking thing and I'm putting a bullet into your stomach." Max took the girl into his arms.

"Me and her are going. That's it for the Nemo Gate," Max said. "No more juice than that."

"What the fuck about me, man? What I do? You're going to let me get butchered here?" The chants were incredible now. There was another hard boom.

He looked me in the eyes and then walked past me and into the Gate. There was an odd popping sound and the smell of ozone. The two of them disappeared into the nothing and I was left there all by my lonesome. I stared in disbelief for a languid moment as the screams and the smell of smoke filled my head. The sound of the storm outside was like a freight train.

"He fucking left me. Cocksucker left me." I felt betrayed, I don't know why. I'd only met him five minutes or whatever before. I was shaking all over, trembling, thinking about those Ni-Perchta coming in and just butchering me like a hog. The chants were getting ever louder, closer.

"Fuck, fuck, fuck." I stepped into the Nemo Gate and of course nothing happened. He was right about the charge running out.

I turned and jogged back to the stairwell. It had emptied out a bit but there was still a helluva traffic jam I could see in the lower parts when I leaned over the railing. A Japanese man in a bathrobe charged past me. He had to be sixty-five but he was running down those stairs quicker than any Olympian I had ever seen.

"That's going to be a death trap," I said to him but I don't think he heard.

And just as I said it, I smelled bananas and rum and all of a sudden there was a boom and the building shook. I landed on my back right on the stairs and it knocked the breath out of me. There was a shudder and when I sort of came to after being disoriented, I stood up and realized that most of the stairwell down below was a smoking ruin. I could see crumples of bodies way far below. I was stuck up here, near the 26th floor.

"Oh Jesus." I saw that the Japanese man was on top of the pile and wreckage. He was moving around, groaning and crying for help in his language.

I went back upstairs. I was cut off unless I decided to take the elevators—I didn't know if they even worked still. I thought they were supposed to stop when the terrorist alarms go off.

I went out into another apartment corridor and saw a man putting on his Mission Security uniform. He was falling and stumbling around.

"Oh thank God," I said, not realizing how fucked up he was.

"Thank nothing, man, I'm fucking here now, motherfucker," he said, slurring his words. He was drunk and out of his mind. He eyes rolled in his head and he smelled bad.

"There's an attack! There's a Ni-Perchta mob out there!"

"Yeah, no shit, funny man. By the way I want my 500 Di-Yaa back or whatever. Your show sucked total shit and I fucking hated your tuxedo. Who wears tuxedos."

"It's my thing," I mentioned absently. "The stairwell is blown out."

"Blow job?" he said, straightening his uniform. He had a gun belt on as well as an ori-baton on him. He pulled his leg up in a very awkward manner to tie his shoe with perhaps his teeth and fell over.

"What a world, what a world," he said. He rolled on the floor, laughing, a bottle of prescription pills falling out of his pocket. Then he started snoring a moment later. Despite the booms. Despite the screams. I couldn't believe this shit. I stepped on his chest and took off his gun belt and he didn't notice shit.

I strapped it around myself. I snapped out the baton, thinking. The asshole Security guy rolled over and I spotted a set of keys on a ring in his side pocket. I grabbed it out of his pocket.

"Hope the best for you," I said to him. He grunted, face down on the carpeted hallway floor.

I walked down the corridor to the elevators and put the key in, switching back to automatic.

"Fuck me," I said. I got into the elevator. The Muzak version of *Walking on the Moon* by the Police was playing like nothing was happening.

I stood in the elevator, thinking about what I could be about to walk into the middle of down below. The Mob was down below. I took out the machine pistol and cocked it back, remembering weekends shooting guns with Jackie Sr. I thought about what floor button I could hit right now. I could go to the ground floor; be a wet spot in twelve seconds.

No, I'm going to the fifth floor. And then figure how the fuck I'm getting out. I guess. I don't know. I wondered how many rounds in the clip in this gun. I didn't even know how to use the ori-baton at all.

For whatever reason, W.C. Fields' last words entered my head. "Goddamn this whole friggin' world and everyone in it." It was so appropriate right now.

I was laughing to myself at the absurdity of me going out like a warrior, and as the doors to the fifth floor opened, and the Ni-Perchta were standing there drenched in blood and viscera, I laughed and laughed as the gun spit out rounds and they still kept coming.

ABOUT THE AUTHOR

Fenton Cooper was born and raised in Detroit, Michigan and graduated with a Master's Degree in Automotive Engineering from the University of Michigan. He currently lives and works in Osaka, Japan and owns a small import/export business (Aisho Motors) specializing in exotic cars and motorcycles for sale throughout Thailand, Japan and Hong Kong. He is the proud owner of a DMC-12 (DeLorean), which he has rebuilt as his own personal time machine. This is his first short story published that his wife of twenty years liked. He has no children and too many cats.

Made in the USA
Charleston, SC
05 November 2016